from dust and ashes

A STORY OF LIBERATION

TRICIA GOYER

MOODY PUBLISHERS
CHICAGO

© 2003 by
TRICIA GOYER

Library of Congress Cataloging-in-Publication Data

Goyer, Tricia.
    From dust and ashes : a story of liberartion / Tricia Goyer.
        p. cm.
    ISBN 0-8024-1554-7
    1. Executions and executioners--Fiction. 2. War crime trials--Fiction. 3. War criminals--Fiction. 4. Austria--Fiction. 5. Widows--Fiction. I. Title.

PS3607.094 F76 2003
813´.6--dc21

2002035754

3 5 7 9 10 8 6 4 2

Printed in the United States of America

This book is dedicated to my grandfather,

Fred E. Coulter
1916–1999

whose personal stories were my first inspiration.

And to the men of the
11th Armored Division.

May your heroic efforts never be forgotten.

PART ONE

We are brought down to the dust;
our bodies cling to the ground.
Psalm 44:25 (NIV)

ST. GEORGEN SNOW

A spot of color
Catches her attention.
Halts her play.
A small hand reaches
For spring's first flower.

Mother pauses from her work
And smiles.
It is a sad smile.
Nursery songs begin again,
Then fade.

Mother and daughter lift their faces
As flakes of white flutter down.
They land gently upon shoulders, on golden hair.
Hand in hand, the two escape indoors,
Where truth is veiled by thin curtains.

Outside, laundry trembles in the wind.
It ripples in the ash.
For in the distance, beyond the gated yard,
Prisoners are released
As smoke from the chimneys.

One

APRIL 28, 1945
ST. GEORGEN, AUSTRIA

Helene breathed deeply and pretended to sleep as Friedrich staggered into the darkened bedroom. He'd been out later than usual. Through the silent, lonely hours her wandering imagination had tried to picture whom her husband was with and what he'd been doing. A hundred scenarios crossed her mind. None of them good.

She could distinguish three scents as Friedrich carelessly fell upon the bed beside her: sweat, vodka, and a sick, flowery perfume. Sweat from beating half-dead prisoners. Vodka to help him face the monster he'd become. And the perfume . . . She pressed her face deeper into her pillow.

Friedrich panted heavily as he leaned over her. She

huddled deep under the thick white comforter and let out a dreamlike sigh, hoping to keep him at bay.

Friedrich lingered for a moment. He twisted one of her loose curls on his finger, then rose from the bed and crossed the floor.

She pulled the comforter back over her body as he moved to the black military chest in the corner. Steel hinges creaked as it opened.

Helene watched from beneath the covers. Any loving wife would awaken to tell her husband good-bye, to help him pack, to assist his escape from the enemy's approach. Helene felt anything but loving.

Friedrich tossed a few items into a small, dark suitcase. She watched him pull his German *luger* from its holster and remove the empty magazine. With the *click-click* of the new magazine, Helene pictured the tormented, rigid faces of the dead strung up on barbed-wire fences like clothes on a laundry line. Sightless eyes reflecting horror, disbelief.

Friedrich shrugged out of his uniform, brass buttons knocking against the wooden floor. He pulled brown pants, a white shirt, boots, and a blue jacket over his muscular frame. Civilian attire. Helene remained motionless.

Over the past few days, whispered rumors had passed from wife to wife at the camp store. Many of the high-ranking guards were leaving. Fleeing the advancing troops.

"The Americans have crossed the Rhine," a friend had shared in hushed tones. "They are fighting their way through Germany and into Austria. Some claim the Russians are coming in fast from the north." Helene knew it was anyone's guess who'd arrive first to discover the nightmare she'd lived since that dark winter of 1940.

Now it seemed the rumor was true. Friedrich was leaving. Abandoning her, his four-year-old daughter, and the child in her womb. Leaving just like that.

Anika cried out from across the hall, and Friedrich swore under his breath.

Helene jumped from the bed and hurried to the child's room. Muted white light from the guard towers filled the room, and Helene could clearly make out Anika's outstretched arms.

Helene sat on the bed. She took the small girl into her embrace and pressed her cheek into her child's sweet-smelling hair. Helene felt Anika's arms encircle her neck, and she willed her daughter to stay calm. "Quiet, shhh, quiet," she murmured.

Anika's body tensed as Friedrich stalked into the room and hovered near the doorway. Helene shivered, remembering the last time he had been drinking. The rantings, the threats.

"Please, just leave," Helene wanted to say. She pulled her daughter tight to her chest and longed for freedom from all that this man represented. Tonight, again, she remembered that winter . . . cattle cars stuck in snow . . . prisoners left to freeze to death because they weren't worth the effort it would take to carry them to the camp.

Her stomach tightened as she remembered the chilling screams that had journeyed through the night air to her window. Urgent pleas from men, women, and children. Then finally, with morning's light, silence.

All through that night, she had implored Friedrich to do something. She had screamed at him, called him a murderer. Still he refused, his cold gaze resting upon her as it surely did now. He told her she didn't understand. He said he was protecting her, but Helene didn't believe him. Instead of standing up to the evil, he allowed it to become a part of him.

"I'll be back to get you," Friedrich said, his voice determined. "I'll get settled and come back for you both."

"You mean us *three?*" Helene corrected, pressing Anika against her bulging middle.

"*Ja,* of course."

She slowly rocked her daughter. "We'll be fine. I'll go back to my father's *gasthaus.* He can always use an extra hand at the inn."

Friedrich cursed and pounded the doorjamb with his fist.

"If Father will take me back," she added.

"He's a foolish, naïve old man. Don't think I'm blind to what he's been doing. I've looked the other way for your sake." Friedrich started to leave, then stopped. He let out a deep breath. "I wasn't a bad guard, Helene," he said, his back to her. "Not like some."

"Of course," she said.

"You will be safe. No one will hurt you or Anika."

"No, I'm sure we'll be fine."

Anika whimpered again. Helene lay down with her, close enough to touch noses. Friedrich whistled a solemn tune that Helene faintly recognized. Anika's eyes grew wide.

What's that song? Helene wondered. But before she could ask, he was gone.

Heavy, booted footsteps crossed the wooden floor and pounded down the stairs. After a brief pause, the front door opened and closed. Shouts echoed in the streets. Nazi trucks rumbled through the night.

He's gone.

Moments passed with the ticking of the old wall clock. Helene felt her daughter's body relax. After a few minutes, the child's fingers crawled up Helene's chest and tickled her chin.

"In there hidden, in there deep, is laughter happy waitin' to peep," Anika whispered.

How many times had Helene recited that simple poem to her daughter during these dismal days of war?

The girl's tickles continued until unforeseen laughter gushed from Helene. It caught both her and Anika by surprise. Then, equally unexpected, with the laughter came tears. And with the tears, Helene's quiet sobs that gently rocked her child to sleep.

Yet for her, sleep would not come. *I'm free, I'm free,* she kept telling herself. But she knew it wasn't true. She felt no freedom inside, only pain. Pain that constricted around her heart like a hangman's noose and cinched tighter with each haunted memory.

The two men ran through the moonlit woods with strength they didn't realize they possessed. Time was running out. The hunters would soon be hunted.

To the one in the lead, the countryside was familiar. Friedrich recognized the landforms, the scent of the air. Despite his sense of urgency, he relished the feeling of his feet pounding on the soft, dark soil. Although dense trees blocked his view, he knew the green farmlands of Germany spread to the north. Behind him, the Swiss Alps veered to the southwest, the Austrian Alps to the southeast. Ahead was the tiny town of Füssen, their destination.

The thick-waisted soldier who ran behind him lacked in both knowledge of the area and in stamina. Arno rumbled through the forest like an armored tank. A crash sounded from the woodland floor, and Friedrich stopped, then swore. He turned to find his companion sprawled in the underbrush like a gunned-downed prisoner.

Friedrich's breathing was labored as he leaned over the man. "Get up, you useless fool," he hissed. "What was I thinking bringing you?"

The man lifted his unshaven face from the soil. In the near-full moon, Friedrich noticed sweat beaded on his companion's brow.

Arno pushed himself up from the dirt and wiped his mud-smeared cheek with his shirtsleeve. "Forget it. We are a day behind schedule as it is," he seethed. "I am going back before they leave without us." He took two steps in the opposite direction.

Friedrich gripped Arno's arm. His teeth clenched as he attempted to calm his screaming nerves. If he hadn't needed an extra hand, he wouldn't have sought help in the first place. Arno had no idea what he was walking away from. Perhaps now the time had come to sweeten the lure.

"I don't care if you come or not, but you have no idea . . ." Friedrich pushed Arno's arm away and lowered his voice. "What if I told you all the golden trinkets we've confiscated over the last five years were merely pocket change?"

Arno's eyebrows lifted, and Friedrich knew the man was picturing towering piles of booty from the camp storehouse.

Friedrich searched the man's round face, weighing if Arno could be trusted. He saw the same dull expression he'd seen every day at work. But he had no choice. He needed help claiming the prize.

He glanced behind him and spoke low and quickly. "I was in Vienna in '38. All Jews were ordered to give a detailed declaration of their valuables. I was a clerk, and those money-grubbers acknowledged enough wealth to make my superiors tremble with greed."

"And you pocketed your own share?"

Friedrich shrugged. "It was easier than I imagined."

"How can you be sure the person holding the loot has not cashed in?"

Friedrich grinned, realizing Arno was once again in his grasp. "If you can't trust your own mother, who can you trust? Besides, we're not too far off course." He dug into his left trouser pocket and pulled out the forged travel papers and his new identity card. "After this, we have one more stop, then on to Italy." He patted his other pockets. Where was the map, the address?

"Something wrong?" Arno asked.

Friedrich shook his head. "It's of no consequence. I left something in the house. But not to worry." He tapped his head. "It's all up here."

The sound of a distant vehicle echoed through the trees. Arno wiped his brow, his eyes hungry. "Does anyone else know?"

A tune lilted through Friedrich's mind. He pushed it out of his thoughts. "*Nein*. No one."

Arno nodded.

"But before we claim the spoils, I need you to deliver this." Friedrich reached into his jacket and produced a clean white envelope. Pulling a three-inch knife out of the swastika-embellished sheath on his belt, he sliced a small gash in his palm, letting a few drops of blood stain the envelope. "A messenger will meet you in front of the stone church on the edge of town. Tell him you found this on my dead body. He'll know what to do. Then wait at the church. There's a hiding spot in a clump of trees near the cemetery. I'll find you. We only have a few hours, so hurry."

Arno snatched the bloodied envelope. The sound of trucks rumbled nearer. "What about you? Where will you be?"

Friedrich pretended not to hear the question. He resheathed the knife and pulled his luger from its holster. "We must split up." He pointed straight ahead. "The church is that way, no more than a kilometer. Now go."

Arno raced toward the town. Friedrich ran the opposite direction. He was close; he could feel it. Soon, he'd have the bounty he'd waited five years to retrieve. By morning, he would be a rich man on his way to Italy. Then Argentina after that.

Friedrich picked up his pace. He spotted the small farm in the distance. A curl of white smoke rose from the brick chimney. *Almost there.*

A branch cracked beside him. Friedrich spun around. Three men crouched behind a large boulder. He recognized their uniforms immediately. Olive-green shirts and trousers. Steel helmets. M1 rifles. *Americans!*

"Halt!" one man called.

Friedrich aimed his handgun at that man. Gunfire sounded.

Then only blackness.

꽃   꽃   꽃

The roar of the trucks reverberated even louder, but Arno couldn't tell which direction they were coming from. He was a fool for listening to Friedrich. Perhaps it was a trap. He'd seen the way Friedrich had played his hand with his superiors, allowing everyone else to do his dirty work while he paraded around town with his lovely wife.

Still . . . the riches were tempting.

Shouts split the air. Arno paused midstep, his heart pounding. Gunfire rang out. He dashed behind a tree and peered in the direction Friedrich had run. He could make out the silhouettes of helmets bent over someone on the ground. *Friedrich.*

Arno cursed. His legs trembled. He couldn't believe this was happening. In one second Friedrich was out of the picture. Even if the man wasn't already dead, he would be soon. Arno vowed he would not be next.

He backed away. His hands shook, but he was determined not to make a sound, determined not to attract attention. When Arno felt he was a safe distance away, he whirled around and sprinted. The woods began to thin as he ran. A church steeple rose in the distance. Arno slowed. Now what?

He stopped and kicked the ground. They would leave without him. Sail away to safety. *And I'll be stuck here. Friedrich, you idiot! Why'd I listen to you? I'll never get out of this now.*

Then Arno thought of the man who awaited him, Friedrich's messenger. Only a small clearing separated him from the church.

Arno stared at the envelope clutched in his hand. He ducked behind a tree and ripped it open. He pulled out the letter, read it, then slipped it back in the envelope.

Then again, he thought, a smirk crossing his face, *perhaps I don't want to leave the country after all.*

℣   ℣   ℣

Arno blew warm air onto his cold hands. He adjusted the thin blanket around his shoulders. The wall he leaned against rose high above him, ending in a jagged line. Beyond that there was only night sky, just beginning to lighten. Friedrich's messenger—not a man, but a boy of thirteen—had brought him to this castle ruin in hopes of finding safety. So far it had worked.

Arno glanced at the boy, sleeping soundly under the stars. Shaggy, straw-colored hair covered most of his freckled face. Over the past few days he'd discovered that Henri was a dedicated Nazi youth and a hired hand to Friedrich's mother. Arno reached over and shook the boy. Henri stirred, then sat up, rubbing his eyes.

"It is time," Arno said. "You will go to the old woman as planned. I will watch from a distance. Tell her Friedrich wants to know if she still has the treasure. Ask if it is safe."

The boy hesitated. Arno knew what he was waiting for. He tossed a few cigarettes to him. "That is a down payment. I am much more generous than Friedrich, ja?"

Henri's eyes sparkled. "Ask Frau Völkner about the treasure. I understand." He jumped to his feet and brushed the dust from his tan shirt and knickers. Together they advanced down the hill, an ebbing moon brightening their path.

When they reached the small cottage, they saw a light flickering inside. Arno hung back in the covering of trees. He watched Henri stroll up to the house and tap on the door. The woman eagerly welcomed him inside.

Arno leaned against a tree and lit up a cigarette. As he surveyed his surroundings, he noticed castles high up on the hill. Not ruins like he'd stayed in the previous night, but two full-fledged castles with tall windows and massive turrets. He wondered what it must have been like for young Friedrich to grow up under the shadow of such wealth.

Arno waited an hour, then two. He'd just about decided to storm the door when the boy emerged from the house, waved, and jogged away. The stooped-over old woman waved back.

Henri sauntered down the road for a while before slipping back into the woods. As he approached, Arno caught a whiff of bacon and eggs. His stomach growled, but hunger was the least of his concerns.

"Well?" Arno asked impatiently.

"Frau Völkner is a nice lady," Henri commented. "She fed me breakfast and told me how her goats were doing, and—"

"What did she say about Friedrich?"

"She laughed when I mentioned treasure. She thought I was joking. She asked about her son. I told her he was doing well." Henri paused. "He is doing well, isn't he?"

"Of course." Arno patted the boy's shoulder. "He has just been detained for a while. Now, go on."

"She's a poor woman, living off the few schillings her son sends every month. She obviously knows nothing about a treasure."

Arno thought back to Friedrich's words: *"If you*

20

can't trust your mother, who can you trust?" Surely the woman knew something. Maybe he'd have to get it out of her himself.

Henri's brow furrowed. "There was one thing—" Arno straightened. "Stacks of Friedrich's letters. He writes weekly and has since joining the military."

A smirk curled on Arno's lips. *That's it. Information about the treasure has to be hidden in those letters.*

"You are going back tomorrow," Arno said, folding his arms across his chest. "Only this time, I am going with you."

Two

MAY 5, 1945
MUEHLVIERTEL REGION, AUSTRIA
ELEVENTH ARMORED DIVISION
FIRST PLATOON OF TROOP D
FORTY-FIRST CAVALRY
RECONNAISSANCE SQUADRON, MECHANIZED

The half-track rumbled like a purring lion. With the tanklike track and the front wheels providing good mobility, this truck was the perfect vehicle for reconnaissance. Cool air from the open window tugged at the corners of the open map as Sergeant Peter Scott rechecked the platoon's location. He calculated the redlined route would not take more than an hour.

Peter's men had arisen before dawn, readied the ammunition, and secured information about terrain conditions and enemy emplacements. They'd received orders to secure a bridge near St. Georgen, Austria. Now on their way, Josef, Peter's driver, focused on the road ahead. Banion, his gunner, sat in the armored box in back, machine guns ready . . . just in case.

One half-track led the way. Peter's was second in line. He glanced at the side mirror, assessing the ribbon of machinery that wound behind. Twenty men in olive-drab fatigues and steel helmets followed in a parade of half-tracks and mud-splattered jeeps.

Troop D's task was to find the bridge and check its suitability for heavy convoys. If the bridge was intact, advancing troops that followed could use it to bypass the heavy fighting in the city of Linz and along other major roads of the Danube Valley.

Even though the fighting had died down in most areas, hinting that an end to the war was in sight, German holdouts were still scattered throughout northern Austria. They were the only barrier blocking the meeting of Patton's Third Army and the Russians. And once the two united, all of Europe would finally be in Allied control.

Peter tried to picture St. Georgen, the small town that would give the Eleventh Armored the passage it needed. Just another stop on the journey from Normandy, through France and Belgium, into Germany and Austria. Another scenic village the war would keep him from enjoying.

Yesterday, when his division stopped for maintenance, Peter imagined how much his sister, Annie, would get a kick out of painting the landscape of rolling hills draped with green and dotted with century-old cottages. Or the high Austrian peaks on the horizon that reminded him of the Rockies near their home.

And even as his mind returned to Montana, his eyes examined the hills, watching for movement in the brush or the flickering gleam of the sun against a German weapon. He knew the enemy could strike at any moment, and often had during their months of movement.

Josef, a nineteen-year-old Austrian American, shifted gears, taking the purr one level deeper. "Kinda peaceful, ain't it, Scotty?"

Peter regarded Josef, wondering what it was like for him to be fighting the men who'd caused many of his people to flee their homeland.

"Peaceful is different from quiet," Peter replied, sliding his palm down the barrel of his trusted carbine. "Quiet it is. Peaceful it's anything but. You ought to know that."

Peter's words sounded harsher than he intended, but over the past few months he'd come to realize peace was simply a lie. Nicknamed Preacher by his pals on the football team back in Columbia Falls, he had dreamed of impacting others with the good news of God's love. That dream had died on the battlefield. Beaches dotted with bodies and open ditches filled with channels of blood had a way of doing that. Now his friends just called him Scotty.

Josef took the cue and focused again on the road.

Peter scrutinized his driver. Josef looked a lot like the dark-haired, light-eyed villagers he'd seen peering from the shuttered cottages they'd passed. But Peter stood out like a carrot in a cabbage patch. With his blond-red hair, green eyes, and tall, lanky build, he was always seen, always remembered. And he used it to his advantage. The memory he determinedly left with his superiors was one of total effort. In the past two years he had done his job well, even learning the German language.

Peter smiled at the thought of what diligence cost. Taking the jobs no one else wanted. Insisting his troops were best prepared. Spearheading through unknown territory.

They passed a sign announcing the town of Katsdorf. The moment they entered the village, Peter knew something was wrong. Villagers' faces—typically some curious, some frightened, others joyous—were not at their usual spots in the windows. Outside of town, road barriers appeared more frequently. Peter tried to remember hearing of any German outposts near this spot, but he couldn't. If some type of camp were close, it was another confounded Nazi secret.

"Corporal Clifton," Peter radioed to the acting scout, "stay alert."

The line of vehicles slowed. Without checking, Peter knew his men had their heads cocked, inspecting the hills for the slightest movement.

A few miles down the road, one man's shout split the airwaves. "On high ground! Germans!"

Peter spotted them. Five Krauts watched from above the tree line on a high hill. They were partially hidden by boulders and shrubs.

On Peter's order, gunfire thundered from the front

half-track, hitting just shy of the boulders. None returned. Was this a trap?

Peter swung his carbine in the direction of the surrounding hillside. The Germans had vanished. He climbed out of the half-track and scrambled to the cover of trees. "Fan out! Search for mines and men."

Soldiers leaped from their vehicles and spread into the low trees that lined the road while the drivers remained to cover them.

"Scotty," a voice called out. "Over here!"

It was Clifton. Peter couldn't distinguish if the strain in his voice carried pain or fear. Perhaps both.

Peter advanced toward the towering oaks. He motioned for a few others to join him, then inched through the heavy foliage. A thick pine scent penetrated the air. Wildflowers grew in clusters. A bird, startled from its nest, flew across the cloudless sky.

Then Peter spotted Clifton. He was crouched in the shadow of a large oak, staring at a large clearing just beyond the trees. Peter followed the corporal's gaze, then pulled out his field glasses to take a closer look.

The terrain was rugged. Boulders lay scattered over the rolling, grass-covered hills. In the distance, next to what appeared to be a steep quarry wall, a ten-foot-high perimeter fence glistened in the sunlight. The fenced-off area held men. Men caged like animals.

"They're less than a mile away," Peter said to Clifton. "And no guards in sight. But we can't get there with our vehicles. It's too risky. We'll have to walk."

Peter glanced over his shoulder. A dozen of his

troops gathered behind him, creating a semicircle of protection.

Peter pointed to the three closest men: Murphy, Banion, and Clifton. "Follow me." As they ventured down the grassy hillside, the breeze captured a sickening smell. The stench became stronger with each step.

Peter stopped when he saw a lone German approaching through swaying wildflowers and grass. The thin man's empty hands were raised. A tattered gray uniform with too-short sleeves hung limply from his shoulders.

"Get on the ground, facedown," Peter yelled in German. "Get down!" He pointed his carbine toward the dirt.

"I have nothing. I have nothing," the man cried in English. He fell to the ground and stretched out his limbs.

"Murphy. Banion. Check him for weapons."

Peter watched them pat the man down, then scrutinized the hillsides, wondering if a full attack would be waged.

"He's clean, Sarge," Murphy reported.

The two GIs yanked the German to his feet, then thrust him toward Peter. He staggered a few steps and dropped to his knees.

"Who are you?" Peter asked.

"I am Wilhelm," he stuttered. Peter wondered why he gave no last name or rank but didn't care enough to ask. More important matters concerned him now.

"What is that?" Peter pointed to the fencing in the distance.

"It is prisoner-of-war camp called Gusen. I take you

there." The German's eyes seemed eager, as if he hoped his assistance would save his life.

Peter lifted Wilhelm's chin with a firm grip. "Who are the prisoners?"

"Refugees from Poland and Russia. Some Italians also."

"Any Americans?"

"Nein. No GIs." Wilhelm's eyes darted. Peter detected the lie. He guessed that if there weren't Americans in the camp now, there had been.

Peter ordered his troops to move back to the vehicles. Then, with a tight grasp on the German's arm, he dragged him up the hill, then slammed him against the door of his half-track. "Call out to your comrades." He pointed his rifle in the direction of the hills. "Tell them to lay down their weapons and surrender."

Wilhelm shouted the commands. A couple dozen filthy men staggered out of hiding with hands high. Their uniforms were neither those of the regular German army nor the SS. These were not trained soldiers. Some were very young, others quite old. Most likely they'd been left behind to cover for fleeing SS troops.

"Line up in groups of ten, five abreast," Peter called. These prisoners were not part of the day's plans, but they would be a fine bounty to present to his Commanding Officer, Captain Standart.

Peter checked his watch. It was only nine o'clock. Still early enough to check out the POW camp and secure the bridge . . . wasn't it? Both were in the same direction. But should he risk going beyond his orders?

"McCoy. Wilks," Peter called. "Restrain them, then wait here. Wilks, you're in charge. Jackson, radio the CO for a pickup. The rest of you, follow me."

Peter pressed the point of his carbine into Wilhelm's side. "Take us to the camp."

"You must go through St. Georgen," he replied, eyes to the ground.

"Then you will lead us," Peter commanded. He motioned to his troops. "Back to the vehicles!"

Wilhelm climbed into Peter's rig, then led the half-tracks and jeeps to an unmanned roadblock at least eight feet higher than any Peter had ever seen.

"Check for trip wires and mines," he instructed. In the distance, he heard the muffled sound of a motor. Peter took out his field glasses and spotted a white touring car traveling down the road toward them. A Swiss Red Cross flag fluttered from the hood.

"What now?" Peter mumbled. "Keep them in your sights," he radioed to his men as their convoy skirted the roadblock.

When the white car stopped before them, a Swiss civilian stepped out. He was a slender man with small, round spectacles and a knee-length white trench coat. The flag on his coat pocket identified him as an international Red Cross worker.

Two German officers climbed out of the backseat. The sleeves of their brown uniforms were wrapped with red armbands, their knee-high black boots spotless. Every instinct told Peter to shoot. To go for those uniforms decorated like Christmas trees. *How many innocent lives paid for those medals?*

Instead, Peter calmly climbed out of the half-track. "What's going on?" he asked in German.

After a few minutes of hurried dialogue, Peter translated for his men. "They say there's a camp with four hundred SS on the far side of the bridge, looking for a U.S. general to surrender to. And there are sixteen hundred prisoners eager to be freed."

Peter searched his men's faces, seeking their response. They waited for his. They all knew this went far beyond orders.

He spoke first in English, then in German. "I am a direct representative of the commanding general of the Eleventh Armored Division." Neither his voice nor his eye contact wavered. "There are hundreds more troops coming behind us." Peter knew the Germans understood his words. He just hoped they believed them.

The half-truth paid off. Soon Peter's radio operator had him on the line with the CO. "Sir, the Red Cross says there are sixteen hundred prisoners depending on us for a fast liberation. They assure me there will be no trouble."

Captain Standart's voice crackled on the other end. "We're already on our way to pick up the Germans you captured an hour ago. How many more prisoners do you need?"

Peter suppressed a laugh.

"Look," Captain Standart said, "your mission was to

secure the bridge. This little side trip of yours represents an unnecessary risk for you and your men."

Peter realized it could be a trap. He also recognized that those POWs behind the fence needed his troops.

"You know me, sir," Peter said, "and I know my men. We're willing to take the chance."

There was a long pause. "On one condition." Captain Standart's voice was firm. "Keep in constant radio communication with me. Do you hear?"

"Yes, sir."

Peter addressed the Red Cross worker. "We're moving out under the lead of the white car. But tell the Germans that if I detect even one false move it will all be over. And be prepared to stop at the bridge before crossing. We will make sure it is secure."

The twenty-three remaining GIs returned to their half-tracks and jeeps. Peter gave the order to move forward, then wiped his sweaty palms on his pants, hoping no one noticed.

Back on the main road, and within a matter of minutes, the entourage wound through St. Georgen. The town curled up to the hills around it, as if seeking protection. A white church with a tall steeple rested in the center. The village circled out from there.

Just beyond the town Peter's troops found the bridge. They checked it for mines and made sure it could handle the weight of convoys. Then Peter left two soldiers to guard it while the rest of Troop D followed the white car over the winding river.

The Red Cross vehicle stopped before a large wooden

gate. A tall wire fence extended from both sides. The three occupants emerged. Peter's half-track pulled up behind, and he jumped out.

Camp Gusen consisted of a series of plank structures set against a white, sandy hillside. On the front and sides of the camp stood tall administration buildings. Beyond that, row after row of dark wooden barracks. Cement guard towers protected the corners. They were empty now, but Peter could imagine Nazi sentries with rifles aimed into the courtyard below. A fog of death hung in the air, filling Peter's lungs with every inhalation. A trembling started at his knees and worked its way up his body, landing in his chest. He used every bit of his will not to gag.

One of the two German officers approached Peter across a carpet of ash. His stride was long and powerful. Peter met him halfway, matching the strut. The officer gave an American salute. Peter kept his arm stiff at his side, wishing for nothing more than to finish him off. But a bullet was too clean, too easy.

Peter glared at the officers. "*Hör zu!* Listen! I'm taking this camp. All Germans must surrender."

The Nazi straightened his shoulders, then barked the command. A siren blared from the towers. Guards scurried from various corners of the camp and lined up in front of Peter, their gun barrels pointed to the ground. Each guard gave an American salute.

Peter had never thought he would witness a day like this. Yet even the scene before him could not quiet his mounting apprehension.

"Secure the Germans," he ordered for the second time that day. "Round them up."

Peter's eyes darted from his men to the Germans to the camp, assessing the situation. When he saw his men easily restraining the enemy, officers included, he allowed his attention to focus on the prisoners.

Crowded behind a wire fence strung on cement poles, wasted figures streamed from the dim buildings. Hundreds of them cried out with joy and tears. Though still alive, their emaciated bodies only vaguely resembled human beings. Some trembled beneath thin blankets or tattered clothing. Others stood completely nude, men and women alike.

Women? This was no prisoner-of-war camp. These people had been chosen for eradication.

Peter and a half dozen of his men marched through the gates of the camp. A wild ovation of cheers rose for the liberators. Hands, bloody and frail, reached out for the slightest touch of freedom.

Peter's legs quivered as if he'd just run a marathon. The thrill of freedom and the anguish of what man could do to man intertwined like cords of light and darkness.

Thin arms punched the air in exhilaration. Bony knees sank into the ground as many collapsed. Trembling fingers covered faces. Peter and his men found themselves surrounded by a sea of skeletal bodies.

Peter sucked in sharply as his gaze stopped on one woman. While most shoulders slumped under the invisible weight of oppression, she stood erect. Her face was unmoving, her eyes fixed on his. Blue eyes, he noted. As blue as the sky above him. Her hair, gray with dirt, was cropped short. She wore a man's striped shirt, which hung to her knees like a cloak, hiding her arms and hands in its sleeves. Something in her gaze drew him. Her mouth moved, but her words were lost in the noise of the crowd. Still, Peter sensed what she was saying. *Thank you. Thank you.*

Peter felt his chest tighten. He stalked back to the half-track. "Jackson, get the CO on the radio. Now!"

Within seconds the commanding officer's voice broke through. "What's happening, Scotty?"

"Sir, this isn't a prisoner-of-war camp. These people aren't soldiers. They're civilians. Thousands of dying people. Far more than sixteen hundred."

"And the bridge?"

"Sir, the bridge is intact and secure. But many of these prisoners will be dead before they're able to leave the gates."

He wanted to say more. He ached to tell his captain about the hands, the faces. The smell. The terror. But no words came.

"Do what you can," Captain Standart answered, "until we get there."

Peter handed the radio back and returned to his men at the gates. "Jones, get the keys and release those who are still locked up. Murphy, find clothing. Anything to cover these people."

"And food," Josef added, his voice shaky.

"You're right. Banion, see what kind of food you can find." His men took off to follow his orders.

"Scotty . . ." Josef's voice trembled even more than before.

Peter followed his driver's gaze to a log pile along the side of a building. Then he realized they weren't logs at all, but bodies. Mouths gaped open in silent screams. Arms crossed over legs. Hair, like cheap wigs, fell over frozen faces.

Josef took two steps, then fell onto his hands and knees, his body convulsing as nausea overtook him.

Peter pulled a handkerchief from his shirt pocket and handed it to Josef. Before he could muster the courage to approach the pile, a commotion drew his attention back to the crowd.

Something had changed. The cries of celebration had transformed into screams of outrage as the prisoners neared the rows of guards lined up outside the wire fencing. Eyes that had shed tears of joy just moments before were narrowed into wicked glares. The prisoners wanted more than deliverance. They wanted vengeance. Now an angry mob, the victims surged toward the gates.

Despite his own feelings of outrage, Peter knew he had to take control. It was obvious that if order was not restored, many lives would be lost—prisoners, guards, and GIs alike.

His men guarding the gates awaited Peter's command, peering grimly down the sights of their M1s. Some weapons were fixed on the guards, others on the prisoners.

Peter fired a round into the air. The commotion stilled.

"Step back," he shouted to the crowd. "We will remove the German guards, and then you will be set free. We are not leaving. We will stay until all is in order." The message was translated throughout the crowd, and the mass of humanity slowly pulled away from the fence.

Peter caught movement from the corner of his eye. Spinning around, gun ready, he found a frail prisoner who had dared to step from the ranks. The man's eyes were fixed on Peter. The man's trembling hands reached upward as he collapsed at Peter's feet. He gripped Peter's leg like a vise. His chest shook and his eyes fixated on a distant vision as one last breath rattled from his body.

The hold on Peter's leg gave way. Peter lowered his gun.

"Sir?" The Red Cross worker hurried to Peter's side. "You cannot stay here. This is only a subcamp." His hands motioned to the mountains toward the east. "The main camp is four kilometers away, on the hill."

Peter's mouth went dry. "Repeat that."

"Mauthausen, the main camp, is up ahead. There are many more guards ready to surrender. More prisoners to free."

Three

Sirens shrilled through the air. Michaela's eyelids fluttered open. She peered through the dim interior and tried to clear her jumbled mind. What was that noise? A bomb siren? After all these months of struggle, would her final resting place be among bomb fragments?

Splinters dug into her fingertips as she struggled to rise from the wooden bunk. The room was filled with the odor of urine and feces too strong to ignore.

A loud commotion drifted in from outside. Michaela pulled herself onto tender feet. Her bare legs, which were once lean and muscular from hikes in the hills near home, were thin and covered with sores. Her hands, which had danced over piano keys and written vivid poetry, were unrecognizable.

She inched across the room. It had been days since she'd eaten, and before that only starvation rations. Michaela struggled to keep her balance. Her mind refused to clear.

Most of the others in the room remained motionless on their bunks, too ill to move. Some were already dead.

Michaela tried not to stare at Hilde's face as she stepped around her friend's rigid body. For months, Hilde had spoken of a reunion with her husband and sons and had sung Polish folk songs to encourage her bunkmates. Now her flesh, stretched over her body's frail bones, littered the floor. Refuse waiting to be burned.

Coming up to a small window, Michaela peeked through its filthy glass. She saw trucks. Not Nazi trucks but brown ones with white stars. A white car led them around the bend. It made no sense.

"*Amerikaner!*" someone screamed from outside.

"Americans," Michaela repeated. "The Americans are here."

Strength she didn't know she possessed surged through her veins. She lumbered to the door and poked her head out. The sun felt warm on her forehead and cheeks. The bright rays burned her eyes like acid.

After a few minutes, Michaela's eyes adjusted to the bright light. She straightened her foul-smelling prisoner's shirt, three sizes too big. In the darkness not many nights ago she had stripped it from a man who lay dead outside her barracks. He had no shoes to take, and as an act of dignity she'd left his pants. Before returning inside, Michaela had closed his nonseeing eyes and offered a silent prayer.

Now, as the sunlight splashed upon her, she noticed that vomit and blood stained the front of the shirt. Still, this was better than the thin, torn one she'd worn before. That thing hadn't even covered her buttocks.

As Michaela moved out cautiously, she noticed the guards weren't at their usual posts. The fog in her mind lifted and she remembered many had left days ago, leaving the prisoners to fend for themselves.

The siren ceased. Crowds gathered. A river of gaunt bodies brushed against her, pulling her into its flow. Gravel dug into the bottoms of her feet with each clumsy step. She felt caught up in something bigger than herself as the crowd pressed toward the front gates. Her eyes darted to the boundaries that had kept them caged for so long.

Don't go there. Turn back! her mind cried as the crowd crossed into restricted areas that before would have brought instant death. She knew those boundaries well.

But she couldn't turn back. The river propelled her along. Her heart pounded in her chest. She couldn't shake the feeling that she was heading for her demise. It must be a trap, leading them all to their final destruction.

Then Michaela lifted her eyes and looked beyond the gates. The trucks stopped. And she saw them. The long-awaited saviors. Whispered rumors of their impending arrival had been circulating for days. She had not believed. Yet there they were, before her.

A sob caught in her throat. A weight shuddered from her heart. Michaela tried to remember a prayer. *Our*

Father, who art in heaven. They were the only words that came. She repeated them. *Our Father. Our Father.* Her thin fingers pressed together in the position of prayer.

Around her, chanting arose in Polish, German, Italian, and other languages Michaela couldn't distinguish.

"Americans. We are free!"

"Home!"

"Nach Hause!"

"Ospizio!"

"Domowy!"

"Domáci."

"Patrie!"

"Free!"

Her hands joined others in the air, and she waved to her liberators as they stepped out of their vehicles. They were young men. Healthy, handsome, and strong. If she had a brush, she would paint them. If a pen, she could fill pages with descriptions of their beauty.

Despite the jumble of people, a man beside her broke out in an awkward dance. His bony elbow jarred her shoulder, and she clung to another man to keep her balance. That man kissed her cheek.

A kiss. If she survived this, she would never forget that kiss.

More screams of *"Home, home"* filled her ears. Michaela gasped as German guards spilled forward from their hidden holes with American salutes. Only then did she truly believe. *This is real! We are free!* A thousand thoughts filled her mind. Ten thousand memories, both bad and good. She pushed aside those musings and focused on her liberators.

"Free!" Her voice joined the others, only to be interrupted by the tears she'd stored for months, for years. She felt their warmness pour over her sunken cheeks, spilling into the hollow of her neck.

Home. The word stuck in her throat, unwilling to break free. Her eyes moved to those around her.

Home? Did they understand what they were saying?

She looked past the gates to the surrounding hillsides. Such a contrast to the dirt and rough wood quarters in which she'd lived. Lush vegetation covered the hills, recently awakened from a deep winter's sleep. And somewhere over those hills, and the mountains beyond, was a place called Poland.

But Michaela knew even in her home country there was no place to rest her head, to pull up a chair, to warm herself by a fire.

"What home?" she found herself yelling among the cries. "We no longer have a home!" Yes, they were free, but free to go where? She thought of her parents, her beloved Georg, her friends. No one was waiting for her return. Their home in Bielsko, the beautiful city spread over twenty hills, probably no longer existed and never would again. What good was freedom now? What was she free to do? Lament for the rest of her life?

Michaela clung to a man next to her to keep from dropping to the ground. He supported her for a moment before moving closer to the gates, to the Americans. The GIs marched into the prison compound, and a wild cheer rose.

Michaela wiped her tears. No, these were not for now. The Americans had fought hard to get here. Should she greet them with weeping?

She struggled to the front of the crowd with straight shoulders and lifted chin. Despite her inner turmoil, she would show them her gratitude in the most dignified way possible.

One American stepped forward as if drawn to the crowd. His hair was the color of the dull red apples that had hung on the tree beside her childhood home. His green eyes were wide, his jaw set firm as if trying to keep his emotions under control. He surveyed the group with disbelief. His gaze rested on her.

"*Danke*," she said, even though she knew he couldn't hear her above the crowd. "Danke sehr. Thank you very much. And may Father God bless you."

The man's eyes flickered with compassion.

The crowd continued to surge around her, and the ground swayed under her feet. Michaela knew she had to get out of their midst. The tight presence of the odorous bodies reminded her of days spent in the cattle cars. Memories she wished forever severed from her mind.

With those memories, a face came to mind . . . Lelia. The teenager had been so full of life when her Jewish family had come to them, seeking a hiding place. Had it really been only four years ago? Then just last winter the two had been transported to this camp together. For months, for years, Michaela had made sure Lelia had remained by her side. Until last week. The influx of prisoners, the final massacres of desperate Nazis, and their weakened condition had made that impossible. Michaela remembered the last time she'd seen Lelia's face as they were herded in opposite directions after roll call. Was Lelia still alive? Michaela had to find out.

She spun around and pushed back through the crowd toward the barracks.

"Excuse me," she said in German to a woman. "Lelia Kubale. Do you know her?"

"Nein," said the woman, pressing on.

"Lelia Kubale? Lelia Kubale?" Michaela asked over and over. Every head shook. Each body pushed her aside in an effort to surge forward.

Just as Michaela was about to give up, one woman stopped. "Lelia Kubale?" she asked.

"Ja, ja. Do you know where she is?"

"The typhus barracks. Not doing well. I saw her two days ago. Perhaps dead by now."

Michaela couldn't bear the thought of the girl coming this far only to die so close to liberation.

"Thank you," Michaela said as she painstakingly hobbled toward the distant barracks. She knew it would be a miracle if anyone came out of there alive.

Michaela paused before the door. She covered her mouth, then pushed the door open. Unlike the other barracks, which had mostly cleared out, this one brimmed with people scarcely alive.

She staggered past the rows of invalids, searching each face. Many eyes were closed. More stared straight ahead, unseeing.

"The Americans are here," she told anyone she believed could understand. "We are liberated." A few of the prisoners uttered words of rejoicing. But most were unable to comprehend her message.

She came to the end of the barracks, with still no sign of Lelia. As she drifted back to the doorway in despair, she noticed a heap on the floor, partially hidden by another invalid.

"Lelia!" Michaela rushed to her.

The girl's eyes were closed, her body folded in an awkward curl.

"Please, God," Michaela cried, collapsing to her gaunt knees. "Please let her be alive!"

Michaela placed her face near Lelia's lips. She felt the softest puff of air caress her cheek.

"Help! Somebody help!" Michaela called. But who could help? *The Americans.* Struggling to her feet, she ventured back into the sunshine.

Yet as she headed for the gates, she noticed the crowds were returning. The jumble of foreign words made little sense as people passed on what little information they had.

She stopped one man she recognized. "What has happened? Where are the Americans?"

"Gone." He shrugged. "But with promises to return."

Michaela's strength gave out. She sank to the ground. *How could they leave?* Perhaps it was a wicked trick after all.

Closing her eyes, she lifted her face to the sun, allowing the stored-up tears to resume their flow.

Four

MAY 6, 1945

Helene slid her trembling fingers through Anika's shoulder-length hair, amazed at the feather lightness of the silken strands. Golden hair. Just like her own.

Helene considered weaving the hair into tiny braids, but she knew it wouldn't stay. The slightest touch, even a gentle breeze, would unfurl it until it flapped like flaxen banners across the girl's cherubic face.

Anika remained motionless as Helene tied her hair back with a pink ribbon.

"There you go." Helene set the soft-bristled brush on the table. As she rose from the kitchen chair, apprehension in her chest made breathing a chore. Try as she might, she couldn't fool herself into pretending today was just another day and their outing simply more errands.

"Come, love." Helene lifted the pot of milk she had thickened with stale bread. She placed it into a large picnic basket along with some bowls and spoons. "The hungry need food . . . and your smile." Yet even as Helene said the words, she didn't want to consider where they were actually going.

The moment Helene stepped out the door, she longed to dart back into the safe womb of her home. The world inside was warm and protected. Outside was chaos.

Dozens of old men, women, and children wandered the streets, many with hands in pockets, looking as if their destination was still being considered. What creatures of habit those in her village had become. Was it so difficult to remember how to think and act for oneself?

The sky was slightly overcast, but the air was warm. As Helene walked through the SS housing units, she was sure she saw a curtain flutter. Then another. People were watching her, like always. She had never truly fit in with the other SS wives. Some of them wore fine clothes pilfered from the inmates. She'd heard that a few wives of the higher officers even had lampshades made from human skin. The thought made her ill.

A jeep drove by with an American driver, and Helene noticed the curtain nearest the road fall. She understood the fear. For so long, men in German uniforms mounted on horseback or riding in automobiles had reigned over the village. They had become as natural to the landscape as the wide Danube River. Now who could the villagers trust?

Helene walked beyond the SS housing into the village, which had barely changed over the centuries. She passed quaint cottages made of brick and garden spots that had been tilled for generations. It was a small town, where every person considered his neighbors as family.

The basket grew heavy on her arm. She clutched Anika's fingers with her free hand and slowed her pace. Ahead, under a pear tree, Alec Weis stooped to pick up a piece of fallen fruit. The sun sparkled against his pure white hair. Not many months before, villagers had scurried through the fields before dawn picking the ground clean. Among other mandates, orders had come down that all fruit must be taken away from the fields and gardens before 6 A.M., lest the numerous prisoners being driven through the fields find even a scrap of nourishment.

And now, *liberation*. The word was so sacred she dared not speak it aloud. The German soldiers' terrorizing faces had changed to the appalled American ones.

Yes, this is real, Helene had wanted to tell the small group she'd witnessed from her window upon the discovery of the camp. *Welcome to our nightmare.*

Anika tripped over a small stone in the path, then righted herself. Mr. Weis tossed the fruit back to the ground and shuffled up the walkway to his cottage. Perhaps he did not know what to do without SS uniforms to mend.

Helene considered how the people in the village had been forced to feed, clothe, and house the guards. What else was there to do but comply?

But now things were different. Now something could be done.

Just this morning a red-haired American solider had approached Helene as she'd hurried back from the store. "In their freedom they cry for food," he said in German. Then he moved on, continuing his plea through the streets.

Finally, Helene thought. *Something I can do.*

She tried not to think of how Friedrich would react to the idea of his wife venturing into the camp to offer help. He considered her too timid. But Friedrich was not around.

Helene could not fool herself into thinking she was not afraid. Her trembling body revealed the true feelings of her soul. Yet greater than her fear was the sense of urgency to help those people. And with Anika at her side, she knew no one would dare confront her for the coward she'd been all these years.

"Anika, child," Helene said softly, "stay close to Mother."

% % %

"Guten Tag." Helene nodded to a soldier as she entered the camp. She gawked at the hillsides outside the gate. Amazingly, they appeared just as green and beautiful from inside the barbed wire. Helene couldn't decide if it was better or worse to suffer in the midst of such beauty.

The American soldier who'd spoken to her earlier

approached and lifted the cover of her basket. The scent of warm milk drifted from the pot inside.

"You're the first from the town to bring food," he said in German. "Danke. Can you bring more later?" His green eyes pleaded even more than his words.

"I'll see what else I can find."

The soldier peered down at Anika with concern, then turned back to Helene. "Come, I'll take you to the women." His voice quivered as he led the way. "They'll be grateful for this."

Helene glanced around. "Will we be safe?"

"Things have settled down. The prisoners are co-operating. Of course, if you'd rather not . . ." Helene couldn't make out the rest of his words as he led her across the noisy compound.

They rounded the corner of a now-empty administration building, and Helene stopped abruptly. A narrow brick structure rose before her. Her heart rate quickened as she recognized the tall chimney that extended above the camp. Helene had seen that smokestack exhale smoke and a fine white mist every day for years. Today it stood cold and empty.

As she drew closer to the center of camp, Helene noticed a large pile of—something. Her stomach wrenched. Bodies. Stacks of them. Left by men who in their haste were unable to hide the evidence of their crimes. Rats gnawed at the bones. She used her clean white apron to block her daughter's gaze. Anika pushed it away. Her eyes grew wide.

Helene pulled her daughter along as she caught up

with the redheaded soldier. *What have I done, bringing my little girl here? I should have just left the food at the gate.*

But before she had a chance to walk away, Helene saw them. Hordes of people huddled in groups, leaning on each other for support. Alarm surged through her at their emaciated appearance. She inched closer to the soldier.

The sound of her shoes on the gravel caused many to turn her direction. Or was it the smell of food?

Helene stared at the ground, attempting to ignore their feet . . . their hands . . . their faces. How pitifully thin they were.

She swallowed the lump in her throat and willed her nauseated stomach to calm. A scrawny hand reached for her. Helene's own hand trembled as she filled a bowl with warm milk and handed it to the woman. As she started to scoop more, she noticed a group in the back who seemed weaker, more in need. She took Anika's hand and proceeded in their direction. The girl's tiny fingers clamped down tight.

Another woman stretched a thin hand from the ground and gently touched the hem of Anika's dress. "A child," the woman whispered. "A real child."

Anika offered a tenuous smile, then turned to gaze at some people sitting along the barbed-wire fence.

Helene's first instinct was to gasp at the frail, skull-like faces and bony arms. Then she noticed one woman speaking gently to a younger one, most likely a teen-ager, who was curled up in a ball next to her. The woman was probably in her twenties, like Helene, but her gaunt face made her appear much older. Her thin hand stroked the teenage girl's equally thin shoulder. Her warm eyes caressed even deeper.

Helene approached the two women, but a strong hand grasped her arm. She looked up to find the redheaded soldier.

"They might be too weak to even eat," he warned. "We gave some of the women in this area meat and bread yesterday." The GI lowered his gaze. "It killed them."

Helene hesitated, but only for a moment. "Warm milk for you," she said to the woman. She lowered herself to the ground and pulled Anika onto her lap. Then she scooped up another bowl.

"I've been praying." The woman's hands trembled as she took the bowl and spoon. Slowly she lifted the spoon to the teenager's mouth. "Here, Lelia, eat."

A knot formed in Helene's throat as she grabbed another spoon. "I'll feed her. You feed yourself."

The woman lifted the spoon to her mouth and took a small taste. Her eyes closed and a euphoric smile lit up her face. "Oh, milk. Warm milk. And a spoon." She took another sip. "How long it's been since I used a spoon."

Helene felt suddenly embarrassed by her rounded figure. She lifted the spoonful of milk to the teenage girl's mouth. Cracked lips parted, and Helene struggled to keep her hand from shaking. Even worse than the helplessness she'd felt over the years was the desperation she felt now. There must be something more she could do. She had to help these women.

"Good?" Anika asked, her eyebrows raised.

"Quite good," the woman said in a voice too beautiful for this place. "You, little angel, make Michaela very happy."

Without thinking, Helene blurted out, "Would you come home with us? We could better care for you there. I live close by."

The woman's eyes grew dim. "Lelia is ill. I'm not sure she would survive being moved. And I mustn't leave her. I promised long ago I'd take care of her."

Helene stroked the woman's shoulder. "I'll talk to the American. The one who speaks German. Surely he can help."

Turning to search the crowd for him, Helene was surprised to see he was not more than a few feet away and had obviously overheard.

"I will help." He looked at the women with compassion. "Of course."

With the aid of the American soldier, Helene fed others too. Hands stretched toward her as the food ran out. "There's no more," she explained. "I'm sorry. I'll have to come back." She packed up her bowls and spoons in the basket, then returned to the two women by the fence.

"Where do you live?" the soldier asked, taking Anika's hand. Surprisingly, Anika let him. He lowered his voice. "Do you really want these women to go home with you?"

Helene suddenly felt foolish for her hastiness. How could she take these women to the SS housing? What would the American think if he knew who she was married to? And what if the women knew? Helene tried to think fast, avoiding the soldier's questioning gaze.

"My home is not suitable, but I have another place in mind. I can be back in a few hours after preparations are made. I will bring more food with me too."

"Danke," the redheaded soldier replied.

Helene took Anika's hand from his, caressing the girl's fingers with her thumb. "*Komm mit.* Come, we must make room. Let's go talk to your grandfather, shall we?"

A look of desperation crossed the face of the woman by the fence.

"I will be back," Helene reassured her. "I promise."

When she was halfway across the courtyard, Helene looked back at the women one last time. As she did, she seared the picture of them into her mind. For their sakes, and for Anika's, she would return to the place she had been forbidden to go. For them, she would approach the man she no longer had the right to call Father.

Five

MAY 6, 1945

The small town of St. Georgen bustled with activity as new American troops rolled into town. Only a few hours before, as she had left the Gusen subcamp, Helene discovered numerous soldiers setting up their tents and supplies just outside the concentration camp gates. Many of the GIs marched through the town in uniform, their olive-drab shirts and trousers dotting the streets. Tanks rumbled over the bridge along the outskirts.

From the town center, Helene could see the large yellow house in the distance. Once used as an inn for travelers, during the war the house had been converted into a storehouse for military supplies. Emptied just weeks ago by the retreating SS, only the man who lived there before the war still remained. It was this man she now sought.

Helene clenched her fingers into tight fists. Her hands seemed empty without Anika's grasp. She thought about the neighbor who'd finally agreed to keep Anika for the afternoon.

Katharina's round face had been blotchy, her nose red. "The Americans came. They said we only have two hours to move out. They're clearing out all SS housing."

"Why would they do that?" Helene asked, bewildered.

"The American army needs space to house their men. What better place for their soldiers to occupy than their enemies' beds?"

Helene stared at Katharina, unable to think.

"I'm sure they will be at your house next. But you, at least, have your father to live with—if he will take you back. Where am I to go? How will I feed my children?"

Helene hated leaving Anika with the frantic woman. But after all she'd witnessed that morning at the camp, she thought it best for her daughter to remain in a familiar setting. There was no way to know what she was about to face by returning to the former inn. For years now, the silence between Helene and her father had widened the chasm between them, until only regret and heartache filled the gaping valleys.

She had heard little about her father's activities during these last few years. "He is well," the grocer had told her occasionally. She supposed the Germans had been supporting him in exchange for use of his space. But what would he do now? Would he reinstate the gasthaus? It seemed only logical. If so, perhaps he would need an extra hand . . . and if he couldn't love her as a daughter, maybe he could benefit from her help as a hard worker? It was these hopes that had brought her here.

Helene started up the walkway leading toward the house. Tufts of new grass poked through the cracks between the large stones. She placed a foot on the first porch step. It was more worn than she remembered. The paint had peeled, and a subtle sway in the step reminded her of the curve of a mare's back. She touched the metal handrail, warm from the sun. Could she really do this?

Two creaky steps up, Helene hesitated. In the far right corner, *MUTTI* was carved into the wooden beam. *Mama.* In her mind's eye, Helene saw herself as a girl of eight. With her light hair falling around her face, she'd painstakingly shaped each letter with a dull knife. Her mother, who had been sick for many years, had breathed her last on that cold October day.

Helene stared at the carved letters a moment longer. Then she continued on, her fingers trailing along the delicate purple clusters hanging beside the steps. She took a slow breath. The air carried the smell of lilacs and river breezes. Sweet, moist scents. It smelled like home.

"Father's flowers," she murmured. Her heart missed a beat as she noticed tall weeds choking the once-beautiful garden beside the house.

She examined the windows for any sign of movement. The drapes were drawn. Helene tried to remember how long it had been since she'd seen the top of her father's hat and his slow gait as he strolled through the streets. Two weeks? Three?

She had often secretly watched him from afar. But where had he been of late? She realized now that she hadn't seen him since the SS emptied his home of their supplies. She cursed her stubborn pride and hurried up the remaining steps, her low heels clicking on each one.

Helene paused with her hand on the doorknob. How natural it seemed to simply twist the knob and enter, even though she hadn't done so for five years. Helene's heart felt drawn to the door and the home beyond. This was what she'd been missing. This place and that man.

She raised her fist and knocked. Nothing.

She tried again, louder. Finally, she noticed a stir in the drapes. Then the door rattled open.

Arms wrapped around Helene before a word could escape her lips. Her well-practiced plea for forgiveness was forgotten as tears overtook her. Her cheek rested on her father's shoulder. Her arms clutched his tall, thin frame. Wool scratched her cheek, and she breathed in the scent of his familiar shaving foam.

"Papa," Helene managed to choke out, and she wondered how she'd ever faced this horrible war without his embrace.

"Shh, *mein Tochter,* my daughter." His voice caught in his throat. "It is over," he said in a hoarse voice. "Welcome home."

Helene felt the embrace loosen slightly. She took a step back and peered into his face. The familiar gray eyes looked tired, his cheeks pale. His smile was tentative— far from the broad, happy one she remembered.

"I'm so sorry I didn't listen," she said. "You were right about him. About them."

Her father raised a hand. Then he limped through the door, as if too weary to stand and listen to her confessions.

She was forgiven. From the first glimpse of him she had known that, felt that.

"Come inside," he called. "We have much to prepare. I heard about the Allied soldiers taking over the SS housing. A wagon will be here soon to help move your things. This is why you have come, is it not? To move back here?"

"Actually . . ." Helene started. But her father was already moving farther inside.

Helene followed him into the quiet house. The same family photos graced the walls. The same furnishings adorned the rooms. The same musty scents filled the air.

New to the landscape was a pile of potatoes in the hallway that reminded her of a tall anthill. She stepped around them.

Her father's arm intertwined with hers as if only days, not years, had passed since their last meeting. He led her to the high-backed sofa and urged her to sit.

"First, we talk." He settled on the couch beside her as if the ticking of minutes didn't matter.

"What are all those potatoes for?" she asked.

Her father ran a hand over his wrinkled face and stroked his thin white mustache, a habit she remembered well. "I have been collecting for the camp all morning. Most people gave me something just to get me off their doorstep." He shook his head. "Things are not good there."

"I know. Katharina told me hundreds of barrack leaders have been murdered since the gates were opened. She's afraid to leave her house, yet she has no choice." Helene pulled her arms tight around her. She thought of her own trip to the camp. A shiver traveled down her neck. She hadn't realized how daring she'd been, or how foolish.

"The camp officials knew what they were doing by placing German criminals in charge," her father said. "The barrack leaders took great pleasure in doing the dirty work. Killing for the sake of killing. But do you think the SS guards concerned themselves with the fate of the barrack leaders? No, only their own." He pointed a finger into the air. "Now the swine are finding little mercy."

Her father rose from the sofa, his voice rising with him. "I heard most tried escaping into the woods, but they were all found. It is amazing what strength the nearly dead can find in the name of revenge."

Years ago Helene had ignored her father's prattling, shrugging off his enthusiasm and his efforts. Now she stared at him in awe. He was, and always had been, a man of principle and action.

"What next?" Her father raised his hands, palms

up. "Who will they turn their weapons on now? The prisoners are angry and have every reason to be. The violence will continue if we do not help."

He crossed to the hallway and plucked a potato from the stack. "You should see the countryside. Prisoners from the camp have robbed the farms, killing animals for food. Two men came by this morning with Angora rabbits from a neighbor's cages and wanted to cook them here. How could I say no? They were half starved. So we all had rabbit stew, ja? But this is only the beginning."

Helene watched him roll the potato in his hands, surprised at how thin and aged they had become. "I took some food to the camp this morning. I plan to take more later." She searched his face for a response. "I never agreed with what they did. I tried to talk to Friedrich, but he wouldn't—"

Her father flinched at the sound of her husband's name. "Ja, ja, good. We will work together now." He pulled back the drapes to look outside.

Helene picked up his blue jacket from the armrest. She rubbed its fabric between her thumb and fingers. The cloth was thin and worn. The past five years had been even harder on him than she'd imagined.

She stood, weighing the tension that hung in the air between them. Yes, she was forgiven. Yes, they could move on and help others. But as Helene replaced the jacket, she considered what she and her father could have accomplished together.

"How is my granddaughter?" His voice interrupted

her thoughts. He turned from the window and beheld her face.

"Anika is fine. Beautiful. Many people from town say she's like me when I was her age."

"And how are you?" The gentle manner in which he spoke overwhelmed her. Gone was his humanitarian air. The man standing before her was simply her father. And she had hurt him deeply.

"*Mir geht es gut*. I am well." She noticed him staring at her stomach. "I am due to have my second child in a few months. Friedrich may be back by then, though I do not know what to do if . . ." She paused, ashamed for again mentioning his name in this place.

"And until then?" He tossed the potato back onto the stack and limped to the coatrack, where he lifted his hat from the hook. "Until then you need to come home. I will help you get your things."

"Wait." She touched his arm, taken aback for a moment at the strong emotion the brief contact produced. "There's not just me. Not just Anika and the baby. I've offered . . . I've offered to care for two women prisoners from the camp."

Helene didn't know what she expected from her admission. She knew her father would agree. He was that type of man. But she hadn't expected the broad smile that crossed his face, causing the worry lines to disappear.

"My daughter has indeed returned. Komm, let us get your things and then prepare the house. We will have many to feed and care for."

Helene hurried into her house and shut the door. Her father's friend had brought a wagon around, and in an hour's time they had loaded most of her things. There were only a few more items she needed. But she knew she didn't have much time before the U.S. soldiers arrived to claim her house.

She surveyed the nearly empty living room and kitchen. For years this had been her sanctuary. The first home that had been all hers. The windows, where bright white curtains had fluttered, were bare. The hardwood floors appeared naked without the colorful rugs scattered across them.

Some items Helene refused to take. On the counter rested Friedrich's radio, a gift from his captain when he became SS *Untersturmführer*. It was still tuned to the official Nazi station. Even now she could imagine Wagner, Hitler's favorite composer, blaring over the airwaves.

The high-backed white chairs remained assembled around the table, reminding her of the pale boys in Hitler's Youth. Those chairs had been Friedrich's too. She'd never cared for their modern style.

An unsteady mixture of emotions swirled through Helene at the thought of leaving. She had become a lover and a mother in this place. It was also here where she'd experienced some of her darkest nights, waiting for her husband's return from the camps.

Helene walked to the window. She looked beyond the crisscross pattern of her fence to the long, metal railroad tracks and the town beyond that. Behind her, out of view, was the camp.

Helene moved toward the desk. It would have to stay. Father's inn had little room for extra furniture, and the shed in the backyard would fill up fast. Still, she needed to sort through the items inside. As Helene reached for the first drawer, she noticed a corner of a photo peeking from beneath the desk lamp.

Lifting the lamp revealed a picture of a young boy in front of a small cottage. Helene picked up the photo. Behind the boy and the cottage, large mountains rose straight up from the fields. On one peak, the tower of a castle spiraled into the sky. Helene used her finger to wipe dust from the boy's toothy grin.

Helene recognized that smile. She turned the picture over, and a handwritten name confirmed her guess. Friedrich. Where had this photo come from? And why hadn't she seen it before? Outside, trucks rumbled down the road. She couldn't worry about that now.

Helene slipped the photo into her apron pocket, then packed other pictures and several important-looking papers from the desk drawers into a small satchel. As she finished, she noticed a piece of paper on the floor where her rocking chair had sat. She picked it up, blew off the dust, and realized it was some sort of hand-written map. A pencil line was drawn from St. Georgen through Germany into Switzerland, then to Italy. Was this Friedrich's escape route? Had he made it to Italy?

Helene turned the paper over, noticing an address in the upper-right corner. PBC, 7002 Chur. Chur? That was a city in Switzerland. What would he be doing there?

She stuffed the map in with the other papers, then left the desk, ignoring the bottom drawer altogether. She already knew what was inside: watches, pendants, and a pearl necklace. Trinkets Friedrich had acquired from the camp. Items she refused to wear. Just the thought of them made her stomach queasy.

With hurried steps, Helene moved to the smaller bedroom on the second floor and rifled through Anika's things. She put small garments for the baby into the satchel, then tried to think of what else she might need.

It all seemed unreal. Helene had to remind herself this was actually happening. Life would never be the same.

She moved on to the larger room. Friedrich's uniform shirts still hung from hooks on the wall. She grabbed one and stared at the bed.

When she'd announced her pregnancy with Anika, she thought things might be different. Friedrich had been overwhelmed and awed at the thought of being a father. He had discussed his own father's death at an early age. He'd even shared stories about his kind mother.

That night, he'd knelt before her, his head pressed to her stomach, and wept. "I want to be a good father. But I cannot bear to bring a child into this awful place. We will go away. We can start fresh somewhere else."

She'd been hopeful that night, and even in her dreams she'd imagined sailing away from the control of the Nazis.

Yet when Friedrich awoke the next morning, it was as if those words had never been spoken. He climbed out of bed the same unfeeling guard he'd been the day before.

On that day, the man Helene married disappeared. Her husband became cold, harsh, and bitter. He even yelled at her for yielding to morning sickness. Over time, Helene found herself shrinking back more and more from his quick temper, drunken rages, and sulky attitude.

She sat on the bed and fingered the roughness of the shirt, then held it close to her face. Instead of the scent of him, the shirt stank of vodka. She threw it to the floor.

What now? she wondered. *What will happen when he returns for me and the children? Does any fragment of that devoted man remain?*

The baby kicked within Helene's womb, and she massaged her ribs. Would the child look like Friedrich? Perhaps this time she carried the son her husband longed for.

The sounds of more Allied vehicles filtered in through the windows. She didn't have to check outside to know that soon it would be her house they parked in front of.

Helene regarded the room one last time, then picked up her satchel and rose from the bed, kicking the shirt behind the door.

She was on the bottom step when the knock came. But it didn't sound like soldiers. *Perhaps it's Katharina bringing Anika back.* She opened the door.

Edda, a neighbor she didn't know very well, stood there, filling the doorway with her presence. Her face was pale, and her hands fidgeted with an envelope.

Helene took a step back. A chill settled over her. What did this woman want? Had she heard of Helene's journey to the camp? Helene still couldn't shake the feeling that she was being watched. That her every act against the Nazi Party was being recorded and reported.

After a few seconds of awkward silence, Helene motioned Edda inside. "I was just leaving, but come in."

Edda did so, closing the door behind her. "I won't stay long," she said, her voice strained. "I have to finish packing. But I have news for you." The large woman shuffled to the kitchen and slumped into one of the white kitchen chairs, pressing her forehead into her hand. Helene glanced at her plump, pink fingers that bore no calluses. Why, they'd probably never performed a stitch of manual labor.

Helene's own hands trembled as she sat, and she fingered a dish towel left on the table. The baby continued to tussle in her womb.

"I'm sorry," Edda said. "This is more difficult than I thought." She fidgeted in her seat. "I've had word from my husband. Arno made it to safety."

"That's wonderful," Helene said.

"I also have news for you."

"About Friedrich?" Helene asked.

Edda lowered her gaze. "He did not make it to Bavaria. He was with a group a few hours behind my husband's. I was told the Americans blocked their path, and when they attempted to escape, the men were captured and killed. Right on the spot. Without even a trial."

A cold sensation washed over Helene. She saw Edda's full pink lips moving but couldn't comprehend the words.

Finally Edda paused. "Do you understand, Helene?" she asked. "He's not coming back."

Helene nodded. Though she wanted to cry, no tears surfaced.

Edda rose. "I have a letter here for you. From him." She placed it on the table. Helene noticed a bloodstain on the corner.

"My husband found it on his body," Edda explained. "A messenger brought it to me. I'm sure he'd planned to send it upon his safe arrival."

Somehow Helene was able to mutter a word of thanks as Edda let herself out. The letter sat on the table. Helene remained on the kitchen chair, her half-packed things by her side, and stared at the envelope.

She lost all track of the ticking clock until a heavy fist pounded on the door. It was time. Helene rose and straightened her hair. She tucked the envelope into her apron pocket next to the photo of Friedrich.

The knock came again. The doorknob twisted.

"Time's up," a voice shouted in German as two American soldiers burst into the room. "This building is now under the jurisdiction of the United States Army." Helene grabbed her things and hurried out, refusing to look into their faces. The satchel dug into her shoulder as she left the gate and scurried down the street. Still heavier were the thoughts of what could have been. What never would be.

Friedrich was dead.

Six

Peter plodded through the gates of Gusen and leaned on the cold concrete pole for support. The sub-camp was small compared to the massive rock structure of the main camp, Mauthausen, where he'd spent part of the previous day. Here, thin wire separated the prisoners from freedom, whereas thick stone walls surrounded the perimeter of the mother camp. While Gusen adjoined the small town of St. Georgen, Mauthausen was a fortress set apart, covering the top of a high hill.

But death was the same in both places. Thousands of bodies, and thousands more dying daily.

Peter's legs felt like lead, and he covered his face with his hands. He'd tried not to look. Had attempted to walk past the man without hesitation, but it hadn't worked.

He glanced back at the body that rested just twenty yards outside the camp gate. It lay there, face to the sky, mouth open. The knees were swollen and bloody, reminding Peter of two large knots on the limb of a branch. The man's chest neither rose nor fell. Peter didn't have to check his pulse to know he was dead.

Peter guessed what had happened. The opportunity for freedom had arrived and the desire to escape had proved too strong. The weak man had crawled from prison into liberty, knowing eternity waited on the other side.

Peter sank to the ground, his back against the pole. It made no sense. Why did this have to happen? How could God allow such suffering? He rubbed the back of his neck and tried to scrub away the deep ache inside.

He placed his head between his knees and took a long breath. It was no use. All he managed to inhale was the scent of death. He'd been told the crematoriums had stopped weeks earlier, yet the stench still blanketed the camp. And even last night, as Peter had traveled back to his base, with thousands of German prisoners in tow, the wind had whistled around him and the driving rain had soaked him to the bone. Even so, he could not escape the foul smells of Gusen and Mauthausen. They had permeated his skin and remained through the night. Perhaps they would always be with him.

Yet even with the mix of smells—human waste, foul body odors, and smoldering flesh—one scent angered him above all. German tobacco. He caught a whiff of it and pictured arrogant guards patrolling the grounds, judging the helpless with possessed eyes. He imagined them smoking their cigarettes while their boots sank into the sticky mud created by the trampling of a thousand bodies.

Peter raised his head and surveyed the camp. His attention rested on one woman. She was too weak to stand. But with all her strength she propped herself onto one elbow. She caught his eye, and he glanced away. He was supposed to be the strong one.

Peter rose and wandered through the crowd, inspecting the caricatures of human beings. Josef approached him, his face pale. "Scotty, we need your help at the graves."

Peter didn't have the strength to ask why. His feet plodded toward the edge of the camp. As he approached the chasm of a mass grave, he noticed a few of his men bent over two people. One was still alive. A young boy—perhaps in his early teens—rested on his knees and leaned over the motionless form of the other.

"He's been here all day." Banion rubbed a hand over his dirty face. "For hours he's just stared at the body. He won't let us take it."

"It's his brother," Josef explained. "He's been begging us to bury him in an individual grave."

Murphy crouched at the boy's side. "He won't eat, he won't sleep. He won't let go."

"Then we'll do it." Peter picked up a shovel that was lying near an open ditch. "Let's make a grave."

Peter's shovel hit the ground and sank into the dirt with little effort. His men quickly followed suit. But soon the soft dirt gave way to stony soil. Rocks blocked every blow. Josef and Murphy gave up their shovels and worked on hands and knees, frantically pulling rocks from the earth. Banion and Peter continued on with shovels, inch by inch, until the hole was large enough.

Peter wiped his brow, then examined the faces of his men. Murphy had been with him when they landed at Normandy. Banion and Josef joined them on other battlefields. But as they laid that frail body in the grave, with the man's brother watching, Peter truly felt he knew them. Their faces expressed both accomplishment and agony as together they fulfilled the boy's wish.

Peter dropped his shovel and stood beside the boy. Tears streamed down the gaunt cheeks as he knelt beside the grave, watching the last clump of dirt fall over his brother.

Josef stood over the grave and chanted the Kaddish, the Jewish prayer for the dead, in Yiddish.

Dropping to one knee, Peter lifted the boy's chin with one finger and gazed deep into his mournful eyes. "It is finished. You must get up now."

The boy trembled, and Peter gently took his bony arm and helped him stand. He staggered a few steps, then fell back to the ground. Peter picked him up and carried him away from the grave.

The boy's face nestled into Peter's shoulder. Peter tightened his grip, pulling him closer to his chest. Tears ran over his sergeant patch.

This is what it's all about, Peter sensed deep inside. *This is what we've been fighting for.*

Peter carried the boy to the barracks. The others stayed at the gravesite, where thousands more awaited burial.

Inside the barracks, a few rays of light fought their way through the slits in the walls. Peter gently set the boy on the nearest wooden bunk.

Former prisoners, scattered around the room, watched him. *What can I do? What can I say to them?* Peter turned away from their distressed gazes. *Nothing.* He could say nothing.

Peter stepped out of the dim barracks and headed toward the gates. He didn't notice her until she was ten feet away. Then there she stood, a lone flower among a field of dead weeds. *"Una donna bionda con due bambini,"* one Italian survivor had called her when she'd brought food earlier. When Peter asked for a translation he discovered it meant "Beautiful blonde woman with child." This time, though, no child accompanied her.

A slight smile brightened her tired face. *How hard this must be for her,* Peter thought. *How brave she is.*

"It is good to see you again," he said in German.

"I have come for the two women. Everything is arranged. Can you still help?"

Peter grasped the arm of one of his men passing by. "Clifton, find me a truck and park it by the front gates."

"You got it, Sarge."

Peter wiped his brow with the back of his hand. The burial of that beloved brother still haunted the fringes of his mind. The boy's tears seemed to burn through his uniform to his skin.

"Have you seen the two women today?" The blonde surveyed the area.

"They were near the back this morning." He led the way for a while, then stopped. "I'm sorry, I should have asked sooner, but what is your name?"

"My name is Helene—" She stopped before giving her last name.

"And where will we be going?"

She pointed toward the town. "To a large yellow house on the west side of the main street."

"I know the one you're talking about," Peter said. "Find the women and wait with them. I'll get a truck ready." He tried to keep his voice steady. "I'll be right back."

The woman, Helene, nodded. Her face looked haunted and weary. Very weary.

Everyone has a story, Peter thought as he scanned the entrance. *I wonder what hers is.* He was curious, but too often the people's stories weighed more heavily upon his heart than the dead bodies. The stories put voice to the horror, where bodies refused to speak.

Peter headed toward the gates. New troops were arriving daily, attempting to bring order to the chaos. Officers moved from building to building, confiscating Nazi documents that had somehow survived the purging. Other troops searched the miles of underground tunnels used to assemble aircraft parts and German weapons. *Bergkirstall,* the tunnels were called. He'd been amazed at how the sand dug from the tunnels had created a man-made mountain just outside the camp.

Peter noted that even reporters and photographers had made their way into the camp, shocking the world with news of survivors, ovens, and mounds of bodies.

Clifton waited at the camp gate, hat in hand. "Sorry, Scotty. The jeeps are blocked by wagons. They're all over the place. Local farmers are using them to haul bodies to a potato field down the road."

Peter watched two men sling a corpse onto a wagon bed. "Never mind." He rubbed the back of his neck. "I'll figure something out."

"Yes, Sarge." Clifton headed back toward the graves.

Peter considered his options. He knew he could carry the women if he had to. Each of them probably weighed less than ninety pounds. Lightweight compared to the packs he'd been trained to carry.

No, he had to find some other way. He'd hauled enough bodies in this war, both alive and dead, to know he never wanted to do it again.

Peter circled around a large truck and spotted a wooden wheelbarrow, carelessly tipped onto its side. He righted it, then lined it with a dirty blanket he found along the fence line. Peter's jaw tensed as he realized that both women's emaciated bodies could fit within the small bucket. Still, he would not let them travel like baggage. He would take them one at a time—through the gates, to freedom, to life.

Peter pushed the creaky wheelbarrow back into the camp, where American soldiers were herding a stream of townspeople. They were mostly older men and boys.

A few women were scattered among them. Many wore Sunday attire.

"What's going on?" he asked the soldier leading the citizens.

"Gravediggers on special assignment," the young GI said with mock authority. "Rounded up from the town."

Peter recognized a few townspeople who'd brought food, clothing, and blankets into the camp. "Under whose orders?" he asked, knowing the chain of command varied depending on who'd left and who'd arrived.

"All the way from the top."

"Patton?"

"Yes. Patton."

Peter watched as shovels and picks were handed out. It wasn't right. These were decent people.

Peter maneuvered the wheelbarrow in front of the GI, stopping him. "Who can I talk to about this, Soldier?"

The man pointed to a colonel Peter had seen a few times when they were stationed in France. He started toward the man, then remembered Helene was waiting.

Glancing one last time at the group of villagers moving toward the gravesite, Peter headed in the direction he'd sent her. The townspeople would have to fend for themselves.

"One thing at a time," he reminded himself, spotting the blonde hair and navy-blue dress in the distance. "One thing at a time."

Michaela's body tensed as a hand touched her shoulder. Where was she? Was she safe? She opened her eyes, wondering whose shadow fell upon her. A man and woman stood over her. A halo of sunlight circled the woman's golden hair, and Michaela wondered if she was peering into the face of an angel.

Then she remembered. She was outside the barracks in the fading sunshine. This woman and the GI beside her were here to help.

Lelia lay crumpled at her side. Dirt streaked the girl's gaunt face. Sores covered her arms. Yet they had made it.

Michaela urged a smile to her lips despite the weakness of her limbs and the pain in her stomach that never seemed to cease.

"We are taking you to my home," the woman said in German, speaking slowly and clearly. "I will care for you there."

Michaela noticed a wheelbarrow in the hands of the soldier—apparently, her ride out of this place. She chuckled to herself before sharing her thoughts with the others. "You are familiar with the German fairy tale about the cinder girl?" she asked the American GI.

"Of course. It's a classic." His voice held a note of surprise. "We call her Cinderella."

After months of captivity, this was one thing Michaela hadn't lost. The stories of her childhood had remained locked away where no human hands could strangle their power. Fairy tales, poetry, parables. Recalling them had kept her mind clear during the endless days and nights.

Michaela stretched out a finger toward the wheelbarrow. "So this carriage will carry me out of the cinders?"

The GI didn't seem to know how to respond. His eyebrows raised, and he eyed her with curiosity.

Michaela stared at her gaunt feet. "Forgive my lack of a fancy slipper."

The man's face brightened. He gently lifted her into his arms. "Your highness."

"Ah!" She winced at his touch. He'd tried to be gentle, but the contact caused a thousand protests.

He cautiously set her on the blanket inside the wheelbarrow, and Michaela suddenly felt embarrassed for her filthy shirt, naked limbs, and matted hair. A cinder girl, indeed.

A moan replaced the lightheartedness of the moment before. A simple memory of a previous wagon ride, with her hair done in bows and her plump hands clinging to the rails, caused a gentle whimper she could not hold in. Was that another girl during another lifetime? A girl as fanciful as the tales she'd read?

The wheelbarrow jostled as the American lifted the handles and pushed. The front wheel sank into the ground slightly, then rolled forward.

"*Gedulden Sie sich bitte einen Augenblick!*" Michaela called out. "Wait, please!" The wheelbarrow stopped. She tried to look over her shoulder, but shooting pains in her neck prevented her. "What about Lelia?"

"Don't worry." The blonde woman squatted at

Michaela's side and rubbed her hand. "We'll come back for her."

"Nein," Michaela insisted. "She must not be left alone." A promise from long ago stirred to the surface. "We were separated once. I cannot leave her again."

"We'll get her next, don't worry." The American pushed forward again.

Sobs erupted from deep in Michaela's chest. Leaving the girl was like leaving her family all over again.

"Wait," the blonde said to the American. The wheelbarrow stopped again, and she leaned over Michaela, a few loose curls falling around her face. "I will stay. Don't cry. I will stay." She turned to the American. Her brown eyes looked so weary that Michaela felt ashamed.

"My father will be waiting for you," the woman said to the American. "There should be a cushion on the front porch. Ask him to keep her company there until I can come and bathe them both."

The GI nodded and resumed the journey. The blonde angel turned back the way they'd come, her steps heavy.

"Danke," Michaela mumbled, suddenly exhausted. She leaned her head back and rested it on the side of the wheelbarrow. The wood cut into her scalp, and she tried not to wince. *A home,* she thought. *After so long, a real home.*

Many eyes followed her as she was rolled out of the camp gates. The prisoners, those she felt a common bond with, appeared both envious and gratified. Though many she knew were young like she was, they all looked so very old.

What a pathetic picture I must appear to them. Like they were to her. *Yet we are the lucky ones. The ones who still breathe.*

Michaela closed her eyes, and her lids turned pink from the sunlight. Still the image of the watching prisoners stayed with her. And as she was wheeled through the gates, those images somehow transformed in her mind. The unfamiliar faces were replaced by familiar ones. She pictured her mother, father, and Georg watching her. Their last prayers now answered.

Michaela suddenly realized that the air around her smelled sweeter than any she'd breathed in a long time. She opened her eyes and noticed she was traveling through town. She stared at the storefronts and homes, amazed that life beyond the gates appeared so normal.

"Goodbye," she whispered to those long lost.

A page in her life story was turning. The nightmare she'd lived for the past few years would be left behind. The thought both thrilled and horrified her. Michaela knew that by leaving the camp, she stepped into a new life without those she loved. And what she feared most was that her newfound freedom would never compare to the memories locked deep inside.

Seven

Peter pushed the creaky wheelbarrow through the village, amazed at how even children looked away when they recognized his human cargo. Shame covered their faces. Conversations halted as he passed. Although many of the townspeople denied knowing the happenings inside the camp, he was certain now that they knew more than they admitted. How could they not hear? How could they not see, not smell?

Outrage at their denial caused his grip to tighten on the wheelbarrow handles. Then he thought of Helene. Obviously she had not agreed with the Nazi annihilation. She'd been the first from town to offer help. Had others felt such compassion? Perhaps some, but not enough. Not enough to make a difference.

Peter neared the street with the yellow house. He

glanced down at the woman, suddenly humiliated for her. The filth, the stench from her body, became more evident the farther he moved away from the camp. Yet she held her chin high. Her wide blue eyes perused the buildings they passed as if she had never witnessed such things. Yet Peter knew she had. She was a normal person just like him. A person who read fairy tales. Who had once lived free.

He rounded the last corner, moving into a residential neighborhood. The large yellow house, partially hidden by tall oak trees, dominated the block. A white-haired man with a thin mustache waited on the porch.

Peter lifted the woman from the wheelbarrow and carried her through the front gate. Softly she uttered what sounded like prayers. Tears dampened her face.

"Your castle awaits, my lady," he announced. The elderly man patted a cushion on the porch, and Peter carefully laid her on it. As he did, she lifted her hands to her face and sobbed.

Curse the Nazis. Every one of them. What they did to these people was something he would never forgive.

After briefly introducing himself to the elderly man, and promising to return with the teenage girl, he left the yellow house. Anger burned within him, and he quickened his pace. The empty wheelbarrow clattered noisily on the streets as he traveled back to Camp Gusen.

The sun was setting over a distant hill. Its rays lighted the clouds with pink and cast shadows over the countryside. Peter's gaze was drawn to a huge cloud of dark smoke rising in the distance. Gusen's large crematorium stacks stood silent, but barracks near the sandy hillside were being burned in an effort to control the disease and stench.

Prisoners who had nowhere else to go burrowed inside makeshift tents just a few yards beyond the camp gates. Peter slowed as he passed and wondered how long they would survive. Wondered how they would start their lives over if they did.

He entered the front gates and spotted Helene sitting on the ground. The teenage girl's head rested on her lap, her eyes open. As he approached, fear radiated from the girl's gaze.

"American GI," Helene assured her, leaning close. The girl seemed to calm, but she did not speak. She clung to Helene's hand as Peter hoisted her into the wheelbarrow. "We are going to my father's house." Helene stroked the teenager's fingers. "Michaela is there. And my daughter, Anika, will soon be there too. Do you remember Anika from this morning?"

Lelia stared at Helene but said nothing. Her eyes glazed over as they exited through the gates.

As they continued on, Helene kept up the casual chatter. This time the entourage received several stares. Men, women, and children peeked out of doorways. Some pointed. Others spoke to each other in low voices. It was not he or the fragile girl who drew their attention, but Helene. Many, Peter noticed, cast hateful glares in her direction. He was sure he knew why. She was helping while they refused. She dared to enter the camps. She was making a difference.

Too bad the town doesn't have more like her. People of character. People who stand up for what's right.

🍂   🍂   🍂

Helene hurried along the narrow lane leading to the small farmhouse on the edge of town. Her shoulders ached, her feet were sore and swollen, but she still had one more task. She had to pick up Anika from the farm where Katharina now stayed.

She was late, but it couldn't be helped. The women from the camp had needed much attention. After bringing Lelia to the house, Helene had bathed both women and dressed them in her old nightgowns. Her father worked with her. And as she washed each one, he gently deloused the other. Helene marveled at the way he'd performed the task without causing them embarrassment or shame. After applying a powder to kill the hundreds of lice, her father had sat there picking them off, telling stories of his childhood as if it were the most natural thing in the world.

The American had returned after his evening meal and carried the women to beds in a guest room across the hall from Helene's bedroom. He brought leftovers with him. Ham and potatoes for Helene and her father, and watery soup for the others' tender stomachs.

With a clean body and full belly, Michaela had beamed appreciatively as her head rested on the pillow. Lelia, on the other hand, worried Helene. The girl, whom she now knew was seventeen, had simply stared blankly, not once moving of her own volition. *Does Lelia even realize she's free? Can she understand what's happening?*

Helene's father had agreed to stay with the women while she retrieved Anika, and even offered to keep watch over them through the night. Helene had gratefully accepted his assistance.

Now the sun had set. The American GI had offered to accompany Helene to get Anika, but she'd refused. He hadn't asked any questions about Helene's life, and she liked it that way. She was certain he'd hate her if he knew. Perhaps he might even find a way to bring charges against her.

As she approached the farmhouse, Helene rubbed her arms, willing the strength for one more task. She spotted a lantern still burning inside Frau Schulmacher's kitchen window. Hopefully someone was still awake.

Helene approached the small stoop and tapped on the door. It cracked slightly. "Go away," the old woman screeched.

Helene stepped back, startled. "Frau Schulmacher, it's me, Helene Völkner. I'm here for my daughter, Anika." She heard movement behind the door, as if a large piece of furniture was being pushed out of the way. Then the door swung open, revealing the two women, Katharina's three small boys, and Anika all huddled around the small kitchen.

"Get in here, girl. Are you crazy?" The woman pulled Helene's arm, quickly shutting the door behind her. "What are you doing out on a night such as this?"

Helene stared at Katharina, silently begging for an explanation.

"It's been horrible." Katharina pulled Helene into the living room, out of earshot of the children. "Prisoners showed up earlier looking for food," she whispered. "They swarmed the place, and we were afraid they'd hurt us. They were so horrible, so grotesque! I can't wait to leave."

"Leave?" Helene wrapped an arm around her friend's trembling shoulders. The light from the kitchen cast shadows into the dim room. "Where are you going?"

"I have received news from Mother and Father. They're sending my older brothers to get the boys and me. They've been living in the countryside in France. Things are better there, they say. Father has connections with the government, you know. He pulled some strings, and he said you could come with us. We'll be safe, Helene. We can leave this horrible place behind."

"I can go too?" Helene released Katharina's shoulders. It had been all she'd wanted since she first realized what the camp was about. "When?"

"Tomorrow. Father promised my brothers would be here by then. We won't be able to take much with us, but we won't need to. My parents will make sure we have everything we need."

Helene's heartbeat quickened as she thought about a new life in France. A chance to start over. An opportunity to leave the horrors behind. Then she remembered the women. She couldn't bring them this far only to leave now. Helene let out a low moan and sank into a small chair.

"What's wrong?" Katharina asked. "It's what we've been wanting."

"I can't do it." Helene recalled the expression on Michaela's face as her head rested on a pillow for the first time in years.

"What do you mean, you can't?"

"I have obligations. I've promised to help some women."

Katharina crossed her arms over her chest. "Just tell them you can't do it. I'm talking about leaving. Starting a new life. I don't care if I never set foot in this terrible place again."

Helene noticed Katharina had said nothing of her SS husband and the part he'd played in this new life. Had she heard any news from him? Or had he been killed, like Friedrich? Helene was afraid to ask.

Katharina lowered her voice. "We will come for you tomorrow and—"

"Nein." Helene stood. "I can't leave my father again either."

"Helene, you haven't talked to him in years. At least think about it. Sleep on it."

"I will. I promise." Helene walked back into the kitchen. She found Anika asleep on a small rug in front of the fire. She lifted her daughter into her arms and carried her to the entrance.

Katharina opened the door. "I'll be by in the morning," she said as Helene headed into the night.

But even as she walked as quietly as she could—her ears attuned to the slightest noise—Helene knew her decision would not change. She would stay. She had to.

For once she'd think of them.

❧ ❧ ❧

Thirty minutes after leaving the farmhouse, Helene eased Anika's sleeping body onto Helene's own childhood bed. She unfolded the downy white comforter and tucked it around the girl's shoulders. Anika's soft blonde hair feathered across the pillow like a halo of fluff.

Was she doing the right thing? Was she putting her children in danger by not leaving this place?

There's too much to consider, Helene thought, settling into a chair by the window. She lifted her apron to her face. The smell of the camp still clung to her.

With a sigh, Helene pulled the shoes off her swollen feet. She felt pressure on her rounded stomach as she bent down, and she rubbed the spot where her baby rested.

When standing, it was still easy to hide her pregnancy. With her long torso, she hadn't shown with Anika until her seventh month. Even now she simply looked plump, like many of the women in the village.

Helene pulled the pins from her hair. It tumbled across her shoulders as she leaned forward to rub her aching arches. But their pain could not compare to the hurt she carried within her heart.

Friedrich is dead, she reminded herself. She had wanted to tell Katharina, but couldn't. She knew the emotions she'd been damming up would break through if she had.

Throughout the day, images of her husband had filled her mind. Not memories of the man he had become, but of their first few months of marriage, when laughter filled their home and humor lit up his eyes. For *that* man she mourned.

Helene straightened in her chair. She found a handkerchief in her apron pocket to wipe the tears dripping from her chin. In that same pocket was the photo she had found on the desk and the letter she'd been putting off reading all day.

Anika stirred on the bed, then settled down again. Outside, Helene heard her father venturing to the outhouse. She had to admit she did miss the modern comforts of the SS housing. But even that made her feel guilty. The two women lying in the next room had survived in utter filth, while she lived in a comfortable home provided by their captors.

Helene rubbed the back of her neck. There was nothing she could do about that now. She must move on. And moving on meant reading the letter from her husband—the last words he had ever penned.

She pulled open the envelope flap and slid out the single sheet of paper inside, trying to ignore the blood and dirt that stained it. Her heart pounded upon seeing the small print that was uniquely Friedrich's. She wondered how many hands it had passed through on its long journey to her.

Unfolding the letter slowly, she noticed it was dated

April 30, just two days after his departure. Was that really only a week ago? Whoever had brought the envelope had done so quickly.

Dear Helene,

As I write this letter, I am in the high hills of Austria, trying to cross the border into Italy. I know I promised to bring you to this place someday, where the edelweiss grows in the crevasses of the highest peaks. Perhaps someday I will. But until that time, remember my love. I promise to find a safe place for us all. A place where we can be the family you've always dreamed of.

As you wait, speak nothing of the things I have told you about my work. THIS IS OF THE UTMOST IMPORTANCE. Many, including the Americans and the Russians, may seek this information. They might be winning the war, but they can never take away our honor.

It would also be wise to destroy all the items I brought out of the camp. You will not want to be found with those things in your possession. I should have attempted to do that myself before leaving, but as you know, I did not have time.

Tell Anika her papi loves her and will come for her soon.

With love,
Friedrich

Helene lay the letter across her lap. What would he say if he knew about the things *she* had brought out of the camp? Surely these women were an even greater testimony than the watches and jewelry tucked away in a desk drawer.

In her mind's eye, Helene was back at home, peeking at Friedrich from under the feather comforter. His jaw locked in determination. His brows knitted in hatred of the never-ending mass of prisoners. No, he would not be happy with what she'd done.

Despite the fact that Helene would never again have to seek his approval, she hated him for succumbing to the darkness. And this hatred was rooted deeper than any mourning could go.

As she snuggled next to her daughter and drifted off to sleep, Helene again thought of the women from the camp. More than anything, she needed to stay and help them survive.

For this was her chance to make up, in a small way, for all that her husband had achieved for evil.

Eight

Peter bolted upright in his cot. His heart pounded as a nightmare chased him into wakefulness. He tried to push the skeletal images out of his mind, but the dream had been almost tangible. *That's because the images are real,* he thought, remembering where he was.

Peter had seen many hideous things. Buddies blown to pieces. American paratroopers hung up in trees, their bellies split open by Nazi bayonets. Yet those men had been trained. They'd advanced through Europe knowing full well the horrors that happened to their buddies could be their destiny too.

With the camps it was different. These people did not choose to be drawn into the fight. They were defenseless. Helpless.

Gentle breathing and an occasional snore issued from the men bunked around him. In the darkness, a lone cigarette glowed from across the room. Peter knew it was Clifton by the way his cigarette swept back and forth in the darkness, as if the university music major were using it to lead an invisible orchestra.

Peter lay back on his cot, his heartbeat still echoing in his ears. He attempted to concentrate on the noises around him. Anything to take his mind off the images. He easily distinguished Josef's snore, Banion's gentle wheezing, and Murphy's deep exhalations that blew like a hurricane. Still, it was not enough of a distraction.

It was the boy we buried, Peter realized, partially sitting up. In the dream, the skeletal figure had tried to escape his rocky grave, his fingers attempting to scratch their way to the surface. Not knowing what to do, Peter had piled more bodies on top of the grave in hopes of trapping the figure. Still the *scratch, scratch, scratch* had continued.

Peter pulled the wool blanket to his cheek and flopped onto his side. In a far window, he saw the first golden rays of sunrise frosting tall evergreens. He thought of the fragile bodies he'd carried out of camp the day before. Had those two women survived to first light? He couldn't remember their names and didn't want to. The more detached he stayed, the better.

And yet, he couldn't stop thinking of how weary that one woman's face had been as he laid her on the bed. And the younger one—it wouldn't be fair for her to die so soon after liberation. Then again, when had this war been fair?

Peter heard Clifton flick his cigarette to the ground and squash it with his boot. Josef's snores increased in volume, meaning he would be waking soon.

Outside, the scratching of shovels started again. More graves were being dug for those who hadn't lived to see dawn.

Something burned against Michaela's eyelids. She covered her face with a thin hand and tried to open her eyes. It was the sun that caused so much pain this new morning. Bright rays streamed through the fluttering curtains, and for a moment she forgot where she was.

Slowly she stretched her aching arms above her head. Then she remembered the blonde woman, Helene, and the bath she'd given her the night before. She rubbed her hand over an arm, awed at the feeling of clean skin.

And the food. For so many months, she'd hungered for that gray soup in the camp, wishing for more and dreaming of just one small chunk of potato. Last night she'd had broth with real flavor. And although she'd only taken a few mouthfuls, it had burned in her shrunken stomach, causing her to fall into a fitful sleep.

Michaela took a deep breath, relishing the scents of a home. The blankets around her smelled of soap and wind. The aroma of eggs frying drifted in from the kitchen.

She noticed another sweet smell too. A vase of flowers rested on a small table beside her bed. Next to the table was the chair where the old man had sat until she fell asleep. Beyond that was Lelia's bed. Michaela clasped a hand over her mouth when she noticed the empty, rumpled sheets. Lelia was gone.

Michaela reached toward the bed. A cry rose from her chest and echoed in the room. Footsteps drew near. Within seconds the door flew open and the blonde woman burst in.

Michaela pointed at the bed. "Is she dead?"

The woman, Helene, knelt beside Michaela and took her hand. "Shh, now. Don't worry. She's asleep on the floor. See?"

With Helene's help, Michaela sat up slightly. She looked over the woman's shoulder and saw Lelia curled in a ball on the floor at the foot of the beds. The girl's head rested on a small rug and a red blanket covered her. A pillow had been pushed to the side. Michaela watched closely to ensure the rise and fall of her chest. *She's still breathing. She's alive.*

Helene settled Michaela back against the mattress. Then she rose and opened the window farther, letting in more of the fresh, clean air. "My father told me Lelia moaned through the night. It reminded him of his time in the first war. After so many days of sleeping on the ground, he said a bed was difficult to get used to."

Helene poured water from a porcelain pitcher into a tin cup and brought the drink to Michaela's lips. The water was clean and sweet, and after a few sips she felt satisfied. She returned her head to her pillow and took a deep breath.

"After my father laid her on the floor," Helene continued, "Lelia went right to sleep." She started toward the door. "I have some warm milk for you. I'll bring it right in."

Michaela stretched out her hand. Helene paused in the doorway.

"Thank you," Michaela said softly. "You saved our lives."

"You're welcome, of course." Helene's eyes glistened with unshed tears. "I'll be back with the milk."

As Michaela lay there, she wondered what the woman's story was. Had she too lost family members? A husband? A mother?

Michaela's mother's words came to her. *Only a tender heart can touch others in such a gentle way.*

Michaela knew Helene's heart was tender. Her touch, a gentle reminder that God had not abandoned them after all.

Peter strode to the mess hall. The flap of the white-walled tent whipped in the breeze, fanning the scents of breakfast toward the line of approaching soldiers.

He was thankful for the fresh, hot food that filled his stomach. After months of K rations, he was sure everyone in his company would quickly fill out their uniforms.

Peter entered the tent and assessed the new faces.

The personnel changed day by day. Some had returned from reconnaissance. Others were brought in to help with cleanup. Medics arrived to assist the ill prisoners. Peter spotted a few of his men sitting at a far table. He got his food and joined them, placing his cup of strong coffee and his plate of sausages and eggs on the table.

Metal forks scraped the plates as they ate. Some men talked about meeting up with the Russians. Others commented about the Austrian girls who were all too willing to show their appreciation to the GIs. A few discussed the war in the Atlantic. Many placed bets on when the Allies' victory in Europe would finally be declared. Only Josef remained silent.

As the men cleared the table, Peter stayed put and motioned for Josef to do the same.

"What's up?" Peter asked, sloshing the last drops of coffee in the bottom of his cup. "How are you?"

Josef glanced up from beneath heavy eyebrows. "Okay, I guess. Kinda tired. Mainly thinking of home."

"Home. Seems like a dream, doesn't it?"

"I'd give anything for a Coney Island hot dog."

"You live near there?"

"Near enough to hit the beaches in search of pretty girls."

"Didn't you used to live here in Austria?" Peter asked.

"Yep." Josef ran his fingers through his thick black hair. "I was raised just a few hours north of here. I remember driving through this area once on our way to Vienna. Man, that seems like ages ago." Josef's gaze seemed to focus on an image in the distant past. "It was pretty much the same then . . . except for the camps, of course. And the roads weren't as well maintained."

"I guess we can thank the Nazis for something," Peter scoffed. "I bet Vienna used to be a beautiful place. It's pretty bombed out now, from what I hear."

"I used to love Vienna. I studied there when I was a kid. I wanted to be an actor."

"It must be hard, coming back. Seeing what's happened to your country."

"America is my country." Josef's chin jutted out with pride. "She took me in, and now I fight for her."

"Of course." Peter tapped his fork on the edge of his plate, trying to work up the courage to ask the question that had plagued him since they'd first approached the camps. "How can you stand it?" he finally asked. "How can you face the death of so many who are . . . like you?"

"Jews, you mean?"

Peter nodded.

Josef's voice softened. "When I see them, I see the faces of my mother, my father, myself. It could have been us out there." He stared out the flap doors, his shoulders sagging under an unseen weight.

Peter rubbed his neck, unsure of what to say.

A new group of men entered the tent, their voices loud and jovial. "Mail's arrived, Scotty," one man called. "Could be a note from your sweetie back home."

Peter cringed. There was no one back home, and they knew it. He waved an acknowledgment and turned to Josef. The young man's tormented eyes were the only giveaway to the raging emotions inside.

"I'll see you later," Josef said, rising quickly. "A few of us are checking out the armament tunnels. I've heard they're a couple miles long, and I guess there were tons of explosives inside, enough to blow it all."

Peter knew about the tunnels. The Germans had used slave labor to manufacture plane parts there. They'd rigged them with explosives, not only to destroy the evidence, but also to destroy the witnesses of their madness: the people in the camps and the nearby towns.

"Be careful. I hear they still haven't explored all the outlets. Who knows, maybe there's even SS hiding inside."

"Yes, sir," Josef said with a salute. Then, with a quick step, he left the tent.

Peter exited the mess hall as well and headed for the mail outpost. Excitement and apprehension battled inside him as he crossed the compound. While Peter always enjoyed hearing from his sister, Annie, he hated reading news about the boys from his hometown—those he'd grown up with who were now scattered across the globe. Some served here in Europe; others fought a different type of war in the Pacific. Some were already home . . . six feet under.

At the outpost, three letters awaited him. He quickly checked the return addresses. One was from his sister. Another came from his high school English teacher, Mrs. McHenry, who faithfully kept in touch with each of "her boys." Peter didn't recognize the address on the third envelope, but the name made his heart sting: Andrea

Gold. He tucked all three letters into his pocket, hoping to find a quiet moment later to read them.

Peter ambled toward town, attempting to focus on the duties at hand. Still, the name would not leave him. Andrea Gold. Wife of his best friend, Donnie Gold—"Goldie."

Peter thought of the last time he'd seen his friend. It was near the Belgian town of Bastogne. Jumping into his tank, Goldie had smiled brightly and called out, "Let's kill some Nazis, Pete. Let's kill some Nazis!" Goldie and Andrea had been the only ones who called him Pete. The only ones allowed to.

Peter thought back to the days at Camp Cooke, when Andrea would bring the car and a friend, and Peter would supply enough gas rations to get the four of them to the Paramount in Las Vegas for a night of dancing and fun. They never drank and didn't need to. Goldie's quick wit was enough entertainment.

Andrea's friends, although nice and fun to hang out with, had never become lifelong companions. Still, Peter rarely refused an invitation. Being around the Golds was like being with family. Andrea was the kid sister Peter missed from back home. And Donnie Gold the brother he never had.

He thought about their trips back to the base. Goldie always loved being first. First to check in and first to make it back to their barracks. "I'll beat you home, Pete," he'd say, jogging away. Only Goldie called training camp "home."

Peter reminisced about the long conversations

they'd had during their rides through the desert. Their talks had often focused on spiritual matters. Discussions of God's plan for their lives. Talks of faith and trust, or of the spiritual battles that were even more threatening than the physical ones.

What fools we were, Peter thought. They'd been young and idealistic about the world around them. Even training for war, they'd imagined themselves put in this position because of God's larger plan for their lives.

But as they faced a baptism of fire on those first battlefields, nothing was as they'd imagined. And when Goldie disappeared, Peter's faith seemed to vanish with him.

Peter wondered how much Andrea knew about her husband's status. Last he'd heard, Goldie's tank had been found disabled, with no sign of him or the rest of the crew. A puddle of blood was their only clue that at least one of the men was in serious trouble.

Is Goldie alive? Or has his body been found? Although Peter longed to know, he couldn't force himself to tear open the envelope. As long as the letter remained sealed, he could still imagine his friend as a prisoner of war—hurt and mistreated, but still alive.

Nine

MAY 7, 1945

Helene ladled warm milk into two mugs and set them aside. She wiped her hands on her apron and watched through the window as the town awoke.

American GIs milled around the general store. They were far enough away that she couldn't distinguish their faces but close enough to make out their playful gestures. The sight of the men caused a stir in her chest. Years before, another group of young men had done the same. At that time, little was known about the Nazi SS. And at this distance, the similarity between the two groups of soldiers was greater than their differences. Echoes of laughter and bright conversation carried down the street.

One soldier left the group and sauntered in her direction. From the easy swing of his arms and his distinctive strawberry hair, Helene recognized him as the one who'd assisted her with the two women from camp. She remembered his strong heart and dedication. Perhaps he'd be interested in helping her feed the women.

Helene gathered the two mugs and prepared to carry them into the back guest room when a glimpse through her bedroom doorway made her stop. Anika sat on the floor surrounded by papers. Upon closer inspection Helene noticed they were photographs.

"Papi!" Anika called, holding up a photo and smiling at Helene.

Helene set down the mugs and hurried to her daughter's side. She recognized the photos immediately. They were of Friedrich and her when they'd first met. She hadn't seen them in years.

She scooped the pictures into a tidy pile on the floor. As she did, she studied the shots. Some were serious, others humorous. There was one with Friedrich in his uniform, and another with Helene posing beside an SS motorcycle. Anyone glancing at them could see this was a young couple in love.

"Where did you get these?"

Anika pointed to the tall dresser in the corner. Helene moved to the dresser and opened the top drawer.

"It's all here." Her hands quivered as she moved on to the next drawer. There were her clothes, her childhood trinkets. Even her diary, just as she had left it. "He didn't touch a thing."

Helene sank onto the bed near Anika. She twisted

the wedding ring on her finger and thought back to that night so long ago when she'd left with only the clothes on her back.

"No daughter of mine is going to marry a Nazi!" her father had shouted when he first saw Friedrich's engagement ring on her finger.

"Well, then, from this moment I am no longer your daughter!" she'd countered, grabbing her coat and hat and running out the door.

Days later, when the impact of their argument sank in, Helene had wanted to mend their differences. But Friedrich had convinced her that he would be her family now, and a clean break was best. Why had she listened to him?

Helene pulled at her ring, struggling to remove it from her swollen finger. When it finally came off, she flung it across the room. Anika watched in stunned silence.

Helene stooped to pick up the pile of photos on the floor. *What a fool I was. Everything's still here, untouched. Waiting for me to return.*

A quick knock sounded at the front door. Helene shoved the photos back into the bottom drawer. "Those stay there. Do you understand?"

Anika nodded.

"Papi is gone." Helene's voice softened as she held her daughter's hand. "He's our secret, between you and me." She released Anika's hand and moved to the door. She straightened her apron, hoping it still covered her round stomach. "Can you keep this secret for me?"

Anika nodded again.

"Run along now. *Opa* is in the yard. Maybe he'll push you on the swing."

Anika did as she was told, letting the back door slam. Helene heard chattering between the two outside. Satisfied, she opened the door, expecting the American soldier. Instead Katharina stood there. Parked in front of the house was a black convertible with two men in the front seat and Katharina's three boys in the back.

"I'm sorry," Helene mumbled. "I should have sent word."

Katharina's face fell. "You're not coming?"

"No." She pulled her friend into an embrace. "But thank you." From over her friend's shoulder, she saw the American GI coming up the steps.

"Am I interrupting?" he asked. In Peter's hand were daffodils and mums she recognized from the neighbor's garden. Frau Chek waved from over the fence, a bar of chocolate in her hand.

Katharina's eyebrows raised at the sight of Peter. Then, with a final good-bye, she gave a quick wave and left. And with her, Helene's final chance for escape.

"She going somewhere?" Peter asked.

"Somewhere safe, I hope." Helene watched the car disappear. When it was finally out of view, she turned to Peter. "Well, come in." Helene felt heat rise to her cheeks. "Let me get a vase for those. They're beautiful."

"I thought the women would enjoy them," Peter said in German. "They're okay this morning, aren't they?"

Helene stared into his deep green eyes as they rested on hers. "Oh, ja, ja, the women." She tore herself from his gaze. "They're fine. Come see for yourself, Officer—"

"Please, call me Peter."

"Thank you . . . Peter." She poured water from a ceramic jug into a blue glass vase and carried it to the guest room. Peter followed. She placed the vase on the table next to Michaela's bed.

Peter chuckled, pointing at the hollyhocks already arranged there. "It seems we had the same idea."

"I just wanted to bring a little beauty into the room," Helene said.

Peter sat in the chair beside the bed and held Michaela's small hand in his large one. "Beauty for the beauty."

"You are kind." Michaela's lips tilted up gently. "Too kind."

Leaving her hand in Peter's grasp, Michaela asked, "How are the others from the camp? Have you heard anything?"

"They're getting help. The 131st Evacuation Unit is setting up a hospital near here. You should visit it once it's ready."

"No need," Michaela said. "I have the best caretaker in town."

Peter glanced in Helene's direction, and she shrugged.

"Still, I mustn't be too much of a bother." Michaela's voice faded. "Helene must be careful with that new babe on the way."

Helene's hands covered her stomach. Of course the

woman noticed; how could she not? Especially last night when Helene's dress had stretched tight over her midsection as she bathed Michaela.

Peter lifted one eyebrow.

Helene waved a hand in the air, as if he should have realized it all along. "Work is good for me. I can't get soft and lazy, can I?"

Both of them stared at her stomach. Helene began to exit the room, her mind searching for a good excuse. "Oh, your milk." She hurried through the door.

I should tell them who I am, she thought as she picked up the mugs. *They're going to find out sooner or later.* Her body felt hot and tense, and her heart fluttered like a nervous moth.

When she returned, she was sure the visitors could read the secret all over her face. But they were focused on Lelia, who'd just awakened. Peter lifted the young lady back into the bed. Helene placed the cups of warm milk on the table between the beds, then pulled the white sheets over Lelia's sore-covered legs. Concern clouded Peter's eyes.

After tucking Lelia in, Peter returned to the wooden chair beside Michaela's bed and guided the cup to her lips. Helene did the same with Lelia. Milk dribbled from the corner of the girl's chin, and Helene wiped it with a clean cloth.

"Last night," Peter said, "I heard about a man who tried to get some food from the Red Cross. They sent him away because they said he'd been through the line earlier. When the man insisted he hadn't, they searched their records and discovered it was his brother they'd seen. The twins were reunited yesterday afternoon." Peter's voice caught in his throat. "They were the only survivors of a family of six."

Lelia raised her hand as Helene lifted the cup, indicating she'd had enough to drink.

"The Red Cross is setting up a system for keeping track of those liberated from the camps," Peter continued. "I've been asked to take your names and add them to the list. The sooner we get the word out, the sooner we can exchange news."

Peter pulled a small piece of white paper and a pencil out of his shirt pocket. "Could I have your full name and hometown?" he said. He attempted to act official, but Helene could tell it wasn't easy.

"Michaela Perl," the woman answered. "P-e-r-l. And Lelia Kubale. K-u-b-a-l-e. I'm from Bielsko, Poland. And Lelia is from somewhere in Germany. I don't know where exactly. I'm sure she'll tell you in her time."

Peter wrote down the names and slipped the paper back into his pocket.

Lelia stared at the ceiling and her lips moved slightly, but no sound came forth.

Peter rose from the chair. "I'd better get back. I told my men I had a quick errand. I'll let you know if I hear anything." He nodded good-bye and left the room. Helene followed.

In the living room, he leaned close and spoke in hushed tones. "I wanted to let you know that a medic conducted an examination on Lelia yesterday morning at the camp, before you arrived. He tested for typhus since Michaela found the girl in the typhus barracks. But as far as he could tell, she doesn't have the disease. She must have just been using that building as a hiding place."

"She's so frail, I'm afraid to touch her for fear of hurting her."

Peter opened the front door and it squeaked loudly. At the same time, the back door opened and Anika scurried in, her cheeks flushed. She ran to her mother, clinging to her legs. Then she peered around Helene's hips and giggled at Peter.

"You're doing a fine job," Peter said to Helene. "You're giving them what they need most: food and tender care. And a family," he added, ruffling the girl's flyaway hair.

Peter moved onto the front porch.

Anika released the grip on her mother and rushed to Peter. "Don't go." She wrapped her arms around his legs and positioned her small feet on top of one black boot.

A tight knot formed in Helene's throat as she watched her little girl interact with the American soldier. "Anika, that's not polite." Helene pulled her back.

Anika shrieked and stretched her arms toward Peter.

Helene felt heat creeping into her cheeks. "I don't understand. She's never like this." Anika pulled harder, and Helene's grip tightened. "Anika, that's enough. He has to go."

Anika dropped to the floor and sat with her arms folded.

"You know what?" Peter bent down and ruffled her hair again. "I have a sister named Annie. Do you think I can call you little Annie?"

Anika nodded.

"Well, I'm sorry, little Annie, but I have to get back to work right now." He held her shoulders gently. "But I can come back. I might even bring you a treat if you obey your mother. Sound good?"

"Good." Anika's pout transformed into a smile.

Helene breathed a sigh of relief. She took Anika into her arms, said good-bye to Peter, then shut the door. "If you act that way, he won't come back." Helene plopped her daughter onto the couch. "And we don't want that, now, do we?"

Anika shook her head heartily, her hair flying about in wisps.

Helene gave a wry smile, letting her daughter know she was forgiven. "Now, go play. I think you left your doll in the bedroom."

Helene returned to the kitchen and stood by the window. She watched Peter head back toward town. She hoped the next time he visited, he'd have news for the two women. Perhaps they had family searching for them. Maybe even a boyfriend or husband?

And how many were there like them? Over the years Friedrich had mentioned several camps scattered across Austria, and she was sure there were others in Germany.

Helene washed the dishes and considered what it would be like to be so ill and completely dependent on the goodness of a stranger. Yes, she'd lost her husband and her home. But she still had her father and her daughter. And as long as she had them, Helene knew she'd be able to face the future, no matter how uncertain it was.

~ ~ ~

Even during the day, Michaela watched Lelia sleep. She couldn't help it. Each rise and fall of the girl's chest brought a sigh of relief. Lelia had made it. Despite all odds, she was still alive.

Michaela sat up in bed and lifted a hand to her mouth as a small cough racked her body. With each cough her stomach contracted, and Michaela willed the food to stay down. Though she had only eaten a few spoonfuls of soup for lunch, her stomach seemed determined to rid itself of the nourishment she so desperately needed.

Michaela heard Anika in the other room, sharing lighthearted banter with her grandfather—"Papa Katz," as he asked to be called. Yet their interaction was odd. Even in playfulness they seemed like strangers.

"Did you know there is a fun attic to play in upstairs?" Papa Katz asked as the two paraded past the door.

Michaela thought of her own family. For so long they had felt far removed from the war in Germany. Then the refugees started arriving—people just like them, who were suddenly homeless. Her father's church

114

had become a haven. Parishioners provided blankets and food. Even when the German army advanced into Poland, their home remained a safe place. Since he was a minister of the state, her father was left alone. And being non-Jewish, their family was able to remain in the area they loved while many others were shipped away.

Then Lelia entered my life, Michaela thought, lying back down. She'd arrived with her father, mother, and sister. From that moment, Michaela had been drawn to Lelia. Only thirteen at the time, Lelia had shiny black hair, thick and curly, hanging to her waist. Her heart-shaped face reflected innocent beauty. Now, four years later, the poor child was only a dim shadow of her former self.

And what about me? What would Georg think if he could see me now?

Georg. The name alone was enough to stir a thousand yearnings. As the war progressed, Michaela had seen him less and less, but even in his absence their love had grown stronger by the day.

Georg. She had been seventeen when she'd confessed to her closest friends the attraction she felt for him. He was twenty and quite serious about his trade as a printer. She watched him every day from afar for two years before he noticed her in the same way. By that time, she had blossomed into a woman. And he became her true prince.

Michaela rubbed her cracked fingernails across the stiff white sheet that covered her and traced Georg's name with her finger.

In the beginning, the war had seemed so distant to the two in love. Then, over time, they found themselves helping as they could. Georg started printing news for the Resistance, and she assisted in the care of refugees.

Michaela stared out the window to the backyard and distant fields. A break in the tree line gave evidence of the Danube River just beyond.

Georg. An image of the last time she'd seen him stirred her thoughts. They had traveled to the countryside on borrowed bicycles with wooden wheels. His mission had been to deliver news reports to a contact in another town. She had joined his journey as part of the disguise. They were to act the part of two young lovers away for a day in the country. It was an easy role to play.

Michaela closed her eyes and could see the wind tugging Georg's light brown hair away from his face. She heard his bright laughter at the silly little songs she made up about their future—their children, their dog, and their house on the edge of the woods. "Happy, happy children three. Children born of you and me. Happy, happy children four. Oops, one scampered out the door."

She knew now their dreams had been foolishness, considering the circumstances surrounding them. But for that day, the songs seemed far more real than their reality. They were in love, making plans for their future. But that future ended two days later, when Georg was captured at his shop and taken into the woods by SS guards for a quick execution. She remembered finding his body, along with two others, in the back of a wagon.

Michaela's shoulders shook. *That's enough,* she told herself. *You're a fool for living in the past, and a coward for not facing up to the future.*

But what of the future? Michaela could not escape the question. Where would she and Lelia go? What could they do? They had both been silly young girls before the war. What type of employment or homes could they possibly find now? They could not depend on Helene and Papa Katz's good graces forever.

She should've told Peter that posting their names would be of no use. Their families, both hers and Lelia's, were dead. She had witnessed it with her own eyes. If it weren't for her promise to protect Lelia—to leave, when everything inside told her to stay with her family—neither of them would be here.

Michaela's eyes closed, yet she refused to allow her body to submit to sleep. As bad as the memories were, at least she could limit them. But she couldn't escape the dreams. The ones where she was home with her family, happy and healthy. Ones where she helped her mother make strudel or worshiped at her father's church. Ones where Georg rode beside her, his cheerful voice carrying on the wind.

☙   ☙   ☙

Helene stood at the basin scrubbing her daughter's hands between hers. She rubbed at the dirt and dipped the small fingers into the cool water, noticing how Anika's slim hands were so similar to her own.

117

She knew she had to tell Anika about Friedrich's death. But how could they mourn without giving themselves away?

While her memories of Friedrich involved more bad than good, Anika seemed to find a decency in her father that no one else could. Once, early in her second pregnancy, when she'd been sick, Helene had watched her husband and daughter in the backyard sharing stories and songs from Friedrich's childhood. Stories of kings and castles. And songs. She couldn't remember the lyrics, but the tunes came to her often.

Helene shook the water off their fingers, then gently dried the small girl's hands with a dish towel still warm from the clothesline.

Anika's voice interrupted her musing. "*Mutti,* why those people so bad?"

Helene released Anika's hands. "What people?"

"The ones in that place Michaela was."

Helene scooted a wooden chair away from the table and sat down. She pulled Anika into her lap. "What makes you think they're bad?"

"They look scary. Some don't got clothes. And they sleep in piles."

Helene pulled her daughter close. *What have I done? I should never have taken her there.* She stroked Anika's silky hair. "Those people aren't bad. They look that way because they didn't have food for a long time. Some are extremely sick. That's why we're trying to help." Helene hesitated, not knowing what to say about the piles of bodies.

Anika caressed her mother's cheek. "Who put them there?"

Your father helped do that, Helene thought as all her tender musings vanished. She tried to ignore the new images Anika's question stirred—the marches through town . . . the raised clubs ready to strike . . . the gunfire. Memories she wished to forget.

"Why not they go home?" Anika asked.

Helene patted the little girl's hand. "Michaela and Lelia are trying to get home, but they live far away. So we will care for them until they're ready to go back."

"Will Papi come home too?"

The kitchen door opened, and Helene's father entered.

"Let's talk about that another time, shall we?"

Without protest, Anika picked up her favorite doll and scampered into the bedroom.

Helene's father said nothing as he unburdened himself of the large burlap sack he was carrying. His other hand grasped the handle of a pail. Fresh milk, still frothy and thick, reached the rim.

Helene wondered if he'd overheard.

"I thought we'd make more soup to take to the camps." He set down the pail. "The Americans are still so overwhelmed with the dead they can't do enough for the living."

"It's understandable." Helene took a few small potatoes from the top of the sack. Her eyes fixed on the man in front of her. She had watched him so often from afar she hardly remembered what he looked like up close. His hair, once brown, was a crown of white.

Tired wrinkles curled around his eyes and mouth. His thin lips were tight as he pulled a large pot off the shelf and carried it outside to the waterspout.

Helene took a sharp knife from a drawer and began the tedious work of peeling the small red potatoes. Sounds of Anika's imaginative play lilted from her room and blended with soft conversation coming out of the door across the hall where Michaela's voice rose and fell.

As she peeled, Helene tried to understand Michaela's words, but she soon realized it was a conversation of one.

She's praying.

Helene thought about how different this prayer was compared to the boisterous, shouted prayers of the Nazi youth. *"Adolf Hitler, you are our great führer,"* boys barely school age had chanted. *"Thy name makes the enemy tremble. Thy Third Reich comes; thy will alone is law upon earth. Let us hear daily thy voice, and order us by thy leadership, for we will obey to the end and even with our lives. We praise thee. Heil Hitler!"*

The hairs on the back of her neck stood on end as she remembered the straight-armed salute that accompanied that chant. Helene rinsed the dirt from the last of the peeled potatoes and wished she could as easily rinse those words and images out of her mind.

She listened more closely to Michaela's prayer, only making out a few of the Polish words. She dropped the potato into a bowl, wiped her hands, and tiptoed toward the room.

Helene stopped a few feet from the doorway and eased her frame onto the floor. Leaning against the wall, she allowed the overheard words to flow over her like a wave of warm bathwater.

What would it be like to pray?

A few minutes later her father found her sitting there. She glanced up at him. He motioned for her to stay where she was, then went back to fill another pot with water.

Helene knew she should get back to work. But her body refused to comply. There was something welcoming and familiar about the prayers. Then Helene remembered.

Her mother had often prayed in such a manner in the early mornings. A vague memory emerged as through a fog, and Helene recalled being a young girl curled at her mother's bare feet.

Helene ran her fingers through her hair, just as her mother had done. Just as she did with Anika. She hadn't thought of that in years.

Mutti, she mouthed. It had been difficult raising a child without her father around, but even harder without her mother.

After a few more minutes, Helene contemplated another similarity between her mother and Michaela. There was something about their eyes. Not the color. Her mother's eyes had been brown like her own. It wasn't the shape either. It was something deeper. Helene couldn't put her finger on it, but that something had made her want to help Michaela.

Michaela's prayers stopped, and Helene rose. As she strode back to the kitchen, Helene knew what she needed to do. She would pray for the words to tell Anika about Friedrich. She would also pray for those people in the camps—pray for a way to help them that would make up for her years of silence. Though never one to give any thought to religion, at this moment it seemed right and good.

"I'll ask her to teach me how to pray," Helene muttered, picking up the knife and another potato.

But for the present, she had work to do. She knew her father wouldn't rest until the two pots were filled with food and taken to the people in Gusen. And for that, Helene was thankful.

Ten

The camps. She would never get used to them.

Helene had been relieved when her father offered to take the two empty pots and Anika back to his house while she stopped for flour and sugar from the grocery. They'd just finished feeding a large group of men, some as young as fourteen. For the healthier prisoners, the U.S. trucked in dark brown bread. But there were many who could barely swallow a few spoonfuls of weak broth.

While she and her father fed the men, they listened to them share stories of their families and homes. One older man had seen Helene coming as soon as she approached the gates. He followed her, then plopped beside her on the ground when she stopped. He talked about his three sons and the clothing store they owned in Berlin. He had big plans to find his boys and reopen their business. Helene didn't have the heart to discourage him with reality.

When Helene finally left for the day, her feet throbbed and her lower back was stiff, but her heart ached even more.

Now, in town, something didn't feel right. She did her shopping, then hurried toward her father's house, weaving through the crowds.

Suddenly, shouts filled the air. A dozen American servicemen with angry expressions lined the street, rifles in hand. They pointed in the direction of the camp. They yelled in English, and Helene couldn't understand.

Before she could get out of the way, Helene felt herself being pushed along. She searched the soldiers' faces for a familiar one but found none. Arms pushed against her. Bodies surrounded her. Neighbors and friends cried out in confusion. With the forceful urging of the Americans, they poured through the gates of the camp.

A woman beside Helene sobbed. An old man stumbled. Helene protected her stomach with her hands, realizing she must have dropped her groceries somewhere along the way.

Helene managed to push herself away from the crowd as they muddled through the courtyard. She approached one soldier and tried to question him. His mouth curved downward in a deep frown. He shook his head, his dark eyes refusing to meet hers, and pointed toward the rest of the group.

Helene's head throbbed as she was led to a section of the camp she'd never seen before. A hill of bodies, piled in a tangled mass, lay beside a spacious shed. She covered her nose with her hand, attempting to block the odor of flesh rotting in the heat of the sun. It did little good.

To her right, an army chaplain prayed over a mass grave as a bulldozer dug more channels. Hundreds of corpses were stacked on top of one another in the ditch. An American soldier stood next to the chaplain. When the prayer ended, the soldier waved toward the bulldozer. The huge machine rumbled toward the dirt pile and pushed the brown mound over the bodies, covering them with mechanical efficiency.

Helene's stomach lurched. The sun glared down upon her, and she wiped a trickle of sweat from her brow. This couldn't be happening.

A soldier approached their group and spoke in German. "All of you, go to that pile and bring those corpses to the ditch. Two of you on each body." The soldier cursed under his breath.

Suddenly Helene realized what was happening. This was their punishment. Chastisement for their silence. For allowing Hitler to return to Austria. For ignoring the cries from beyond the razor wire.

A young woman next to Helene let out a mournful cry. Others around her joined in.

Helene followed the soldier, shocked by what she'd been asked to do. The pile of bodies stood shoulder-high. She refused to look into the face of the man who

125

lay on the top. But she couldn't tear her gaze from his hand. The fingers were curled into a fist. Burgundy numbers were tattooed on his arm.

Helene reached for his hand. It was warm from the sun. The skin was soft, the fingers rigid. The sky seemed to spin.

"Are you all right?" A man next to Helene tilted back his hat. "You're shaking. Perhaps you'd better sit down."

Helene released the dead man's stiff hand. The buildings, bodies, and guards started to fade, as if all color was being drained from her vision.

Helene leaned on the man beside her for support. The gray landscape swirled around her and vanished, and she was overwhelmed with a flood of black.

℞   ℞   ℞

Nausea overtook Helene as she came to. A crowd had gathered around her. A soldier she vaguely recognized leaned in close and said something she couldn't understand. Then he stood and cupped his hands around his mouth, shouting something in English. Helene picked out Peter's name among his words.

Within minutes, Peter was leaning over her, his face red. He yelled at the soldiers, then leaned down and helped her from the ground.

"They said they didn't realize you were pregnant," he muttered in German, leading her to the nearest building. "They have to find a better system. This is inexcusable."

Before long, Peter had set up a makeshift cot for her in the former commandant's office. As she lay down, she noticed a faded outline on the wall, hinting where a Nazi eagle had once hung.

A medic entered and placed a cool, damp cloth on Helene's forehead. Her hands fidgeted at her sides, and she willed them to stop trembling.

"Rest a minute more," Peter said. "You'll feel better soon."

"I was on my way home when I was rounded up," she muttered. "I must have fainted in the heat." She didn't mention the body or the feel of the dead man's hand in her own.

The medic pressed on her stomach to check its size. He said something to Peter in English.

"He says they never should have had you out there," Peter said, "especially in your . . . condition. He also says you're due in less than three months."

A sob escaped Helene's lips, though she wasn't sure why. She knew the baby would be fine. It was her heart she was worried about. She had to do something, had to make a difference. She couldn't just sit at home and do nothing.

"Your husband . . ." Peter said gently. "Was he in the German army?"

Helene glanced away. "He was."

"Is he gone?"

"He's dead."

Peter took her hand. "You've been doing too much.

You need to rest. I'm sure you've hardly slept with caring for the women and your daughter."

The medic spoke again, and Peter translated. "He wants to know if you've been having any pains. Signs that anything's wrong."

Helene rubbed her round belly. "Nein. Everything's been fine . . . until today."

Peter interpreted her answer for the medic, then addressed her again. "He wants to examine you, and then he says I can take you home."

After Peter left the room, the medic felt her stomach, listened to the baby, and checked her pulse. When he was finished, Peter was brought back in.

"Easy does it." Peter helped Helene to her feet, his arm around her shoulders.

"Really," Helene protested, "I can walk on my own."

"Maybe so, but it's better to be safe than sorry. The medic said you're underweight. The baby's healthy but small. You need to start paying more attention to your health."

Deciding not to fight him, Helene wrapped her arm around his waist as they shuffled through the courtyard. The sun had dipped into the horizon by the time they exited the gates.

Peter helped her into the first available jeep, then drove toward town. The car wove in and out of wagons, soldiers, and civilians as it rumbled toward her father's house.

Several men stared as they drove by. Peter kept his focus straight ahead. Either he didn't notice the stares or he simply ignored them. With her free hand, Helene tucked her knee-length skirt tight around her legs. The wind whipped her hair.

She was glad her father's home wasn't far. And glad that he wasn't waiting by the door when she arrived with no groceries.

Peter helped her out of the jeep and into the house. Inside, all was quiet. Anika was curled into a ball on the sofa, taking a nap. Voices from beyond the back door told Helene that her father was in the backyard talking with neighbors.

Peter led Helene to her room and watched her climb into bed. Helene pretended to be absorbed with arranging the blankets around her. She couldn't look into those green eyes of his. They asked too many questions.

"I'm going to check in often to see if you're resting," Peter said, forcing sternness.

"But the people, the food—"

He held up his hand, cutting her off. "If you'd like to continue cooking, I'll send some men to pick up the food. You don't need to be going out. A new commander has jurisdiction now, and he will continue to round up villagers to help bury the dead. I've heard that tomorrow all townspeople over twelve will be forced to attend a mass funeral."

Peter sighed. "The commanding officers are overwhelmed with the tasks of caring for the people. They try to do their best, but they have little understanding of the situation here. They blame the townspeople for not doing more for the prisoners, for not stopping the horror. And they feel the villagers should help deal with what they didn't stop."

More than anything, Helene wanted to tell Peter she had tried to speak out. She'd wanted to help but couldn't. She was as much to blame as the rest.

Peter stepped toward the bedroom door. "I'm going to see how Michaela and Lelia are doing before I leave."

"Thank you so much . . . for helping me." Helene pulled the blanket up to her chin and noticed her hands still smelled of the camp. She told herself she would get up and wash as soon as he left. But she settled deeper into the bed as her body relaxed. She yawned, and her eyelids grew heavy.

"I'll see you tomorrow," Peter said. Then he headed into the room across the hall. Was it Helene's imagination, or did he comb his hair and straighten his uniform before entering?

Helene pictured how Michaela had looked that morning. Even in her frail state, her peaceful smile hinted at her former beauty.

Helene drifted into a fitful sleep. As she was dozing off, she could hear Michaela's laughter joined by Peter's. Their laughter and talking carried on as the shadows moved across the wall, finally encompassing the entire room with night.

Helene wasn't sure when their true conversations ended and the ones in her dreams began.

ᴸ   ᴸ   ᴸ

MAY 8, 1945
ST. GEORGEN, AUSTRIA

An air of celebration replaced the somber attitude when the end of the war in Europe was announced. Victory in Europe, V-E Day at last!

"We need a photo to commemorate," Murphy called out. "Can you snap us?" He tossed Peter his camera.

A dozen or so soldiers gathered around. Three of them hunched down in front. Two more stooped over behind them with hats in hand. The rest lined up in a long row, faces beaming. Peter peeked through the eyepiece and noticed Banion with his hand tucked in his shirt, imitating Napoleon. Josef held his hand up, his fingers V'd for victory.

Peter couldn't help but chuckle. "Okay, on the count of three." The camera clicked and the group dispersed.

All available liquor had been rounded up from town. Music poured from the radios late into the night. Peter celebrated with the rest. But he caught himself glancing often in the direction of the yellow house. Were those women celebrating tonight?

In the midst of the carousing, Peter knew the same questions raced through every man's mind: *Do I have enough points to be sent home, or will I have to remain with the occupational forces? Or worse, will I be sent to the Pacific now?*

Peter's mind wandered to thoughts of Goldie and the letter he had received from Andrea. While the other letters had brought news of home in an effort to cheer him up, the one from Andrea was different. Blurry spots, which Peter knew were caused by teardrops, dotted the page. The handwriting was difficult to read, but the questions were even more troublesome. *"Have you heard any news? Can you find my husband?"* she'd asked. Then, *"What do you know about the treatment of American prisoners of war? I saw a photo of a POW in* Life *magazine. Surely that's not how they're all treated."*

Peter did what he had to. He lied. *"No news is good news,"* he'd answered. *"Under the Geneva Convention all prisoners must be treated well."* He didn't dare tell her the kind of treatment the prisoners he helped had received.

♂   ♂   ♂

MAY 15, 1945

For a long, full week, Peter tried to ignore his nagging questions about Goldie by helping Helene care for Michaela and Lelia. Most of his help came after hours, when his work around Gusen and Mauthausen was finished. A few times he even stayed late into the night, monitoring a fever that had caught Michaela by surprise and pressing a cool cloth to her forehead. He'd told himself to stay uninvolved. That he had enough work to do with overseeing his men and dealing with the masses of prisoners. But something kept drawing him to that house. Especially to Michaela.

He clearly remembered Michaela's face that day when he'd first spotted her behind those locked gates.

132

Though barely able to walk, she had stood tall. Despite her filthy appearance, he had seen beauty in her gaze. Beauty that grew deeper each moment he spent with her. *What was it about her that drew him so?*

Peter thought back to two days ago when he made the trek to the large yellow house. That morning he heard a church bell chiming in the distance and realized it was Sunday. The market was closed, and he spotted some of his friends lounging on a front porch. They had playfully saluted as he passed.

Even though horror had greeted him when he first entered this town, Peter now felt at home in St. Georgen. Obviously his friends did too. More so than anyplace they'd been in the last four years. As he made the same trek this evening, he knew that saying good-bye would be difficult.

Peter rounded the last corner and paused. Two women sat on the porch in the shade of giant oaks. Helene and Michaela smiled broadly and waved. Peter jogged toward them, his boots pounding on the ground.

"What a greeting!" He took the porch steps in one leap. "How did you get out here?" He took Michaela's hand. Her soft dark hair had grown out some and now framed her face.

She blushed. "Helene's a patient woman." Michaela smiled appreciatively at her friend. "She encouraged me on, step by step. I think it took an hour."

"Not quite." Helene brushed a blonde curl from her cheek. "I'm glad you came tonight. It will be your job to get her back." Her laughter danced on the night breeze.

"That shouldn't be a problem. Are you ready now?"

"I think so." Michaela's voice betrayed her weariness.

Peter dropped to a crouch and scooped Michaela into his arms. She looped her hands over his shoulders. Peter took a few steps, then pretended to stagger. "Whoa, maybe this wasn't a good idea after all. I think someone has put on a few pounds."

Two playful swats landed on his shoulders, and Michaela feigned a frown.

"Just kidding." He righted himself and carried Michaela back to her bed. After setting her down, he moved to the chair beside Lelia, who was reclining in a half-sitting, half-lying position, staring out the window.

"Why, you sure are a sight for sore eyes," he said.

Lelia faced him but her expression was blank. She didn't speak a word. Peter wondered if she was really there. Though her body was improving, her mind seemed to be someplace else.

After carrying on a one-sided conversation with Lelia for a few minutes, Peter returned to Michaela. Helene arrived with a bowl of soup. Anika entered behind her and scampered to Peter's side.

He cleared his voice. "While you're all here, there is something I must tell you." Everyone turned his direction, even Lelia.

He took off his cap and ran his fingers around the brim. "I've just been reassigned. I have to leave tomorrow."

Helene set the bowl of soup onto the table with a

thud. Broth sloshed over the rim, leaving a large orange-brown spot on the white tablecloth.

"Leaving?" Michaela rose to her elbows. "Are you going to the Pacific?"

"No, I'll be stationed in Germany. At an SS prison in Landsberg."

Helene took a corner of her apron and attempted to wipe up the mess she'd made. Her face looked pale.

"I might make it back on leave. Maybe in a month or so—"

"Will trucks take you? Will you be gone for long time too?" Anika asked with an odd expression that Peter could not decipher.

Peter looked to Helene for an explanation, but her eyes were fixed on her daughter. Her intense gaze resembled the one Peter's mother had given him when he was a child and his words had crossed the line.

Anika said no more. She shuffled to her mother's side.

"I will write." Peter took Michaela's hand and glanced at Helene.

"Of course you will." Helene picked up the bowl and drifted toward the doorway. "And we'll be able to get news to you too." She padded to the kitchen, and he heard the metal spoon clang against the pot as she ladled more soup.

"Thank you for all you've done," Michaela whispered.

Peter tried to smile at her. His attempt was as weak as hers.

"I will write," he said again.

"Of course," she answered.

He patted her hand and waved to Lelia, realizing that if he didn't go now, he probably wouldn't be able to tear himself away until late in the night, and he still had packing to do.

"Good-bye." He waved one last time. Then he slipped out of the bedroom and joined Helene in the kitchen. She stood with her back to him, staring out the window into the darkening sky.

"I'll ask some of the guys to stop by and check on you."

"We'll be fine." Her voice held no emotion. "My father's here."

"Well, just in case. You never know."

"No, you never know." She picked up the full bowl of soup. "Lelia needs to eat too. I'd better get this in there."

"I won't keep you," he said, though his body blocked her passage.

"Thanks again," she murmered without looking up at him.

"No, thank you." He angled himself so she could get past him.

Helene took a few steps down the hall. Then she stopped and glanced back over her shoulder. "I'll take care of Michaela for you. She's a good woman."

Peter ran his fingers over his chin, thankful she understood. "Will it be okay to send my letters here for her?"

"Ja, of course."

Then with one last farewell, Peter stepped out the door and into the cool evening.

Dear Annie,

A lone candle burned in the corner of the tent. The flickering light danced on the clean white sheet of paper. Peter had been writing a letter to his sister in his mind for the past few days. Now it was time to get those words on paper.

Last week, the end of the war in Europe was declared. It was celebrated in small ways among the troops, but it's hard to be too jubilant when we're still trying to live with the aftereffects. A lot has happened since I wrote last, and I've seen and experienced things I'll never be able to express in a letter. Perhaps soon I can tell you in person.

My troop took part in freeing the prisoners of a concentration camp. It would take pages to describe the horror, the stench, the piles of bodies, the starving people.

Although I've helped many, there are two prisoners I've been able to spend more time with. One of the townspeople, a young woman with one child and another on the way, has taken these prisoners into her home. One of them isn't doing well. She is young—seventeen, I believe—and she refuses to speak. The other is a nice young woman named Michaela. She is Polish, but we are able to communicate in German.

Helene, the woman caring for her, works tire-lessly. It is quite the sight to see how much help she can offer in a day! She is a true saint. I'm enclosing her address. I hope you can find a way to help her. I don't know what you could do, but perhaps you'll think of something.

I have to leave tomorrow, as I'm being stationed away. At least I'm not heading to the Pacific, like many I know. Not yet anyway. It's hard to believe our boys are still fighting and dying, and that some of my friends might soon be among them.

Please pray. Who knows, maybe it will work for you. These are difficult times, and things are not going to get easier any time soon. The land is torn by the ravages of war, and so are the people. Those like Michaela have lost everything. Although she hasn't said, I'm sure her whole family is gone. While many wait for news from loved ones, she never asks. Maybe because she already knows the answer.

Please write soon. I expect the postal system to become more effective than it has been. I'll write again once I get settled.

> *With all my love,*
> *Your big brother,*
> *Peter*

Peter folded the sheet, slipped it into an envelope, and blew out the light. Then he climbed into the cot. "Good night, St. Georgen," he whispered. Tomorrow he would be in another place. But at least it wasn't another war.

Although his mind should have been planning the movements of his men the next day, it concerned itself instead with only one thing. *When will I see her again?*

🍂   🍂   🍂

MAY 16, 1945

The first light of dawn was just breaking through the tent flap when Peter sensed a body moving toward him. His eyes opened to find Murphy reaching for his shoulder. He sat up with a start.

"They found him." His friend's face was solemn. "Cap said to get you."

Peter stood and pulled on his pants. "Found who?"

"Goldie. Somewhere in Germany."

Peter buttoned his pants and pulled on his shirt. "Is he dead or alive?"

"The old man didn't say. He just told me to get you quick."

As Peter finished dressing, he thought of his buddy. *Let's kill some Nazis,* Goldie had said. As Peter followed Murphy to the captain's quarters, he realized he had no greater desire than to do just that. *Every last one of them.*

Captain Standart had set himself up in a house on the outskirts of town. It was a monstrous brick building with a porch running from one end to the other. Peter jogged up to the front gate, then took the porch steps two at a time.

A soldier led Peter toward the front drawing room. The captain sat by a large picture window, sipping his morning coffee. Peter gave a full salute.

"At ease, Soldier," Captain Standart said. "Have a seat."

Peter did as he was told, choosing a chair across from the captain. He leaned forward, elbows on his knees.

"Donald Gold is alive," the captain said simply.

Peter let out the breath he didn't realize he'd been holding.

"But barely."

Peter's folded hands rested against his lips.

"The First Army found him in Stalag Twelve. In Limburg, Germany." The captain took a drink from the mug in his hand, the steam momentarily fogging his black-rimmed glasses. "You know those walking bones out there? Well, that's what we found. Our men, thousands of them. Half starved and mostly dead. They were discovered weeks ago, but word is just now getting to this end of the occupational zone."

Peter peered into the seasoned warrior's face. "And my orders, sir?"

"I'm sending you to Limburg for a few days. Then I have an assignment for you in Czechoslovakia."

"Czechoslovakia instead of Landsberg, sir?"

"I have a dozen guys who can take your place in Landsberg, but this trip to Czechoslovakia is vital. The camps are taxing us, and our supplies must be replenished. I've received information about a warehouse full of German medical supplies outside Prague. A med-

140

ical officer is assembling trucks and men. They should be ready to head out as soon as you return from visiting your friend. They'll need you along in case they face any opposition. I trust you, Scotty. Besides, that will give you a good three days to see Goldie. It will work better for everyone this way,"

"Yes, sir. Thank you, sir." Peter left with a salute, his thoughts on the way he and his buddy used to light up Las Vegas.

Later that day, as a jeep carried Peter across the border of Germany, all of Europe seemed to be on the move. Frail-looking men and women struggled on as if in mass exodus—some coming, some going. A few with carts, others on foot, all cradling their meager possessions as if they were rare treasures. Each hoping a better place awaited them.

How strange it was, Peter thought, that he had come through this war physically healthy and unscathed. Images flashed through his mind of young men who would never return home, and those who were still fighting in the Pacific.

Why them? Peter wondered. *Why not me?*

At the end of a long day's travel, Peter's driver announced their arrival at the town of Limburg. "Home of the famous cheese," he proclaimed. Although war-torn, the town's former beauty could not be denied. The half-timbered houses were still embellished with a wealth of carvings and sculptures.

The driver pulled up to a hospital, and Peter disembarked quickly. A nurse, tall and lanky, greeted him at the front desk with a crooked smile.

"Donald Gold?" Peter asked.

She examined her charts. "Oh, yes, here he is. Nice fellow. Too bad."

"Too bad?" he echoed.

She clucked her tongue. "Typhus. It'll be a miracle if he makes it."

Peter felt his jaw tense.

The nurse started down the hall. "Follow me."

The hospital, like almost everything else in Germany, had been "liberated" for use by the Americans. It was old, and one section had been destroyed by artillery fire. The area Peter was stumbling through seemed ready to crumble.

He followed the nurse into a dim room where a decrepit old man lay on the bed with his eyes closed. Peter frowned at the nurse, certain she had made a mistake. He was about to inform her of her error when a gruff voice called from the bed.

"What's the name of Mickey Mouse's girlfriend?"

"Minnie," Peter answered, smiling at the old password used to flush out Krauts trying to pass as Americans.

One wrinkled eye popped open. "Hey, Pete."

Peter stared at the old man on the bed. "Goldie?"

"Hard to believe, ain't it?" Goldie's voice sounded the same, but quieter, as if he strained to talk.

Peter neared the cot. "Hearing you were alive made my day."

"Yeah, mine too." Goldie laughed, but the laughter became a deep cough that rattled his body.

Peter pulled a handkerchief from his pocket and handed it to his friend. When the coughing ceased, Peter saw that blood stained the white fabric.

Goldie's body was as thin as any Peter had seen in the camps. His hair had receded and two frail arms poked out from the hospital gown. Had it only been four months since he'd last seen his friend?

"They treated us worse than dogs, Pete."

Peter pulled up a chair, still in shock.

"Eighty pounds. Can you believe it? Thank God Andrea doesn't have to see me like this." At the mention of his wife's name, a moan tore from Goldie's lips. His gnarled body trembled.

"She's been writing me," Peter said, "asking if I've heard any news. She's been sick with worry. All she can talk about is how much she loves you and misses you."

Goldie stretched out a thin hand and grasped Peter's. "Whatever you do, don't tell her you saw me like this. They're sending me to England for a few months. Tell her I'm healthy, but they're keeping me around for some rest."

Peter didn't have the heart to tell his friend that not even two months of care in England would bring his life back to normal.

When Peter didn't answer, Goldie squeezed his hand tighter. "Promise me."

Peter patted his friend's shoulder. "She'll never be the wiser. Before you know it, you'll be jitterbugging just like the good old days."

Goldie gave Peter a tired grin.

Peter searched his mind for a light subject. "Hey, how did the Peabody go? I've been trying to remember in case I find a pretty girl to dance with."

Goldie moved two fingers along the mattress as if they were feet sliding across a dance floor. "Remember, you have to glide, not step. Glide, not step."

Peter laughed. It felt good to laugh with Goldie again. He stayed with him through the night and most of the next day. Later, they swapped stories, just like the old days. Only this time, Goldie talked about his time as a prisoner of war. Peter, too, shared about their final stand against the Germans, the day they crossed the Rhine, and, of course, the camps.

But that first day, Peter joked with his buddy and they both laughed. More than anything, Peter needed to see his friend laugh. Somehow that seemed to guarantee Goldie would recover.

Eleven

MAY 25, 1945

Warm wind, perfumed with the scent of apple blossoms, blew in through the open window of Michaela's room. The calendar would soon flip from May to June, and she could think of only one thing: her father's birthday. June 7 was less than two weeks away, and for as long as she could remember it had been the turning point of her year. June meant the end of school. It meant strawberries and cream. Lemon cake, three layers thick. It meant longer days and carefree sun-filled afternoons with her family. At least it used to.

Michaela twisted a piece of thread between her fingers and broke it off with a jerk. Her hand shook slightly as she worked the needle through the small garment on her lap. She heard the front door open and wondered whether Helene was coming or going. Over the last few weeks Helene had brought in bags from the shed for Michaela to sift through. They were filled with clothes, shoes, silk stockings, and sewing supplies.

Michaela didn't ask where the items had come from, but she'd made herself useful by taking down hems on Anika's colorful frocks and adding side panels to Helene's clothes in an effort to keep her expanding waistline from popping buttons.

A few white petals blew through the open window, and Michaela thought of her mother's practical summertime favorite, Karpatka cake. She rehearsed the recipe in her mind.

"Butter, flour, baking powder, water, eggs. Yes, four eggs," she mumbled. Remembering little things like that had helped during the dark days in the camp. For some prisoners, remembering the past hurt too much. For her, it helped to think of life before the pain. The Germans had dragged her from her homeland, stripped her bare, even replaced her name with a number, but they couldn't disrobe her faith or her memories. She'd kept them concealed deep inside. They were her inward smiles hidden beneath salty tears.

After one dress was done, Michaela moved on to a second. Anika's voice called from the other room.

When Helene didn't respond, Michaela quickly tied off her stitches, then laid the garment on her bed. Lelia stirred slightly, pushing a strand of hair from her face. Though Michaela guessed she was awake, the girl didn't bother opening her eyes.

Leaning on the small table for support, Michaela

pulled herself from the chair and eased across the room. Helene's hand-me-down dress swung loosely on her frame as she moved to Anika's bedroom and opened the curtains. Sunshine drizzled into the room. Anika wrinkled her button nose and reached out, playfully grabbing a handful of Michaela's dress in her fist.

Michaela perched on Anika's bed and allowed the girl to climb onto her bony lap. The child's touch felt wonderful, warming her even more than the sunshine.

"Can we go for walk?" Anika asked, stroking Michaela's arm.

Michaela laughed. "Is that all you think about?"

"Ja." Anika blinked. "And chocolate."

"Well, at least you're honest." Michaela noticed how thick and foreign her words sounded compared to the young girl's native German tongue. "Perhaps there will be no chocolate today."

Anika grinned, obviously not believing this could be true. Peter had left, but many of his friends still worked around town. They delivered bread, transported displaced persons, cared for the sick. A few even took time to check on the occupants in the large yellow house.

"Ja, we can go for a short stroll. If it's okay with your mother. But not too far."

Anika tumbled from Michaela's lap. "Choc-o-late," she called as she ran down the hall.

Michaela mentally prepared herself for the vision of town. While Anika focused easily on the clean, neatly pressed GI uniforms, Michaela couldn't get past the former prisoners. In small groups or alone, they clumsily staggered from place to place with white-wrapped Red Cross packages tucked under their arms.

The survivors' thin arms dangled at their sides and their jerky movements seemed unnatural. They reminded Michaela of the marionettes that had performed in the theater near her home. The worst part was, Michaela knew she looked the same.

When she got to the kitchen, Michaela found Helene buckling Anika's shoes. A bright yellow handkerchief was coiled around Helene's head and a few blonde curls peeked from underneath. A mop bucket sat next to her. The kitchen smelled fresh.

"I hope you're up to this." Helene gingerly rose from her crouched position and rubbed her side. "If you're at all too tired—"

Michaela squared her shoulders, trying to appear strong. "I can make it down the street and back, certainly." She held out her hand for the young girl.

Helene put her hands on her hips. "I'm sure of that. But I would feel better if you had some decent shoes."

Michaela examined the old brown loafers Helene had found for her. The soles were nearly worn through and offered little protection from the pebble-covered asphalt streets.

"Remind me to trace your foot later." Helene reclaimed the mop with a flourish. "I'm sure I can find a better pair somewhere." Michaela knew better than to argue.

Anika tugged on her hand. "Walk, walk."

"Ja, ja, I'm coming." A knowing smile passed between Helene and Michaela as the mop swooshed across the floor.

🦢　　🦢　　🦢

Not long after Michaela stepped into the street, she knew something was wrong. The town crawled with frantic movement as trucks, soldiers, nurses, and ex-prisoners jostled toward the camp.

She stood on her toes but could not see what was drawing the people. *Maybe I don't want to know.* Her fingers tightened around Anika's hand as they walked. The young girl protested and she loosened them slightly.

Toward the end of the block, near the camp, a group of men shoved past her. She recognized their uniforms. Former SS guards. It appeared they hadn't bathed in weeks.

GIs corralled the motley group like shepherds herding scraggly sheep. Only these men weren't sheep. They were wolves. Even as prisoners their presence was frightening. Michaela had to get away.

As she turned back toward home, a group of towns-people and dozens of former prisoners surged past her.

"Ziereis," a man in the crowd called. Michaela halted. Commandant Ziereis had been the head officer over Gusen and Mauthausen. His name had been greatly feared among the prisoners.

Michaela could still picture his piercing stare as he inspected the fearful, bedraggled prisoners, daring any-one to confront him. Michaela had glanced into those

149

eyes for only a fraction of a second, but even now, in freedom, the remembrance was enough to make her knees grow weak.

Michaela heard the name again as a man shouted and pointed. A few blocks away, the stream of people grew as they swarmed from the evacuation hospital to the gates of Gusen.

Michaela picked up her pace. She had to get back to the safety of Helene's house. She had to get some space between her and that name.

Anika tugged at her hand. "Let go!"

Before Michaela could understand what was happening, Anika pulled free. Michaela spun around, as if in slow motion, and watched the girl's small leather shoes pound down the street toward the camp.

"Anika, no! Stop!" Michaela's heartbeat quickened as the young girl lunged toward the crowd. "No!"

Chocolate. She must be going after the Americans' chocolate. Michaela willed her body forward. The girl's blonde tresses bounced as she ran. *Please, God, make her stop.*

Forcing her feet to move as fast as they were able, Michaela followed Anika as she skipped off the sidewalk onto the road. An army jeep screeched to a stop within inches of her. The girl paused for a second, then took off again.

"Anika!" Michaela pressed forward. She stumbled slightly, then caught her balance, hobbling on, ignoring the ache in her limbs and the shooting pain of her feet on the pavement.

"Anika, stop!"

Anika continued to run, calling out something Michaela couldn't comprehend. The distance between them grew.

"Stop her," Michaela called in German as Anika ran past two GIs. But the men didn't respond.

People continued to swarm the gates, and now Anika was among them. Rocks dug into Michaela's feet with every step. Her chest burned.

Anika was about to cross the threshold when a soldier grabbed her arm. "Let me go!"

Wheezing, Michaela approached them just as the GI lifted Anika into his arms. Michaela noticed concern on the man's face. Then she recognized Peter's friend. *Josef.*

His eyes narrowed. "You shouldn't be here," he said over Anika's cries. The girl in his arms squirmed to get loose.

Something hanging in the air to her right caught Michaela's attention. She turned, then gasped. Just inside the camp gates, a man's body swung between two poles. His bloated chest showed evidence of a bullet wound. His neck was stretched to an unnatural length. He was naked and rigid. Michaela quickly averted her eyes.

"Franz Ziereis." Michaela's trembling hands covered her mouth.

"Take the child and leave here." Josef tried to put Anika into Michaela's arms, but she didn't have the strength to carry herself, let alone the child.

Michaela reached for Josef's arm to keep from collapsing. Anika lunged, escaping their hold, and bolted away. Josef ran after the girl, weaving through the crowd.

"Papi!" Anika cried.

No. Helene's husband can't be here, can he? Michaela had overheard he was dead.

Anika ran past an armed guard and darted through the slats of a temporary fence that surrounded a group of Nazi prisoners.

Josef was just about to grab Anika when the young girl flung her arms around the waist of a tall man inside the fencing. His blond hair was overgrown and ragged. An SS uniform hung from his wide shoulders.

Even over the noise of the crowd, Michaela could hear the girl's cry, "Papi!"

The man scowled down at Anika from beneath bushy eyebrows. She shrank back. Josef pulled her into his arms as Michaela neared. Anika clung to Josef's neck.

"Are you her father?" Josef asked the man in German.

"Nein," the prisoner growled.

"That's all I needed to know." Josef wrapped his free arm around Michaela to hold her up and led her to the shade of a nearby building.

Michaela collapsed onto the ground, unsure of what to think, uncertain of what to do. The familiar odors of the camp pressed down around her, and she longed for a fresh breeze.

"How did this happen?" Josef knelt beside Michaela. Anika's arms remained tightly wrapped around his neck.

Michaela tried to catch her breath. "We were walking and she slipped away. I tried to stop her—"

Josef shook his head. "Nein. Not that. How did she pull it off? An SS wife, pretending to be a helpful citizen?"

"Helene?"

Josef leaned close. "Don't you see? This little girl thought that prisoner was her father. His uniform is that of an SS camp guard. Has Helene mentioned anything about her husband?"

"Not really."

Though she hated to admit it, it made sense. The missing husband, the fine clothing, awkwardness at her father's house. Helene was an SS wife.

Michaela curled her legs up to her chest and tightened her arms around them.

Josef patted Anika's trembling back. "She must have thought she would be above suspicion," he whispered. "She fooled us all."

"No," Michaela blurted out. "It can't be." She thought of Helene's kind eyes and cheery attitude. It wasn't an act. "Helene is a caring woman. She may be an SS wife, but entering that camp was a sincere act of compassion. She cares." Tears stung Michaela's eyes.

Josef shook his head. "Think of the bodies we're burying. Helene's husband was a part of that. That means she was too."

Michaela didn't know what to say. She knew nothing of Helene's past, but she was certain of how the woman treated her now.

"We have to get you out of that house," Josef muttered.

"I won't leave." Michaela lifted her chin. "She saved

153

my life. I have no one else but her. I will go back to the house and ask her. I will listen to what she has to say."

"Fine then." Josef released Anika. "But she's done getting help from me. She purposely hid this from us." Josef's eyes flickered with hatred. As he stood, Michaela noticed a Jewish star hanging from a chain around his neck.

Michaela grabbed Anika's hand. "We need to go back now. Your mother will be worried." She rose awkwardly and headed toward the road. It was clogged with people coming to view the hanging body.

Michaela rubbed her aching limbs. Feeling Josef's arm grab hers, she turned to him. He pointed his chin at Anika. The girl was wiping away tears with the back of her hand. Michaela felt her chest constrict. She wanted to reach out to the girl, to comfort her. Instead, Michaela pulled out of Josef's grasp and began the long walk home. With every step, she braced herself to face Helene.

༺   ༺   ༺

Helene searched the street through the lengthening shadows. Clouds gathered in the distant horizon. *Where are they? What could have happened? Why can't my father find them?*

She realized now how foolish she'd been for giving Michaela so much responsibility. The woman wasn't well. What if she'd collapsed or lost her way? Would Anika know how to get home? They were only supposed to go to the end of the street, which was within view of the house. *That was over an hour ago.*

Helene sank onto the sparse grass in front of the gate. *It will be all right. They'll come walking around the corner any minute.*

Helene's father had come home thirty minutes earlier and had tried to calm her fears, but it hadn't worked. Especially after he shared the day's events. She listened breathlessly as he relayed the death of Franz Ziereis and the hanging of his body just inside the camp gates. Her father had urged her to stay at the house in case they returned. Then he left again to search for the two.

The commandant's death had been no surprise to Helene. News had come days ago that Ziereis had been found in the Alps and was shot while trying to escape. Helene had also heard he'd given a confession before his death. Perhaps his confession pointed to other Nazi families still in the area. Maybe that had something to do with Michaela and Anika's disappearance.

She was just about to head into the house to get her sweater and pocketbook when four figures appeared in the distance. Michaela was limping, her father and an American GI helping her along. Anika toddled closest to the houses, holding her opa's hand.

"Thank God," Helene cried out. But as she jogged toward them she could tell something was wrong. When she neared, Helene noticed Michaela's sober expression and Anika's tearstained face. Her father refused to look at her. The dread of his disapproval fell upon her afresh.

Helene slowed, partly because of the awkwardnes of jogging and partly because of the look on the GI's face. A tight knot formed in the pit of her stomach. She felt vulnerable and ashamed. He knew. They all did.

"Anika," she cried, ignoring the stares of the others. The girl released her grandfather's hand and ran to her. Helene bent down and embraced her daughter. Then she looked up at her father, silently pleading for an explanation.

He continued on to the house without a word. Josef waved to the others, then left. His contemptuous frown as he left stung as sharply as any physical strike could.

The group shuffled into the house in silence. Anika occupied herself with a slice of buttered bread. Michaela sat on the sofa and took off her tattered shoes.

Helene's father pulled her aside and spoke in a low voice. "Your daughter saw an SS officer and thought it was your husband." His gray eyes searched hers. "You have caused a lot of unnecessary pain, Helene. Did you not tell her he's dead?"

"I started to explain, but it was too difficult," Helene said softly.

"I'm so sorry." Michaela's voice was thick with emotion. "I tried to stop her, but she was too quick for me." Helene expected to see repulsion and disgust in the woman's blue eyes. Her expression was questioning but not hateful. A weight seemed to lift from Helene's chest. *Does she really know who I am?*

Helene took a deep breath. She knew she had to tell her. Had to confess what she should have revealed in the beginning. She stepped forward.

"It's not your fault. Really. It's mine. I—" Though

156

she wished more than anything to divert her gaze, to hide her shame, Helene looked into Michaela's eyes. "I should have told you sooner. You need to understand why Anika thought that man was her father. Her father, my husband Friedrich, was an SS guard."

Michaela looked away, but not before Helene caught a glimpse of betrayal. "I don't know what to say. I can't say I understand your choices. I don't know what happened then. But from the first moment I saw you I knew you cared. It makes no sense. . . ."

Helene knelt before Michaela and placed a hand on her knee. Michaela took it and gave it a gentle squeeze. If only she were the person Michaela had believed her to be.

"I'm afraid the Americans won't be as understanding," her father said sternly. "I'm sure even now Josef's trying to locate Peter."

Peter. At the mention of his name, heat rose to the base of Helene's neck. She sat on the sofa. "Will they come after me? Will they punish me for my husband's actions?"

"I doubt that." Her father ran a hand over his mustache. "The Americans usually try to listen first. Now, if it was the Russian army . . ." His voice trailed off. "Besides," he added, "you have no crimes to pay for."

Deep down Helene felt otherwise.

Anika straggled in from the kitchen, rubbing her eyes. "Can I have a nap now?" She climbed onto her mother's lap.

Helene carried her to the bedroom. She felt her

father and Michaela watching her. Now more than ever, she wished she could take it all back.

Yet, as she tucked Anika under the handmade quilt she had snuggled under as a child, Helene felt freer somehow. The secret was out. They could either accept her or hate her. Either way, she was tired of pretending. Tired of hurting alone.

Twelve

MAY 26, 1945

Peter had enjoyed reminiscing with Goldie again. Once he'd overcome the shock of his friend's physical appearance, it was easy to connect with the man inside. The man who'd survived while so many other POWs had not.

Goldie had soberly shared about starvation rations, inadequate living quarters, and the punishments brought on by minor infractions. Peter, in turn, discussed the camps and the survivors, but he didn't broach the subject of Michaela and Helene. One word about them and Goldie would have him pegged. Peter couldn't pull off a nonchalant attitude with the person who knew him best. So he didn't even try.

Instead, Peter told Goldie about their group of twenty-three men freeing the prisoners of Gusen. He talked about the camp orchestra playing the American anthem as he and his men entered the gates of Mauthausen. The group was made up of the finest musicians in the world, reduced to rags, now living as displaced persons. He related the story of how he found an American prisoner inside the camp. Though frail, the lieutenant had been strong of will and heart.

What brought the most pleasure to Goldie's face was the description of the SS guards upon their capture. Even before the U.S. entered the war, every American was aware of the mighty SS. Black-and-white newsreels played before every movie and showed rows of fit, handsome men marching as one.

Goldie had sat in silent admiration as Peter described what it was like to have the SS under his control. It was a far different group of men that had straggled back to the American outpost on May 5 under the guard of Peter's twenty-three GIs. Two thousand Germans had trudged along, five deep, as the rain poured from the sky. With shoulders slumped and heads bowed, they looked more like bedraggled puppies than seasoned soldiers.

Although the two could have shared a dozen more tales, the stories eventually had to stop. Peter wished his friend another good-bye. Only this time, before parting ways, there were no theological discussions, no long talks of God and faith. All Peter needed to know was that Goldie would be okay—and he saw that by the faith and hope in his friend's eyes.

"I'll race you home, Pete," Goldie said. "And when

my feet touch home soil, I'll say a special prayer for your safe return."

Peter knew his friend wasn't just talking about returning to America. He was sure Goldie saw his spiritual wanderings too.

Yes, Peter might be able to fool everyone else, but not his friend. Never Goldie.

      *   *   *

Peter was on the road again. This time in Czechoslovakia, with a line of trucks following behind his. He'd gone back to Austria, but not for long. Close to St. Georgen, but not close enough.

When he'd arrived at Linz, he found the ten two-and-a-half-ton trucks he'd requested to carry medical supplies. A driver and assistant for each truck waited with them. Peter quickly rounded up German prisoners from the POW camp for extra help, although he was sure they would never have volunteered had they known they would soon be entering the Russian zone.

Now the worst part of the trip was over. The warehouses had been found, the supplies loaded. And the trucks were winding through the tree-lined country roads of lower Czechoslovakia. It was their third day on the road. So far there had been no problems. Warm sunshine fell upon the convoys, and Peter scratched the place where his Red Cross armband encircled his uniform sleeve. All the men on this trip wore these now. It was safer that way.

Yet unlike any official Red Cross representative, at Peter's side was a .30 caliber pistol. He prayed he wouldn't have to use it. Another few hours and they'd be back in the American zone. Back to safety, and perhaps back to St. Georgen.

Peter glanced into the mirror, keeping an eye on the last truck, in which the German volunteers were hiding between boxes of bandages and blankets.

"Do you know where those POWs are from?" Peter asked his driver, who was resting his arm on the back of the seat.

"Cap says they're from the Lake District in Germany. Too bad, though. I would have loved to rub it in to that one obnoxious fellow that I'm sleeping in his bed."

Peter raised one eyebrow.

"Not like that." The driver laughed. "I'm staying in one of the SS houses we cleared out a few weeks ago."

"Really?" Peter cocked his head.

"Right in St. Georgen. I'm just sorry the lady of the house didn't come with it." He let out a low whistle. "She sure was a pretty thing, all blonde and curvy. Kinda reminded me of Ingrid Bergman, only with lighter hair. Her man must have abandoned her or was killed, 'cause he wasn't around to help her pack. She had a little girl, though, I know that."

"A little girl?" Peter repeated.

"One room had a tiny pink bed." He chuckled. "You should have seen my buddy climbing into it. He . . ."

Peter didn't hear the rest of the story. A hollow ache hit the pit of his stomach. *Blonde woman? Little girl?*

162

Peter wanted it to be a coincidence, but deep down he knew it wasn't. St. Georgen was a very small village.

It had to be Helene. She was an SS wife. He'd suspected it all along, but he'd forced himself to ignore the signs. He'd let her get close, catching him with his defenses down.

Then a new thought hit him. Did Michaela know? He hated to think about what such knowledge would do to her. He had to get back soon. Had to find some way to tell Michaela himself, before she suffered anymore.

The driver started a new story about finding a boat loaded with accordions on the Danube, but Peter wasn't listening. He rolled the window down to get some fresh air.

He opened the map again, and a warm breeze ruffled the corners. Captain Standart had outlined their route in red. The captain had also highlighted a second road just a bit to the west that seemed a lot shorter. *Perhaps, if we shave a couple hours off the return trip, we could be back in Linz by late afternoon, and maybe to St. Georgen by morning.*

"How 'bout we try a shortcut?" Peter held the map up for the driver to see. "It looks like this turnoff should be within the next few miles. Want to try it?"

The man grinned. "Anything to get out of this truck sooner. I've got one aching back."

Within five miles they found the turnoff. The area was heavily wooded. Their convoy was the only traffic. Peter stared off into the distance and tried to imagine what Helene would say when he confronted her with the truth. He could almost feel Michaela's hand in his own.

The truck jerked. "What the—" The driver slammed on his brakes. The tires skidded to a stop. The trucks behind did the same.

A Russian soldier had appeared out of nowhere, pointing a burp gun directly at their cab. Peter glanced at the pistol on the seat beside him, then pushed it behind his back, out of view. He lifted his hands in the air.

"No sudden moves," Peter whispered to the driver, hoping a platoon of the man's friends wasn't hiding in the woods behind him.

"What does he want?" the driver mumbled, also lifting his hands.

"Looks like we'll soon find out."

The Russian approached the open passenger window and pointed the small submachine gun at Peter's face.

"Hello, comrade," Peter said first in English, then in German.

The man held the gun steady and rattled off something in Russian. His volume rose with every word. His dark eyes flashed with contempt.

"I don't understand. Do you speak German?" Sweat trickled down Peter's brow. He willed himself to keep his eyes off the end of that barrel.

"Give him something," the driver muttered. "Bribe him."

Peter motioned to his musette bag. "Chocolate? Would you like some food?"

The Russian nodded him on. Peter opened the bag slowly. He grabbed a candy bar and held it out.

The Russian's gaze softened. But he wasn't paying any attention to the chocolate. Instead he focused on Peter's watch, glistening in the sunlight. Before Peter knew what has happening, the watch was off his wrist and in the man's hand. The candy was tossed into the dirt.

The man slipped the watch into his pocket. While he was distracted, Peter touched the pistol behind him. His finger wrapped around the trigger.

The Russian scratched his head with his free hand, then raised his gun into the air. Peter released the breath he'd been holding. The Russian shot a single round, then lowered the rifle with a sarcastic smile. His teeth were yellow, and one was missing altogether. Then, as quickly as he came, the man disappeared into the woods.

The driver let out a sigh. Peter released his gun. The two stared at each other for a moment; then Peter shook his head and laughed.

"That was close," the driver muttered, stepping on the gas. The other trucks followed. "I swear I could hear my heart hammering. Sorry about the watch."

"It's no big deal. I can get another." Peter relaxed into his seat. "Can you believe they're on our side?"

"Who knows? He might be the one sleeping in that Nazi's bed soon."

Peter glanced at him. "What do you mean?"

"Haven't you heard? A portion of Austria is going to be annexed to Russia. And if my sources are right, the Muehlviertel region will be included."

Peter sat up straighter. "St. Georgen?"

"St. Georgen, Gusen, Mauthausen. Everything from the Danube to the Czech border."

Peter thought of Helene. If she really was an SS wife, the Russians would take revenge without asking questions.

Peter rubbed the spot on his wrist where his watch used to be. "Rumors. If I had a nickel for every rumor that never amounted to anything, I'd make Rockefeller look like a hobo in comparison."

The driver drummed his fingers on the steering wheel. "You don't have to believe me. But taxiing you around hasn't been my only gig during this war, if you know what I mean."

Peter tried to ignore the disturbing feeling in the pit of his stomach. Now that he knew she could be in danger, Peter's harsh feelings for Helene softened. Perhaps she wasn't a traitor after all. He thought about all the time she spent helping the former prisoners. She certainly seemed trustworthy. And she could be in trouble. Along with everyone in her house.

Thirteen

MAY 27, 1945

After Michaela's discovery, Helene tried to keep as low a profile as possible. It wasn't that Michaela did or said anything to make her uncomfortable. But Helene sensed the awkwardness as easily as she felt the cold winds that blew in from the east. Michaela was polite, and Lelia had even started getting up and around more. Still, Helene wondered if things would ever be right again.

On the second day, Helene went for an evening stroll by the Danube. When she returned, her father and Anika were playing in the backyard. And inside, she discovered Michaela sitting on the sofa alone, her eyes red and puffy. Helene stepped closer, concerned that the woman's fever had returned. Yet when Helene neared, she realized Michaela had been crying.

The woman's frail legs were stretched in front of her, covered with a blanket Helene's mother had crocheted. Michaela's eyes were still sunken in and her cheekbones hollow. Yet there was something about her that made Helene want to risk breaking down the walls she'd so carefully built around her emotions.

Michaela patted the space beside her. Helene felt a chill pass through her. She moved to the sofa with awkward steps, then sat, straightening her blouse over her round stomach.

"I won't say I'm not sorry to discover who you are." Michaela's voice broke the silence. "I have to admit I wanted you to say it wasn't true. That our conclusions were mistaken."

"I wish I could say they were." Helene lowered her gaze. "I am what they say."

"Can you tell me the whole story?" Michaela asked. "Help me understand why you would marry an SS camp guard?"

The words caused Helene's heart to pound. She wet her lips and inhaled deeply, summoning the courage to relive her past.

"I was young and stupid," she began. "Just seventeen when I met Friedrich."

"Lelia's age now," Michaela whispered.

"My mother died years earlier, and my father seemed like an old man who didn't understand me. We had to work hard to keep the inn going, and I resented him for it. It was busy in those days—before the Nazis came. There was always someone to cook and clean for.

On weekends, when my friends went to the cinema in Linz, I had to stay behind to work."

"It must have been difficult," Michaela said.

"Ja. But I didn't see it as hard, just constricting. I wanted freedom, and Friedrich offered that. Or so I thought."

"Did you meet him here at the inn?"

"No, in town. At the beginning of the war. I was doing the daily shopping, and he and some friends were sitting on the front steps of the store. Our eyes met as I climbed the stairs. He was so handsome. Tall, with blond hair and a contagious smile. That is what drew me most, his smile."

Michaela tilted her head, obviously intrigued. "Did he say anything when he saw you?"

"Not then, but later—on the walk home. He offered to carry my groceries. He asked my name, about my family, and a million other questions. It wasn't until we arrived at my walkway that I realized I'd been talking the whole time."

"When did you find out who he was?"

Helene tapped a finger against her lower lip. "Friedrich told me right away that he'd come to town with the *Waffen* SS. The war had already begun, and Hitler was building a work camp for prisoners of war. Friedrich guarded the construction site during the evening hours."

Helene twisted a strand of hair around her finger. "The main camp, Mauthausen, had been on the hill for a few years at that point, but I really didn't know much about it. I'd seen some prisoners as they journeyed from the work details back to the camp. At that time I thought a subcamp would be better for the prisoners because they would be closer to their work." She shook her head. "How foolish I was."

Michaela's gaze was intent.

Helene took a minute, trying to decide how much to share. Finally she began again. "We started seeing each other every day after that. Friedrich would wait by the tree near the road and walk me to the store. Then he'd take me home again. None of my friends nor I knew much about the Waffen-SS or how it compared to the regular German army. He wore a uniform, was proud of his nation and willing to fight for its honor. He'd traveled in Germany and Belgium. I'd hardly left St. Georgen. I was stunned that he'd be so interested in me, and honestly, I felt an incredible need to have someone love me after so many years of just me and my father."

Helene gauged Michaela's expression but could not determine what emotion stirred in her eyes as she waited to hear more.

"The townspeople adored Friedrich," Helene continued. "What they didn't see, hidden behind the charming facade, was a haunted soul that could attack at any moment." She paused, trying to quench the flood of memories. "Friedrich was like a pup you instinctively want to pet, yet if you stroke the wrong way, he'll turn on you."

Michaela pulled the blanket tighter around her.

"Of course, I was fooled in the beginning. I was sure he was my perfect match. But my father didn't feel the same."

"What did he do?" Michaela asked.

"One day he caught Friedrich sneaking me a kiss behind the apple tree. Father was furious. He dragged me inside the house. He said no daughter of his was allowed to find comfort in the arms of a Nazi! That took me by surprise. I didn't know my father's beliefs before then. At that time it was dangerous to go against Nazi ideals, so he thought it better I not know."

Helene took a deep breath, amazed at all she'd just shared. The darkness outside and the lamplight within the room had transformed the window into a mirror, perfectly reflecting the two of them. Weeks ago they had resided on opposite sides of a literal fence. Today they sat together physically, but the barrier between them was thick.

Look at us, sharing the same sofa, a prisoner listening to the cares of a Nazi wife. Helene only wished she had a more heroic story to tell.

"I left home and stayed with a friend. I swore I'd never come back. A few months later, when my Aryan heritage had been proven, Friedrich and I were married before a Nazi magistrate. Those first few weeks of marriage were everything I'd ever hoped for. Then one night . . ."

"One night?" Michaela's gaze met Helene's in the reflection.

Helene wrapped her arms around herself. Michaela placed a hand on her shoulder.

"The cattle cars couldn't make it into camp. It had been snowing all day. I'd seen the cars before but never

171

gave them much thought. They went in, they went out. I knew prisoners were loaded on them, and I just assumed they were enemy soldiers. But that night—"

Her voice caught and the words refused to budge. Michaela's touch moved from her shoulder to her hand.

"I heard their voices," Helene said finally. "Women and children." Her voice faltered. Helene glanced at Michaela and noticed tears in her eyes. She felt ill.

"I'm so sorry," Helene blurted out. "I didn't mean to cause you to hurt all over again."

Michaela brushed the tears from her cheeks. "Don't be silly. The hurt is there. It always will be. But crying is a good thing. My mother always said tears water the garden of your heart. If there were no tears, there would be no life."

Helene thought about Friedrich's lack of emotion in the last few years. His smile had vanished, and so had his tears.

"Friedrich pretended to sleep." Helene rubbed her stomach. "But I could tell he was awake. I begged him to do something, but he refused. I put on my boots to try myself, but he wouldn't let me leave. He pulled me away from the door and threw me across the room."

Helene choked back a sob. "My husband died that night. The next morning a new man took his place. A man who didn't flinch over the cries of dying children. One who could ruin lives without batting an eye."

Helene's fingers clenched into fists. "But I kept listening, kept seeing, kept living with the ache. I knew the moment I stopped weeping for the suffering, my heart would die along with Friedrich's . . . and my soul with it."

Helene turned to Michaela. "When Friedrich left for good, I—"

"You came to the camp," Michaela said. "To us."

"Yes. I finally had a chance to do something, to put into action what my heart had felt all along. Unfortunately, for many, it was too late."

"You are brave." Michaela wrapped a thin arm around Helene's shoulder the way an older sister would. "And for that I owe you my life."

"If I could have found a way to help sooner, maybe others would have been saved."

"The Lord knows, Helene. He knew when the time was right. He knew when you were ready. He knows your heart. Trust in that."

A breeze stirred the air, and Helene realized the window was still open. She heard the new leaves rustling on the aspen outside.

"Now I must admit something to you," Michaela said. "There were many I should have helped. Whenever I see Lelia, I wonder if I could have done more for her family, or even mine. It's easy to notice the faults of others while ignoring your own." She squeezed Helene's hand. "God brought us together. I know that."

"I've never thought much about God," Helene admitted. "Do you really think He had a part in bringing me to you?"

"I know He did."

Helene rested her head against Michaela's shoulder. "How?"

"You came during the darkest moment of my life. The Americans had too many prisoners to try to help, and Lelia and I were very sick. So I prayed. I prayed for an angel of deliverance to lift me out of hell."

Helene's heart stuck in her throat. The thought that she could be the answer to someone's prayers astonished her.

"To be honest," Michaela continued, "I was praying for death. Death surrounded me. In piles of bodies, in walking skeletons, in ash that fell on my head. I longed to become that ash, to be free from the pain. But instead, God sent you."

"I'm far from an angel." Helene rose. "You know that now."

"God works in mysterious ways indeed." Michaela smiled. "Perhaps He knew the prayer of your heart also. Maybe He knew you needed me as much as I needed you."

Helene saw no pride in Michaela's face. Yet it was true. Michaela had given her far more than she ever would have imagined. "I guess you can say we are each other's answered prayers." Helene closed the window. "An answer to a prayer I didn't know I'd prayed."

Helene gazed at the reflection. Their images shimmered through her unshed tears, and for a moment she caught a glimpse of the woman Michaela must have once been. Helene's heartbeat quickened and a strange tingling shimmied down her arms.

Then Helene focused on her own reflection, and an even more amazing thing occurred. For through her tears, she saw not who she had been, nor who she was, but who she could be.

🐦   🐦   🐦

Arno stood on the edge of the woods, his hands clenching and unclenching. He'd seen the transport in the distance. This was his chance. His one shot. In the next few minutes he was either going to pull off the biggest ruse of his life, or he'd just signed his own death warrant.

Friedrich's mother's cottage was still visible from where he sat. Arno had to admit, he liked the old woman. She was everything her son was not. Kind, generous, witty.

After sending Henri to deliver Friedrich's letter, Arno had stayed almost two weeks with Mrs. Völkner, saying he was Friedrich's closest friend—which wasn't far from the truth. The old woman had shared stories of Friedrich's childhood and his time in service to his country. She even shared news about her daughter-in-law and granddaughter, although she hadn't had the opportunity to meet either one.

"This terrible war keeps me from my grandchild," she'd said in frustration.

He'd patiently listened to the woman's prattling, then helped her with handyman's work around the cottage. But Henri's first assumption had been right. She knew nothing.

After the first week, the old woman began to show him Friedrich's letters, starting back with his first SS training days at Dachau. The young, impressionable soldier had written of the inspiring Avenue of the SS, which faced Eike Plaza.

"It's a wide two-lane road with a lawn down the middle," Friedrich had written. *"Massive administration buildings and barracks line the roads. Everything is neat and orderly and beautiful."*

As he read, Arno wondered why Friedrich hadn't also mentioned the death camp and prison. Had he thought it too offensive for his venerable mother?

A stack of letters later, Arno learned Friedrich had indeed been stationed as a clerk in Vienna. *"We SS soldiers are held to higher standards and are subjected to the strictest discipline,"* Friedrich wrote during his first days in the service. *"I strive to do my job well."*

Arno continued reading. A few months into Friedrich's stay in Vienna, the news took on a more social nature as obviously the young man discovered that the life of a respected solider drew the favor of many.

"Last night, I was treated to an amazing performance of Richard Wagner's 'Götterdämmerung' at the State Opera. 217 people were in attendance, but I was lucky enough to enjoy row 12."

It was foolishness. The later letters were filled with even more descriptions of useless daily activities and boring stories. Tales only a mother could choke down.

So after two weeks, Arno left the place with a kiss on Mrs. Völkner's wrinkled cheek and a promise to return. His visit had confirmed that Friedrich had been involved with something in Vienna. But what? *Perhaps Friedrich's wife will know more.*

Arno thought of their last moments together. Friedrich had mentioned leaving something behind with Helene. Throughout that night Arno had weighed whether or not he should chance going back to St. Georgen. Not only was it dangerous, but he hated the thought of being there again. Hated the way the others had looked down upon him. He'd risen to the ranks of the mighty SS only to be treated like a simpleton by his comrades and superiors. Always passed up for promotion, always put on the gruesome jobs. Even Friedrich, Arno knew, had befriended him for his own benefit.

But he would show them. He would return. He'd find the treasure. And while the others still ran for their lives, he'd be living like a king.

Now the line of American trucks roared closer. Arno had watched the group from the castle ruins the night before and knew their plan was to deliver men from the regular German army—those the Americans now considered harmless—to their homes throughout Germany and Austria.

Arno decided to join them. Not only to obtain a ride, but also for the permission to return to St. Georgen. He was no fool, but he'd gladly act like one to get his way.

Arno waved, and the first truck slowed to a stop. The others in line did the same. Arno's heart quickened. He ran his fingers through his overgrown hair.

The GI on the passenger side leaned out the open window, rifle pointed. Arno knelt on the ground.

"Get off the road," the GI yelled in German.

"P-p-please," Arno stuttered, wagging his head. "I s-s-surrender. A-all I ask is for a r-ride home."

The GI glanced at his buddy, then back again. "You in the regular Germany army?"

"Ja, ja." Arno bowed lower.

"Where you headed?"

"St. Georgen," Arno answered, daring to lift his gaze.

At an order from the driver, the passenger climbed down from the rig. He glanced back at the driver and asked a question in English.

The driver looked at Arno and spoke again, rolling his eyes. The two GIs laughed.

Arno made the sign of the cross and crouched as low as he could.

The soldier stepped closer, kicking dirt into Arno's face. "Get up, fool!" Arno rose slowly.

"Man, Hitler *was* getting desperate, wasn't he?" The driver smirked.

The soldier patted Arno down, then motioned to the back of the truck.

"Danke," Arno said, climbing over the tailgate. The back was already packed with men, all of them filthy and battle torn. Thankfully, none he recognized.

One man scooted over, making a narrow spot. "Danke." Arno muttered again, sitting. The man didn't respond.

178

PART TWO

He raises the poor from the dust
and lifts the needy from the ash heap.

Psalm 113:7 (NIV)

CONNECTED

I've heard it said
That only God, who made hearts,
Can join them.
Perhaps my broken heart, joined with yours,
Becomes more complete somehow.

I never should have called you friend.
For the world considered us enemies.
Yet here we are,
Listening, understanding.
Knowing.

In our reflection I see
What compassion is all about.
It's about sitting side by side,
And the only obstacle between us
Is the warm air we breathe in as we whisper.

Fourteen

Lelia laughed.

Outside the wind howled and a late spring storm showered the countryside with rain. But the girl's laughter was enough to brighten the whole house.

Michaela had needed the feather bed that afternoon, her muscles still aching from her run to the camp a few days before.

Helene had visited the room with hot tea and biscuits. The awkward tension of the previous days was gone. Michaela's heart felt as light as the feathers that fluffed the bed, and in a way she felt even closer to Helene than before. She had finally sought God and had put her relationship with Helene in His hands.

"Look at me!" Anika had called out as she scampered into the room dressed in her grandfather's tattered gray-green coat and favorite alpine hat with braided trim. Her small face barely peeked out from under the brim, but it was the sight of her upper lip that caught everyone by surprise. Beneath her upturned nose was a mustache made of soot from the cookstove.

When Anika imitated her grandfather's slow gait, Michaela's laughter started as a trickle and grew into a roar. Then, without warning, Lelia's laughter joined in. All eyes focused on her as she giggled like the teenager she was.

"What do we have here?" Helene asked, hands on her hips.

Something must have struck Lelia funny about Helene's wide-legged stance and her stomach, which seemed to have doubled overnight, for the girl's laughter grew even louder. Soon all of them were chuckling so hard that tears streaked their cheeks.

Helene struggled to catch her breath. "Lelia, thank you for that gift of laughter." Michaela watched as Helene pulled a chair up beside the girl's bed and grasped Lelia's hands.

"You are welcome," Lelia said quietly, smiling.

Michaela's chest warmed. *Her first laughter and her first words. Perhaps things will turn out all right after all.* In God's hands, it was just a matter of time.

☙   ☙   ☙

The storm stopped late that afternoon, and Helene took it as her opportunity to make a trip to the store before it closed. She whistled as she strolled, searching for her father's profile among the crowds.

Lately, he had been spending most of his time visiting friends, talking politics, and planning for their future. Everyone, it seemed, lived on rumors these days. Rumors of Russian occupation. Of the possible rebuilding of the Austrian government. Of who would rule when.

Part of the future, Helene knew, included reopening their home as an inn. They'd been living off the generosity of others. The "extra" rations from poor farmers, and meager offerings dropped off by those her father had somehow helped during the war. They also received bread passed out by the Americans. But soon they would need an income.

Her black leather shoes splashed in the shallow puddles dotting the street. The air smelled fresh. It had been ages since such a sweet scent had risen on the wind.

Rounding the street corner, Helene hesitated. Disbelieving what her eyes told her was true! A man from her past sat on the steps of the tailor shop smoking a cigarette. He was thinner than she remembered, but his disturbing grin was the same.

Arno Schroeder. Friedrich's friend. The man who had found her husband's letter on his dead body. *What's he doing here?*

Helene's fingers tightened around her metal shopping basket and for a moment their eyes met. She resumed her pace but could still feel him eyeing her. She smiled politely to a couple passing by, while everything within her told her to turn around and go back home. She refused. She would not to give in to those urges. Would not be intimidated by his stare.

Aren't the Russians after him? Or the Americans? How could he so easily return to St. Georgen?

A smirk rested on Arno's lips as he assessed her pregnant frame. His gaze traveled up her body, making her stomach churn. She stalked past without a word, nearly passing the grocery store altogether.

Her father's call from the doorway drew her attention. He frowned when he saw her face. With three quick steps he was at her side, leading her up the store steps.

Her eyes shot to Arno, then back to her father. "What is he doing here?"

"The Americans found him in Bavaria and graciously gave him a ride home." Her father's voice sounded calm, but Helene detected anger in his tone.

"But don't they know who he is?" Helene asked. They paced the aisles together, examining the near-empty store shelves.

"Nein. He most likely lied and said he was in the regular army. They're taking all those soldiers home." He jutted his chin into the air. "They are no threat now that the war is over."

Her father spoke a little too loud, in Helene's opinion. Perhaps she would never again be used to speaking one's mind in public. Helene dropped the conversation but couldn't shake the uneasiness of seeing that man.

"Maybe we should tell them," Helene said. "We could go to Josef and—"

Her father rubbed his chin. "And do you really think Josef will listen to what you have to say?"

The words stung, but she knew he spoke the truth. No, she could not go to Josef.

"I don't see anything here that interests me today." Helene stopped perusing the store shelves. Her mind wasn't clear enough to recall her shopping list anyway. "Will you walk me home?"

This time as they passed, Arno's wife and two teenage daughters were with him. Helene quickened her steps, but not enough.

"Helene, Herr Katz, so good to see you," Edda called from the doorway. "Did you see Arno has returned?"

Edda's cheeks were red from the exertion of running to Helen's side. Helene paused and attempted to smile. She looked into Edda's face, refusing to even glance at her husband.

"Your family is indeed lucky," Helene said in her most pleasant tone. Her father's fingers tightened around her arm, and she knew he was warning her to watch her words. "How . . . how good for you."

The woman's eyes widened as she scanned Helene's stomach. "Why, I didn't know you were pregnant. You do know how to keep a secret, don't you?"

Helene smiled stiffly. "Friedrich and I were waiting for a good time to announce it. But, as we all know, a good time never arrived."

"How foolish of me. You're right. I'm so sorry. I'd forgotten he's gone."

Her father lifted his hat as a farewell. "Please excuse

us now. My daughter is needed at home," he said curtly, then pulled her down the street.

"It makes no sense," Helene said when they were out of earshot. "Anika has no father. And this baby won't either. Our lives have been completely upturned, and others move on as if nothing happened." Her basket hit her leg with every step, but she didn't care.

When they were almost home, her father finally spoke. "And what do you think would have happened if Friedrich had returned? What would he think of where you live now and what you are doing?"

Michaela and Lelia's faces flashed in Helene's mind. Anika's too. She thought of the laughter of that afternoon. "You're right. I could never go back."

Her father patted her shoulder. "Nor would you want to."

They trudged through the gate and up the front steps.

"You've been given a second chance," he said simply. His hand clung to the railing. "I won't say it will be easy without a husband. Heaven knows how difficult it's been without your mother. But you are becoming a woman of strength and courage. The evidence of both is now taking root from the seeds your dear mother planted deep in your soul."

Strength and courage. Helene let those words roll over in her mind as she walked through the front door. They were the exact traits she'd need with a man like Arno Schroeder back in town.

Fifteen

MAY 29, 1945

Do you have a photo of him?" Michaela asked Helene as they sat on the sofa reading.

Helene glanced up from her book. Michaela's hair was now a cap of dark curls. In the light of the flickering oil lamp, her eyes appeared as dark as her hair.

"My husband, you mean?" Helene asked.

"Yes."

Helene's mind raced as she moved to her room. Why did she ask? What if she recognized him? How would it be for her to stare into the face of a captor?

Helene opened the door quietly and tiptoed to the bureau. Anika slept soundly on the bed. Helene knelt, then slid open the bottom drawer and pulled out a few shots. She chose the ones of her husband when they'd first met. Her heart pounded, and she held them to her chest. For a few minutes she remained there in the near-dark, holding the black-and-white images.

Did I do enough? she asked herself as she struggled to rise. *Could I have done anything to make him love me more than the Nazi ideals?*

Anika snored softly. Helene leaned over her, brushing a lock of blonde hair from her face. She saw him in her. Though she tried to ignore it, often an expression or a gesture would be all too familiar.

She wandered back to the living room, still unsure. Without a word, she stood before Michaela and handed over the photos. Michaela took the pictures and slowly thumbed through them. If Michaela recognized Friedrich, her expression didn't let on. She appeared as natural as if she were looking at photos of a friend.

"Handsome," Michaela said.

"Ja." Helene wiped her hair back from her face and tucked it behind her ear, trying to hide the quivering of her fingers.

Michaela flipped through the photos again. The one on top was one of her and Friedrich together.

What a child I was, Helene thought, looking over Michaela's shoulder. Her long hair, hanging down to her waist, was wavy due to the braids she wore back then. At Friedrich's insistence she had let down her hair, allowing it to fall over her shoulders for the photo. She was dressed in a simple handmade frock. A ring of white daisies floated upon her golden hair.

She examined it more closely. Though the girl in the photo was smiling, her eyes told another story. Although supposedly in love, Helene knew the young woman was just starting to realize what she'd left behind.

Michaela tilted the photo toward the lamp to get a better view. Helene studied the image of Friedrich. Though not dressed in uniform, his power could not be denied. He was proud of his country and of the Aryan beauty by his side.

"I'm just trying to understand," Michaela said finally. "Understand how people can be so different. How some can be drawn to good and others to evil. If I had seen him on the street, I would never have guessed . . ."

"He was a handsome man," Michaela said again, handing the photos back. "Anika has his eyes and his chin." She laughed quietly to herself, then glanced away as if deep in thought. "My mother always did that," she finally said.

Helene placed the photos on the floor in front of her. "Did what?"

"Pointed out features. When we'd visit friends with new babies she'd go on about 'his father's nose' or 'her great-uncle Holder's hairline.' I always thought she was making it up. A baby just looked like a baby to me." Michaela gave a slight smile. "Now listen to me. I'm doing the same."

Helene moved to Michaela's side. "Tell me more about your mother. Did she look like you?"

Michaela chuckled again. "Not much. She was short . . . and round. A true Polish mother. I remember getting lost once at the market and approaching four women before I found the right one."

Helene laughed. "And your father?"

A smile curled on Michaela's lips. "My father was German. Blond hair, blue eyes. Similar to your Friedrich. He was a pastor. As a young man, he visited our town to evangelize the Catholic population. Rumor had it he was leaving town when a farmer's daughter caught his fancy, and he retraced his steps and took up residence as if that had been his intention all along."

Helene could barely utter her next question, although she was sure she already knew. "Are your parents dead?"

Michaela stared at her lap. "Yes."

"I'm so sorry."

Michaela's voice softened. "In the summer of 1941, four Jews arrived from Germany and asked my father for shelter and help." She spoke matter-of-factly, as if relating someone else's story. "Marian and Sarah and their daughters, Leah and Rebecca, stayed with us for three years. Their names were changed, as well as their identities. The girls became my cousins from Warsaw who had lost their parents. Since they were young and smart, my family taught them the Christian faith in order to hide their Jewishness. Only our closest friends knew that Leah and Rebecca's real parents hid in our basement."

"So Lelia is Leah," Helene said, putting the puzzle together.

Michaela stared at her hands. Her voice was barely audible. "In 1944, Gestapo men arrived in the village. As they approached our home, my father told me to take Lelia and run. He assured us the family would be safe, but something in his eyes said different."

Helene rubbed the spot where the baby tussled.

"Lelia's parents and her sister were in extremely poor health. Thinking back now, I realize Lelia and I were the only strong ones. My father knew that. I believe he hoped we, at least, could make it."

Helene tried to picture what it must have been like for Michaela to have to leave her family behind. "Then what happened?"

"When the Gestapo arrived, Lelia and I escaped out a back window. We hid in the woods until they were gone. I'll never forget it as long as I live. The image of those men dragging my mother. It was awful." Michaela gulped back a sob. "I was angry with my father for many months. Perhaps he could have made it if he'd tried. My mother too. But they didn't even attempt it."

"Did you ever find out what happened to them?"

Michaela took a steadying breath. "I found out days later that they were all arrested. They were being transported to a concentration camp with a large group of people when, without explanation, they were all taken off the train and shot. Men from our town were rounded up to bury the bodies."

Helene couldn't begin to imagine such horror.

"After hearing of my family's death, I returned home to retrieve some of their things." Michaela's eyes teared. Helene felt hers doing the same. She patted Michaela's hand, not knowing what else to do.

"Then, not knowing where to turn, Lelia and I went

to the home of my father's dear friends, Jacek and Lidia. They welcomed us and fed us. But the next day someone reported us." Michaela shook her head. "The rest is just a blur. The transport, the camps. Nothing was right again until you brought us here to care for us. And for that I'm forever grateful."

Helene took Michaela into her arms, surprised at how thin she still was. Yet deep inside that delicate body was a strength Helene envied.

Sixteen

MAY 29, 1945

I can take you to the top so you can get a better view." The GI's voice held a note of pride, like a zoo-keeper showing off his prized animals.

Peter shielded his eyes from the bright sun and squinted at the four towers. One stood at each corner, with a high barbed-wire fence strung between them. There were no buildings or vehicles inside the fence. Only men and dirt. It reminded him of the steer corrals back in Montana. Across the field stood the large brick prison of Landsberg.

If ever there was a time when Peter had wanted to disobey orders it was when his commander sent him to this prison in Germany instead of allowing him to re-turn to St. Georgen. *Trying to get this continent in or-der sure is inconvenient at times*, Peter thought. One minute, the officers and men seemed almost free to move as they pleased, and other times—like now—their work and movements were more restricted.

Peter followed the soldier up the wooden steps to the guard tower. When they reached the top, he saw that the walkway completely encircled the caged area. Two soldiers, one on each side, stood at attention with rifles in hand and watched over the men inside the stockade.

"So that's the mighty SS?" Peter said with a low whistle.

"The best of the best."

He studied the men below. *Waffen* SS, Hitler's elite. Gone were the lightning bolt runes on their right collar tabs. Gone were their silver SS eagles and field-gray wool tunics. These men were dressed in tattered, filthy street clothes. And it was clear they'd spent weeks exposed to the elements.

In an area the size of a football field, the prisoners had dug small caves out of the soft dirt in an effort to stay out of the weather. Their hair was shaggy and tangled. Those recently brought in were easy to spot. They showed a slight trace of cleanliness.

Many of the prisoners shifted in groups, smoking cigarettes and talking. The once-elite now appeared as the animals they really were. The corners of Peter's mouth lifted in a smirk.

The soldier giving Peter the tour called out to a man, then leaned over the tower's railing and spit. The spittle landed on the head of a prisoner below. The man didn't even flinch.

"Look at that," the GI boasted. "The guards who manned the concentration camps make excellent prisoners."

"Are any of them from Austria?" Peter asked, thinking of Helene. If her husband hadn't already been killed, he likely would have ended up here.

"Yeah, a few guards. And a couple of commandants are in the big prison next door."

"Did you hear about Ziereis?" Peter asked.

"Oh, yeah. I heard they strung him up after he croaked . . . but not before he had a chance to hang his own guys out to dry." The soldier laughed. "So, you think you can handle the job?"

"Transporting more men here? Not a problem."

Peter followed his guide back down the stairs, glancing occasionally at some of the prisoners. He wondered if any had been in Gusen. Perhaps some of these men had even contributed to the horror Michaela had faced.

"So, where's the next pickup?" Peter asked when they reached the bottom of the stairs.

"They found a small group in the mountains close to where Ziereis was hiding."

"That's back in Austria, right?" Peter's heart leapt.

"Yeah. Have a problem with that?"

"Not at all. In fact, I was hoping to get back soon. I'm due for some leave."

"Sounds like you have a girl there. Tsk, tsk. No fraternization, you know."

"Don't worry, she's Polish," Peter bantered.

The soldier stopped. "A displaced person?"

"Actually, she is."

The GI chuckled. "Yeah, right. That's what they all say."

Peter didn't argue. He would have come to the same conclusion himself. While all soldiers were ordered against fraternizing with German or Austrian women, there was no rule against being friendly with children or displaced persons. Peter had been to more than one dance where grown women swore they were only twelve, or wore borrowed DP armbands.

Peter knew no one would understand his concern for a frail prisoner. He didn't understand it himself. Yet he found thoughts of Michaela swirling through his head more each day.

Of course, he often thought of Helene too. Her generosity. Her beauty. But it was easier, safer, to dwell on the thoughts of Michaela. Helene had been married to a powerful man. She had strength and . . . no, it was Michaela who needed him most.

Peter toured the medical tent and the soldiers' quarters, then returned to his jeep, where a driver waited.

"Where to?"

"Why don't you take me back to my quarters."

"Sure thing." The jeep rumbled away, stirring up a cloud of dirt. Peter glanced over his shoulder and saw the dust descend on the prisoners, just as ash had done not too many weeks before.

His body jolted with each pothole the vehicle hit, but he barely noticed. *How much should I reveal to*

Michaela? What if sh
was a soldier. He need

I'll write about wh
decided. Michaela nee
idea. Imagining what
country. Realizing how
someday progressed tha

"Thanks for the rid
jeep. *Dear Michaela,* hi
as he strode to his barra
well and happy.

"Michaela, Michaela,
Bing Crosby's song "Acc
compound's loudspeakers

Peter changed his tune,
as he crooned along with I

Peter shrugged off th
waltzed into his office. He
the wall and sang all the w

"I guess seeing Krauts
Scotty's day," one GI called

"What turnip truck di
quipped. "No one acts th
love."

Peter tapped his pencil o
he muttered to himself. *So th*

Michaela? What if she has no idea of my feelings? He was a soldier. He needed a plan.

I'll write about what life in America is like, he finally decided. Michaela needed to start thinking about the idea. Imagining what life would be like in a different country. Realizing how much he could offer—if things someday progressed that far.

"Thanks for the ride," he called, jumping from the jeep. *Dear Michaela,* his mind was already composing as he strode to his barracks. *I hope this letter finds you well and happy.*

"Michaela, Michaela," he sang before noticing that Bing Crosby's song "Accentuate" was playing over the compound's loudspeakers.

Peter changed his tune, and his voice rose in harmony as he crooned along with Bing.

Peter shrugged off the stares he received as he waltzed into his office. He flung his cap onto a hook on the wall and sang all the way to the desk.

"I guess seeing Krauts caged up really brightened Scotty's day," one GI called from down the hall.

"What turnip truck did you fall off of?" another quipped. "No one acts that goofy unless they're in love."

Peter tapped his pencil on his lower lip. "In love," he muttered to himself. *So this is what it feels like.*

sun-kissed head to reappear. When a minute passed, Helene awkwardly rose from her blanket. She stood on her toes to see if she could spot her daughter but saw only two things from her place in the quiet hollow: the church's steeple and the chimney of the crematorium.

Helene shook out her blanket and folded it. The trek home would take at least thirty minutes. They should start home now if they hoped to make it back in time for dinner. Along the way, Helene decided, she'd finally tell her daughter about Friedrich. The girl needed to know her father wasn't coming back.

"Anika!" Helene called, moving toward the hill where the girl had disappeared. Helene mumbled under her breath at Anika's increased disobedience. Friedrich had seemed harsh at times, but he *had* been successful in raising a child who obeyed.

Helene rounded the crest of the hill and stopped. Anika sat under the shade of a large oak tree with a man. Helene quickened her steps. As she neared, she recognized the dark shaggy hair and disturbing profile. Arno! Helene suddenly felt foolish for taking her daughter so far from home. What if they needed help? Who would hear Helene's cries?

Heat rose to Helene's cheeks as she approached them. Arno was lying on his side, talking to Anika in low tones. He glanced Helene's way as she approached.

"Finally, there's your mother."

Helene tucked the blanket under her arm and took Anika's hand, pulling her to a standing position. "What are you doing with my daughter?"

Seventeen

Helene plucked a white-haired dandelion from the green grass and blew on it. The tiny parachutes fluttered on the breeze and floated over the pasture where she sat with Anika. As she lost sight of them on the wind, she imagined them lifting over the cottonwood trees and the rippling waters of the Danube.

The shadows of the trees swayed gently over the ground. Anika plucked her own dandelion. She blew at it, but the parachutes didn't budge.

"Try this." Helene picked another dandelion and shook it. The seeds scattered.

Anika tried. "It works!" She jumped to her feet and chased the seeds.

"Don't go too far," Helene called as her daughter disappeared over a small hill. She waited for Anika's

"Talking to her. Protecting her. Entertaining her with stories of her father. Really, what type of mother would let a little girl wander like that?" Arno twirled a blade of grass between his fingers. "Would you like to hear some of the stories too, Helene?"

"Thank you, no. We have to get home." She turned in the direction of town.

Arno jumped to his feet and snatched the blanket from her arm. "I'll walk you."

Helene grabbed the blanket back. "There's no need." She continued with a quickened pace, yanking Anika along.

He fell into step beside her. "Really, it would be my pleasure. I need to talk to you."

Helene kept her vision straight ahead, the steeple as her guide.

"I know things about him. Where he was going. What he was up to. Things he kept secret from you. Things that could change your life."

Helene didn't respond.

His stride matched hers. "Wouldn't you like to know what happened after he left? The promises he made? I was there. I can tell you—"

Anika cried out, and Helene realized she'd been squeezing her daughter's hand much too tightly. She loosened her grip, but only slightly.

Arno stepped in front of her and cursed. Helene stopped abruptly.

"Just tell me one thing," he growled. "Did you find anything he left behind? A piece of paper, maybe?"

Helene knew what Arno spoke of. The map. The address. But if it did mean something, Arno was the last person she'd tell.

"Friedrich left a lot behind," she said gruffly. "He left piles of dead bodies. He left his family and his home, just to save his own life."

"Is that all?" Arno grabbed her arm. "There has to be something else."

Helene glared at him in disbelief. "Isn't that enough?" Her voice shook. "Why don't you leave us alone? That part of my life is over."

Arno's fingers tightened. Helene winced. "You are being very foolish, especially if you think I believe you. You're a smart one, bringing those camp filth into your home, befriending the enemy. You know how to play this game better than most." He released his grip on her arm. "But I'll be watching your every move."

Arno began to leave, then stopped. "One more thing. It's not over. It will never be over. You know too much. So do I."

Helene refused to watch him walk away. Refused to give in to the panic his words stirred inside. Instead she turned her attention to Anika, grasping her hand gently. The girl seemed close to tears.

"Just remember, Helene," Arno's voice carried on the wind. "It was you who refused to listen."

Michaela sat on the front porch and swatted the air, attempting to shoo away the fly that buzzed close to her ear. White clouds streaked across a sky as blue as the jay that hopped along the fence.

"Really, I should be doing that," she called to Helene, who was attacking the debris in her father's flower beds. Dry leaves, weeds, even bits of newspaper had entangled themselves among the new sprouts climbing toward the warm June sun.

"Not a chance." Helene scratched her nose with the back of her hand, leaving a smudge of dirt. "My rear aches from sitting. Besides, I've always liked the feel of my fingers in the dirt."

Helene had been quiet and moody ever since returning from a walk with Anika the previous day. But today, Michaela noticed, she rolled up her sleeves and toiled with vigor.

Michaela shook her head. "You can hardly bend over with that stomach of yours."

Helene rubbed her belly. "The baby is growing, isn't it?"

"Like a weed." Michaela chuckled. She drew a long breath, taking in the scent of rich, moist soil. The smell stirred images of her mother repotting geraniums that she'd purchased from the farmer's market. In a child's eyes those robust flowers had appeared as tiny blooming trees. *Mother.* She sighed. *Home.*

Michaela was stirred from her thoughts when, in the distance, she saw Papa Katz, Lelia, and Anika coming back from town.

"Mail call," Papa Katz called as they neared. While civilian mail was sporadic at best, military mail—especially between the army stations in Germany and Austria—took no more than a week.

Anika ran through the front gate, waving an envelope. Her red-and-white-checkered dress and blonde curls swung as she ran.

Anika paused at the front steps and held out the envelope to Michaela. She took it, running her fingers over the blue-and-red stripes on the flap. She felt her face growing warm but told herself it was from too much sun.

"Another letter from Peter?" Helene asked. Michaela searched for any sign of disappointment behind her friend's smile. There was none.

"Third one this week," Papa Katz commented, stroking his thin white mustache. A web of lines crinkled around his eyes. "And you should have seen all the attention Josef gave Lelia in town. I think both of our girls have admirers."

Lelia glanced up from beneath her dark lashes and blushed.

"Read it, read it," Anika chanted.

Lelia sat down and leaned close as Michaela slid her finger under the flap and tore it open. She pulled out a thin white sheet of paper with words written in German.

"Dear Michaela and all," she read out loud. "Another day has passed, and thankfully I found a friend to assist me with my letter writing. I can imagine how troublesome it has been for you to make your way through my many spelling errors. I speak German far better than I write it.

"First and foremost, I must ask why you haven't replied. It would bring me so much joy if you did. I hope your health is returning. If I can't get back before long, I'm going to ask one of my buddies to take a picture of you. I'd like to see the results of Helene's nursing. I'm sure she's given you the best care possible."

Michaela peeked up at Helene.

"Well, go on," Helene said, waving a dirt-encrusted hand at her.

"During the course of my army career, I've never run around as much as I have during the past few days. I've been transporting prisoners from all parts of Germany and France. While many of the cities are nothing more than rubble, there are some places the Allied bombers missed. A few cities appear almost normal. I was even able to ride the Metro during a short stay in Paris. It reminded me of the subway in New York. I've been to the Big Apple (that's what they call New York) a few times, and I like it there. But it's the long dirt roads back home that call to me most often. Sometimes I try to imagine what your response would be to Montana's gentle people, tall mountains, and the big sky that seems to go on forever. Or I try to guess if you'd favor my sister's canned raspberry jam or her peach preserves. Perhaps someday I'll find out."

Michaela cleared her throat, then continued reading. "Well, I think I smell dinner cooking in the chow hall. Give my best regards to all, and plant a special kiss on little Annie's cheek for me. I'm looking forward to a reunion soon. Peter."

Michaela refolded the letter and tried to make sense of its words. Why did he write these things? And to her especially? It hardly made sense.

"He's looking forward to seeing you again," Helene said as she plucked a deep-rooted thistle from the earth.

Michaela examined the envelope. "I'm sure he's excited to see us all."

"Sounds like it will be soon." Papa Katz hobbled up the porch stairs, favoring his right leg. "I would like to hear more about what he's seeing out there," he said as he disappeared into the house.

Michaela pulled Anika onto her lap and placed a kiss on her petal-soft cheek. "That's from Peter."

Anika giggled. "No, it not, it from you!" She hugged Michaela, then studied Lelia, who sat contentedly beside Michaela. "You want to play doctor?" Anika's voice was as soft as her smile. "I take care of you."

Lelia stretched out her hand. "Ja, I will play." She strolled into the house with Anika chattering at her side. Michaela smoothed her skirt and tried to think of something to say to Helene. She had to admit Peter's letter did stir heart-tingling feelings. Emotions she hadn't felt since Georg.

Still, the thought of going to America troubled her. She'd never been one for travel. Although she enjoyed reading stories from around the world, she'd always been content to stay at home near the people she loved.

The blue jay started a song from its new place upon the rooftop. Michaela closed her eyes and pretended she was sitting on her own front porch back home. She thought of the nursery school down the street and the large church next door. Did those places still exist? Did the people? She'd give anything to know.

Though she was happy here, Michaela couldn't imagine never returning to Poland. The thought of seeing familiar faces and entering into the house of worship where her father had preached made her heart stir. She fanned her face with the envelope.

Michaela noticed Helene staring at her with a curious expression.

"You looked like you were making a wish." Helene attempted to rise from the ground, with little success.

Michaela giggled at the clumsiness of her pregnant friend. "Did I? Actually, I was just thinking of someplace special." She descended from the porch and extended a hand to Helene. Their fingers intertwined.

With a gentle tug from Michaela, Helene rose to her feet, then attempted to wipe the dirt from her dress.

"Helene?" Michaela asked.

Helene stopped her brushing.

"Would you be interested in walking to the church with me? I've been drawn to that steeple for so long. It would feel good to enter a house of worship again."

"Tomorrow perhaps." Helene's smile disappeared. "I feel like sticking close to home today."

Helene plodded up the stairs. "Or perhaps my father

could take you. That might be even better," she said before disappearing into the house.

"That would be fine," Michaela said to no one.

Over the past few weeks she'd prayed with and for Helene. But while their friendship grew, Helene obviously still struggled with Michaela's faith. She seemed drawn to it and fearful of it at the same time.

She needs to find forgiveness, Michaela thought as the spring-swept air ruffled her skirt.

Michaela returned to her seat on the porch and thought about the photos Helene had shown her of Friedrich. In her mind's eye she could see the two of them posed in their wedding attire, kneeling before the Nazi flag that had been displayed over the podium. Friedrich's power, strength, and influence over Helene could not be denied.

A cold chill coursed down Michaela's spine. That was it. *How could Helene get over her own guilt of not doing enough, when she still struggled to get over the man who'd taken her down that path?*

Somehow she knew forgiving Friedrich would be the key to unlocking Helene's heart.

Eighteen

The sounds and smells of breakfast cooking drifted in from the kitchen. Helene attempted to roll over to check the time on the clock beside her bed, but the size of her stomach made that small task difficult to accomplish.

She heard Anika's singsong voice intermingled with her opa's low tones. The scent of bacon was strong, and Helene covered her nose. She uttered a low moan.

Soft footsteps entered the room. "Are you okay?" Michaela placed a cool hand on her forehead.

Helene hugged her stomach. "I think I'm coming down with something. The smells from the kitchen are making me ill."

Michaela opened the window, letting in the fresh morning breeze.

Helene took a deep breath, expanding her lungs as far as her stomach would allow. "That's much better, thanks."

Michaela poured a glass of water from the pitcher on the side table and handed it to Helene. "It's not time for the baby, is it?"

"Nein." Helene took a long drink, then handed the glass back to Michaela. "I have a few weeks yet. Besides, this doesn't feel like it did when I had Anika."

Michaela leaned closer. "Perhaps we should have a nurse stop by just in case?"

"Oh, no." Helene snuggled back under the covers. The image of the SS doctor came to mind. Just the thought of him made her skin crawl. "I'll go see my mother's old friend later. She's a midwife and has birthed half the babies in town, including me. Right now, I'm just really tired."

Michaela's hand rested on her shoulder. "You sleep. I'll help your father. He was planning to visit some friends at the evacuation hospital today."

Helene's eyelids felt heavy. "And Anika?"

"We'll take her with us. She's always a welcome visitor there."

"Danke," Helene mumbled, but Michaela was already on her way back to the kitchen. Helene took another deep breath of fresh air, then succumbed to the weariness coursing through her.

🦢   🦢   🦢

"Stop! No, stop!" Helene begged.

Friedrich's face closed in on her. She smelled liquor on his breath and tasted it in his unwelcome kisses. He pressed her body between his chest and the wall.

"Please, you're hurting me." Helene tried to wriggle free from his hold. As she did she felt a warm sensation on her legs. *Blood?* He had brought home the blood from the camps, and now it was on her.

"No!"

Helene opened her eyes. The room was bright. Blankets entangled her arms and a hot tightness stretched across her abdomen. Her inner thighs felt wet.

Oh, no. Not now. Helene pulled back the blanket. The sheet beneath her was drenched. "My water broke," she cried out. There was no response.

Her mind still groggy, she tried to remember what day it was. *Wednesday. I wasn't feeling well, so Michaela went with my father. I have to get help.*

Helene struggled to untangle the covers. She pulled her body into a sitting position. Suddenly she winced in pain, remembering this unique sensation all too well.

"Why is this happening now?" When the contraction passed, another thought seized her. *It's too early. Something's wrong. I'm going to lose the baby.* Tears welled in her eyes.

Helene stood, her knees wobbly. She took three steps, then grabbed the chair for support.

"Help," she called, feeling the strength in her legs give out. She slumped into the chair. A sob shook her chest. Not only could she not stop this, but she was alone. Alone to face what lay ahead.

After a minute or two, another contraction mounted. Helene's hair dangled in her face as she gripped the chair.

"Oh, God, please. Somebody help me."

"Helene?" a voice came from the doorway.

Helene looked up. "Lelia, thank God."

Lelia stumbled into the room. "You need to get in bed." She placed one hand on Helene's back and another on her elbow. Helene stood. Fluid dripped down her legs.

"I can't believe this. It's too soon."

Lelia stripped the damp sheets and replaced them with a clean blanket. "Here you go." She helped Helene back into bed. "Don't worry. Everything will be fine."

Helene tried to relax on the bed. But as she did, another contraction hit. The room started spinning. "I think I'm going to be sick."

Lelia rose. "I'll go get help."

"No! Please stay. I don't want to be alone."

Lelia remained by her side, holding Helene's hand, rubbing her back, and offering words of encouragement for what seemed like hours.

Each contraction demanded all of Helene's focus. Between contractions she prayed. Simply and honestly like Michaela had taught her. She prayed for strength and for her father to get back soon.

"Where are they?" Helene cried.

Lelia rose. "I don't want to leave you, but the baby's

coming too fast. I have to get help. There are nurses at the camp. I'll hurry—"

"No!" Helene felt a strong pressure between her legs. "There's no time. I can feel the baby coming. You can't leave now." Tears filled her eyes, but her hands shook too much to wipe them away.

Terror filled Lelia's face.

"Please stay with me," Helene begged again. "I can't bear to be alone right now." The last word faded as another pain started.

"Of course I will stay." Lelia took Helene's hand. Her gaze took on a look of determination.

When the contraction passed, Helene studied the girl's face. Instead of fear, she saw resolve.

"My aunt had a baby," Lelia said, as if just remembering. "I watched the birth, and my mother showed me what to do." Her voice was steady. "I can help you."

The contractions continued to mount.

Lelia wiped Helene's forehead. "Look at me." She gripped Helene's jaw and turned it toward her. "Focus on my face."

Helene did as she was told.

"Everything will be fine. You're doing very well. We can do this."

Helene panted.

"Now," Lelia said, patting Helene's cheek, "I'm going to check the baby, ja?" Lelia examined Helene as if she had done this every day of her life. Then she returned to Helene's side. "The baby's close. I need to get some things ready. Whatever you do, don't push." Lelia hurried from the room.

Helene's fists twisted the bottom blanket. "Oh!" Her cries grew louder as the pain swelled. It felt like small shards of glass ripping her apart in tight, heart-stopping pains. She had to remember to breathe.

Lelia, her mind screamed, *where are you?* Helene felt a strong urge to push. *Please, God, let this baby be okay. Let my child live.*

Lelia returned, her arms laden with scissors, string, towels, and a bucket of water. Helene clenched the blanket as another pain tightened her abdomen into a fiery ball.

Lelia set down her items and crouched between Helene's knees. "The baby's coming. I can see the head." Lelia's voice rose. "Push when you feel the need."

Helene grabbed her thighs and pressed her chin to her chest. With each push, Lelia encouraged her on.

After a few pushes Lelia gasped. "The head is coming."

Helene wailed in both joy and pain.

"The head's out," Lelia said. "One more."

Finally, the baby slid into the world. "It's a boy!" Lelia shouted.

Helene exhaled her breath and waited for a cry. It came. Loud, angry, and beautiful.

Lelia worked quickly, cutting the umbilical cord, then clearing out the infant's mouth and nose with a small cloth. "He's beautiful."

Helene leaned up on her elbows, panting, and

watched Lelia use a damp towel to wipe her son's face. Lelia wrapped him in a soft blanket and placed him on his mother's stomach. Helene began to shake, then cry. "My baby, oh, my baby."

The babe puckered his lips and attempted to open his eyes. Tiny strands of blond hair stuck to his head. Helene snuggled him to her chest, then reached out to Lelia. "You saved us. I couldn't have done it without you."

Lelia blushed, and Helene noticed a transformation in the girl's face. The silent victim was gone, and Helene caught a glimpse of the young woman hidden inside.

The front door opened and closed. Lelia covered Helene with a clean blanket, then hurried to the living room.

Helene heard squeals, then a shout of worry from her father. Three nervous, excited people entered the room. After ensuring that Helene and the baby were fine, Helene's father went for a nurse. "Just to be safe," he said, flying out the bedroom door.

Michaela kissed the baby's head, then took Lelia into an embrace.

Anika, who'd stayed by the door, ran up and peeked at her baby brother. "He so little," she said in a quiet voice.

"Little, but healthy," Helene said. "Come sit with me." Anika climbed onto the bed and laid her head on Helene's chest. The breath of her two children caressed Helene's skin. Their faces tilted in her direction. She kissed them both, and swore to herself to protect them with all the strength that was in her.

"Thank you," she said to Lelia. "Thank you."

Lelia sank onto the chair. Her shoulders trembled as if she were just realizing what had happened.

"I'm so proud of you both." Michaela crouched by Helene and studied the baby's tiny feet.

Lelia's smile assured Helene that all would be well.

Helene contemplated her baby's perfect face. "Petar," she murmured.

"Oh, yes, we must get word to Peter." Michaela rose. "Perhaps your father can—"

"No, wait," Helene said. "That is his name. I will call him Petar, after our hero."

"Baby Petar." Anika cradled his tiny fist in her palm.

By the time Helene's father returned with a nurse, Michaela had cleaned up the mess and Lelia had fallen asleep in the chair. The nurse, who wore an American uniform, examined Helene and the baby, taking time to wash them both thoroughly. Lelia, who had awakened when the nurse arrived, watched closely.

"Everything's fine," the nurse said. "I couldn't have done a better job myself," she added with a wink at Lelia.

"Now you need to rest. I'll check you again tomorrow." She patted Helene's shoulder.

Lelia showed the nurse to the front door, then went to her room to change clothes and lie down. Helene's father pulled up a chair by his daughter and gently tucked her hair behind her ear.

"Just look at them." His gaze was tender as he peered down at his grandchildren. Anika had fallen asleep at her mother's side. The baby slept too, his soft snore sounding like the purr of a kitten.

"I can put Anika on my bed," he whispered. "Then you can rest." He reached for the girl.

"No, leave her. Just for a while."

He nodded. "A grandson." He sighed.

"Friedrich always wanted a son." Helene's voice caught in her throat.

"Let's not dwell on the past. The time for mourning is past. A time of rejoicing has come."

Helene's lower lip quivered. She let her head sink deeper into the pillow. *If only the mourning could truly be over.*

But the more she thought about it, she realized that sometimes good did result from pain. Michaela and Lelia in this home. Being reunited with her father. Two beautiful children. These were the things Helene thought of as she drifted off to sleep.

Beauty from ashes. Life from pain.

Nineteen

Every morning during the first week of his life, the baby's cry had preceded even the neighbor's rooster in stirring the house to wakefulness.

"Sh, there's no need for that." Helene lifted the small bundle from the cradle her father had found in the attic. In just a few days Petar had regained his birth weight of 2.27 kilograms, or as the American nurse said, 5 pounds. Helene kissed the top of Petar's soft blond hair, marveling at the scent of him.

The baby rooted his head toward his mother's breast and settled as she brought him close to nurse. Helene studied him in the dim light, noticing how his miniature earlobe perfectly matched his sister's.

At a gentle tap on the door, Helene lifted her head. "Come in," she said just above a whisper.

Lelia, still in her nightdress, poked her head around the doorframe. A few black curls peeked out from under a scarf. "I can take him when he's through," she said shyly.

"I'd like that." Helene yawned. "I promised Anika we'd bake a cake to celebrate Petar's birth. A few more hours of sleep would be nice before I have to start the day."

Lelia padded into the room and sat down in the chair.

"I just can't believe he's here." Helene wrapped her son's fingers around her own. "I couldn't have done it without you."

Lelia stared at her hands in her lap. "I did what I could."

"No, really, you have a gift, Lelia. I nearly fainted when I saw all the blood, but it didn't even faze you. Perhaps you should consider becoming a nurse."

Lelia beamed. "I will think about that."

When Petar finished nursing, Helene lifted him to her shoulder and burped him, then passed him to Lelia. She pulled him close, kissing his button nose.

Helene snuggled back under her quilt. "I hope he didn't wake you." She yawned again.

Lelia wrapped a blanket around the baby. "He did wake me, but not in the way you think." She paused and stared at him a moment. "When I came here I couldn't think. I didn't want to be alive." Her eyes looked past Petar and far away. "So many people were gone. My family—"

Helene leaned up on one arm. Petar opened his eyes as if he too were listening.

"Then he came. You needed me. I felt alive again." Her voice faded. She patted Helene's arm. "Now, you get some sleep, and don't worry about him." She caressed Petar's cheek, then carried him out of the room, letting the door close softly behind her.

Helene wanted to say something more than thank you, but words didn't seem to be enough. So Helene just lay there, in awe of the miracles taking place around her.

After a few minutes, she closed her eyes. *Thank you, God, for giving me Petar. And for giving us Lelia back too.*

And as she considered what else to pray, it seemed that her words to God never said quite enough either.

Helene felt better after a few hours of sleep. She was busy helping Anika with the cake when a loud knock at the door startled her. She handed the wooden spoon to Anika and wiped her hands on her apron. "Keep scooping batter into the pan."

"I keep going." Anika licked the spoon once before sticking it back into the batter. Helene chuckled quietly.

The knocking sounded again, and Lelia and Michaela approached the door as well.

Upon opening the front screen, Helene saw a huge bunch of wildflowers and a package wrapped in glossy blue paper, tied with a white satin bow. The face behind them wasn't distinguishable, but she could make out an

American army uniform. She moved her hand to her chest and was about to call out Peter's name when a face moved from behind the flowers. It was a face she recognized—one of Peter's friends. But not Peter.

"Please come in," Helene said, willing her heart to cease its wild beating. She hoped her smile hid her disappointment.

"I come bearing gifts from Peter," the GI said. "He's sorry he can't be here himself."

Helene stepped out of the way so he could enter. After taking a long sniff of the flowers, she placed them on a side table. "I'm sorry. I don't remember . . ."

"My name?" He grinned. "Clifton. Corporal Dan Clifton, at your service." He bowed, then looked around. "Well, where's that new baby? I have direct orders to check out the little guy."

They all tiptoed to Helene's room and peeked into the cradle. Petar was asleep, his tiny fist curled next to his cheek.

"What did you name him?" Clifton asked when they returned to the living room.

"Petar," Anika announced.

Clifton folded his arms across his chest and grinned. "Now, that's something I'd love to report." He pointed at the gift. "Well, are you going to open it?"

"Oh, I almost forgot." Helene smelled the flowers one more time, then picked up the rectangular box.

"The flowers are from several of us guys." Clifton ran a finger around his belt buckle. "We sure got plenty of ribbing for picking wildflowers."

Helene sat on the sofa and untied the white satin bow. Then she worked on the shiny blue paper.

"That's from Peter," Clifton said. "I have no idea what it is, but it was quite a task transporting it from Germany without mussing it up."

"Is Peter doing well?" Michaela asked.

"Oh, yeah. I only got to see him for a few minutes, but he did seem to have a spring in his step."

"I wanna help!" Anika grabbed one end of the paper and pulled. With a swift jerk, the lid came open, revealing a wooden train set.

"*Wundervoll!* Wonderful!" Anika cried, grabbing the caboose.

"Anika," Helene said sternly, "that's for your brother."

"But I tell him to share," Anika answered in a serious tone.

The four adults couldn't help but laugh.

"Okay," Helene conceded. "He can share."

Within minutes, Michaela and Anika had the train put together and were pulling it around the room by its long yellow string.

"What a special gift." Helene folded the wrapping paper and placed it on the table. "I'll have to write Peter a thank-you note."

"Or tell him yourself. He should be here within the week."

Baby Petar cried from the other room. Lelia started to rise, but Helene waved her away. "No, you sit and visit. I'll attend to him."

A week, Helene thought as she hurried to the bedroom. *What will it be like to see Peter again? And what will happen between him and Michaela?*

"Let's just take one day at a time," she whispered to Petar as she picked him up from his cradle.

After Petar finished nursing, Helene returned to the living room, where she found Clifton on the floor with Anika. The girl pulled the train around the room and quietly hummed a tune. Michaela and Lelia watched from the couch.

Clifton looked up as Helene entered, then cocked his head. "Anika, that's a lovely song you're humming. Can you hum it a little louder?"

Anika stood straight and tall and did as she was asked. Helene's eyebrows furrowed as she sank into a chair. It was the tune Friedrich had taught her.

"Do you know what that is?" Clifton asked.

Anika shook her head.

"It's 'The Bridal Chorus' by Richard Wagner. It comes from one of his operas." Clifton sat up straighter. "Haven't you heard of it? It's very popular in the States. There we call it 'Here Comes the Bride.' I'm partial to Wagner's title myself."

"I'm familiar with Wagner," Helene said.

"How do you know so much about music?" Michaela asked their visitor.

Clifton tried to hide a grin. "In my prewar days I majored in music at Chico State University. I actually joined the service hoping to visit the countries of some of my favorite musicians." He laughed.

"So have you seen anything memorable?" Michaela asked.

"I saw Wagner's Concert Hall in Bayreuth. The guys gave me a hard time for that, Wagner being Hitler's favorite composer and all."

Helene smiled, but her mind hardly comprehended what Clifton was saying. Instead, she patted her baby's back and wondered why Friedrich had chosen to teach Anika that tune. She knew Friedrich liked Wagner, but why "The Bridal Chorus," of all things? Then Clifton said something that caught her attention.

"I'm sorry. Can you repeat that?" Helene asked.

"I was just saying that soon I'm going to be transferred to Füssen, Germany. While I'm there I hope to see—"

"Füssen?" Helene asked, recognizing the name of her husband's hometown. "Someone I once knew was raised in Füssen."

"Really?" Clifton sat a little straighter. "Then you must know about Neuschwanstein and Hohenschwangau, King Ludwig's castles. You can see both from Füssen. That crazy king was devoted to Wagner's work. So much, in fact, that the rooms of Neuschwanstein were built to be stages for Wagner's operas."

Clifton continued on, giving Michaela and Lelia a music history lesson. But Helene's thoughts drifted. She handed the baby to Lelia and excused herself. Slipping into her bedroom, Helene shuffled through the papers and photos she'd taken from her home.

"Here we are," Helene said, finding the photo she was

looking for. She tilted the black-and-white picture toward the light coming in through the window. She studied the image of the small boy and the cottage, then examined the rolling hills and the castle huddled into the folds of the mountain behind. Was that one of the castles Clifton spoke of?

Helene took the photo into the other room and handed it to Clifton. "I'm sorry for interrupting, but can you take a look at this?"

Clifton took the photo. "It's Neuschwanstein. Amazing. You can't see it from this view, but just a few kilometers away is Hohenschwangau." He studied the photo more closely. "Who is the boy?"

"That was my husband when he was a boy," Helene said, sitting back in the chair. "His mother still lives there. Interesting . . . I never realized the connection between Wagner and those castles."

Clifton handed the photo back and stood. "I'm afraid I need to be going now. But it certainly was a pleasure meeting you ladies."

After Clifton left, Anika started softly humming the tune again.

"Anika," Helene asked, "why did your father teach you that song? Is there a story behind it?"

The cord to the train she'd been pulling dropped to the ground. "I not tell." She placed a finger over her lips. "I promised."

♪   ♪   ♪

Later that day, Michaela sat at the table in her room, fidgeting with the piece of writing paper as she tried to think of how to sign the letter.

"'With love' would be good," Lelia urged from her place on the bed.

"I don't know. It sounds too forward." Michaela bit her lip and twirled a strand of hair in her fingers. She felt twelve again, awkward and uncertain.

Helene entered the room with the baby in her arms. "Lelia, would you mind changing him? Clouds are building, and I'm afraid it will rain on the laundry if I don't bring it in right away."

Lelia stood and took the baby. Helene started for the door, then stopped when she noticed Michaela brooding. "What are you writing?"

She sighed. "A letter to Peter."

Helene sat in a chair beside the desk. "What did you say?"

Michaela shrugged. "I just told him about daily life around here. How your father is always busy helping the townspeople. Anika's humorous antics. About you and baby Petar, and Josef's dates with Lelia."

Lelia swatted Michaela's arm as she juggled the baby. "They're not dates."

Michaela grinned. "Well, if you don't call three walks in three days *dates*, I don't know what they are." She looked at Helene. "I'm just not sure how to end the letter."

Helene scooted closer, craning her neck to get a better view of the paper. "How you end it depends on how you feel. How do you feel?"

Michaela sensed warmth spreading through her. "Strange. I mean, I don't even know if Peter's interested in me."

Helene and Lelia both gave vigorous nods.

"Well, then, I do care for him." She lowered her head. "Not the way I did for Georg, though. With him, it seemed our lives were entwined into a single cord. I thought of him every minute of the day. I never could understand why God would take him when we had so much love between us."

"Would you marry Peter if he asked?" Helene questioned.

Michaela thought for a minute. "Oh, I don't know. Well, maybe I would. It's really too soon to even think about that. I suppose the feelings I have for him could grow into love. But get married? Move to America? That seems too much to think about."

Lelia patted the baby's back. "I think about it."

Helene raised one eyebrow, then placed a hand on Michaela's shoulder. "Don't worry about that now. Just sign the letter and be done with it. What about 'With care'?"

"I like it." Michaela moved the fountain pen across the paper.

Lelia leaned back on the bed and hummed to the baby. The sound of raindrops tapped against the window.

"Oh, the laundry!" Helene rushed from the room.

"I'll help," Michaela called after her. She placed the letter on the table and followed.

The rain fell on their heads in fat drops as they scurried outside. *Too many questions. Too many changes,* Michaela thought as they worked quickly to get the clothes off the line. It was true that many romances had blossomed immediately after the liberation. Numerous weddings took place at the displaced person's camp and around town every day. Still, it seemed too soon. Michaela had concerns as countless as the falling raindrops. And serious questions that couldn't help but dampen her spirit.

Michaela yanked the last of the laundry off the line, then noticed Helene. Her friend's face was tilted to the sky, her eyes closed. Raindrops fell over her cheeks like tears. Michaela tugged on Helen's shirtsleeve, and the two hurried into the house.

"What were you doing?" Michaela asked, squeezing the moisture out of her hair.

"Looking for answers," Helene said flatly.

"Pardon?"

"Oh, Michaela, I'm so confused. Maybe it's just my mixed-up emotions after just having a baby, but that thing about Wagner and the castle keeps bothering me." She took a half-wet towel from the pile of laundry and patted her damp head. "What was Friedrich doing when he taught Anika that chorus? I mean, he hardly spent any time with his daughter, and that's the one thing he chose to teach her?"

Michaela wrapped an arm around her friend's shoulders. Helene smelled like baby and wet hair. "Why don't we pray? God has all the answers, and it seems we both could use some about now."

229

Twenty

Helene knew the time had come for her to tell Anika about Friedrich's death. Her father had gone into town. Michaela was already in bed. And Josef sat with Lelia on the front porch, his interest in the girl having won out over his disgust of Helene.

After Helene tucked the blankets around Anika, she kissed her soft cheek. "My lamb, I need to tell you something, but first I have a question. And I need you to answer Mutti truthfully, all right?"

Anika nodded.

"What did your father make you promise not to tell me?"

The little girl pressed her lips into a thin line.

Helene took a deep breath. "Sweetheart, your father . . ." She blinked away the tears that threatened to flow. "Your father has died, my dear. Do you know what that means?"

"It means he's not coming back. His body isn't alive anymore. People buried it."

"Who told you that?"

"Opa. He say Papi still loves me. Even if he's gone. He always love me."

Helene tried to swallow, but her throat felt thick. Her father never ceased to surprise her. "Your opa is right. Your papi loved you very much." She stroked her daughter's silky hair. "But now that he's gone, it's all right for you to tell me his secret. In fact, it could help me a great deal." She looked into her daughter's innocent blue eyes. "Does it have to do with the song?"

"Ja." Anika kicked her feet under the blanket. "Papi say he going away. He say when he come back, we live in a house big like a castle. I be a princess, and he buy me pretty clothes. And we listen to music together."

Helene stroked her daughter's head. *Why should that be a secret? Didn't all fathers like to imagine such things with their daughters?*

Perhaps there was some hidden truth behind his words, and Friedrich had resources she didn't know about. Helene hated to think of where he could have obtained such riches. No, maybe Anika had just been confused.

"That's everything?"

"Ja," Anika said simply. "He say you didn't know about surprise." She yawned. "Now you sing to me? Sing me one of your songs?"

Helene knew which songs Anika meant. Songs from her own childhood. Songs she had sung to Anika from birth.

"Sing '*Stille Nacht*'?" Anika asked.

"But 'Silent Night' is a Christmas carol."

"I know." Anika snuggled deeper under her blanket. "But I like it."

Helene sighed. "If that's what you want."

Anika clapped her little hands.

"*Stille Nacht, heilige Nacht,*" Helene sang. "*Alles schläft, einsam wacht. Nur das traute, hochheilige Paar. Holder Knabe im lockigen Haar. Schlaf in himmlischer Ruh'. Schlaf in himmlischer Ruh'.*"

Before the last line was sung, Anika was sound asleep. Helene sang the song again, this time for herself.

Heavenly peace. That's what she needed. Peace from all the questions. From all the uncertainty surrounding Friedrich.

As she sang the chorus a third time, Helene prayed for exactly that.

⁊ ⁊ ⁊

Michaela stood in front of the full-length mirror as Helene fretted about. Her body was fuller now, but only slightly. Her hair longer, but not long enough. It curled behind her ears in an easy wave.

She smiled at her image, then frowned. She was alive. She had friends and an admirer. She should be excited. Why wasn't she?

Perhaps it is because of Georg. She thought of all the days she had dressed and primped solely for the look of admiration in his eyes.

"It's not the latest style, but the color does compliment your eyes." Helene removed the last pin from the waistband of the simple, short-sleeved frock that buttoned all the way down to the hemline. "There." She stood back for a better view. "I think that will do just fine."

A knock sounded at the door and both women jumped.

"He's here," Michaela heard herself saying. Anika's voice cried out the same from the other room. Michaela glanced at the stack of letters that sat on the bedside table, a testament to the recent correspondence between her and Peter. *What will it be like to see him after two months?*

Helene hurried to the door, then stopped. "You should answer it. I'll go get the baby."

Michaela twisted the knob. Anika hopped in anticipation beside her. She opened the door. "Peter," she said as he pulled her into a hug.

Michaela pressed her cheek into his uniform shirt. With a deep breath, she took in the scents of soap, cologne, and summer sun.

Peter held her at arm's length. "Let me get a good look at you." He smiled, then noticed Anika at her side.

"Little Annie!" The young girl jumped into his arms. Balancing her on the crook of his right arm, he pulled a chocolate bar from his left pocket. "For you," he said with a wink.

Michaela took a step back. "Please come in. Lelia is with Josef. Helene's gone for—"

Before the words were out of her mouth, Helene entered the room with a sleeping bundle in her arms. A blond baby head and a tiny fist poked out from the blanket.

"The baby," Peter exclaimed, setting Anika down. His booted footsteps crossed the room, and he peered down at the little face.

"That little Petar," Anika said as she struggled to remove the wrapper from her chocolate bar.

"Petar," he said. The name seemed to catch in his throat.

"Would you like to hold him?" Helene motioned to the living room.

"Would I ever," Peter said. "Michaela's written all about the little guy, but he's even more . . ." Peter sat on the couch. "Well, more than I imagined."

Anika stood at Peter's side, and Helene placed the baby in his arms.

Peter glanced at Helene. "I'd love a dozen of these," he said, trying various ways to hold the child.

"Sit here, Michaela," Helene suggested. "Next to Peter."

Michaela settled onto the cushion beside him. She watched Peter's hands as they cradled the infant, amazed someone so strong could also be so tender. She remembered those hands cradling her when she'd been so close to death. He would be a good father someday.

The baby opened his squinty eyes. Peter laughed.

"Why, just look at him, would you?" Little Petar let out a cry. Peter bounced him, but the crying only increased.

"I believe he's hungry." Helene lifted the baby, and he quieted. "I'll go feed him. Anika, can you come get a clean diaper for me?" They left the two alone in the room.

Peter searched Michaela's face. "I was hoping to take you out for some fresh air," he said softly. He rose from the couch and extended the crook of his arm.

Michaela stood and put her arm in his. "I would like that."

"That's a lovely dress," he said, opening the door for her.

"It was Helene's. We had to make a few alterations, but it works."

"Works? It's fantastic."

They strolled quietly down the street toward the little white church with the large bell tower and steeple. Michaela had often viewed it from a distance and even visited a few times with Papa Katz.

A low stone wall surrounded the church and outer buildings. Peter sat on it and pulled Michaela in front of him. He looked so handsome in his uniform. His hair seemed lighter than it had that spring. His smile more brilliant. He gazed admiringly at her.

"I've enjoyed your letters," he said.

"I've enjoyed yours too."

"You might have guessed something by now."

She gazed into his green eyes.

"My thoughts are continually drawn back to this place. To the three remarkable women in that house. I have feelings for you, Michaela. I want nothing more than to spend more time with you. There's something about you . . . I guess I'm just trying to say I think you're pretty special."

The leaves above them rustled as a warm breeze blew. A warm wind also stirred in Michaela's heart.

"I was going to wait until we had spent more time together," he said. "But I can't wait. I've never been good at waiting."

He ran his fingers through his hair. "There's a song I want to sing to you, but the words are in English. It's by a guy named Bing Crosby. I don't know all the lyrics, but the chorus is something like, 'All day long I'll be saying your name, and then for forever I'll be doing the same.' Something like that." He hummed a few bars. "Anyway, I've only known you a short time, but what do you think the chances are for two people like us?"

"What are you asking?" Michaela pressed the palm of her hand to her neck.

Peter's eyes seemed to dance. "I know we come from two different worlds, but I'd like you to consider thinking of me as more than a friend." He slipped off the wall and faced her. "Michaela, is that too much for me to ask?"

Michaela felt a stirring inside her chest. Yet it wasn't light and happy as she had expected. Something inside told her to wait. To give it time. She felt unsteady and unsure.

Michaela gazed into his eyes, so full of tenderness. How could this not be the right thing?

"I'm honored, Peter," she said, "That sounds nice."

Peter grinned and pulled her into a big hug. Michaela laughed and pressed her face into his neck. A man rode by on a bicycle and cheered.

Yet even as Peter released her, she felt the world spinning too fast. She pushed herself back.

"But wait." She sat on the wall again. "I answered too soon. I must talk to you first. I don't know what the future holds. For so long I didn't even know if I'd have a future. I think it's only fair that I tell you a little of my past. You need to know . . ." Michaela thought of Georg. His face. His tender kisses. Perhaps the love she still had for him was the reason for these feelings of uncertainty.

Peter caressed her hand. "You don't need to tell me if you don't want to. I know horrible things happened during the war."

"It's not that. There are other things. Good things."

He settled beside her.

"It's about Georg."

Peter's boyish grin disappeared. "Is he still alive? Could he be out there somewhere? I've seen many reunions. I—"

Michaela shook her head. "No, he's not alive. But before we become any more serious, I have to tell you what he meant to me."

"I should have known there'd been someone else. A girl like you, someone so special . . . of course."

Michaela fiddled with the buttons on her dress. She pictured Georg's face. She thought of the way his hand had caressed her cheek, her neck. She remembered the feeling of her fingers in his thick, dark hair.

"I will start by telling you of my home. I have mentioned some of it in my letters. But not enough."

Peter leaned in close, his face inches from hers. "I'm so sorry. I should have asked more. I've just been thinking about myself."

Michaela covered his mouth with her finger. "I will tell you about my life. As a start, you must know who I was and where I came from." She took a deep breath. As the air escaped, so did the words she'd been holding for so long. "I was born into a Christian, middle-class family in Bielsko. Bielsko is noted for its textile industry. They have an abundance of sheep, and electric power from the mountain streams."

"I remember the first time I walked to the market with my mother. The large buildings with their domes and towers seemed enormous. A three-story courthouse is not that tall, but to a child it's like a castle."

Peter laughed. Michaela noticed the shadow of the steeple falling across them.

"My father's church was much like this one."

"He was a minister?"

"Yes, and a great one." Michaela smiled, but the happy memory faded quickly. "That was before the war, of course." She was quiet for a few minutes, wondering if her father's church still stood. Oh, how she would love to walk through its doors again.

"I remember picnics to the countryside. Rolling hills. Clusters of leafy trees and lush grass. And I'll never for-

239

get the autumns. In late September, the trees replace their green leaves with crowns of gold."

"It sounds wonderful."

"It was. The people were all friendly and outspoken," she rattled on. "Each neighbor was a friend, especially those from my father's church. We were often invited to dinners. *Barszcz,* beet soup, for Christmas. *Pierogi* with meat and cabbage."

Peter wrinkled his nose and Michaela laughed. He took her hand. "And what were your favorite things to do?"

Michaela lifted her face to the warm breeze. "I loved reading romantic poetry. My favorite poet was Adam Michiewicz. But my father said I shouldn't only read Polish writers, so he picked up foreign books for me when he traveled, including fairy tales."

"Cinderella, yes, I remember now."

"I loved going to the theater. That was before 1939." She shook her head. "On September 1, I was returning from my friend Gerda's birthday party when German fighter planes appeared overhead. Two days later, on Sunday, they began bombing. Many people fled the city that horrible night. My family hid in our basement through the intense shelling. Many people we knew did not make it. In fact, Georg's older sister was killed when the building she was in collapsed."

Michaela shivered with the memory. "After they found her body, I went to the family's home to comfort Georg. The house was filled with mourners. Suddenly we heard a tremendous roar. Two German soldiers raced down the street on a motorcycle crying '*Heil Hitler.*' A red, black, and white flag fluttered from the window ledge of the theater down the street. I swore to myself I would never enter that place again. And I never did."

Peter's eyes remained intent on her.

"In the summer of 1941, a section of Bielsko was transformed into a Jewish ghetto. A year later the ghetto was liquidated. Every man, woman, and child was taken to a camp in Auschwitz."

Tears formed in the corners of Michaela's eyes. "Despite the law that said anyone caught harboring a Jew would be killed, my parents took in a family with two daughters."

"Lelia's family?"

"Yes." Michaela played with the ends of her short hair. "My father wanted so much to help those girls."

Peter wrapped an arm around her. "If this is too hard for you, you don't have to—"

"I need to tell you one more thing." Michaela rubbed her bare arms. "Just before the war started, I fell in love with a man named Georg. He was like you in many ways. Strong. Brave. Handsome." She blushed. "I loved him more than I thought was possible. He was killed while working for the Resistance. I need you to know that I will always have a place for him in my heart. I will never forget him."

"Of course not. I will never ask you to."

"I guess I shared all that just to say . . . can we take a few—just small—steps together to see what happens?"

Peter squeezed her tightly. "That's all I could hope for.

And know too that I understand. Sometimes my emotions get so mixed up with all that's happened with the camp, with you, with Helene. If you're willing to explore the future—a future of us getting to know each other better —then that's the best news I've had in a long time."

Michaela rested in his embrace, soaking in his warmth. It felt good to be cared for and protected. She liked Peter. He was a good man.

Georg, she thought. *Papa, Mama, am I doing the right thing?*

Michaela stood before she could change her mind. She took Peter's hand. "Let's get back and tell the others."

He hopped down off the wall and brought her fingers to his lips. "Are you sure?"

"Yes," Michaela said, not willing to lose love again.

"All right, then. But I have one condition."

"What is it?"

"That you share more with me later. I want you to tell me all about your previous life."

My previous life. Yes, that's what it was. It was not her life anymore. She clutched Peter's hand as they wandered back to the large yellow house.

This man was her future. He would be her life now.

Twenty-One

Michaela and Peter entered the house unnoticed and sneaked into the kitchen. Lelia sat at the table with Anika on her lap. Helene sat across from them, rocking the baby and discussing dresses and hairstyles. Josef stood by the back door with Papa Katz, mug in hand.

The room stilled as they entered. Helene's eyes widened, and Michaela realized her hand was still enclosed in Peter's. He noticed too and quickly released it.

Peter strutted across the room and shook hands with Papa Katz. "Good to see you again, sir." He nodded at Josef. "You're looking well."

Helene raised the baby to her shoulder and winked at Lelia. "Go ahead. Tell them."

The young woman placed Anika on the floor, stood, and embraced Michaela. "Josef and I are getting married!"

Michaela wrapped her arms around her friend. *Married? They've hardly been courting for two weeks.*

"Josef, old man, it seems we've both found love within these walls," Peter announced.

Lelia took a step back and gawked at Michaela. "You too?"

"Well, we're not getting married. Nothing like that," Michaela responded. "But we have decided to consider getting to know each other as more than friends."

Lelia grinned and pulled Michaela into another tight hug.

"It looks like a double celebration," Papa Katz said. "Helene, why don't you make your famous punch?"

Helene seemed to ignore him, intently rewrapping the baby in his blanket.

"Helene?" her father said again.

She rose from the table. The color drained from her face. "Punch, of course. Let me just get Petar down for his nap. Then we can celebrate." She scurried to the bedroom.

Anika bounced from person to person, bubbling from the energy in the room. Josef and Peter discussed dates and locations for a wedding. Josef kidded Peter that perhaps he'd be making the same plans before long. The words swirled around Michaela like a dust storm.

"Will you excuse me for a moment?" A heaviness settled upon Michaela, and suddenly she wondered why she'd allowed things to go so far.

Michaela followed the path Helene had just taken. She pressed her cheek against the wood of Helene's door and found it ajar. She knocked gently. "May I come in?" she asked through the crack. Then she entered without waiting for a response.

Helene was sitting on her bed, her back against the wall. Petar lay on her lap, half asleep.

"Are you all right?" Michaela asked.

Helene sniffed softly. "Of course."

Michaela sat in the chair beside her and patted her leg. "Now, I know better than that."

Helene tilted her head back. "It's just that I'm going to lose you both. One of you would be hard enough to bear, but two?"

Helene caressed the baby's cheek.

"You're not losing me," Michaela protested. "Peter and I are still just getting to know each other. There's no telling what will become of this. Peter is still in the army. Who knows how much we'll even see each other?"

Helene was quiet as she considered Michaela's words.

Michaela's thoughts turned back to Lelia. "Did Josef and Lelia say when they will be married?"

"Next week. Saturday, I believe."

Michaela bit her lip. *So soon?*

Helene handed Petar to Michaela, then moved to her dresser. Michaela lifted the pudgy baby to her face, kissing the soft skin of his neck.

"I want a dozen of these," Peter had said. And so did she. But could she conceive a child? She no longer knew if that was possible. The starvation, the beatings,

and the unsanitary living conditions in the camp had changed her body into a stranger.

Helene pulled a wedding photo from the bottom drawer. "Besides the births of my children, my wedding was the happiest day of my life." She handed the photo to Michaela. "Do you like this dress?"

Michaela admired the high waist, the low V-neck, and the delicate flowers embroidered on the bodice and long sleeves. Narrow pleats hugged Helene's hips and fell to the floor. Helene's hair touched her shoulders in long blonde waves. Friedrich stood beside her in full uniform.

"It's beautiful." Michaela handed the picture back. "You were stunning."

Helene placed the photo back in the drawer. "I still have the dress. It was one of the things I brought back with me." She paused, then looked at Michaela. "Someday you might need a wedding dress. Who knows? It might even be with Peter. And if that happens, I'd like you to wear it. It would look gorgeous on you."

Michaela felt the heat rising to her cheeks.

"I don't know . . ."

Helene's face brightened. "Really, I would like to do this."

It was all too much for Michaela to comprehend. Just a few months ago she'd wondered if she would even live. She'd longed for any scrap of food. She'd slept in lice and watched those around her killed without reason. In a few months, could she change from wearing a dead man's shirt to being offered expensive bridal wear?

Michaela pressed her fingers to her temples. "Really, we don't need to get so carried away. That's still so far off. Give me, give us some time."

Helene's countenance fell. "Oh, I didn't even consider that you may not want to wear a dress that was used in an SS wedding. I'm sure you and Peter—"

"Nein. It's not that. I am just . . . not ready for that yet. I just want to be open to what God wants."

Helene hugged her friend, careful not to squish the baby on Michaela's lap. "Of course. What was I thinking?" She leaned back. "I'm just happy that you have someone as wonderful as Peter; I really am."

Michaela kissed baby Petar's head. "Ja, so am I." Her words sounded flat even to herself.

🕊   🕊   🕊

Helene rolled over in her bed for the hundredth time that night. The blankets were too warm, the air too cool. Anika's gentle snoring, usually a source of joy, seemed loud and obnoxious. *Just like her father,* Helene thought as she flipped the pillow over.

Helene tried counting, but that didn't help. The lack of sleep reminded her of the long nights she'd waited for Friedrich to come home. Her shoulders tensed, and she tried to push those thoughts away. If only she could find someone like Peter . . . but she didn't want to think about that either.

The sound of iron pans clanging together carried in from the kitchen. Someone else was having problems sleeping. Probably Michaela or Lelia, excited about boyfriends, weddings, and new lives in America.

Helene pushed back the covers and stood, the cool floor causing her toes to curl. Careful not to bump the cradle, she grabbed her robe from the chair back and slipped it on. Then she tiptoed into the kitchen.

As she entered, a warm lantern's glow greeted her, along with her father's wink. He stood by the stove, stirring a pan of milk with a wooden spoon. Yesterday's bread waited on the counter.

Helene sat in the rickety old kitchen chair. "I feel ten years old again. How did you know I would need milk toast tonight?"

"You always need it on days like today, whether it be good news or bad." His voice was soothing. "Remember the time your name was announced as the finalist for the school spelling bee? Or the day we received news that your mother was down to her final days? Milk toast was the only thing that got you to sleep."

Helene traced the wood grain of the table with her finger. Within minutes, a bowl of bread soaked in warm milk and sprinkled with a hint of sugar was set before her. She took a bite, appreciating the softness and comfort of the food.

"So, which do you think today was?" Helene asked when her bowl was half empty. "Good news or bad?"

"Well, that depends whether we're considering the future of our friends or ourselves. It seems their joy will ultimately lead to our loss."

"I didn't think I'd feel this way until my own children

were grown." Helene swirled the milk toast with her spoon, forming the shape of a heart. "I don't think they're ready for serious relationships. They're just beginning to get well."

She licked the spoon. "Take Lelia, for example. A month ago she could hardly speak and now she's to be married? And how long has Josef been coming around? She's too young, and she doesn't really know him."

Helene's father chuckled, and the realization of her words hit her. Not too many years before he'd felt the same about her. She'd been young. She'd hardly known Friedrich. Yet no one could have told her not to marry him.

Helene considered how difficult it must have been for her father to let her go. Not that he'd had a choice. She had been a determined young woman. Nothing could have stopped her from being with the man she loved.

"The world is changing, my daughter. Good changes and not-so-good. I've been to meetings in town, talked to key people. Just when the war is over, it seems we'll soon be under a new government."

Helene focused on his face. All humor was gone.

"I didn't want to ruin the glorious announcements earlier, but U.S. troops will be leaving sooner than I imagined. Austria will again have her own borders, but we will be divided into four occupational zones."

He swept his hand toward the window. "This whole area, from the river to the northern border, will be Russian territory."

"The Russians?" Helene had heard rumors of their brutality, especially to anyone associated with the Nazis. Tens of thousands of Russian men had been killed without a trial in the camps near her home. And what of the Americans? She'd found comfort in their presence. The brown jeeps with white stars, the tent hospitals and sprightly nurses, the jazz music and gum-chewing soldiers.

"How many days do the Americans have left?"

"From what I've heard, less than a week."

"And Peter?"

"He hasn't said. But I imagine that's why these relationships are moving along so quickly. The men won't be able to come back after their military forces leave the area."

"Not ever?"

"Nein." Her father leaned against the counter. "Not unless they get special permission or come on government business. Courting a young lady won't fall under those terms." He paused. "So I'm sure, even now, Peter's thinking of a way to get Michaela out."

Helene's head pounded, and the milk seemed to curdle in her stomach. She pushed the bowl away.

The baby's cry sounded from the other room. Helene stood, then decided to ask one more question. "How far will the Americans go?"

"To the other side of the river. The banks we can see on the other side will be in the American zone."

Her heart filled with a grief she'd come to know all too well. "So they'll be close."

Her father stroked the white stubble on his chin. A

strand of hair as fine as spider's silk fell across his high forehead. He raked it back with a finger. "Close, but not close enough."

As Helene returned to her room, the darkness of the situation seemed blacker than the night outside. A wide, watery chasm would soon separate her from those she cared for.

Helene lifted Petar from his cradle. The small wooden bed rocked, but her thoughts seemed to rock with an even greater force. She nestled into her own bed and held the baby to her chest to nurse.

"At least I'll still have you," she murmured to the infant. "You and your sister and your grandfather."

It will be enough, she decided. It had to be. Helene leaned against the plaster wall. The baby was cradled between her thighs and her chest, protected and loved. Helene rocked back and forth. Not to soothe her infant but to calm the shaking of her shoulders.

Oh, God, will it be enough?

Twenty-Two

A knock at the front door woke Michaela from her fitful sleep. She rubbed her eyes. From the light that filled the room, she knew it had to be after 9 A.M. When was the last time she had slept so late? It had been years, she was sure. But after the tossing and turning with a million thoughts of life and love, Peter and Georg, she'd finally drifted off.

The knock sounded again, and she wondered where everyone could be. She climbed out of bed, pulled on her cotton wrap, and hurried to the door. She swung it open just as three visitors started to leave.

Michaela stepped out onto the porch. "If you need a room," she called, "we'll have some available in a week."

The three turned, and she noticed a Red Cross armband on one woman's arm. Michaela glanced at the frail man and woman standing beside her. Their heads were lowered, and their bodies moved with strange effort. While they appeared to be young, both were dressed in ill-fitting clothes and showed the effects of malnutrition and suffering.

The Red Cross worker shook Michaela's hand. "I'm from the DP camp in Linz," she spoke in Polish, "and I'm looking for a Michaela Perl."

"I'm Michaela."

The frail woman standing next to the Red Cross worker grinned. Michaela recognized that smile. "Kasia?" She peered closely at the man. Her heart leapt. "Marek!"

"Michaela!" Marek cried.

Michaela wrapped her arms around the two ghosts from her past and pulled them into her embrace. "These are dear friends from my father's church in Bielsko," she explained to the Red Cross worker. "Come in, all of you!"

The Red Cross worker helped Marek and Kasia climb the porch steps. "They arrived last night on the train. You should have seen their faces when they saw your name on the list of survivors. I brought them over as soon as possible."

"Michaela, it is a miracle you're alive." Marek grabbed her face and kissed both cheeks.

Tears streamed down Kasia's gaunt face. Michaela felt her knees grow weak. These were her friends. The beloved ones her father had worked so hard for. Two of his Jewish friends, converts to the Christian faith.

Michaela led them to the couch in the living room. "Have you heard news of anyone else? Where have you been? What has happened to you, to our other friends?" she rattled in Polish.

Marek grabbed her hands. "So much has taken place since you were captured. Many from the church were rounded up. Several Jews were found in hiding. Someone reported us all, but I will not go into that now."

"Did Jacek and Lidia survive?" Michaela dared to ask. They had been her parents' close friends and had graciously welcomed her and Lelia into their home after their families had been murdered by the Nazis. Michaela could hardly imagine life without them.

"I am afraid not." Marek shook his head. "They were killed, along with their whole family."

Michaela gasped. "And their children?"

Marek released his grip. "The baby, Sabine, was at a friend's house. She alone survived."

Michaela's heart went out to the toddler who, like so many others in this time of war, would grow up without ever really knowing her parents.

Kasia placed a hand on Michaela's knee. "The last I heard, Rahel was alive, but that was months ago."

The mention of Georg's younger sister quickened Michaela's heartbeat. That was one memory she was still not ready to delve into. "Jacek and Lidia had a neighbor named Filip. He was very nice to Lelia and me when we returned to my parents' house. Do you know if—"

"I do not know. Marek and I were taken by transport to many camps," Kasia said, looking uncomfortable. "We finally ended up at Ebense—not far from here. It is a miracle my brother and I survived."

"Kasia is still not well." Marek took his sister's hand. "We are only traveling on her insistence. Poland is calling us home."

"You're returning?"

"How could we not? It is our home. I miss the scent of the air, the food, the ways of the homeland." He lowered his head. "I would like to visit the graves to say good-bye. I know many were simply thrown into the ground with no one to pray or remember. It meant so much to us years ago when your father performed that ceremony for our mother. His words of eternal life and heavenly rewards gave us such hope. I would like to share that hope with others."

Michaela studied his face, so familiar yet so different. His head was shaven and covered with sores. Sharp cheekbones jutted out. Even more noticeable were the dark circles under his eyes. Yet, looking into their depths, Michaela saw the hope her friend spoke of. She took Marek's slim hand in her own.

"My father would be proud." She rubbed his rough hand in her soft ones. "He always said God's calling was on your life."

"As on yours," Marek responded.

Michaela released his grasp. Like the memory of a dream that resurfaced through fog, her father's words spun through her mind.

"Share the gospel with these dear people," he had said. *"Protect Lelia. Never leave her side. Without you she is like a lamb to the slaughter. Promise me you will care for her and those who remain."*

"I promise, Papa," she'd said during their last embrace. It was that promise to protect Lelia that had kept her strong through the capture, through transports, through the camps. And she had done her best, keeping the girl with her as long as it was humanly possible. But had the whole promise been fulfilled? *What about the others?*

The Red Cross worker interrupted her thoughts. "I've asked these two to stay in the hospital at St. Georgen for a few days to get some much-needed rest before moving on. I was hoping you could help convince them. But a few days is all we have. Even now the hospital is preparing to relocate."

Michaela didn't understand this talk of relocation. She would ask Papa Katz about that later. And it was obvious more than a few days of rest was needed. "Yes, please stay. Rest would be good. And—" She paused for full effect. "You must be here for the wedding."

"Wedding?" Marek asked.

"Is it someone we know?" Kasia's eyes lit up.

Michaela grinned. "Lelia is marrying an American GI next week."

"Lelia survived?" Kasia asked in a low voice. "Praise the Most High."

"How wonderful it would be to attend a wedding again," Marek said. "*Tak,* yes, we will stay."

Michaela rose and gave each of her friends another hug. "I will get dressed, then prepare breakfast. I have so much to tell you."

As she hurried to her room, Michaela realized she hadn't shared what should have been the most exciting news of all—her own budding relationship with Peter. The thought of his handsome face and the care in his eyes should have been enough to chase away any doubts. But still, that unsettling feeling refused to subside.

She pulled her nightgown over her head and slipped into the light green dress Helene had given her. She washed her face with cool water from the basin, then ran a comb through her short dark hair.

As Michaela prepared to rejoin her friends, she knew the path she'd agreed to the day before needed further consideration. Perhaps she should go back to Poland. Back to the people her father had loved and given his life for.

Peter's face flashed in her mind. His kind eyes. His smile. His caring heart. How would she ever tell him?

❧   ❧   ❧

Helene and the children returned just as Michaela was finishing the breakfast dishes. After introductions were made, Helene begged the Red Cross worker to leave Marek and Kasia in her care. There was, she insisted, plenty of room, and she was quite experienced in looking after camp survivors. The Red Cross worker agreed and left with a promise to come back in a few days to check on the pair.

When Lelia returned from her outing with Josef, she found them all in the kitchen, enjoying tea. The sight of Marek and Kasia seemed to stir even more excitement in Lelia. With laughter and hugs, she embraced each of them and chattered in Polish about their time with Helene.

Michaela watched the exchange with elation. Would anyone have believed this was the same girl who rarely spoke and who had been so close to death just months before?

"Oh, and did Michaela tell you her good news?" Lelia asked. "She has a new beau. He's a handsome American, and he's quite smitten with her."

Marek and Kasia blinked at Michaela. Helene rose and turned her attention to a ball of bread dough that had been rising on the counter.

"No, we did not hear." Marek's brow furrowed. Michaela knew he was thinking about Georg. She suddenly felt like a traitor in the presence of her friends.

"It's not that serious yet," Michaela said hurriedly. "In fact, I must talk to Peter. I'm unsure—" She paused. "I'm not sure what will happen now." Michaela took a sip of her hot tea, trying to hide behind her teacup.

Helene stopped kneading the bread dough.

"You aren't breaking it off with him, are you?" Lelia asked in German.

Helene wiped off her hands on her apron, then placed them on Lelia's shoulders. "I'm sure Michaela has a lot to think about and a lot to discuss with Peter.

Come, I want to show you some fabric I found. I believe it would make a perfect dress for your wedding."

Lelia shot Michaela one more glance, then did as she was told. The room fell silent. Marek and Kasia continued to sip their tea. Michaela rose and started kneading Helene's bread dough.

A knock at the door punctured the silence. "That must be Peter." Michaela wiped her hands on a towel. "He promised to come by today." She headed for the door. "Come, you must meet him," she called back to Marek and Kasia.

Michaela opened the door. Peter stood there with his arms open wide. His olive uniform was perfectly pressed. His reddish hair was slicked back. He smelled wonderful.

Peter took her into his arms and planted a soft kiss on her forehead.

Michaela took a step back. "I have some people I'd like you to meet. Old friends from Bielsko."

Marek extended his hand. "I am Marek. This is my sister, Kasia," he said in rough German. "We are friends with Michaela. We too survived the camps."

"It's a miracle," Peter said. He lifted Michaela's chin. "Another reason to celebrate."

She led him into the kitchen. "Would you like to join us for tea?"

"Of course." He followed the others to the table. "Then I was hoping we could talk. There is a lot happening in this area soon, and I have some things I need to discuss with you."

"Tea first." She placed a white china cup in front of him. She needed time alone. Time to formulate her thoughts and words.

As they sat around the table, Marek and Kasia entertained Peter with stories about Michaela's childhood.

Marek tapped the side of his head, as if trying to stir a memory. "Remember when you visited—how you say it—the place with the animals and acrobatics?"

"*Der Zirkus*," Michaela said.

"Tak, yes, the circus." Marek smiled. "The whole school went to the circus, and the next day Michaela was so enchanted by the tricks she tried to control the *zwierze*—"

"Zwierze?" Peter asked.

"It means 'beast' in Polish. He was a neighborhood dog that frightened all the children." Michaela's face flushed.

"She took one of her mother's chairs and marched down the street." Marek chuckled. "We didn't notice until after she opened the gate. I rushed in and scared the dog with a stick. Georg swept her up and raced out of the yard."

"He was my hero from the age of eight." Even now Michaela could see the way his dark hair flopped over his determined face as he ran. "He saved me from certain death. Or so I thought."

"Do you still have the scar?" Marek asked.

"Among many others." Michaela rubbed the spot on her arm without lifting her sleeve. Mere inches below the dog's mark were the numbers imprinted by

261

beasts equally as vicious. The atmosphere of the room instantly sobered.

Kasia, who had been quietly listening to the conversation, yawned and rubbed her thin neck. "I'm getting weary," she said in Polish. "Helene has prepared a room for us. I think I'll rest for a while." She stood on shaky feet. "Marek, will you join me?"

Marek frowned. "I was just going to tell about time Michaela—"

Kasia placed her hand on Marek's arm. "Another time, Brother. I believe Michaela and Peter need time. Alone."

"Tak, tak, of course. Yes, a midmorning rest would be good." He rose and followed his sister.

"Nice friends," Peter said. "It's a miracle they found you." He leaned back in his chair and crossed an ankle over his knee. "I'd love to hear more of Marek's stories."

"Another time perhaps." Michaela raised her teacup to her lips. When she noticed it shaking, she returned it to the saucer. "Now, about us."

Peter rose. "Yes, I've been talking to some of the guys, and they've heard there are jobs available for translators in Germany. Communication with the DP's has been a problem. I'm not sure how long it'll take for the paperwork, but we'd get to see each other more—"

"Peter, I really—"

"I told some of the guys about you, and they can't wait to meet you." He paced the kitchen. "And maybe when Josef and Lelia get married, they can be transferred close by."

Michaela clenched her hands at her sides. "Peter, please."

Peter stopped his pacing. For a second Michaela almost talked herself out of what she had to say. Then she thought about Marek and Kasia and the members of her father's church. Her church family. She thought about her promise . . . and her calling.

The anxious feeling that rose in her chest reminded her of the day when, as a little girl, she'd been separated from her mother in the market. Horror had choked her heart when she realized she was following the wrong swishing blue skirt. The woman's face was kind but not the right one. Michaela felt the same despair now, realizing she had been clinging to the wrong dream.

She winced at the confusion etched on Peter's face. "I'm so sorry. I cannot allow us to get carried away. I can't begin a relationship with you—anything more than friends. I've known all along. Deep inside I've always known." She turned away from him, unable to face his look of disbelief.

Michaela wrapped her arms around her stomach. "I have to go back to Poland. My father's church is in shambles. The families there need me. They need to hear the Word of God preached again. I want to help rebuild what has been torn down."

Peter's voice rose behind her. "They need you? What about your needs? You're still weak. You've been through so much. You need someone to take care of you." Peter caressed her shoulders and gently turned her to face him. "I want to be that someone."

Michaela cringed at his tender touch. "God will take care of me. He will—"

Peter interrupted with a harsh laugh. "Just like He took care of you in the camps? Just like He took care of all those people who are now ash? I have a hard time believing that."

Michaela placed a hand over her mouth, trying to hold back the sobs that threatened to break forth. It was no use. The emotions she'd tucked away refused to be silenced any longer. Michaela's knees weakened.

"I'm sorry, Michaela. I'm so sorry." His arms wrapped around her.

"It has to be this way. It has to."

Peter helped her to the chair and eased her into the seat. He kneeled before her, and she rested her head on his broad shoulder.

"We'll talk about this. We don't have to make a decision now. We have time. I'm so sorry I hurried you."

Even as the tears flowed, Michaela knew time would make no difference. What she had to do would not change. The stirring inside had confirmed God's calling. There were people at home who needed to hear the good news of Jesus, especially now.

And even as she cried into Peter's shoulder, Michaela knew she was making the right choice. Though she mourned the thought of leaving this wonderful man, a steady peace settled in her heart. She would return to Poland with Marek and Kasia. She would pick up where her father had left off.

Twenty-Three

The day of the wedding finally arrived. After Michaela's decision to journey back to Poland, only one commitment kept Peter in St. Georgen. He had promised to be Josef's best man.

Though he had worked hard at helping the Americans prepare to leave St. Georgen, every turn down every street bent his thoughts to the large yellow house. Was she considering the "what-ifs" as he was? Knowing that Michaela's decision was a hard one didn't make living with it any easier. His friends, who'd celebrated the fact that Scotty had finally found a girl, had remained distant after he broke the news. Peter knew they were uncertain of what to say, and he was equally uncertain about what to do. All he knew was he had to get out of this town, out of this country, off this continent.

Peter rose from his bed and wandered down the hall of the newly liberated house he shared with some of his men. Josef stood in the tiny kitchen, pressing his dress uniform. The heavy iron swished back and forth almost effortlessly, and Josef whistled a little tune. Two other GIs sat around the dining room table playing cards, drinking, and swapping war stories.

The whistling and conversations stopped when Peter entered.

Peter shook a fist in the air. "I'm going to knock you guys on the side of the head if you keep that up." He punched Josef's shoulder. "How would you feel if every time you entered a room it immediately fell silent?" Peter pulled up a chair. "Life goes on. I don't want the whole world miserable just because I am." He strained to smile, and it seemed to work. Josef resumed whistling, and the card game started up again.

"Hey, buddy," Peter said, digging into his pocket. "Do you have a wedding band?"

Josef smirked. "Not yet. I promised Lelia we'd get one in the States. She's not worried about it. I've assured her she'll be well taken care of. My mother told me to bring home a good Jewish—" Josef stopped when he saw Peter pull a tiny ring from his pocket.

"Will this work?" With a flick of his wrist, the band of silver flipped from Peter's fingers, landing on the ironing board.

"Scotty, no. I can't take this."

"What am I going to do with it?"

"But Scotty—"

Peter rose. "I won it in a poker game last week. It's just a simple band. Really, I would consider it an honor if you used it."

Josef held it up to the window. It glimmered in the sunlight. "I don't know what to say." He slid it on his smallest finger. "It's so tiny. It's sure to fit Lelia."

Peter patted Josef's shoulder. "See you at the church."

Josef's smile broadened. "Yeah."

The church, Peter thought. The place where he and Michaela had spent that wonderful afternoon. The chapel where Michaela would be standing next to Lelia, and he next to Josef. It was the last place Peter wanted to be. But he had no choice. He'd go, and laugh, and dance. And behind his happy facade, he'd ache at the sight of her.

৯   ৯   ৯

"There, now, let me get a good look at you." Michaela took a step back and held Lelia at arm's length. "Good gracious, you look like one of those American film stars."

Michaela's days had been consumed with catching up with Marek and Kasia and in helping Lelia with her wedding preparations. It was hard to believe the day had arrived, the church was filled, and Lelia would soon be married.

Lelia blushed. She was seventeen, but she looked twelve. Her face was still too gaunt, her hair too short, but those things were insignificant compared to the gleam in the young woman's eyes.

"Helene did a fine job helping you with that dress," Michaela said, taking in the light-yellow checkered pattern with bows at the bodice and waist.

"Did you see the shoes?" Lelia asked. "One of Josef's friends brought them as a gift. A little tissue in the toes and they fit fine." Lelia lifted her foot and pointed her toe to give Michaela a better view.

"White leather. They're beautiful." Michaela pulled Lelia into an embrace. She hoped the emotions building in her chest would stay hidden until she could be alone. Lelia had been her constant companion for almost all of the past four years. Caring for the girl had kept her going.

"Your parents would be so proud," Michaela said in Polish, touching Lelia's cheek.

"You think they would be pleased?"

"*Tak jest,* of course. You found a nice Jewish boy who loves you and will take care of you. And you're having a traditional wedding besides. They would be very happy."

"I'd give anything if they could be here. To see them, hear them—"

"*A gezunt ahf dein kop,*" Michaela said in Yiddish.

"Good health to you too," Lelia said.

Michaela patted Lelia's cheek. "I'm sure the rabbi will have a more appropriate prayer, but that's the only Yiddish I remember."

Lelia laughed. "Health is good," she said. "Good indeed."

Helene burst into the room. Her blonde hair was swept up in a twist at the nape of her neck. Her face glowed. "You should see it out there. The church is packed. And such excitement. After so much pain, a real wedding to celebrate!" She took a deep breath. "It was a good idea sending word to the DP camp."

Helene produced two white gardenias. She tucked one behind each of Lelia's ears. "A finishing touch."

A man's voice came from the doorway. "Greta Garbo, watch out!"

Michaela whirled around and spotted Peter. Josef stood at his side, transfixed and speechless.

"I was wondering if you were here." Helene gave Peter a one-armed hug. "We've missed you."

Michaela repositioned the flowers in Lelia's hair.

Josef approached tenderly. "Are you ready?"

Lelia nodded and slipped her arm into his.

"I'd better check on Papa and the baby." Helene fled the room in the direction of the sanctuary.

Michaela turned to Peter. "We should get out there."

"You look incredible," he said in a hushed tone. "There's just something about you—"

"Thank you." Michaela smoothed her sky-blue dress with her palms. "The dress is Helene's. She's letting me borrow it."

"Blue is your color."

Michaela felt as if she could read a story in Peter's eyes. A longing for love and an uncertainty of where to find it. She quickly looked away. "It's almost time for the *Aufruf*."

"Aufruf?"

"The Shabbat, the holy prayer offered before the wedding. Josef and Lelia will bless God for the reading of the Torah, and then the guests will throw candy to wish the couple a sweet life together."

"Ouch," Peter said.

Michaela squeezed his arm. "They're supposed to throw gently. And besides, Josef will use his *tallith,* or scarf, to protect his bride."

They paused at the door to the sanctuary. "You know a lot about their customs," Peter said.

Michaela chuckled. "I've been to a few Jewish weddings. And Lelia has been my life for many years."

When they entered the sanctuary, Michaela was pleased to see the *chuppah* set up and the rabbi—who not long ago had been a prisoner himself—standing under it.

Peter leaned close to her ear. "This is so different from what I'm used to," he confessed.

A young boy started playing a violin before Michaela could answer. She focused her attention on the bride and groom. Lelia and Josef would soon be bound together as man and wife. But Michaela knew a different path awaited her.

Lelia and Josef passed under the chuppah. With slow steps Michaela walked on Lelia's left side and Peter on Josef's right. Marek and Kasia watched from the front row.

The violinist's bow moved gracefully over the strings as if it had a mind of its own. It played a tune of celebration, but the melody also held a note of mourning. *Yes, this is a time to rejoice*—the music seemed to say—*but let us not forgot all who are gone.*

Michaela also felt a deep mourning in her soul. Not only was she turning Lelia over to another's hands, but she was also doing the same for herself.

I will follow, her heart cried to God. *Lead me, and I'll follow.*

The ceremony continued, each part taking on a deep meaning of faith, love, and commitment. And as Michaela watched her friends' union, a private ceremony seemed to be taking place within her soul.

Before she knew it, Lelia and Josef were pronounced husband and wife, and the celebration and dancing began. The *hora* and other Jewish dances were taught to all, and soon the lawn outside the church was filled with bodies in motion.

During one dance, Michaela found herself face-to-face with Peter. He bowed, and she curtsied in return. Their hands clasped and released; then they moved on to other partners. When they were reunited, Michaela murmured a quick thanks, then released her hands with a flourish as the dance ended. She was free. She felt it deep inside. Free from her commitment here. Free to return to her homeland.

While the music played, Michaela scanned the room in search of Marek and Kasia. The time to plan their journey had arrived. Poland was calling her home.

℘   ℘   ℘

Peter picked an empty glass bottle off the street and threw it against a low brick wall. It shattered into a flurry of pieces. Shards flew through the air like the wedding candy had done only hours before. Someone shouted from behind, but Peter didn't care. If he were a drinking man, Peter knew he'd find comfort in a bottle such as the one he'd just thrown. But there'd be no comfort in a bottle. No comfort anywhere.

Music poured from the courtyard behind him. It filled the streets with song. Peter kicked at a clump of grass that grew through the sidewalk. *Why can't I find that kind of love?* He swore under his breath. *What's wrong with me?*

Peter stared at the celestial canopy above. How many nights over the past year had he counted those stars? In silent foxholes with ears attuned to the slightest sound, he'd counted them and had considered the God who put them there.

He pressed his fists deeper into his trouser pockets. The sky didn't even seem right. Nothing was right in this new world of light and color, civilians and soldiers. In the former land of blackout curtains and open fields, the sky seemed closer, more real. Too much light flooded this new world. It somehow seemed foreign. False light had filled his soul with false hope.

Peter passed a local tavern, and English voices mixed with the music behind him. He pressed the palms of his hands to his ears and quickened his steps.

I have to get out of here. At the wedding Peter had announced his plans to leave Austria. He would be permanently stationed in Germany, near Landsberg, as if "permanent" meant anything in this place. But even that was not far enough away.

The house where he was staying was just ahead. Peter charged past a buddy who was smoking a cigarette on the porch. In his room, he flung open the door to the wardrobe, where his clothes hung neatly. Peter yanked his army bag from beneath his bed. Clothes, canisters of film, letters from home, other mementos. Into the bag they went.

Peter paused when he came to a small stack of photographs. In one, three smiling female faces peered into the camera. In another, a small girl was picking flowers in a yard while her mother hung laundry in the background. *Anika. Helene.* He murmured their names, then returned the photos to the stack.

The final picture in his hand was worn around the edges and creased from being carried around in his jacket pocket. Soft black curls framed Michaela's face. A white ribbon was tied in her hair. Her clothes were ill-fitting but clean. Her eyes were filled with happiness. Peter shoved it in with the rest and pulled the cords on the top of his bag, tying it closed.

When he tramped back outside, his roommate called to him. "Hey! Where you heading off to at this hour?"

"Anywhere that offers a ride," Peter said, stalking through the gate and down the street. "Tell Josef I'll write him in a few days," he called back as an afterthought.

The image of Josef laughing and dancing with his

bride, her arms intertwined with his, flashed through his thoughts. Peter's long stride became a jog.

A jeep drove by with three GIs on board.

"Where you headed?" Peter called.

"Gmunden," a soldier answered.

"Perfect. May I join you?"

The jeep slowed, and Peter jumped in. He had no idea where Gmunden was or what he'd find when he got there. But he still had a few more days before he was due to report in Germany.

Gmunden it is, Peter thought as the jeep rolled out of town. They drove down the main street, and he looked the other direction as they passed the large yellow house.

He would leave it behind. Just like he'd left Normandy, France, and the battles at Bastogne. This place too would someday be only a distant memory.

Yet even as he pushed the memories out of his mind, Peter doubted they would stay there. This hurt jabbed a place even war hadn't touched.

Twenty-Four

Helene ambled through the dark streets of St. Georgen with Petar clutched to her chest and Anika's hand in hers. Her daughter was exhausted, and Helene felt the same.

"Just a few more steps," Helene coached, spying her father's house in the distance. "We're almost there." Anika's sluggish steps plodded on.

The house seemed vacant from this distance. And Helene realized it would soon be that way. She'd already said goodbye to one friend that night, and Michaela and the others would soon leave too.

A jeep rumbled up the street. Helene pulled Anika to the side of the road and waited for it to pass. Two soldiers laughed and talked. One leaned out with a wave and a whistle. To Helene's dismay, Anika waved back.

Just as they passed, Helene noticed a hunched figure in the backseat, facing the opposite direction.

"Peter?" she whispered as the moonlight caught his reddish-blond hair. She felt a need to call to him, to invite him over for coffee. They could talk about the coming changes and exchange a formal farewell.

But the jeep passed by too quickly. "Good-bye, Peter," she murmured.

He didn't even glance at the yellow house.

Helene's heart went out to him, riding away alone, running from the pain. "Godspeed," she called softly into the night. "Come back soon."

Then she remembered. The Russians would be taking over shortly. And when that happened there would be no returning.

The jeep turned a corner and disappeared from sight. Helene continued homeward.

What did he do to deserve this heartache? she wanted to cry to the heavens. She would be alone soon, she knew. She would lose her friends, lose Peter. But she deserved this punishment. She deserved this for every time she ignored the horror.

But Peter? He'd only helped. Only provided.

It doesn't make sense. None of it makes sense. Helene moved through the front gate and up the steps.

Within minutes, her children were tucked into bed. Helene kicked off her shoes. She collapsed onto her bed, too tired to undress.

She decided to pray for Peter. She'd been finding much comfort in prayer lately. And as she considered her words to God, Michaela's prayers came to mind. Even now she could hear their gentle cadence in her mind. The prayers were like a soothing balm. Yet she still didn't understand how Michaela could have such faith. She'd barely escaped a death camp. She'd turned her back on a relationship with a wonderful man in order to return to the place of her betrayal. And yet, she was not bitter.

It's hard to make sense of it all, Helene thought, fighting sleep. *Unless . . . unless the balance of good and evil doesn't depend on what we've done or what happens to us. Perhaps it really does depend on the life and death of Jesus.*

Could that be part of the answer?

Helene thought of her mother, and of the story Michaela had told her just a few nights before.

When I felt near suffocation in that cattle car, I knew this was not natural, Michaela had said. "*Evil is wrong. A person being slain like an animal is horrible. But then I thought of Christ's life. His service. His love. The way He laid down His life for His friends. My heart tells me that's how life was meant to be lived.*"

The words replayed in Helene's mind, and they made more sense each time she considered them.

That's the reason I felt so guilty, Helene realized as she rolled over onto her side. *If a God of love is the truth, He's the reason hurting others feels wrong, no matter what the popular belief. And why helping others, although difficult at the moment, feels so right in the end.*

Helene flipped over onto her back. She felt weary,

but good. Difficult concepts—truth, faith, hope—were beginning to make sense. She pulled the blanket over her body, still dressed in wedding attire.

More than anything, she realized, she wanted what her heart cried was natural. She longed for what her soul told her was right. She needed what she'd been missing all these years.

If Christ is truth, then I either have to accept Him or reject Him. If she had learned one thing during the war, it was that there was no middle ground.

So before Helene surrendered to sleep that night, she embraced the One who was her hope after so many years of hopelessness. She prayed to Michaela's Savior and made Him her own. And in doing so, she found the gate to freedom. As a prisoner once chained by sin, the doors were now opened through a new life in Christ.

For the first time in years, Helene drifted off to sleep in sweet, sweet peace.

Helene woke with morning's first rays. Her eyelids felt heavy, but her heart was light.

Petar had awakened numerous times to nurse. Instead of becoming frustrated, Helene had kissed his soft baby head and prayed the prayers she had been storing deep inside for so many years.

Sometime during the night, her father and Michaela, Marek and Kasia had returned from the wedding. Michaela had tried to muffle her prayers, but in the quiet of the night Helene could not mistake them. Days before she had wondered why Michaela had made the decision she had. Now she understood a little better. Michaela's greatest joy was to please the Lord. Helene had sensed that joy herself last night, and she still did now.

As she sat up, the scent of lilacs drifting in through the window reminded her of an old Austrian tale. As she thought about it, she realized it made a perfect illustration of God's love.

Helene stretched her arms, then flipped the covers back from the bed. Her bare feet touched the cold wooden floor. As much as she wanted to tell Michaela about her decision, there was one person she wanted to share it with even more.

She pulled stationery and a fountain pen from the bottom drawer of her dresser. The image of Friedrich's smiling face flashed before her as she spotted the photos that lay there. It was too much to try to rationalize his part in the evil schemes. Today she must concentrate on the good.

Sitting in the chair, she used a book for a table and began to write.

July 29, 1945

Dear Peter,

Guten Morgen, my friend. I cannot help but wonder where you are waking up this morning. Only a few hours have passed since you left our town, but so much has happened that I can't wait to share. For without your help I would not be experiencing the joy I feel now.

Oh, dear Peter, where do I begin? First, I will go back a bit and share a story that is popular with all young Austrian girls. It is a story about true love. You see, up in the highest peaks of the Austrian Alps a simple flower grows. It is small and white, but it's the spirit of the flower that matters even more than its beauty. In order to grow, the edelweiss must survive the harshest conditions and bloom in the most challenging weather.

When I was young, every year there would be reports of young men who scaled the Alps and died in their attempt to pick a bunch of edelweiss for their true loves. It was a sign of ultimate devotion. As silly as it was, I would always dream of a man being so in love with me that he would risk his life to bring me a flower. Imagine that! But for many years that was my fantasy.

Then the war came, and romantic thoughts disappeared. Until you came. That is when I first realized that perhaps good does still exist in this world. You risked your life. You went out of your way to save lives, and you helped me, your enemy. Why, if it wasn't for you bringing Michaela, I would never know the love I now have.

By your example, and Michaela's prayers, I have finally discovered the truth behind the edelweiss. I was no foolish girl. Each of us wants to be loved *like that. Although I've never had a man hand me such flowers, I feel that same type of love at this moment.*

Michaela often speaks of a God who loves us so much He gave His life for ours. This morning I discovered this truth: Like a lover wanting the best for his true love, God not only sought a way to prove His love, but He did so knowing full well He would die on that mountain. Last night, I finally realized He died for me.

I have accepted Christ, Peter. Do you know what that means? Like America, Austria has been known as a Christian country. But I've lived many years not knowing what that could mean to me personally.

Now I do.

I hadn't meant to write three pages, but I had to tell you first. I wanted to tell you about the freedom in my soul. Thank you. Thank you for bringing Michaela here. And thank you for showing me that heroes still exist.

My little Petar is waking. I will write again. I hope to hear from you soon.

With friendship in my heart,
Helene

Helene put down the pen and let out a sigh. She folded the letter in thirds and sealed it in an envelope before she could change her mind.

"Shh, little one." She lifted Petar from his cradle.

She struggled to put on her robe with one hand and balance Petar with the other, already missing Lelia's helpful pair of hands.

"I'm sorry to keep you waiting," she cooed to the baby. "But I had a very important letter to write."

Anika awoke and blew a kiss to Helene. Helene started to return the gesture when a pounding on the bedroom door startled her. Before she could respond, the door flew open. Marek stood there, his face drained of color.

Helene pulled her robe tighter around her chin.

Marek's panicked expression quickly transformed to one of embarrassment. He took a step back. "So sorry."

"It's all right. What's going on?"

"I apologize for the intrusion," he said in broken German, "but I need Michaela. We must leave at once. The Russians—"

"They're here?"

"Tak, yes," Marek said. "They closed down borders sooner than expected. The Americans have moved out."

Helene thought back to Friedrich's rantings about the Russians. *"They are animals,"* he had said with a vile curse. *"Hardly men."*

"Does my father know?" Helene asked.

"Oh, yes. He is meeting with the town council right now."

Helene stared out the window. A robin bounced from branch to branch on the large tree outside, seemingly without a care in the world.

She turned back to Marek. "I'll start packing for

more, I'll miss you. You saved my life. I can never repay you."

Helene tried to speak, but the words wouldn't come. She tried again. "I thought I was the one helping you. But I was the one saved. I only offered bread. But what you gave me—" Helene placed her hand over her chest. "What you gave me, I can never repay. The life you showed me lives here. I have found a new life. Your work here is complete."

Michaela stood on her tiptoes and kissed Helene's cheek. "That is the only reason I can let you go," Helene continued. "God has called you to share this good news with others as you did with me."

The train whistle blew again, and Helene took a step back. Michaela crouched before Anika. The young girl released her mother's skirt and flew into Michaela's arms. Helene glanced at those on the platform around her. After years of knowing her every move was being watched, she couldn't help but wonder who at the station was observing this scene. What did they think of an SS child in the arms of a former prisoner?

Michaela's lips moved, and Helene knew her friend was saying a prayer over Anika. Michaela stood and placed a hand upon Petar's head and did the same for him.

"As soon as I arrive, I will write," Michaela promised.

Helene nodded, pulling Anika toward her. "Go now. Before you miss your train."

Michaela stepped through the train doors. Helene waved to Marek and Kasia in the window and caught a glimpse of Michaela's face before the train rolled forward and disappeared down the tracks.

The platform still buzzed with the motion of dozens of bodies—serviceman, displaced persons, and villagers. Yet Helene felt more alone than ever.

She took Anika's hand and hurried toward the house. The rain continued to fall, and by the time they reached the front door they were soaked.

She would bathe the children, dress them, feed them, and play with them. Perhaps she'd prepare a tea party with Anika and bounce her son upon her knee.

Still, Helene knew that her heart would not be there. Through the rest of the day and into the night, her thoughts would be with the train as it increased the distance between them.

꒳   ꒳   ꒳

That night, after her children were tucked into their beds, Helene lay awake, unable to sleep. She heard a train's whistle and wished it signaled her friend's return. She imagined the Red Army's heavy-booted footsteps and willed them to stay away.

Austria had been carved like a side of beef, with the four Allied powers choosing their own cuts. St. Georgen rested north of the Danube—the border of the Russian zone. Only a river crossing away, Helene knew, dwelt the symbols of those carefree months after the war. Peter, Coca-Cola, bubble gum, and jazz music had receded to the opposite bank.

But God is with me, whichever side of the river I'm on, she reminded herself. *And in Him I will trust.*

Later, during the darkest point of the night, a clamoring outside stirred Helene from her bed. She heard a woman's scream, then men's laughter.

Wrapping a blanket around her shaking frame, Helene approached the front window. On the small street that ran alongside their house, a Russian jeep was parked with its headlights off. The men's shouts were directed at a helpless young woman. They pulled her into the jeep, then sped away.

Where are they taking her? What will they do? Helene stepped back from the window. She jumped when a hand touched her shoulder.

"It's just me," her father said. He tucked her under his left arm. A rifle rested in his right hand. "This is a gift from Peter," he said. "Liberated from the Germans."

Helene understood. "You warned me they were coming."

Her father stepped to the window. "Thirty thousand of their comrades were killed in that compound on the hill. They're here for revenge."

"But the guards are gone. All those involved have left." Even as the words spilled from Helene's mouth, she knew it wasn't true. She remained. And her father, who'd kept supplies for the Nazis, had stayed. Even the priest who once housed a dozen men was still there. Although most of these people had no choice at the time, they could still be considered sympathetic toward the Nazis.

A new oppression had come to their town. Helene snuggled deeper into her father's arms.

⁊   ⁊   ⁊

The next morning, Helene's father was gone when she awoke. She peered at the spot where the woman had been taken the previous night. The memory of her screams caused Helene to jump at the slightest noise. The streets were quiet now. But she knew, out there somewhere, the Russians lurked.

She fed her children and then gave Anika paper and scissors. As the girl played, Helene stood at the window, watching for her father. Finally she saw him, moving toward the house in quick steps, his brow lined with worry.

"It's as we thought." He quickly entered the room and latched the door behind him. "A group of prisoners has already been taken to Siberia."

Helene gasped. "Prisoners?"

"Ja, those considered enemies of the Russian state. Nazi sympathizers. They're accusing many of cooperating with the enemy. Those already taken are being sentenced. Only those who are 'of service' to the occupational forces will remain. Even now Russian tents are being set up where American ones recently stood."

"How many of them are here?"

"The men you saw are only the tip of the sword. They have come to protect the borders. The full occupational forces have yet to arrive."

Helene glanced at Anika, who was cutting a piece of red paper into the shape of a heart. She lowered her voice. "Are the borders closed?"

"Ja."

"All of them?"

"All of them."

Helene collapsed onto the chair. *I deserve this. I am an enemy.* But as soon as the words filled her head, others took their place. She could hear Michaela's voice. *No, you are forgiven. Your slate has been wiped clean.*

In God's eyes, perhaps, but not to the rest of the world. To the Russians she was simply the wife of a former guard.

"There is a way out." Her father sat in the chair beside her. "It is risky, but it is our only chance."

Helene stared into his gray eyes. He seemed so old. So tired.

"There are many who want to get out. Even Jewish survivors who are still weak. Farmers are rowing them across the river." He placed his hands over hers. "I want you to go tonight. With the children."

"In a rowboat? Across the Danube? But it is so wide and strong. Nein, it's too dangerous." She stood, then leaned against the table. "I can't. If anything happened to them—"

Her father stood and placed his hands on her shoulders. "There is no other way. You know you will be found. Too many know. And even those most loyal can be bought . . . or threatened."

"What about you?"

"I have already been sought out. First by the Nazis for storage, then by the Russians for men. They want to use our home for boarding." He kissed her head. "As long as I provide a room and *schnitzel,* I will be taken care of. I am an old man. I pose no threat."

"I can't leave you again. I couldn't bear it."

"Be strong, my daughter. Think of the children. When things settle down, then perhaps I can join you."

"Either you come too, or I'm not going."

His eyes flashed vulnerability for a moment, and then the willful expression returned. "You don't understand. There are dynamics I cannot begin to tell you about." He held her face in his hands. "The Lord knows I'd do anything for you and for the children. But I cannot leave. Not yet. You have to trust me in this."

The determination in his eyes told Helene he wasn't going to change his mind. "But cross the river? Isn't there another way?" Her thoughts went again to the man she had depended on so many times over the previous months. "What about Peter? Can we get word to him? Can he come to help?"

"Nein. From the moment of surrender, no U.S. soldier has been allowed into the Soviet zone. You must go. They are already collecting names. Names of former Nazis."

"But even if I get across, where will I go?"

Her father took a knife from a kitchen drawer and carefully sliced the stitching on the lining of his jacket. He pulled out a paper from inside, neatly folded, and handed it to Helene.

She unfolded the sheet and saw the seal of an American eagle. The date on the paper was two weeks old.

Dear Captain Standart,

By my own witness, and by others of the Eleventh Armored Division, the bearer of this paper, Helene Völkner, compassionately helped the troops of our division in their efforts to save the lives of the victims of Nazi atrocities.

In return for protection for herself and her children, Mrs. Völkner has agreed to cooperate with the U.S. Department of Investigation in their efforts to secure the names and ranks of SS officers and guards at Camp Gusen.

If you have any questions about Mrs. Völkner, please feel free to contact me.

Sincerely,
Sergeant Peter Scott

Helene held the paper to her chest. "You want me to disclose the names of the guards?" A knot formed in her stomach. "You've had this planned all along. You and Peter. You knew, when faced with danger, I'd have to comply."

"We were hoping it would not come to this. We knew no American servicemen would be allowed in, but we had no idea the Russians would shut down the border to locals so quickly."

Helene considered the danger of giving out such vital information. She thought of Arno Schroeder. His face, his taunts, his threats. He was just one man. There were hundreds like him who had disappeared, never wishing to be found. Many who would do anything to keep her silent.

Then again . . . maybe she'd have a chance to work for the side of good rather than evil.

"Could you give the names?" he asked.

"Of course. I know them all. Their positions. Their wives. Their families. After all, I attended their parties. I visited their homes. I was one of them."

Helene refolded the letter and set it on the table. She thought of Peter's care, his interest in her and her friends. Had it been real? She thought of the American actors in the movies set up for the GIs' amusement. They played their parts well. Had Peter's interest been just an act? Had he played the part of an honorable hero only to win her confidence? Maybe he'd known who she was from the beginning. After all, who else but an SS wife could give the U.S. Army all the information they could ever need?

Helene tried to control her shaky voice. "When did he approach you with this idea?"

"He did not approach me, but I him . . . just in case it came to this."

"So, this was your plan?"

"Our second plan. Our first was to have you leave with Michaela if she had chosen to move to Germany." He lowered his gaze. "You could not leave with Peter alone. Nonfraternization, you know. But you could safely travel with her, especially if she were employed by the U.S. Army. After all, she had no laws about who she could befriend."

Helene dropped her head. The more she heard, the more she realized she didn't want to know. "But Michaela went one way, and Peter the other."

"So here you are."

"Still, that doesn't answer my question. What will I do when I get to the other side?"

"Someone will be waiting to take you to Linz. Once there, find an American serviceman. Give him the letter and ask to be taken to Captain Standart. He will know how to contact Peter, and Peter will connect you with the right people."

"Peter is expecting me?"

Her father rubbed his mustache. "He knows it's a possibility."

"I have to think about it."

"Of course." He paused. "But remember what you saw last night. Leaving will be dangerous, especially with two little ones. But staying could be even worse."

Helene didn't need to hear any more. She picked up the letter and shuffled to her room. Anika still slept on the bed, Petar in his cradle. Her heart swelled with love for them. They were so helpless. They didn't realize who they were in the minds of the Russians. They didn't know their father had been an accomplice to the murder of thousands as their mother stood by and watched.

Oh, God, it is so difficult. She dropped onto the bed and curled into a ball. The foolish decisions she'd made long ago mattered so much now.

Helene knew what she had to do. It was the only way. Her father knew it. Peter did too.

Helene gazed about the room, taking it all in. She would leave everything behind again. Her father. This place. The memories, both good and bad.

Helene noticed something glimmering on the floor in the corner, half covered with dust. She rose from the bed and reached for it.

My wedding band. How many weeks ago had she pulled it from her finger and thrown it across the room? Yet even so, she had not been able to escape its hold. She would forever be Friedrich's bride.

Helene slid the ring onto her finger. She would go. She would give the names. And as she kissed her sleeping baby, Helene hoped more than anything God would go with her.

Twenty-Six

AUGUST 2, 1945

Helene repacked her satchel for the tenth time. How could she possibly reduce everything she needed for herself and her children into one bag? Their identification papers, ja. Old photos, a few. She put those in the bag, then picked up the map she'd found. She had studied it again after Arno came around asking questions, but still it made no sense. Nevertheless, she stuffed it into the satchel just in case.

At 2 A.M. her father came for her. He lifted Anika from the bed. The girl stirred slightly but didn't wake. Helene lifted Petar to her shoulder. Then she picked up her satchel with her other hand. The weight of a life's possessions pulled against her fingers.

"Did you give them your grandmother's special tea?" her father asked.

"Ja. I hope it works."

The two made their way down the back stairs. The slivered moon seemed far too bright, their footsteps too loud. Helene followed her father through the back streets. Her side ached and her breathing was labored as she balanced a sleeping baby and a satchel that felt like it was full of rocks.

"When you get to the other side," her father whispered through the night air, "watch for a blue two-door sedan. My friend said it's the color of a robin's egg, and it should be the only car out there."

"You found a ride for us?"

"I hope," he said. "My friend is nervous. He has a family too. He said as long as there was no danger . . ."

No danger?

Near the water's edge they trudged through the woodsy shoreline toward a small boat. Her father took the lead. As Helene followed, something in the bush stirred. *It's only an animal,* she told herself, her heart pounding.

Suddenly something leapt from the bush—a man. Helene tried to call out, but before she could say a word, a hand clamped over her mouth. Another hand grabbed her arm. She stumbled but somehow managed to hold on to the baby and the satchel.

Heavy breathing exploded in her ear, and she smelled beer on the man's breath. She held Petar tight to her chest as the man pushed toward the water's edge.

This is it. It's over. The Russians. The woman's screams from the night before flashed through her mind. Helene silently cried out to God. *Please let my children escape.*

Her father looked up from the boat where he'd laid Anika. His face registered fear, then confusion. "Arno! Get your hands off her."

Arno? Friedrich's friend had escaped with his family days ago, hadn't he?

Helene's captor pulled his hand from her mouth and pushed her into her father's arms. Petar stirred. "Shh," she said, bouncing him. His eyes opened for a few seconds, then fluttered closed again.

"I need you to take me across with you," Arno said, nose-to-nose with her father.

"And what if I say no?"

Arno opened his jacket. A pistol was tucked in a holster on his side. "Then I'll just take the boat myself."

"You dare threaten an old man, and a woman with children?"

"No threats." Arno buttoned his jacket. "Only a request."

"Fine, get in," her father said in an angry whisper. He waved a hand toward the rowboat. Helene climbed in. The boat rocked as she settled onto the seat near Anika. Arno sat in the center.

Down the riverbank not more than a hundred meters, Helene saw other forms piling into a similar craft. Her father pushed off and then jumped in.

She surveyed the shoreline. She spotted headlights coming their direction. Other lights flashed through the trees. Helene held her breath. The truck slowed but kept moving.

Thank God.

The current was strong. Her father fought it with every stroke, heading toward their landing point slightly upstream. At least it would be easier for him to make it back. Helene glanced into the dark water and thought of the rumors of entire transports of bodies dumped into the river. Goose bumps rose on her arms as she imagined the icy waves driving her body into the river's current. She caressed Petar's head.

A cold wind blew on Helene's face, and she adjusted Petar's blanket to block the wind. It did little good. Petar stirred and let out a cry.

Arno shot her an angry glare. "Shut that kid up, now!"

Helene pressed Petar to her chest and rocked him, but the muffled cries escalated.

Her father glanced back. "Please, Helene, do something."

"Mutti?" Anika asked, rubbing her eyes. "What wrong? Where are—"

"Quiet," Helene rasped as she fumbled to place a blanket over her shoulder and lift her blouse. Petar latched on to her breast. His crying stopped. Her fingers trembled as she stroked his cheek. Then she pressed a hand on Anika's back.

Strong waves tugged against the boat and splashed water over its side. Her father's breathing labored as he struggled to keep them moving forward. When it seemed her father could row no more, Arno took the oars. Helene was grateful for Arno's assistance, but his presence still worried her. What would he do when they got to the other side? Would he follow her? Would she be safe?

Helene tried to make out the other boat through the darkness. She finally caught sight of it downstream and noticed it moved neither as fast nor as gracefully as theirs. *Perhaps Arno's presence is a gift in disguise.*

With a grating sound, their boat finally hit land. The jarring motion startled Anika. She sat up and clung to the side. Helene motioned for Anika to be quiet as her grandfather lifted her to the shore.

"Thanks for the lift, old man," Arno said as soon as they were unloaded. For a split second a small object glistened in the moonlight. It landed at her father's feet.

"Something for your troubles." Arno sneered.

Her father bent to pick it up, then cursed. "A tooth." He threw the object into the water. "A gold tooth."

Arno muffled a laugh, then jogged away with a wave.

Helene's stomach lurched. She balanced Petar on her hip, flung the satchel over her shoulder, and took Anika's hand. "What a sick man," she seethed. "First he threatens our lives, then he waves good-bye?"

Her father stared at her intently. "Do you have the letter?"

"Ja, pinned to my underclothes."

"Good. You must hurry. Do not stop. The car should be waiting on the road. My friend will take you to Linz. It's only about six miles south of here."

"I know," Helene assured him.

"Remember, Linz is also divided into four segments. The American section will be the first one you come to from the main road. Don't waste time once you get there. Ask for the captain and give him the letter. Then, and only then, will you be safe."

"Oh, Papa." Helene released Anika's hand for a moment and wrapped an arm around her father's neck.

"My little girl." He rocked her gently. "God be with you." She felt his chin tremble against her cheek before he released her.

"Can't you come? I'm sure Peter can help you too."

Her father shook his head sadly. "Nein. I must stay. There are those who still need help. Besides . . ." A twinkle lit his eyes. "Just like the Germans, I am sure the Russians are easy with their words when they are drunk. Nights around my living room with a few drinks often leads to information that can help many."

Helene chuckled despite her tears. *So that's what he's been up to all these years.*

Her father embraced her one last time, then kissed both children. Tears glistened on his eyelashes as he returned to the boat and pushed off.

Anika whimpered.

"Don't cry." Helene grabbed her daughter's hand and plowed up the riverbank. "I need you to be strong. We have to go now. We have to—"

Helene heard the sound of footsteps down the bank. Not far from her, others struggled up the sloping shoreline toward freedom. She spotted a car in the distance.

An older-model blue sedan parked on the side of the road. She and Anika had made it nearly halfway to the road when spotlights bounced over the waters.

Across the river, a truck stopped at the water's edge. Bright headlights flooded the distant riverbank. Helene spotted the two rowboats struggling to cross. Her father's boat was in the lead.

Russian shouts and gunfire split the night air. Bullets splashed the river's surface.

A spotlight flashed on the other boat. The man in the boat stood, hands high in surrender. Gunfire erupted again. His body trembled, then slumped like a puppet with its strings cut. Helene watched in horror as he hit the wooden side and splashed into the cold depths of the river. Another victim swept beneath the silent waters.

Papa! Where was he? As the lights swung that way, Helene located his boat on the far shore, empty. It was a miracle he had made it across so quickly. But was he safe? She didn't have time to think of that now. More gunfire rang out. One of the trucks was moving across the bridge in their direction. She looked toward the car again. Would she have time to reach it before the truck was upon them?

She yanked Anika's hand. "Hurry!" The girl did her best to keep up as they ran awkwardly through the trees.

The Russians had returned to their trucks and now aimed their large spotlights at the grass not more than ten feet behind Helene and her children.

"Anika, faster!"

The young girl cried out as Helene pulled her along.

"Run!"

Helene struggled forward, clinging to the satchel and the whimpering baby. As she neared the blue sedan, she noticed the young driver's face was pale with panic. In the seat next to him sat Arno, gun drawn.

Before Helene could decide what to do, the car lurched forward, speeding off down the road.

"No, wait!" she screamed. Petar woke in her arms. The Russian truck neared. She dropped to the ground, pulling Anika down with her.

Helene's heart pounded as she searched for a place to hide. She spotted a hollow where the tree's roots met the ground, making a perfect bowl for them to slide into. Helene's dress tore as she scurried into the pit. She held both hands over her crying children's mouths as the truck approached their secret lair.

Keep going, she begged. *Please don't search the woods.* The truck's engine roared. Tires screeched. Gradually the noise faded, leaving behind the smell of scorched rubber.

After several minutes, Helene crawled out from beneath the tree. She heard no other sound and wondered what had happened to the others who'd crossed.

She took a deep breath and considered her options. Traveling the road would be faster, but Helene didn't want to take any chances. So, with her arms laden and Anika at her side, they plowed through the low brush and trees parallel to the road.

After they'd gone no more than a mile, Anika slumped against a tree. The baby squirmed in Helene's arms. The satchel burned on her shoulder. She had to come up with a plan. They'd never make it to Linz at this rate.

Helene squatted to the ground and rifled through her things with one hand. She pulled out a knitted sweater and laid it on the ground, then placed Petar on it. He started to fuss, but she worked quickly. Within a matter of minutes, she'd formed a sort of sling. She moved her son to her back, carefully sliding one sweater arm over her shoulder and the other under her arm. She secured it with a tight knot, then stood and bounced to see if it would hold. It did.

Now for her daughter. Helene lifted Anika, wrapping the girl's legs around her waist. She picked up the satchel with her other hand. It wouldn't be easy, but it would work.

Through the night, Helene plowed through the woods past houses and farms. A cow mooed near one fence as she passed. A light from inside a farmhouse flicked as if a lantern was being lit. A few vehicles passed, but Helene made sure to stay out of sight.

As she pressed on, the waif-like figures from the camp clambered through her mind. Michaela had been just one of many. There were thousands more with stories of hard labor and death marches. With each step, Helene understood a bit more of what they had faced.

Finally, at dawn's light, Anika was able to walk on her own, allowing Helene to swing Petar to the front and nurse as they walked.

"You did it, my darling," Helene praised her daughter as they reached the army base. "You are so good."

Helene smoothed her hair, then approached the GI guarding the gates.

"Please help," she said in German. "I need to see your captain." The man pointed toward the evacuation barracks, where former prisoners of war were beginning to rouse. *I am a displaced person,* Helene realized. But she couldn't make the man understand.

After four attempts, she found an American who spoke German.

"My superior?" he asked.

"Ja," she said. "I have a letter stating that I am of value to your country. I can assist you in finding Nazi criminals."

The man smiled, first at her, then at Anika. "Really? Anyone who can do that deserves to see the big chief. Follow me."

The GI led Helene to a former Nazi building that had been transformed into U.S. Army housing. She remembered being there once for a Nazi Party dinner. That seemed like ages ago.

Helene paused when they entered the building. "May we, uh, use the water closet first?"

"Take your time." He showed Helene to a room with running water and a working toilet. She changed the baby and fed Anika some bread from the satchel. A few minutes later she reappeared, feeling slightly refreshed. The baby slept on her aching shoulder.

"Danke," she said to the soldier who waited. He led them to an office. He asked for her letter, which she gave to him, then he disappeared inside.

"Captain Standart will see you tomorrow," the GI said when he returned. "I'm supposed to find accommodations for you in the meantime." The man seemed more distant than before and refused to meet her gaze.

He led them across the road to a housing unit that had once been used for SS guards. Small rooms divided the brick building. Inside each room a high window gave dim light. A cot rested against one wall; a small table with a washbasin and a chair graced the other. The cement walls were painted a disgusting shade of green that reminded Helene of the cooked spinach her mother had forced her to eat as a child.

The soldier pulled a chocolate bar from his pocket and handed it to Anika. Despite the flight for their lives, the young girl grinned.

"Danke," Anika said.

The soldier left, and Helene and Anika collapsed onto the cot with Petar snuggled between them.

Helene took one look at Petar's sweet baby face and Anika's chocolate-stained lips and let out a deep sigh.

Through the wall, Helene could make out a radio broadcast. Though she couldn't understand any of the words, the American jazz melodies lulled her to sleep.

Twenty-Seven

AUGUST 2, 1945

Helene and the children slept through the day, and when she awoke the room was dim. Strains of American jazz still frolicked in the air, but softer than before. Every now and then she detected footsteps in the hall outside her door.

Somehow Anika had gotten Petar off the bed and onto a blanket on the floor. Helene shifted to her side on the cot and reached for the baby, stroking her fingers through his fine hair. When Petar spied his mother, his face brightened. Helene pulled him up beside her and held him tight, kissing his soft cheek.

"I'm hungry," Anika said as she climbed on the bed.

"I have some bread." Helene lay the baby on the cot and picked up her satchel. She rummaged through it and pulled out bread wrapped in wax paper.

"I'm tired of that."

"I know." Helene tore off a piece and handed it to her, then took a bite herself. "But this is all we have."

Anika played with her bread, squishing it between her fingers. "Can we go to store?"

"Nein. We have to stay here till tomorrow."

"I have to go potty."

"I'll take you in a minute. Let me nurse your brother first."

Anika slumped onto the floor and crossed her arms. "I want to see *mein opa*."

"He's not here." Helene's voice was strained as she pictured her father's face. "Do you understand? We have only a little money, and we can't go back."

Helene heard heavy footsteps outside the door. She clicked on the electric light. "Come here, my lamb," she said, trying to control her frustration. "You've been a good girl. I'm proud of you." Helene pulled her daughter close. "How about a book?" She found one of her daughter's favorite picture books in her bag and took it out. Anika squealed with delight and started quoting the book before Helene began reading.

When she'd finished the story, Helene held the girl's face in her hands. "I know this is scary. You have to be a big girl now. Will you show Petar how to be a brave boy?"

Anika's bright blue eyes grew solemn. She nodded, then quietly ate her bread.

Helene popped a piece of the bread into her mouth but couldn't swallow. Like a torrent, last night's events flooded her mind. The journey across the river. The man's body slipping into the water. The long trek through the woods.

Helene knew she couldn't dwell on those things now. She had to keep going. For her children. Petar gazed at her with curiosity as he nursed. Anika nibbled silently.

After the baby was fed and changed, Helene ran a comb through her hair and traded her wrinkled dress for a fresh one. She hid her paperwork under the cot mattress and tucked her satchel beneath the iron frame.

Helene's arms ached as she lifted Petar to her shoulder. She stretched out her hand to Anika. "Come, let's find the water closet, and maybe some food."

The hallway was long and stark. Electric lights flickered from the ceiling. As Helene passed room after room, she pictured this place swarming with haughty SS guards, throwing their blood-splattered clothes down the laundry chute and perhaps remembering their victims in their dreams.

After using the water closet at the end of the hall, they followed the smell of food. Helene checked the coins and bills in her pocket, hoping she had enough.

She found the mess hall in the basement of the building. The scents of sausage and yeasty white rolls made her hungry stomach rumble.

A sea of male faces turned her direction as she and her children entered. Helene felt heat rising to her face and pretended to ignore their stares. Soon, their conversations resumed.

Helene squared her shoulders and strode toward the

supper line. She approached a soldier who was ladling biscuits and gravy onto metal trays.

"*Bitte,* may we purchase a meal?" she asked in German. She pulled out some money and offered it to him.

The soldier turned to his buddy as if unsure what to do. Obviously, they couldn't understand her.

Helene searched for a familiar face among the room full of laughing soldiers. Finally she spotted the man who had shown her their room. She approached him cautiously.

"Excuse me for interrupting." The man looked up with curiosity. Helene gulped. "I was wondering if I might purchase some food for my children."

He laughed, then answered in German, "You're kidding, right? You don't have to pay. Just help yourself." He waved her toward the line, then continued talking to his companions.

Helene's cheeks burned as she returned to the line and stared at the stack of metal trays. She stood there for a moment, trying to figure out how she could balance the baby and a tray—even if she could pry her fingers from Anika's—when a woman approached. She was shorter than Helene by a few inches and wore a crisp white nurse's uniform. A pointed white cap perched atop her brown, styled hair, and her red lips offered Helene a warm smile.

"Men," the nurse sighed, speaking in German. "Why do they not offer more help?" She grabbed two trays and signaled with a tilt of her chin for Helene to follow. Within minutes the trays were filled with ham, fried potatoes, sausage, and warm buttermilk biscuits.

"Follow me." The woman found an empty table. She set the trays down, then took a seat. Helene sat beside her with Petar on her lap and Anika at her side.

"I'm Rhonda." The nurse shook her hand. Rhonda pushed both trays in front of Helene and Anika. "Eat up, ja?"

"I thought one of those plates was for you."

"Nein." The woman waved a hand in the air. "I've already eaten. But, honey, you are so thin. This will put some meat on your bones."

Compared to Lelia and Michaela, Helene thought she was doing well. Still, the food tasted delicious.

"Here, let me hold the little one." Rhonda pulled Petar onto her lap and cooed at him. "What a cutie you are. Such a precious little button nose. And look at those cheeks. It just makes me want to squeeze them." She tickled Petar's nose with hers, and he attempted a smile.

"So I hear you're a Nazi wife," Rhonda said casually.

Helene nearly choked on a piece of sausage. "Yes." She put her hand to her mouth and swallowed. "He's— My husband . . . is dead now."

"I understand, sweetie. I heard many young women were forced to marry and have babies against their will. Future soldiers for the one-thousand-year Reich and all."

Helene didn't argue, but she had a hard time swallowing.

"I hear you're going to help us now," the nurse said, cuddling Petar.

Helene wondered what else the woman knew.

"Do you need me to watch your children while you meet with Captain Standart? Tomorrow's my day off."

"Oh, if you could. That would help." Helene had no choice but to trust this woman.

"Not a problem. I'll be at your door at ten minutes to eight." She checked her watch. "But right now I have to get back to work. My shift isn't quite over."

With a hasty good-bye and one last kiss on Petar's cheek, Rhonda handed the baby back to Helene and hustled out, turning soldiers' heads as she did. Helene was again alone amidst the mass of uniformed men.

"Where's Peter?" Anika asked, standing on the chair. "I don't see him."

"He's not here. He's far away."

"Opa's not here, or Peter, or Papi." Anika lifted her hands, palms up. "Who will take care of us?"

Helene squared her shoulders, attempting to appear confident for her daughter's sake. "God will," she said, taking another bite of buttery biscuit. *God will.*

Twenty-Eight

Michaela tucked the brown paper sack close to her chest and hurried through the predawn streets. Although the war was over, she knew from the hostile stares she'd received since returning home that prejudice and hatred had not ended with the Nazis' defeat.

Many Polish townspeople expressed outrage when the camp survivors staggered back into their country. The Russian occupiers were even more incensed. Jews had been unwelcome in much of Poland for hundreds of years. Now, those associated with them were also despised.

Michaela's initial welcome back into Bielsko was having a rotten apple thrown at her. It had hit her leg with a thud, splattering at her feet.

She shuffled past the bombed-out buildings to a small apartment that had somehow remained standing.

She opened the basement door and crept in. Marek and Kasia still slept in the corner under threadbare blankets. Michaela pulled back the soiled curtain and searched the night sky, longing for morning's first light. There was no chair or bench in the room, so she perched on the packed-earth floor.

Marek rolled onto his side, yanking on his thin blanket. He opened one eye. "You finished?" he whispered.

Michaela rubbed her aching fingers, sore from pushing a thick needle through even thicker fabric all day and into the night. "Ja. And look what payment I received." She grinned, opening the bag.

He leaned on one elbow. "A loaf of brown bread and three hard-cooked eggs for two days of work?"

"And this." Michaela reached into the sack again and brought out the treasure she'd worked extra hours to afford.

"A book?" Marek sat up and peered through the dark. "How will that fill our stomachs?" He took it from her, flipping through the pages. "It's blank!"

Michaela took the book back and caressed the hard cover. "My mind is already filled with more words than these pages can hold. And my hand has been itching for pen and paper."

Marek grunted and lay back down. "You'd better get some sleep. You'll have more than your share of work tomorrow."

"Tomorrow's Sunday," Michaela said, curling up next to Kasia. "I've been waiting years for a chance to worship God with my old friends."

She closed her eyes, but Michaela knew she wouldn't sleep. Her mind was full of images that begged to be transposed into words on paper. As soon as the first morning light stretched its rays, she planned to do exactly that.

゜ ゜ ゜

The summer sun shone hot on Michaela's head. She shielded her eyes and tried not to stare as she passed the gutted shell of her father's church and the cottage next door that once housed her family. *"The church burned not long after you were taken away,"* a friend had told her. *"And the house was turned over to Communist supporters."*

Oh, Father. What has this world come to?

During her captivity Michaela had imagined roaming these streets again. She'd pictured the snowcapped mountains in the distance. Thought of seeing the people she'd known all her life and chatting happily with them along the way. Yet, as she ambled past the church, an unexpected loneliness burned deep in her soul. True, she had Marek, Kasia, and other old friends. But friends were not the same as family. And her family was gone forever. Being here made that fact all the more real.

Tears trickled down Michaela's cheeks. Maybe it would have been better to go to the States. Or to stay with Helene. Then she'd never have had to experience this emptiness.

No, she told herself. *I can do this*. She wiped her damp cheeks and raised her chin.

When Michaela rounded the last corner, she saw the small crowd gathered in the park. Many faces peered at her, and she waved. Today they would sing, and they would cry. They would remember those who were gone and offer words of hope for their future.

She thought about a Scripture she had memorized when she was a child. The words of the prophet Isaiah, in chapter 61, had never been more appropriate than they were right now.

He hath sent me to bind up the brokenhearted, she recited in her mind, *to proclaim liberty to the captives, and the opening of the prison to them that are bound; to proclaim the acceptable year of the Lord, and the day of vengeance of our God; to comfort all that mourn; to appoint unto them that mourn in Zion, to give unto them beauty for ashes, the oil of joy for mourning, the garment of praise for the spirit of heaviness.*

In the gospel of Luke, the Lord Jesus had spoken those same words at the synagogue. The promise from the Old Testament had been proclaimed again in the New, and she clung to that promise for them now.

Michaela whispered a prayer for wisdom and strength. *Jesus will be our gentle Shepherd,* she thought as she approached the faithful members of her father's church.

Her chest tightened as she scanned the crowd. There were so many missing. Some were dead. Others had betrayed them, causing those deaths.

318

Arms opened to her, and Michaela received their hugs. Her eyes burned to see their tears. Her father's sheep. Those he loved. They were her calling now. Her destiny and her future. She would share with them the love of the One who had guided her father—and had been her only comfort in the dark days in the camps.

Two old friends, Pawel and Rozalia, waited until last to approach her. Rozalia held in her arms a small girl with light brown hair and creamy ivory skin.

Michaela gazed at the little girl. "Is this . . ."

Pawel nodded. "Jacek and Lidia's daughter, Sabine. She'll be three next month."

Michaela placed her hand over her mouth, realizing how much the girl resembled the friends she would never see again. She opened her arms to the girl. Amazingly, Sabine reached for her in return.

Michaela took the child into her embrace, pressing her face into the girl's neck. Tears flowed freely as an amazing grief filled her again. Only this time it wasn't those from Bielsko she cried for. But those in Austria she'd left behind. As she held Sabine she thought of Anika and the baby. She thought of Peter and Helene. She thought of Peter's short note to her, saying that Helene planned to leave St. Georgen with her children.

Michaela knew Peter would help Helene and the children as he was able. *At least,* she thought, *they have each other.*

Twenty-Nine

AUGUST 3, 1945

Helene's stomach knotted as she entered the dimly lit office. She clasped her hands, hoping to hide their trembling. A lone window in the far corner gave scant light. The room was sparse except for the large metal desk in the center. The gray walls seemed to absorb color.

That morning, Rhonda had arrived as promised. Anika was excited about staying with the perky American nurse . . . especially when she saw the floppy, red-haired Raggedy Ann doll Rhonda had brought for her. Yet Helene's arms felt empty without her baby and her daughter.

The man sitting at the desk wore a white uniform that seemed unnaturally bright in contrast to the room. His hair was gray at the temples. His face showed no emotion. Beside him stood a young soldier in the familiar olive-drab uniform.

"Mrs. Völkner, I presume." The young soldier spoke German in a monotone voice.

"Yes."

"Have a seat."

She did, sliding into the cold metal chair, tucking her skirt around her legs.

The young soldier introduced the officer behind the desk as Captain Standart. The officer said something in English, and the young soldier translated. "It says here you are the wife of a former SS guard, Friedrich Völkner?"

"Yes," she stammered. "That is correct."

"And what has become of your husband, Mrs. Völkner?" the translator asked as Captain Standart tapped his pen on the desk.

Helene's voice shook slightly. "He was killed . . . when he attempted to escape the country."

"I see. It also says you wish to divulge names of other guards from the Gusen compound?"

"Ja. It is the only way."

"The only way?" The translator's eyebrows raised.

"For my safety. I have two children. I must protect them."

"And how will Captain Standart know you are telling the truth?" the translator asked. "How do we know you won't lead our investigation team on a wild-goose chase?"

She gawked at the translator. Captain Standart adjusted his black-rimmed glasses.

"I will speak with honesty." Helene stumbled over her words. "I have no reason to lie."

She stared at the translator's fidgeting hands. *They don't trust me. What will I do now?*

"I will vouch for her honesty, sir." The German words came from behind Helene. She turned. A man emerged from the shadows. It was Peter. His face looked weary, his eyes tired. She wanted to laugh and cry at the same time. Her chin quivered, and she held back the urge to run to him.

"Sergeant Scott. You say this woman can be trusted?" Captain Standart's voice held a hint of amusement as he spoke in German.

"Yes, sir, I do."

"And how do you know this woman? There is a law against fraternization with Austrian and German citizens."

Peter approached the captain's desk. "I first saw Mrs. Völkner when she brought food to the liberated prisoners of the Gusen camp, sir. She was not forced to do so, yet she risked her life to help."

Helene's attention bounced from one man to the other as they spoke. The young soldier stood at attention and stared into space, his translation services no longer required.

"Can others validate your statement?" Captain Standart questioned.

Peter spread a half dozen sheets of paper on the captain's desk. "I have signed statements here from Private Josef Wottitzky and his wife, Lelia. Mrs. Wottitzky is a liberated prisoner who was helped by Mrs. Völkner. And she's doing well." Peter glanced at Helene and showed the slightest hint of a grin. "Private Wottitzky often visited Mrs. Völkner's home during his courtship."

The captain readjusted the glasses on his nose and studied the letters, tilting each one toward the lamp on his desk.

"There are also letters from Miss Michaela Perl of Poland and others who were aware of Mrs. Völkner's work in the camps," Peter continued. "Miss Perl was another ex-prisoner Mrs. Völkner helped. She too is doing well."

Helene impatiently awaited Captain Standart's response. To her surprise the officer cracked a stiff smile. "I see you've done your homework, soldier."

"Only trying to help someone who helped the troops and DPs while the war was going on, sir."

As Captain Standart finished reading, Helene felt Peter's gaze, but she was too timid to look his way. Doing so, she knew, would break open the dam of emotions churning inside.

The captain removed his glasses. "Everything looks in order. She can stay here for now and take her meals in the chow hall."

Captain Standart reached across the table and gave Helene a firm handshake. "We appreciate your help."

Helene sighed. "I'll do my best."

"You will report to me at 0800 hours," he stated. His voice softened. "That's eight o'clock in the morning."

"And my children?"

"They will be well cared for." His eyes twinkled. "Until we can find a better arrangement, one of the nurses can watch them for a few days." He laughed. "Compared to their regular duties, I'm sure any one of them would jump at the chance to play with a couple of kiddies."

Peter joined in the captain's laughter, and Helene felt the tension melt from her shoulders like a chain-mail cape falling to the ground. She considered requesting her new friend Rhonda, but she wasn't sure if that would be appropriate.

"What do you call the little tykes?" Captain Standart asked.

Helene looked to Peter, unsure of the question.

"Your children. He wants to know their names."

"Anika and Petar."

The captain raised an eyebrow. "I see. I'll tell the head nurse to send someone to your room first thing in the morning."

Peter placed his hand on the small of Helene's back. His touch felt warm and protective.

Helene took a few steps toward the door, then turned back to the captain. "Uh, sir."

He glanced up from his paperwork.

"I'm sorry, but I . . . I don't have any way to tell the time, and I don't want to be late."

"Sergeant Scott," Captain Standart said with an amused lilt in his voice, "could you find this lady a watch?"

"Will do, sir." As Peter escorted Helene from the room, she could hear the captain chuckling.

The long hall was empty, and as soon as the door was shut Helene fell into Peter's arms. Her shoulders shook as the realization of what she'd faced over the past forty-eight hours hit her again.

"Everything will be okay." Peter stroked her hair. "They called me back from Landsberg. I'm here. I'm here." His breath felt warm against her ear.

"What would I do without you?" She nuzzled her face into the crook of his neck. Peter's arms closed around her.

Helene pulled back. "I'm sorry," she murmured.

Peter took her face in his hands. With his thumb he wiped a tear that had managed to break free. "You've been through a lot. Why don't we get you back to those children? I can't wait to see them."

They proceeded down the hall and out the door, then headed across the compound. Peter's easy swagger reminded Helene of a lanky adolescent boy—slightly slouched over, arms swaying gently.

The morning sun was at half-mast and golden light crept over the distant mountains. High Alps towered in the distance. Behind Helene and Peter loomed another set of hills. And beyond that, a small town where Helene knew her father was thinking of her.

"Peter," she asked as they stepped through the door of the barracks, "do you think you can get word to my father? Let him know we're well?"

"I don't know. The full occupational forces have arrived. No one is allowed in or out. It's a miracle you made it."

Helene thought of her prayers. She sensed Michaela was praying too. *Yes, a miracle.*

"Even a simple telegram?"

Peter ran his fingers through his hair, then glanced at her. "I just don't think it would be safe. It would draw too much attention. The lower the profile he keeps, the better."

"Of course," she answered. "It was too much to ask."

Peter looked up and down the hall, then spoke in a low voice. "You don't know, do you? You still don't realize who he is."

"He's an innkeeper. His property was used to keep military supplies, and—"

The look Peter gave her indicated that wasn't what he meant.

"What do you know that I don't?"

He led her to a corner of the hall farthest away from the doors. He leaned close, his voice scarcely audible. "I wish I could tell you more. But just know your father is a great man. His assistance saved many prisoners' lives. And his work is not finished."

Helene thought back to the last time she'd seen her father. "Trust me," he had said. But obviously, from the secrecy Peter and her father maintained, it was she who could not be trusted.

Thirty

AUGUST 3, 1945

Peter couldn't comprehend what was happening. He understood Mr. Katz's reasons for convincing Helene to leave the Russian zone. And Captain Standart's eagerness to receive her statements made perfect sense. But the fact that the sight of her made Peter's palms sweat and his mouth dry out—that was the mystery. Wasn't it Michaela he had longed to be with? Wasn't it the petite Polish girl he cared so much for?

When they returned to Helene's room, Peter was greeted with a huge hug from Anika. He squatted and pulled her into his arms.

"Why, Scotty, is that you?" a female voice asked.

Peter looked up, recognizing the pretty nurse from one of the hospitals he'd visited while picking up German prisoners. "Well, hello, Rhonda. What are you doing here?"

She juggled little Petar in her arms. "One of Captain Standart's more enjoyable orders." She laid the baby on the cot and smirked at Peter. "So, why are *you* here?"

Peter stood, holding Anika in the crook of his arm. He patted Helene's shoulder. "I'm helping a friend."

Rhonda regarded them with amusement. "A friend, huh? Baby Petar indeed." She cocked her head and raised her eyebrows. "Well, have fun . . . but not too much fun."

Peter noticed Helene's cheeks flush. She thanked Rhonda for her help, and the nurse winked at Peter on her way out.

Swinging Anika to the floor, Peter sat on the cot and leaned over the month-old baby. "Look at you. You're so big." He tickled Petar's feet and the baby squirmed. "You don't look like a little blob anymore, no, you don't."

Helene laughed. She sat down next to them on the cot and folded her hands in her lap. Peter longed to weave his fingers through hers, but resisted the urge. "I'm glad you made it."

"It wasn't easy. I'll tell you all about it sometime."

He studied her face. "I'd like that."

Anika introduced Peter to Raggedy Ann. Then she twirled the doll in a wild dance, her dress poufing out like a bell around her legs. Peter laughed. Encouraged by his attention Anika danced about the room, humming a lively melody.

"You remind me of Carmen Miranda," he said.

"Who?" Anika asked, her feet still bebopping.

"A Brazilian lady who dances with fruit on her head."

"Carmen Miranda, Carmen Miranda," Anika chanted as she continued dancing.

"Thank you for the letter you wrote to Captain Standart for me," Helene said. "We'd still be stuck in the Russian zone if it wasn't for you."

"No problem," he answered.

"So you've heard from Michaela? And Lelia?"

"They both sent the letters I needed to convince Captain Standart of your validity." He pulled two slips of paper from his pocket. "And they each sent a note for you."

"You were able to get notes to them so quickly?"

Peter smiled. "It's amazing what buddies crisscrossing the continent are able to accomplish for you."

Helene opened the one from Lelia first. "Would you like me to read them out loud?"

"If you don't mind."

Helene cleared her throat. "Dear Helene. It has not been long, but I miss you already. I am in France at a camp for military wives. Josef is finishing his duty. I would be lonely here except for the other women. Most of us get along well. I will try to write more later. Give the kids a hug for me. Love, Lelia." Helene laughed. "She never was one for many words."

Peter smiled. "No, I would never accuse her of that."

Next she opened the note from Michaela. "Greetings, my friend! Peter wrote and said you might have to leave St. Georgen. I understand, although it must be hard to leave your father. Is there any chance he could join you? My country is also occupied by our friends from the North. First the Nazis, then . . . But I really shouldn't write too much. I also shouldn't complain. We found a place to stay, and I have a job sewing for a woman in town. She has a personality that is almost as bland as the soup at the camps."

Helene chuckled, then continued reading. "At least I can work for a little food. Our 'church' will be meeting under a large oak in the park until we can find a building. I just have to remind myself that my Savior's favorite place to worship was in the open fields and hills of Galilee. I'd better say good-bye. Tell Anika I miss her giggles, and give baby Petar a peck on the tip of his nose for me. Also tell Peter I think of him often. Not an hour goes by when I don't ponder your friendship. Sending all my love, Michaela."

Peter suddenly felt the room growing warm. The mention of Michaela, the closeness of Helene. He had to admit it felt good to have her beside him. Helene had always fascinated him. He remembered her determination as she'd carried that first pot of milk into the camp. Her tender concern for the weak and dying. He thought of the time he had caught her watching him from the window of the big yellow house.

"Thank you for sharing the letters," he said. "But I should get going."

Helene rose. "I understand." She rubbed her hands along her skirt, attempting to press out the wrinkles. "You have work to do."

Peter didn't tell her he had the day off. "It's a nice walk around town if you want to get out," he suggested. "Who knows? Maybe I can meet you for dinner at the chow hall."

"That would be nice."

"See you then?" he asked.

"Yes," Helene said as she closed the door behind him.

Peter drifted into the hallway. He leaned against the wall and rubbed his chin as he seared another one of Helene's expressions into his memory. This one said "I miss you" before he even had a chance to leave.

☙   ☙   ☙

A letter was waiting for Peter when he arrived back in his room. He recognized his sister's loopy script.

Sinking onto his bed, he tore the end off the envelope and shook it. Three folded sheets fell out. One was a newspaper clipping from the *New York Times*, May 8, 1945. The headlines read:

THE WAR IN EUROPE IS ENDED!
SURRENDER IS UNCONDITIONAL.
V-E WILL BE PROCLAIMED TODAY.
OUR TROOPS ON OKINAWA GAIN.

The center-page photo showed a wild crowd. The caption read, "Thousands fill Times Square in spontaneous celebration."

Peter ran his hand over the photo and tried to imagine what it would be like to be on American soil. It was all his men talked about. He couldn't bear the thought that most of them would likely set foot in Japan before the United States. Rumors circulated that some of the Eleventh's equipment was already being transported in that direction.

Peter unfolded the other two pages.

July 17, 1945

Dear Big Bro,

I thought you would enjoy seeing the clipping from V-E Day. Quite a celebration, don't you think? Things were not as wild here, but a few of my friends and I went out for a night on the town. Dinner and the cinema! I'm sure things are different where you are. (Just where are you? Ha, ha!)

One of the things I'm most excited about is the thought of some of our boys coming home. We've heard through the grapevine that some may return home for leave, or even for good. Who knows? Perhaps by the time you receive this letter the war in the Pacific will also be over. Wouldn't that be wonderful?

Around here all people talk about is transports in and transports out. Remember the Italian internees who were being held in Fort Missoula? Well, word is they'll be returning to Italy now. My friend Jeanie is trying to talk me into driving down to the fort with her to wish them farewell. I told her, "No way." It's not worth a two-hour drive.

Although we try to keep merry attitudes for the sake of those returning, every soldier who comes home stirs memories of those lost. I try to keep a happy face, but I feel I can tell you the truth. I've attended enough memorials for a lifetime.

I had been holding off telling you, but if you're coming home anytime soon, I might as well. I'd hate for you to be shocked by what you discover when you get here. Three guys from your class have been killed. David C., Billy, and Allen. Also gone is the entire eleven-man starting lineup of the 1940–41 Montana State College football team. Remember when we used to go to their games? I just can't imagine a whole starting lineup gone.

I hate to end this letter on such a sad note, but it's time to sign off. I have to be at work in an hour. Please write and let me know if you'll be one of the lucky ones coming home soon.

Love,
Annie

P.S. As you requested, I sent a package to the woman you mentioned. It should be there soon. I could tell by your note that your interest lies in more than just her health and welfare. Don't be shocked, big brother. A sister can always tell. Please let me know if I might expect to be an aunt soon. And send photos too!

Peter dropped the letter onto the bed. An aunt? Wherever did Annie get that idea? Unless . . . unless she thought it was Helene who had caught his fancy, not Michaela.

Peter scratched his head. What had he written in that letter?

🐾   🐾   🐾

The day passed slowly for Helene. Even after a stroll around the compound, lunch, and naps, it seemed forever until dinner. By the time they made their way to the chow hall, Anika was a bundle of energy. Petar weighed heavy in Helene's arms.

Entering this time, Helene felt more confident. She again noticed many eyes on her. But as before, the men soon resumed their eating, their conversation accented with the chinks of metal forks hitting metal plates.

Helene searched for Peter's face, his shoulders, his hair, but he wasn't there. She sat Anika down at an empty table and gave her the baby to hold. Then she filled up two trays and brought them back. She held the baby with one arm, and ate with the other hand while she watched the door. Did she feel so desperate for Peter's company because he was all they had left? Michaela was gone, and so were Lelia and her father. Peter had become the only familiar face.

Or was there more to her feelings than that?

Helene chastised herself for thinking such things. But she had to admit her feelings toward Peter had changed, though she couldn't pinpoint exactly when the transition had begun. When she'd first met him, she considered him nothing more than a kind American hero. After that, she enjoyed him for the wonderful person he was. His sense of duty. His tender heart.

But he cared for Michaela. And Michaela was everything she wasn't. Helene knew she shouldn't become hopeful of what could never be. Besides, how could she be sure of her feelings? She had made wrong decisions before. Helene knew if she ever decided to become involved with a man again, she'd have to chose someone who loved God and could join her on her journey of faith.

Helene was almost finished with their meal when Anika let out a happy squeal. Before Helene could stop her, the girl jumped from the table and ran toward a soldier standing in the doorway. It was Peter. He lifted Anika into his arms and waved. Helene waved back.

All the reservations she had a moment before melted away.

Peter sat beside her. "If I told you I've arranged for some friends to watch the kids tonight, would you be interested in taking a stroll through town?"

Helene placed her fork and knife on her plate. Friedrich had escorted her through the streets of Linz many times before. She remembered the Nazi parties, the drinking, the cursing, and the blonde escorts that had hung on the arms of party members like trophies. The thought made her shudder.

But this was different. Peter was different. *Oh, Lord, help me to know.*

Then again, what could be wrong with a simple stroll?

"Should I change?" As soon as she said it, Helene chastened herself. She had brought only three dresses with her. One she wore, one was filthy from traveling, and the other would need to stay clean for tomorrow's meeting.

He smiled. "You're perfect just the way you are. I wouldn't change a thing."

Helene felt heat rise to her cheeks.

Peter walked her and the children to his house, where they dropped off the children with a few buddies of his. After promising to be back before Petar's next feeding, the two headed toward the center of the old city.

"See that building with the dome?" Helene said, pointing. "It's the Palais Kaufmännischer Verein, where congresses, fairs, and balls are held."

"Of course." Peter dug his hands into his trouser pockets. "I should have known you've been here before."

Helene twisted a blonde curl around her finger. "Many times. I was dragged to Nazi parties and forced to mingle with people I had no desire to know. I had to act interested in their families, their landholdings, and their travels. I'm sure many thought less of me because I was a simple peasant from St. Georgen."

Peter seemed intrigued. "Perhaps you should be giving me the tour."

"I'm sure you've seen everything before. But there is

something I'd like to show you. It's my favorite." Helene led him onto a side street, down an alley, and into an open courtyard. "This is Linz's main city square, Hauptplatz. Those pastel-colored buildings are from the seventeenth and eighteenth centuries. And see that large pillar? It's beautiful close up."

They quickened their steps and soon reached it. It stood taller than the surrounding buildings. A gold sun and cross graced the top.

Peter tipped his head back. "It's massive."

"That's the Dreifaltigkeitssäule, or Trinity Pillar. It was built in 1723. The people of the town built it in gratitude for salvation from war, plague, and fire. It had been a bad few years."

"Kind of a gaudy thing, don't you think?"

"I think it's a beautiful symbol."

Peter looked at her, rubbing his neck. "Well, I'm so happy the war in Europe's over I could build a pillar too."

"Oh? And what type of pillar would you create?"

"It would be a statue of a beautiful woman. The saint of Camp Gusen."

Helene stared at the white marble. "Michaela would be honored."

Peter touched the base of the pillar, his fingers tracing the delicate design. "I was talking about you."

Helene took a step back, nearly bumping into someone passing by. "Me? A saint? Far from it." She shook her head and began walking again. "Truly, Peter, you shouldn't tease."

He caught up to her and matched her pace. "You don't think the army would let you stay here if they didn't think your help was special, do you? Saving the lives of many people is nothing to be humble about."

Helene stopped. "But I was weak. My help came too late for many."

A group of soldiers passed by, casting her appreciative glances. Helene lowered her voice. "Besides, it was I who received so much. My whole life is different because of Michaela."

They resumed walking, their arms touching every now and again. In their closeness Helene caught a whiff of Peter's cologne. It reminded her of pine trees after the rain.

"You got my letter, didn't you?" she finally asked. "And what I wrote about my newfound faith?"

"Yes." Peter dug his hands into his pockets again. "And I'm happy for you."

They strolled past the Old Cathedral. Music poured from its doors.

"Do you believe in God, Peter?"

His brow furrowed. "I did before the war. I guess I do now too. It's just so confusing. Too many questions. Like, why am I still here and so many others aren't? Why does my best friend still fight for his life in a German hospital? Why do people like Michaela end up in death camps?"

"I wish there were easy answers."

They meandered down a narrow street that was a strange mix of bombed buildings and unscathed ones.

Their footsteps echoed on the cobblestone. The street ended at a park. Lamps had been lit along its borders, and crickets could be heard from the river beyond. Up on the hillside a castle hovered over the town like a hen over her chicks. It reminded her of the castles near Friedrich's childhood home.

"We should get back," she said finally. "I'm sure my children are tired, and I'd hate for your friends to have to deal with that."

Peter chuckled. "Oh, they'd love that." They headed toward the army base. When they were nearly there, Peter stopped. "I almost forgot." He pulled a folded piece of fabric from his shirt pocket. Unwrapping it, he took out a delicate silver watch and held it out to Helene. "For you."

She was enchanted by the intricate band and tiny face. "It's beautiful."

"My orders," he said with a grin.

"Oh, but I never expected—" She took it from him and attempted to place it on her wrist. The clasp slipped from her fingers.

"Here, let me help." Peter took the watch. Helene held up her arm, and he carefully fastened the clasp. Then he gently took her hand and held it up. "Just how I imagined it."

Helene pulled her hand from his grasp, and they continued on to his house, where her children awaited their return.

After talking with his friends for a few minutes, Peter followed Helene and her children to the door. "Are you sure I can't escort you back?"

Helene kissed the top of Petar's sleepy head. "I can see my building from here. There's no need."

Peter gave her a tender smile. "Thank you for the tour. See you in the morning?"

"In the morning."

Helene glided across the compound, the cool night air caressing her skin. Anika hummed a tune that Helene identified as American jazz.

A few scraggly trees lined the sidewalks, reminding her of the oaks back home in her father's yard. As she passed one, a stirring in the leaves caused her to look up. She thought she saw legs dangling from a branch. Before she could run or cry out, the figure jerked, hurling something at her.

Helene bent to protect Petar, and a hard object struck the side of her face. She stumbled, almost losing her grip on the baby. Pain stung her face.

Suddenly a jagged rock crashed into the sidewalk in front of Anika's feet. "Mutti!" she screamed, tugging on Helene's arm.

Petar wailed.

"Mutti, carry me!"

"No, Anika, run!" Helene darted toward her housing unit, her vision blurred. Something else struck the sidewalk behind them.

Anika's screams intensified as Helene dragged her along. "Mutti, my arm!" Helene noticed blood on her daughter's sleeve. She grabbed the girl's hand, clutching Petar even tighter, and ran.

When they finally reached the building, Helene released Anika's hand and grasped the doorknob. It was locked. She pounded against the metal door. Her knuckles stung from the impact. "Let us in!" She looked back over her shoulder, expecting to see her attacker right behind her. Instead he dashed across the lawn away from her.

The door opened. Helene pushed past a soldier, her body trembling under heavy sobs. She scrambled to her room, hearing shouts but couldn't understand the words. She released Anika's hand and opened the door to her room.

As Helene laid little Petar on the cot, she noticed blood on his shoulder. She gasped and searched for the wound. Not finding anything, she touched the side of her head. Blood soaked her fingers. Anika screamed.

The soldier who'd let them into the building appeared in the doorway. "Are you all right?"

She begged him to get a doctor, then pulled Anika to her and collapsed on the cot next to Petar. Within minutes a medic with a white armband came in. He checked the cut on her head, cleaned it, and placed a cloth over the wound. Then he took her hand and placed it over the cloth. Although she couldn't understand his words, she knew he was telling her to keep pressure on it.

Just as the medic left, Peter burst through the door, his eyes wild. "Are you okay?" He knelt beside her cot. "This is my fault. I should have walked you back."

The baby had fallen into a fitful sleep on the cot.

Anika stood beside the cot, her breath coming in gulps. "Somebody threw stuff at us."

Peter held out his hand. In it was a broken piece of brick. "We found this outside. Someone knows you're here. I'd just like to know how he got onto the base."

Helene stared at the brick. On it tiny words were written in white. Her name, Friedrich's, Anika's, Petar's, and her father's. On the other side it read, *Open your mouth and you will lose them.*

Helene didn't understand. Friedrich was already dead. Her father was still in the Russian zone. "Why would anyone do this?" Helene sobbed. "Is it because my husband was a Nazi? Because my children are the babies of a Nazi?"

A haughty face popped in her mind. *Arno.* The one person who knew where she was. The only man who was with Friedrich at his death. She opened her mouth to tell Peter of her suspicions, when he cut in.

"We have to relocate you," Peter said.

"What should I do?" She rubbed Anika's back, trying to calm her daughter and herself.

"Nothing tonight. I'll talk to Captain Standart first thing in the morning. In the meantime, I'll make sure guards are stationed by your door and window."

"Thank you." Helene's head throbbed and her eyelids felt heavy. She thought again about telling Peter about Arno, but decided it could wait until morning. It would be too much to try to explain with her head aching so.

Peter crossed to the door. Helene couldn't help but

344

notice how handsome he was, couldn't help but realize how much she needed him.

"You're a strong woman, Helene. I'm proud of you." Then he left without another word.

Helene succumbed to the urge to sleep. When Petar awoke during the night, she could hardly stay awake. As he nursed, she touched the bandage on her forehead.

Why is this happening, Lord? Since confessing her faith in Him, it seemed her life had become even more difficult than before. Wasn't everything supposed to turn out all right for God's children?

But even as Helene thought that, she knew it wasn't true. Michaela was a strong believer, and look at the hardships she had faced.

And perhaps was still facing.

ə   ə   ə

Michaela tied the red scarf around her hair. "Thank you, Marek. It's perfect."

"I thought it would protect your head from the hot sun." He picked up his walking stick. "Are you sure you're up to this?"

She glanced down at her sturdy shoes and examined the trail before them. "Tak jest, of course. I used to hike this in ten minutes."

Marek frowned. "You are not as healthy as you were then. Besides, I wasn't talking about the walk. Are you ready in your heart?"

Michaela pressed her fingers to her temples. Many

times she had imagined the day she'd visit Georg's final resting place. Over the years she'd composed various eulogies, things she would like to say, emotions she'd share. Now the time had come. "I'm ready," she said solemnly, taking the lead.

They had only been on the woodsy trail a few minutes when Marek grabbed her arm. She'd been so taken by the dark green branches shading their journey and the numerous birds chattering among the trees, she hadn't noticed a man approaching. She recognized him immediately, though he was older and sadder than the last time she'd seen him.

"Filip," she called. It was Jacek and Lidia's neighbor who had been so nice to her and Lelia long ago. She started to wave, but Marek caught her arm.

"No, Michaela, you will regret it. Let's leave."

"What are you talking about? It's Filip." Her smile faded as she noticed the scowl on Marek's face. "What's wrong?"

"Don't you know?" He released her arm. "He is the one who reported your family, turned in you and Lelia."

Michaela felt the strength drain from her limbs. "No." She glanced back to where Filip had been standing, but he was no longer there. Confusion and anger surged inside her.

Marek took her hand. "Come. We will do this another day."

Michaela followed, but now a new conversation played in her head. The peaceful thoughts of the moment before were replaced with seething words. Anger she hadn't experienced since the camps pumped through her. The next time she saw that man, she'd be prepared. She'd let him know exactly how she felt about his betrayal.

Michaela ripped the scarf from her head, trudging back the way she'd come.

Thirty-One

You'll be moving to a town called Gmunden," Peter told Helene the next day, lightly touching the bandage on her face.

The name sounded familiar. "Isn't that by Lake Traun?"

"Yes. An American headquarters has been established there. It's a nice place." He grasped her hand. "We're taking you there tonight. The army was foolish to think they'd suppressed all Nazi supporters. You and I should never have walked so openly in town."

"I should have known better," Helene admitted.

"I'll be back for you tonight. Until then, there are many arrangements to make." He gave her hand a quick squeeze.

"Don't worry. I won't go anywhere."

"Come in, Sergeant," Captain Standart called from behind his desk.

Peter entered the dimly lit room. "Captain." He saluted.

"At ease." Captain Standart pointed to the chair, and Peter sat. "I heard about the incident last night. We should have known there'd be some who wouldn't want that young lady to open her mouth." He leaned forward. "What do you propose we do? Gmunden will work for a while, but we need a more permanent solution."

Peter cleared his throat. "I think the only way she'll really be safe is to leave the country altogether. Perhaps, after Helene's given us the information we need, she could be moved to France or Great Britain."

"Maybe even leave the continent?" Captain Standart raised an eyebrow.

"Sir?" Peter asked.

"How about I put in a request for a United States visa? The quota is filling fast, but it's worth a try."

The thought of Helene moving to the States made Peter's head spin.

"I'll file the papers today. We should have an answer in a few weeks."

"Thank you, sir." Peter rose, holding back his elation. He turned to leave.

"One more thing," the captain called to his back.

Peter did an about-face. "Sir?"

"Don't mention it to her yet. I can't make any promises."

"Yes, sir." With a parting salute, Peter left the room.

The day passed slowly. Army personnel brought meals to Helene and her children. The food tasted good, and she appreciated the personal attention, but it hardly compensated for being caged within four bare walls.

Anika was in a difficult mood. Nothing pleased the girl—not stories, songs, or the few meager items Helene had found for her to play with.

Helene's head ached. Every time she moved, a throbbing pain shot through her temple. "Please just leave me alone," she begged Anika when the girl insisted on climbing over her. Helene found the Raggedy Ann doll and gave it to her daughter. "Here. Go play over there."

"Over there" consisted of a bare corner of the room. Anika's lip trembled, and then her chin jutted out in defiance. Helene recognized that expression all too well. The thought of her daughter picking up Friedrich's bad habits made Helene's head pound even more.

Anika plopped down facing the wall, her doll tucked under her arm.

Helene rifled through the satchel. She had to do something to make herself useful. She decided to make a list of the items she needed to acquire in Gmunden. She'd need soap. There was laundry to do—especially Petar's diapers. She glanced at their clothes, some of which had been torn during their escape. She needed thread for mending.

Before she could find pen and paper, Helene's thoughts were interrupted by Anika's clamor in the corner. The girl threw Raggedy Ann against the wall. "Undress! Line up. Filthy vermin."

Helene's heartbeat quickened. She knew where her daughter had heard those words. They'd blared from the camp loudspeakers day and night when they'd lived with Friedrich. During quiet nights, the shouting filtered into the house, even with the windows closed.

Anika picked up her doll and shook it hard.

Helene lunged from the cot. "No!" She lifted Anika to her feet. "What are you doing? What are you saying?" Helene's grip tightened around Anika's arms. Anger and horror surged through her. Anika winced, then began to cry.

Helene let out a guttural moan and released her grip. Anika sank to the ground and glared at her mother, then curled in a ball against the wall.

"I'm sorry." Helene slumped to the ground and stroked her daughter's head. Although the crying stopped, Helene's chest felt heavy. *What have we become?*

Anika cautiously climbed into her mother's lap. Helene clung to her daughter and rocked her gently on the cold, hard floor.

"Please don't say those things ever again," she whispered in Anika's ear. "Those are bad things. We must forget." Even as she said it, Helene knew forgetting was impossible.

Peter came in. He undoubtedly noticed their somber mood, but didn't ask. "Is this all you have?" He gingerly lifted the satchel.

Helene rose from the ground and hoisted the baby to her shoulder. "Ja," she said, feeling vulnerable and overwhelmed.

"We'll have to do something about that later," he said as he led her and the children down the hall.

Helene didn't argue. She was just happy to be leaving this place.

The few hours' drive to Gmunden was beautiful, lifting Helene's mood. The summer air felt warm, even with the gentle wind of a topless jeep. A golden moon clung to the dark sky and reflected light against the sharp slopes and deep crags of the mountainside. Peter drove in silence, and Helene wondered if he was thinking about the view around him. Or, like her, was he attempting to keep his thoughts and fears unspoken?

Her children slept to the lull of the engine and the creaks of the vehicle. What would happen to them? Where would they all be a year from now?

She glanced at the man beside her, wondering again what part he would play in her new life. Helene knew she couldn't depend on his help forever. There would be a time when she'd have to face the hardships of this world alone. Peter, after all, was not her source of protection.

Peter broke the silence with talk about the war. "Our division, the Eleventh Armored, has been alerted for shipment to the South Pacific. They're sending our equipment ahead, which can only mean one thing. The invasion of Japan."

Helene's heart raced. "You might be returning to the battlefield?"

He glanced her way, and she caught a look of apprehension. The wind picked up slightly, the jeep slowed, and a river roared as they passed over a small bridge. "Looks like it."

Helene couldn't bear the thought. It would be difficult enough to lose Peter if he returned to the States, but to lose him in another war?

They passed the Gmunden sign and entered the village, which rested comfortably by a lake so wide she couldn't see the other side. The black waters tumbled in slow motion. Shadowed flowers nodded in the breeze. Light shone from the windows of a few buildings, but for the most part, the town slept.

"This is a beautiful place," Helene said.

Peter pulled up in front of a small cottage near the edge of the water. "You need to stay inside as much as possible. There's a tall fence in the backyard that will keep you out of view. No one should bother you here." He stepped out of the jeep and came around to her side. "I'll pick you up in a couple of days, and then you'll meet with the person who will take the information from you." He placed a warm hand on her shoulder. "Don't worry. It will be over soon."

"And you?" Helene cradled Petar against her chest. "Will you let me know if you have to leave . . . for the States . . . or the Pacific?"

He grinned and hoisted a groggy Anika into his arms. "That won't be happening quite yet. The captain pulled some strings. I have two weeks here—unless the invasion of Japan moves forward sooner than we expect."

Helene felt a weight lift from her shoulders. Together they carried the children and her few meager possessions inside.

The house was sparse but clean. The living area and kitchen comprised one room. A small bedroom held two beds. Helene laid Anika on the one farthest from the door. The baby would sleep with her.

When both children were settled, she returned to the living room where Peter waited. He looked especially tall under the low ceiling. Tall and strong. Peter rubbed his chin, a gesture that reminded Helene of her father.

Helene sank onto the old sofa. If only she knew her father was all right. If only she knew things would work out for her and for Peter. She didn't want to think of him fighting his way through Japan. Her head ached beneath the bandage.

After a moment, Peter sat beside her and flipped one of her blonde curls back over her shoulder. More than anything, she wanted to lean into his embrace. But too many things clouded her thinking. Her previous bad choices. Michaela.

Peter pulled his hand away and stood. "I need to get going. Tomorrow's Sunday, so I won't be around, but someone will be by with food for you. I'll be back on Monday."

Helene followed him to the door. She heard the lake

lapping against the shore. A distant train whistle called from a mountain pass.

"Get some sleep," Peter suggested.

Helene shrank back inside the door. "Danke." The simple thanks seemed insufficient. She soberly waved as he drove away.

The room was stuffy when she finally climbed into bed, but Helene couldn't bring herself to crack open a window. The sound of her children's breathing was her only comfort.

I'm safe, Helene tried to convince herself. Still her mind would not rest. She jumped at every sound. She thought again of Michaela and wondered if she was doing well in Poland.

Would anything ever be right again?

🕊   🕊   🕊

Peter made the long drive back to Linz feeling like a puppet being yanked by its strings as he served his country and also tried to protect those he cared for. When he entered the army housing late that night, jovial cheers greeted him.

"New York City, here I come," Jackson yelled. "Bright lights, big city, beautiful girls."

"What's going on?" Peter asked, catching a copy of *Stars and Stripes* that was tossed to him.

"You know anything about atomic bombs?" one soldier asked.

"A little. Why?"

"Well, one's been dropped on mainland Japan. Wiped out a whole city. You can bet the Japs will surrender now."

"And if they do," Jackson exclaimed, "we go home."

"Oh, yeah, smarty?" another guy called. "What about occupational forces? Some of us will be around here for a while. And they'll need troops in Japan too."

Boos erupted throughout the room. Someone tossed a pillow, nailing the doomsayer in the head.

The door opened and a soldier Peter didn't recognize staggered into the room. "What are you sitting around here for?" he asked with slurred speech. "The Austrian gals are dancing in the streets!"

The room cleared out within minutes, and Peter moaned at the mess left behind. Empty cognac and champagne bottles littered the floor. How had they even managed to find the alcohol?

A few hours later, when the sun was just beginning to rise, Peter had the common area pretty much straightened up. He'd attempted to sleep, but the noise from the celebrating troops had kept him awake. That and the questions that continually plagued his thoughts. Was the end of the war really right around the corner? Would he be returning home? How would things play out with Helene? Would she too become just a distant memory?

As the sun came up, the racket on the streets died down. Peter's thoughts returned to Gmunden by the lake. He'd first fled there after Lelia's wedding, needing

357

distance from one girl. Now he was going back there to help another woman find safety from enemies unknown.

🎵   🎵   🎵

On Monday morning, Peter picked up Helene at exactly 8:00. Two nurses had delivered food and household items the day before, and earlier that morning they'd come to watch her children. Although Helene knew her babies were in good hands, she still hated the thought of leaving them. What if someone tried to harm them while she was away?

"We'll only be a few hours," Peter assured her. "We can be back in time for lunch." They stepped through the door, and Peter handed Helene a colorful scarf and a pair of dark sunglasses. "You'd better wear these, just in case."

Helene tied the scarf over her hair and donned the sunglasses. Then she climbed into the jeep, feeling like an American movie star. Looking around, she realized that in the daylight Gmunden was the perfect movie setting. The water seemed more like an ocean than a lake. The morning fog concealed both the distant shore and the mountains beyond.

They drove to a dilapidated office building converted for army use, and Peter led her to a room at the top of the second-story stairs. A pad of paper and a fountain pen sat on a table. Two chairs faced away from the door. Sitting on one, Helene noticed that outside the tall window was a beautiful view of the lake. Birds covered

358

the docks like a feathered carpet. Through the fog, the outline of a lone boat zipped across the water.

"Do you know who will be questioning me?" Helene thought of the kind captain in Linz and wondered how the new person would compare.

Peter sat beside her. "You're looking at him." He winked. "You're my new assignment."

"Really?" Helene gazed into Peter's face. For the first time she noticed how light his eyelashes were and how perfectly they framed his green eyes. Helene picked up the pen. "Where do we begin?"

Peter straightened in his chair. "First, you need to make a list of every Nazi you can remember. Every guard and commander, their duties and where they lived."

Helene squirmed in her seat. She wrote one name first. Arno Schroeder. She added a few more names, then paused as the realization of what she was doing struck her. Yes, these were the men who ran the camps, but they, for a time, had been her husband's closest friends. With each name penned, she thought about their wives and children. Their humor, or lack thereof. She thought about their roles as camp guards, their work with the dogs, their supervision over the armament facilities in the Gusen caves. She filled one page, then another.

Helene paused, considering the engineers who had worked in the caves. Mechanics too, making sure the weapons and aircraft parts were up to standard. Should she list them as well?

Helene thought about Friedrich. She didn't even want to consider what he would think about what she was doing.

Peter examined the list as she worked. Every now and then he questioned what she knew. When did that man arrive? Did you ever see him with the prisoners? When, approximately, was his last day of service? As he interrogated her, Helene saw Peter as the professional he was.

"Now, this is the important part," he said. "I need you to think hard and try to imagine where these men would hide. Think about the parties you attended. The conversations over coffee. Did they ever talk about family in Germany? Did they discuss moving to another country? We have hundreds of former inmates who can give us names and provide detailed descriptions, but only you, someone on the inside, can give us clues to where they might have disappeared to."

"I understand." Helene scoured her memory. She pointed to one of the names. "This mechanic was from Holland—Amsterdam, I believe." She indicated another name. "That guard has family in Berlin. I remember he received a postcard once, and Anika liked the photo on the front, so he gave it to her."

Peter's eyes brightened. "Good. This is exactly what we need. With information like this, the army is going to bend over backward for you."

After a few hours of writing, Helene was exhausted. Her hand cramped. Her mind was weary.

"That's enough for today." Peter stood and stretched his arms over his head. "Let's see how the kids are doing."

When they arrived back at the house, one nurse was giving Petar a bottle. Anika and Peter disappeared into the backyard.

Helene thanked the nurses as they left, and her hands trembled as she stroked her baby's cheek. It took a while for her to shake the helplessness, fear, and anger that revisiting those dark memories had invoked.

That is not my life anymore, she told herself. Most of those men were gone. Some dead. Others imprisoned.

Still, many were unaccounted for, hiding somewhere. She touched the bandage near her eye. *There are others still out there. Watching. Like Arno.*

Helene laid the baby down for a nap, then joined Peter and Anika. Here in the mountains the weather was not as warm as in the valley. The cool breeze felt refreshing on her face and neck. Her skirt fluttered around her legs.

Anika raced around the yard, trying to catch the dandelion puffs Peter blew into the wind. Helene chuckled at the sight of them and sat on the back steps beside the woodpile to watch.

For a moment Helene imagined this was reality, and had been all along. She imagined Peter chopping firewood on a frosty morning. She pictured herself wrapping her head in a wool scarf and bringing him hot cider. He would sip it and laugh at her cold, red nose.

But in the quiet of that afternoon, she knew a different reality had been hers. Dogs barking, spotlights shining, voices shouting, prisoners crying. Instead of piles of wood chopped by her beloved, she'd witnessed stacks of bodies she'd never forget.

Thirty-Two

The subsequent days passed similarly to the first. Helene and Peter drove to the office building, and Helene wrote down as much as she knew, which was more than she had at first realized.

She remembered that two of the guards were cousins and had grown up in a small town near the Swiss border. Another guard was from a wealthy family who provided for his extravagant lifestyle. There were men who had enjoyed their cruelty and others who were known to let things slide. She told dates and events, mostly of the final months. They were not only the most recent, but also the most vicious as the guards became overwhelmed with the masses. Mauthausen and Gusen were the farthest camps from the front lines, and the Nazis had marched tens of thousands of prisoners there in an effort to keep their atrocities hidden from the Allies.

At the end of each day, Peter and Helene returned to the small cottage and spent a few hours playing with the children, sharing jokes and laughter. Peter and Helene also made it a habit to have dinner together and talk into the night about anything besides the camps.

A few times, Peter brought letters from his sister and translated them for her. He told Helene about his home in Montana, and the Rocky Mountains that ran down the western quarter of the state. He told stories about cowboys who worked on cattle ranches. And how schools, churches, and community organizations worked together for the war effort. He told her about the Indians who still lived on reservations, carrying on their old traditions. His stories were so interesting that sometimes even Anika stopped to listen.

When Saturday arrived, Peter broke the usual routine by surprising Helene at the door with flowers. "It's the weekend. No work today," he explained. "I brought a baby-sitter, and I'm taking you for a ride. We'll be back before midnight, I promise."

Helene was unsure about leaving Petar and Anika for so long, even though Petar was doing fine with a bottle. She was about to decline when a familiar face peeked around the door.

"Rhonda!" Helene exclaimed, pulling the nurse into a tight embrace.

"Look at you," Rhonda said. "You have circles under your eyes. What has Scotty being doing to you?"

Peter raised his hands in mock defense.

"Well, you certainly do need some time away. And I'd love to help. Now, where's that precious little girl of yours? I brought her a book I think she'll like."

Anika squealed with delight when Rhonda brought the brightly colored picture book out from behind her back.

Helene knew she couldn't say no to Rhonda. So she kissed her children good-bye, slipped on her scarf and sunglasses, and jumped into the jeep.

Peter grinned as he started the motor. "Here we go."

Helene settled in for a breathtaking ride. As they drove through the Alps, she was awed by the sharp peaks that jutted into the sky. They drove through tunnels drilled through the mountains and emerged to find quaint villages nestled between the folds of ridges, overlooking deep valleys.

"Want to hear some good news?" Peter asked after they'd been driving for a short time.

Helene nodded eagerly.

"Japan started peace negotiations with the U.S. yesterday. It sounds like the end is near."

"So you won't be going away?"

"Not anytime soon. Not that I know of, anyway."

Helene lifted her face to the sun, soaking in its warmth. She was sure this was one of the most beautiful days she'd ever experienced. "I've never been to this part of Austria before," she said, changing the subject.

Peter steered with one hand and shot her a carefree glance. "Just wait, baby. I'm gonna show you the world."

Helene chuckled, but inside she questioned if there

was some truth in the jesting. She had come to enjoy her time with Peter, but could he ever care for her as he had for Michaela? And if he could love her like that, would developing a relationship with him get in the way of her newfound commitment to God? As the wind whipped through her hair and scarf, hopeless questions spun through her mind.

It was too much to consider. So Helene decided simply to enjoy the conversation, the scenery, and her day with this wonderful man.

When they arrived at the town of Hallstatt that afternoon, they stepped out of the jeep, and Helene did a full circle, taking in the view around them. It was as if the small town rested in a bowl, with mountains all around and a lake in the middle. The houses clung to the side of the mountain and appeared as if a strong wind could blow them into the lake.

Peter guided her to a small building surrounded by army jeeps. Music drifted out through the doors.

Helene laughed. "You drove me all this way to go dancing?" She glanced down at her wrinkled dress that Peter had already seen her in three times that week.

"Actually, we passed about a dozen dance halls on the way, but I figured this was as far as I could come and still get you home before midnight. After all," he added, grabbing her hand, "don't you think the conversation and scenery were worth it?"

"Of course," Helene said, following behind as he pulled her inside. Jazz music filled her ears. Helene didn't understand the lyrics, but the tempo was intoxicating.

Young soldiers danced with nurses and local girls. But all Helene could focus on was Peter. She didn't want to weigh her options anymore. Her heart told her what her mind was still trying to figure out. As Peter pulled her into his arms for a slow tune, she refused to second-guess herself any longer. When she snuggled her face into Peter's neck, he held her even closer.

The time passed much too quickly. When each song was finished, they promised themselves just one more.

Finally, near midnight, they forced themselves to leave the dance floor, Peter's hand engulfing hers. "The children will be missing you," he said, kissing her forehead.

"Children?" she said dreamily. "What children?"

Peter laughed. "Stay here. I'll get the jeep."

Helene pouted as he released her hand. "Don't take too long."

He bounded a few steps, then stopped. He looked up at the stars for a moment, then walked back to Helene. "This has been one of the best weeks of my life." He caressed her hair, then let a finger trail down her neck. "I'd like to talk to you about something on the way home. About my crazy, mixed-up feelings." His face drew closer. "And about how I think I've finally figured them out. You're amazing, Helene. Your strength inspires me."

"I can't wait to hear what you have to say," Helene said, soaking in his words.

Peter kissed her lips. Then, before she could respond, he started jogging to the far side of the parking lot where the jeep was parked.

Helene sat on the bench outside the dance hall. The streetlamp that illuminated the sidewalk seemed dim compared to the star-filled night. Her chest felt so full she didn't think it could contain all the happiness. Peter was in love with her. Even before he said the words, Helene knew it. She could see it in his eyes.

She'd told herself over the past few months that her attraction to him was because of his help during the dark days surrounding liberation. Now she realized that she had cared for him from the beginning. Cared in a way a woman shouldn't care for a man unless he was her intended.

Helene sent a heartfelt thanks up to her Father in heaven. *Everything really is going to be all right. I know You're taking care of me.*

She let her finger trace the pattern on the rough-hewn wooden bench. Then she stretched her legs out in front of her, remembering the soft kiss that still tingled on her lips. *As soft as peaches,* she thought.

Across the parking lot Peter started up the jeep. Helene gazed into the night sky and wished she knew the name of the constellations. Maybe she'd ask Peter about them on the way home—after their talk, that is.

The music started again, and Helene felt the vibration through the wall. The wind blew slightly, as if joining in. An empty cigarette pack and a newspaper ruffled on the bench beside her. The newspaper was printed in English. The front page flapped in the breeze. She couldn't understand the words, but the pictures caught her attention.

Helene peered at a center-page photo of a group of men. And in an instant, her warm, tender feelings washed away in a flood of fear and disbelief.

No, it can't be.

There in black and white was a photograph of ten camp guards. The second one on the right was Friedrich.

Helene grabbed the paper and stood to inspect the image under the dim lighting. Her husband was thinner than she remembered. A worried expression lined his face. He wore strange clothes. And his arms were pulled behind his back as if he was restrained.

Where did this picture come from? It was current, she knew. Taken within the last year. She noticed the faint white line of a scar across his cheek, caused by a bar brawl the previous winter.

Did the Allies take this photo upon his capture? Did they snap it as a record of the men they were planning to slaughter?

The approaching jeep honked. Helene jumped, pulling the paper to her chest.

Peter hopped from the jeep and dashed toward her. His feet barely touched the ground, and in the glow of the headlights she noticed a childish grin on his handsome face.

"Ready? It's still a four-hour drive back, but if we leave now, we'll beat the dawn." Peter's smile faded as his gaze met hers. "Are you okay? You're white as a ghost. I was only gone a minute."

Helene pushed the crumbled paper into his hands. Her voice quivered. "Tell me about those men."

Peter stared at her a moment, then read the article. "It says they're ex-Nazis who were captured on the German border. Some as early as April. Others only recently. They're being held by the Americans in Landsberg, where they will face charges for—" He looked up, as if finally making the connection. "Helene, do you know these men?"

She nodded. Her stomach ached. "I don't understand. They were captured? And they're still alive?"

"That's what it says here."

"The date." Helene pointed to the masthead, her voice cracking. "What's the date?"

"August fourth. Last week."

She sank back onto the bench. "It's a mistake. It has to be."

Peter sat beside her. "Can you tell me what's going on?" He lifted her chin with his finger. "Is one of these men . . . your husband?" His eyes pleaded with her to say no.

"The tall blond one. Second from the right." She covered her face with her hands.

Peter's leg pressed against hers. She felt the warmth of his skin through their clothes. Only minutes ago that touch would have made her soul soar. But now, her soul felt paralyzed.

"But Friedrich is dead. That's what I was told."

Peter stood and started toward the jeep.

Helene rose and stopped him. "Peter, you have to take me there. I need to see him. I just won't believe it until I do."

"Are you crazy? They're not going to let us in. Besides, it's a full day's drive . . . in the opposite direction of Gmunden."

Helene squared her shoulders. "He's my husband. I need to see him." Her voice rose. "Don't you understand? I have to know for sure."

For the longest time Peter didn't move. Helene watched his resolve languish away.

"I'll have to call the captain to get permission." He wiped away something on his sleeve cuff that didn't exist, refusing to look at her. "And see if Rhonda can stay with the kids a while longer."

"There's a pay phone by the bench."

"It'll take a few minutes." His voice was quiet. "Will you be okay waiting here in the jeep?"

"I'll be fine," Helene said, climbing into the passenger side. *Or will I?*

Peter strode to the phone booth. Helene noticed the paper still on the bench where Peter had left it. For a moment she considered retrieving it, but changed her mind. She didn't need the photo.

Friedrich's scarred and weary face was already burned into her mind.

PART THREE

But your dead will live;
their bodies will rise.
You who dwell in the dust,
wake up and shout for joy.
Isaiah 26:19 (NIV)

IN THE SHADOW

In the shadow of the tower,
I felt oppression, fear.
In the shadow I longed for escape.
Escape has now come—
Or has it?

    Why do chains still bind?
    Why do memories
    Again draw tears?
    I seek God, and He answers,
    "Forgive him."

But if I forgive, will wrongs become right?
If I forgive, will I then forget?
So I cling to my pain
Until the heaviness grows too great
And I give it to my Lord.

    As He lifts the burden off my shoulders,
    I look into my Savior's eyes
    And see my enemy reflected in Christ's gaze.
    He sits in darkness, hurting, alone.
    "Now, go to him," Jesus whispers. "Go to him."

Thirty-Three

Dark shadows melded with the night sky, making it difficult to tell where the land met the heavens. Even in the blackness Helene could feel they were moving into unknown territory, far away from all she knew.

The ribbon of the road wound upward, and the jeep followed as if on rails. Gnarled tree limbs waved in the wind. A sliver of moon illuminated Peter's face. His strong hands gripped the steering wheel like those of a drowning man clinging to a life preserver.

The drive had been silent except when Peter offered her a blanket from the backseat. Helene had accepted, wrapping it around her trembling legs. She'd wanted to say something, and her mind tried out numerous combinations.

"Please, Peter, try to understand."

"I'm sorry, Peter, there's no way I could have known."

"This is something I must do."

But how could she verbalize her own jumbled emotions?

She considered asking him to turn around, to take her back to Gmunden, to pretend she had never seen the photo. But it was too late for that.

She needed to find Friedrich, to ask him why he'd deserted her, endangering the lives of their children. She had to look into his eyes to find out what had become of the man she loved, then hated, then mourned.

The jeep skidded around an especially sharp corner, and Helene gripped her seat to keep from sliding into Peter.

"Sorry," he muttered, slowing.

"It's all right," Helene answered.

Around the next corner, the mountains opened up before them. Below, a gigantic lake glimmered like a sea of broken glass.

Peter cleared his throat. "I need to tell you that I won't be around anymore. My work is done. I told the captain we have the information we needed. And because of the circumstances—well, things have changed."

Helene didn't know how to respond. While she should have felt relief at not having to revisit that place and those people again in her mind, she didn't. And, even worse, how could she admit to herself that she would miss being with Peter, when that was no longer an option? Instead of trying to put words to her mixed-up sentiments, she remained silent.

"We're almost to Germany," Peter said.

"This will be my first time there," Helene admitted. How many nights had she sat at SS banquets listening to the Nazis brag about the glory of the Third Reich? Now she would enter, not to see its renown, but to witness its ruin.

"Peter?" She studied his profile.

His eyelid twitched slightly but he made no other indication he'd heard her.

Helene faced the road again, rubbing the scratchy woolen blanket between her fingertips. Helene thought of her children. Thankfully Rhonda had agreed to watch Anika and Petar for a few more days. Still her arms ached to hold them, to be near them.

She thought of Friedrich. It was nearly four months ago that she'd last seen him. He had promised to come back to them. Now she knew the real reason he hadn't.

Helene had finally broken free from his influence . . . or had she? Could she ever be free from the man who'd haunted her life so completely?

🍂   🍂   🍂

The sun was high in the sky as Arno watched through the filthy kitchen window. An army jeep approached with two occupants: the familiar GI and Helene. Arno snickered as he let the drapes fall.

He'd had enough gold to buy both this little shack near Landsberg and the clunker parked outside. The Audi DKW rattled when it ran, and its imitation leather seats were worn through in several places, but it would work for his purposes.

Arno had been foolish for allowing Friedrich's wife to get away from him in Linz. He hadn't known Henri would have such good aim with the brick. He'd merely wanted to scare her out of talking. He had no idea she'd leave town.

But as soon as he'd seen Friedrich's face on the front page of that American paper, he knew she'd go to him. And he wasn't surprised when it was the American who brought her. Arno wished he could see Friedrich's face when he spotted Helene with her new "friend."

"Henri," Arno called. The boy sidled up to him from a shadowy corner of the room. "Watch the window while I pack the car. I don't expect them to come back this way for a couple of hours. They might even stay a day, though I doubt it. Still, don't let her get past you, no matter what. She can't escape again."

🐂   🐂   🐂

Peter's jeep drove into Landsberg about noon. During the war the town had been one of Hitler's top three command posts. Helene remembered Friedrich traveling here before, returning with stories of parade grounds and extravagant feasts in honor of *der Führer*. Hitler had once been imprisoned at Landsberg, before his rise to power. *And his men are here now,* Helene thought. Only this time they did not march through the streets as a well-designed war machine. Instead, each waited behind bars, separate, alone.

378

Peter parked near the prison and led Helene inside. Captain Standart had called ahead. A guard waited, offering to take Helene to her husband. Helene looked to Peter. *"Don't leave me,"* she wanted to say. Yet did she really want him to be there when she saw her husband again?

Peter stepped back. "I have to move the jeep. I'll follow shortly."

Helene knew it was an excuse, but she didn't argue. A guard led her down a long hall. Helene's heels clicked and echoed in the silence. As they exited through the back door, the tall fencing loomed before them. Guard towers were stationed on each corner of the yard. Men mulled around, filthy and thin. They looked a lot like the prisoners they had once ruled over.

The guard called out Friedrich's name. Many men turned around. In a far corner one man rose. Helene recognized his stride. His footsteps quickened when he saw her. Like a man lost in the desert, he ran to her as if she were an oasis.

"Helene, darling!" Friedrich's filthy, hungry hands reached through the fence and caressed her hair.

Helene fought a strong urge to pull back.

"You found me." His lips trembled.

Helene studied his face. He'd aged. Thick lines stretched from the corners of his eyes and mouth, and his hairline had receded. "I thought you were dead. Arno's wife brought me a letter. She said you'd been killed."

"I did that for your safety. Please forgive me." He reached through the fencing and wrapped a blonde curl around his finger. "I believed if they thought I was dead, they would leave you alone." The explanation tumbled from his lips, almost as if rehearsed.

"You did it for me?" she repeated.

Now, just when she thought she might have a good man in Peter, a love based not on childhood fancy but on triumph over hardships and sorrows, Friedrich was back, a humiliated and humble man, stealing her future. How could he say it was all for her?

His hands grappled for her through the fence. "You have to get me out," he begged. "Please." He pulled her into the metal meshing and kissed her lips, the wire pressing against her cheek.

"No, Friedrich, stop." She pushed back from the fence.

The guard behind her cleared his throat. Helene spun around to find Peter standing there. As she beheld his face, Helene was sure she'd never seen more pain in a person's eyes. Their green depths were clouded with a fog of unshed tears.

Friedrich cursed in German and spat at him.

"Friedrich, stop." She glared at him. "Peter has been a great help to me. And to my children."

"You mean *our* children," Friedrich sneered. "We need no help from an American!"

"Peter is a friend," Helene insisted.

Friedrich's face calmed for a moment as he stared at Peter. Helene knew well how his mind worked. She could tell he was considering how to use her friendship with Peter to gain his freedom.

"You're right, of course," Friedrich said, instantly changing his tone. "Forgive me." He gave Peter an American salute. "Thank you for bringing my wife to me."

"So it's true." Peter crossed his arms over his chest as if trying to hold in his emotions. "Your husband is alive." Without another word, he walked away.

Helene longed to follow, but should she? As she stepped toward Peter, Friedrich exclaimed, "Helene, you're no longer pregnant."

She placed her hands over her flat stomach. "You have a son."

Friedrich's face exploded into a grin. "What is his name?"

Helene swallowed hard. "Petar."

Friedrich's grin transformed into a sneer. "You named my son after the American?"

Helene stood her ground. "I named him after my friend."

Vulgar curses flowed from his lips. Helene started to leave.

"Wait," Friedrich called. "I need your help. There is something very important you must do for me. Something that can save us."

Ignoring his plea, she ran to the building. She had to put some distance between her and that man. She raced back through the long hall. "Where is Sergeant Scott?" she asked the man at the front desk.

The soldier pointed to the doors. "He's outside, ma'am. He said he would wait."

Helene blasted through the door. Peter's back was to her. "Peter?"

"Yes?" he said without turning.

"I'm so sorry. Could you take me back now? I need to leave this place." She struggled to hold back her tears.

His shoulders straightened. "Are you sure? We just got here."

"Please. I have to go home. My children need me." What she didn't admit was how desperately she needed them.

An hour later, as Arno finished packing, Henri shouted that the jeep was returning. The GI and the woman were already leaving Landsberg.

Arno jumped into the Audi and leaned out the window. "I'll be back in a couple of days. Have everything ready."

"Sure thing," Henri said.

Arno placed a cap on his head and yanked it down to his brows. He started the sputtering engine, then pulled onto the road behind the army jeep.

"Now, little lady," he said, changing gears and speeding up, "where have you been hiding?"

Thirty-Four

AUGUST 13, 1945

In a little over forty-eight hours, Peter and Helene arrived back in Gmunden. Rhonda met them at the jeep, and after a quick thank-you Helene stumbled into the house, aching to get out of her limp, dirty dress.

"Mutti," Anika called, running to her mother.

Petar reached a chubby hand toward Helene, and she scooped up both children before collapsing onto the sofa. She rocked them back and forth, gazing into their faces—realizing how much they resembled their father.

"I can stay if you like," Rhonda offered. "Peter just left. He asked me to tell you good-bye. He said you might need some help for a while."

"I'm fine, really. It's bedtime for all of us. But thank you for all you've done."

"No problem," Rhonda said with a wave of her

hand. "It beats wiping the rears of injured soldiers any day." She tried to appear lighthearted, but Helene saw concern on her new friend's face as she left.

Helene remained on the sofa with her children snuggled against her chest. Anika placed little kisses on her cheek as she soaked up their closeness.

The growing shadows painted patterns on the wall. Outside, crickets began their serenade to the rising moon. In the distance, gentle waves lapped against the concrete shoreline.

Hours later, Helene woke. She still lay on the sofa, her children nestled against her. Her neck kinked in an awkward angle, but she dared not move for fear of waking them. Their peaceful sleep contrasted sharply with the wild thoughts whirling inside her head.

Where to go? What to do? Helene thought of the lists of SS officers penned by her own hand. She had felt safe relaying that information with Peter by her side, but what about now? She knew he wouldn't stay around. And the United States Army couldn't protect her forever.

Helene wondered how many of the SS men she'd exposed had been captured. Not enough, she knew. Even one would pose a threat.

Most of all, Helene thought about Friedrich. Her husband lived. Her children still had a father. A man who might one day gain his freedom.

Helene sat in the darkness, her mind spinning with possibilities. The sound of a flowerpot crashing from the window box beside the front door burst through the silence.

They've found me!

Anika stirred. Helene slipped first one child and then the other out of her arms. Afraid even to breathe, she tiptoed to the kitchen. A scraping sound against the side of the house startled her. Helene pulled a knife from a drawer and raised it high over her head.

A shadow moved in front of the kitchen window. Helene screamed. A head bobbed up from below the sill and let out a bark. The knife clanged to the ground as Helene placed a hand over her racing heart.

"It's just a stray dog," Helene muttered with relief.

"Mutti!" Anika called from the couch.

Helene lit the lamp in the kitchen and slid the knife back into the drawer. "I'm right here, darling." She scurried to her daughter's side.

Within minutes, she'd coaxed Anika back to sleep. Helene slumped to the floor and rested her hands on her knees, her heart still racing. After a few brief moments of prayer, she noticed something.

On a small side table near her sat a book. Helene hadn't remembered seeing it there before. She picked it up. It was a Bible translated in German. *Did Rhonda leave it?* Helene opened the front cover, and her breath caught at the sight of her name printed inside. And under her name a note.

> *To Helene,*
> *To help you on your journey of faith.*
> *Love,*
> *Peter Scott*

"Peter." Helene ran her fingers over his name. When did he leave this? Perhaps he'd given it to Rhonda to bring into the house.

She flipped the page. There, written on a folded slip of white paper, she found the answer.

Helene,

I had planned to give this to you when I dropped you off after our night of dancing. Of course, my plans changed. I wish I could say I'm happy your family is once again intact, but I'm not. I also wish I could say all your hard questions could be answered within the pages of this Book, but mine haven't been. I just hope the words here will somehow ease the pain and worries you'll face in life.

Helene, Helene. It seems everything associated with the war in Europe has become a curse to me. I'm going to try to make the next transport home.

Wish me luck.

Peter

P.S. If you do find this Book holds all the answers, let me know. I have a thousand questions that torment me like hounds from hell.

Helene read the letter three times before tucking it back between the thin pages. The book smelled of dust and mildew, but to Helene it was beautiful.

"Thank you, Peter," she whispered into the night.

No matter what his note said, to her this Book was a glimmer of hope after a day of terror.

Helene flipped through the pages. Inside, she knew, were many stories she had heard Michaela recite from memory. Even now she could picture Anika at Michaela's feet as she told the tales of David and Goliath, Noah and the ark, Joshua and the walls of Jericho.

Turning page after page, Helene stopped at a section where small black print was scribbled in the margin. *When we get to our lowest points, it is there when we truly see God,* someone had penned. The passage beside it, Job 42:5–6, was underlined in black ink.

"I have heard of thee by the hearing of the ear: but now mine eye seeth thee. Wherefore I abhor myself, and repent in dust and ashes."

At first Helene was taken aback. *Repent in dust and ashes?* She'd had her share of both. The dust of the dead, the ash of the camp.

An owl hooted outside. The wind played on the branches of an old tree. Petar breathed a contented baby sigh. Helene flipped the pages backward. She had to know what Job's message could mean, and why she felt a stirring in her heart as she read those words.

※   ※   ※

The morning sun caught Helene by surprise. She had never been much of a reader, but through the night she had visited Job and his so-called friends as they attempted to explain good and evil and why the innocent suffer.

Helene stretched from her place on the floor where she'd stayed through the night. Outwardly she felt useless, but inwardly she was renewed. She had hope.

Picking up the Bible, she read the verse again. "'I have heard of thee by the hearing of the ear: but now mine eye seeth thee,'" she read out loud. "'Wherefore I abhor myself, and repent in dust and ashes.'"

As she read the words, something burned inside her. And as she prayed, a fog of confusion began to lift. She had heard of God many times through the years. Her mother had believed in Him. Her father too in his own way. The Third Reich had created their own image of God. Still, it wasn't until recently that she saw Him as Lord. Her Lord.

Helene had witnessed for herself what one man with limited sovereignty and control had accomplished for the side of evil. She had seen nations conform to his madness.

But God's way was different. Through Michaela's example she had seen that sometimes God didn't lead His people in triumphant victories, but rather with simple, quiet comfort. Like the comfort that had come to her that night through the reading of His Word. The comfort she felt even now, despite the uncertainties surrounding Friedrich.

Helene heard another noise outside. Rustling near the front door. She glanced to the children, still sleeping on the couch.

There it was again. She groaned and bustled to the door. *Stupid dog.*

"Scat!" she yelled, opening the door. "Get out of here!"

"Is that any way to treat an old friend?" The words rolled off Arno's tongue. "Really now, Helene."

"No!" Helene attempted to shut the door, but she wasn't fast enough. Arno pushed through, slamming the door behind him. Helene ran to the kitchen, diving for the knife. She pulled it from the drawer and spun around.

Arno held Anika in a tight grip. The girl's arms extended toward Helene. "Mutti," she wailed. Petar awoke, his scream joining his sister's.

"Put down the knife, and no one will get hurt," Arno said calmly. His fingers caressed Anika's cheek. "We're going for a little ride."

Thirty-Five

AUGUST 14, 1945

The Audi rattled down the road. Though Arno refused to tell Helene where they were going, or for what purpose, she knew. She recognized the road to Landsberg from the day before.

Helene let out a low moan. She had needed some space between herself and her husband. Needed time to think, to pray. But apparently that wasn't going to happen.

"I wondered how long it would take you to find out about Friedrich," Arno said. "It was sooner than I expected."

"If you knew all along," Helene asked, holding Petar secularly in her arms, "why did you have Edda tell me he was dead?"

"I believed him to be dead. For a while anyway."

Arno focused on the road. "Until I saw him listed as a captured Nazi. Of course I was thrilled he was alive. Your husband has information I need. And you're the one who can get it for me."

Helene glanced at her daughter, sleeping in the back seat. "What happened to your wife and children? Where did you leave them?"

A smirk crossed Arno's face. "Thanks for caring," he said sarcastically. "They're safe at her mother's."

"In Vienna?" Helene questioned, remembering a conversation from long ago.

"Ja," he grunted. "They didn't need to be entangled in this."

"So why do we have to be involved? How could we possibly help you?"

"You've already helped." He held up a piece of paper.

The map. He must have found it when he was packing her things. *So that's why he dumped everything out of the satchel before he filled it up again.*

"You lied to me," Arno feigned offense. "You said you didn't have any information."

Helene refused to face him. "How was I supposed to know it meant anything?"

"You kept it, didn't you? You had to pack light, but one of the few things you held on to was this." Arno drove in silence for a moment, then started in again. "So, do you know what it is?"

"Nein, and I don't care. I just want to start a new life."

Arno clicked his tongue. "And do you really think you can? My father used to tell me, 'If you play with darkness, you'll end up married to evil.'" He laughed. "Too bad I didn't listen. Too bad for you too."

Helene rubbed her finger against her son's cheek. Arno was wrong. She'd found a new life. One that could only come from discovering a God who loved her despite her past mistakes and poor judgment. She shot up a silent prayer as the car sputtered on.

Long after nightfall, Arno pulled over in front of a small, dilapidated house off the main road. Helene spotted the lights of Landsberg in the distance. If she could only get away—escape to the U.S. Army base. But how could she flee with two small children?

"Home, sweet home," Arno said, opening the car door.

Helene shuddered. A cobweb filled the outside window and a spider the size of her baby's fist waited in the center of it for its evening prey. "I'm not taking my children in there."

Arno pulled her from the car. "As if you have a choice."

She held Petar close and watched Arno lift Anika into his arms. The sleeping girl snuggled into his shoulder, not realizing who carried her.

Arno opened the front door, motioning Helene inside. She entered the room. A lantern burned on the table. Filthy blackout curtains hung in the windows. Helene jumped when she noticed movement from one corner. Her breathing calmed when she realized it was merely a young boy.

"My lady." Arno pointed to a jumble of blankets in

the corner. Helene kneeled onto them. They smelled of soured milk and decay.

"This will never do." She held Petar close. "Can you please get my things?"

"Henri, do as she says," Arno said, seemingly amused.

The boy quickly brought in the satchel. With one hand, Helene stacked their clothes and extra food into a neat pile. Then she slipped the baby inside the satchel, setting him on the blanket.

"What about the girl?" Arno asked impatiently.

Helene spread out her extra dress next to the satchel. "At least it's clean," she murmured.

Arno handed Anika to Helene. The girl moaned once as Helene laid her on the dress. Then she nuzzled against her brother without waking.

Helene stood. "Now, will you tell me what's going on? Why do I need to see Friedrich? What could he possibly have that you want? You have the map, whatever that means."

The boy, Henri, sat up straighter.

"Your husband promised wealth beyond my imagination, then promptly managed to get shot and captured. I'm only after what he pledged."

"And you think he'll tell me?"

"First of all, you're the only one able to see him. Second, you can use those pretty little eyes of yours, that charming smile. Cry. Talk about your future. Tell him the lives of your children are at stake. And if he no longer cares about those things, tell him I'll find witnesses for his trial. Witnesses that will get him a date with the hangman's noose."

Helene crossed her arms in front of her. "Are my children's lives at stake?"

"Only if it'll help me get what I want."

Helene sat down next to her daughter. "You won't hurt them," she stated bluntly.

"Then you'll do what I ask." Arno strode toward the door. "I'll be outside for a minute. I don't want to hear a sound from in here, you understand?"

Arno lit a cigarette and motioned to the boy. Henri followed him outside. They argued, but Helene couldn't make out the words.

Who is that boy? Helene guessed he was no more than twelve or thirteen. She thought she'd detected a hint of compassion in his gaze when she entered. How did he get involved with Arno? And why?

Just then Petar woke up with a hungry squall. Henri charged into the house. "Quiet that baby, now!"

Helene clasped Petar to her breast. No, no compassion there.

How am I going to get out of here? Helene spent the night waiting and praying for a way to escape. None came.

꩜   ꩜   ꩜

AUGUST 15, 1945

Helene lowered her sunglasses as she approached the prison. Getting past the guard at the main entrance hadn't been a problem. He remembered her from a few days before. But would she be able to make it all the way to Friedrich?

She paused, knowing she could turn Arno in. He was a wanted man, a camp guard. But Arno knew this too. That's why her children had become hostages, guaranteeing her compliance.

She thought of Anika's and Petar's frightened cries as she drove away that morning. "Mutti will be back shortly," she'd promised Anika. The girl struggled in Henri's arms. Instead of getting angry, the boy stroked her head, trying to calm the girl. That made Helene feel a bit less uncomfortable about trusting him with her babies.

She clenched her fists. *It is better to cooperate. I need to keep them safe.*

Helene neared the front desk, noticing a different soldier than the one a few days ago.

"Ma'am?" he asked with a tip of his cap.

"I'm here to see my husband, Friedrich Völkner."

The man studied the papers on his desk, then viewed her with suspicion. "I'm sorry, but your husband has been transferred to Dachau."

"Dachau?"

"Ja. They have a permanent facility. All former guards have been sent there until the trial."

"But I was just here a few days ago. I saw him."

"Sorry. Looks like you're a day too late."

"Thank you." Helene turned to leave.

"Ma'am?"

She stopped and looked back.

"Just so you know, you'll need special permission before you visit, and that usually takes a week or two."

A *week or two*? She wanted to get this over with. "Can you do that for me, obtain permission?"

"I can fill out the paperwork." He pulled a sheet from his desk. "Name?"

"Helene Völkner."

"Prisoner you wish to visit?"

"Friedrich Völkner, my husband."

"Purpose for visit?"

Helene paused.

"Purpose for visit?" he asked again.

"I . . . I would just like to see him again, and . . . to show him his children. He has yet to see his son."

The man lifted an eyebrow as he wrote the details.

"All right. If your visit is allowed, you will know at Dachau in a few weeks."

"Danke schön." Helene put on her sunglasses and headed toward the Audi. She again considered running back and telling the soldier about Arno. But no, she would wait. She had to give Arno what he wanted.

℘   ℘   ℘

"I can't believe he's not there!" Arno picked up a chipped ceramic plate from the table and flung it across the room.

Helene winced as it hit the wall and shattered, tumbling to the ground in shards. Petar flinched and let out a cry. Helene pulled him tight against her. "Shh, shh, it's okay," she murmured to him, knowing it wasn't. Thankfully, Anika was outside with Henri.

Arno pushed his dark hair back from his face. "Two weeks is too long. I have to get out of this country." He paced across the room.

Helene finally got Petar settled just as Arno seemed to make up his mind. "Maybe we don't need him. You probably know more than you're letting on." He stood before her, his grimy nose almost touching hers. "Do you have any more secrets, Helene? Anything else you're keeping from me?"

Instantly, the image of Anika humming "The Bridal Chorus" popped into Helene's mind. But she kept her gaze steady, refusing to give away any information. "I know nothing."

"Let's just see about that. Between you and his old mother, there has to be something. I refuse to believe Friedrich was perfect in hiding his secrets. Get your things. We're heading to Füssen."

❦   ❦   ❦

As they drove, Arno persuaded Helene to tell him all she knew about Friedrich's mother, which wasn't much. Mostly, she knew of Friedrich's obsession with writing to her every week.

"I told her to keep every one of my letters," Friedrich had told Helene once. *"And I have no doubt she will. They'll be important someday . . . important for the children."*

Henri provided more information. He spoke of Mrs. Völker's kindness and simple lifestyle, and Helene felt sorry for not meeting the woman sooner.

"There has to be something in those letters," Arno spouted like a man possessed. "I will show them I am no fool!"

Although Füssen was no more than a two-hour drive from Landsberg, heavy traffic and hordes of displaced persons clogging the road made it much longer. Füssen, Arno explained, was a small town in southern Germany near both the Austrian and Swiss borders—thus a perfect escape route for anyone trying to leave the country.

Before they reached the town, an American checkpoint loomed before them. Helene's fingers tightened around the door handle.

"Don't even consider it." Arno pushed his jacket to the side, displaying his gun.

Helene returned her hand to her lap, feeling utterly hopeless.

When they stopped, Arno handed over their papers. The American soldier scanned them. "Everything appears to be in order. Thank you, Mr. Reichmann," he said, motioning them forward.

"Mr. Reichmann?" Helene asked after they were down the road.

Arno fluttered his hand in the air. "At your service." He clicked his tongue. "Poor Friedrich. He's rotting in jail, and soon I'll be the one with everything he's worked so hard for."

Henri spoke up from the back, where he sat with

Anika. "I don't understand. Why all the lies? I thought you were working for Friedrich. Trying to help him. Trying to save his life. You said he was only detained for a while."

"I told you last night, there will be no more discussion," Arno snapped.

"You won't hurt Friedrich's mother, will you?" Henri asked.

Arno snorted. "Of course not."

"Or his wife? His children?"

"Nein! Once I get what I want, we'll all be happy."

Helene grimaced at Arno's lies.

A few minutes later, the old Audi pulled up in front of a small cottage.

As Helene climbed out of the car, the view overwhelmed her. When they were first together, Friedrich had told her about this place, but his stories of childhood poverty hadn't portrayed the enchantment of the region. Two breathtaking castles overlooked the small valley. Just down the road a quaint stone church rested in a pasture filled with blooming wildflowers.

The cottage looked like something from Anika's book of nursery rhymes. Helene knew immediately it was the house from the photo. The one where young Friedrich had spent his childhood days.

"Those letters contain the clue to where the treasure is," Arno said again. "A code. Encrypted messages. Something."

He pushed her forward. Helene balanced Petar on her

hip. Anika stood close by her side. She took a deep breath and knocked. Arno stood behind her, Henri beside him.

"Smile pretty," Arno whispered in her ear.

The door opened and a young man answered. Tattered clothes hung on his thin frame. Helene instantly knew he was a camp survivor. In addition to his appearance, she could see it in his sunken eyes.

Arno must have known too. He pushed past her and barreled through the door, shoving the man backward. The two men tumbled to the floor.

From somewhere in the house a young woman let out a scream. "Niklas! Please, don't hurt him!"

Helene turned to Henri. An expression of horror crossed his face. She handed Petar and Anika to him. "Here, take them. Run to the car." Then she darted into the room, refusing to be a bystander any longer.

Arno had the man pinned to the floor. Helene ran up and kicked him as hard as she could. "Get off!"

Arno hardly flinched. He shook the man beneath him. "Where is she? Where is the old woman?"

"She . . . she was ill. She could hardly move when we arrived. She died," the man choked out. "We tried to help her."

Helene searched the room for something to stop Arno. She spied the young woman huddled in the corner, hands over her head. Another survivor. *Dear God, help.*

"You filthy vermin Jew!" Arno snarled, slugging him in the jaw.

Helene grabbed a chair, but Arno had already released the man, running to the woodstove. He crouched before it, staring into the flames. "What did you do?" he wailed. Helene noticed piles of letters. Some in stacks. Others crumbled. Some simply ash.

"How many did you burn?" Arno croaked.

The man shook, wiping blood from his lip. "I . . . I am not sure. We had no wood for the fire, only those papers."

"How many?" Arno repeated, his eyes red as a mad bull.

"A few dozen? A hundred, maybe."

"A hundred?" Arno moaned. "One of them could have held the answer!" He pulled the gun from his belt and pointed it at the man's head.

"No!" the woman in the corner cried.

"No!" Helene echoed. She ran to the man, clinging to him.

"Get out of the way!" Arno yelled, lowering the gun. "Now!"

"No. I will not let you do this."

He aimed the gun at Helene. "Fine. You are no use to me anymore."

A shot exploded through the room. Helene clutched the frail man, every muscle in her body tense. A man's voice screamed. It took a second for Helene to realize it was Arno, squealing in pain as his gun clattered to the floor. He crouched in the corner, cradling his bloody elbow.

Helene lunged for the pistol. A tall figure stood in the doorway, light framing his form. Helene aimed the gun, then faltered when she recognized the uniform of the United States Army.

"Whoa, now," the man from the doorway called, lifting his hands in surrender.

She lowered the gun, her hands trembling. The soldier stepped toward her and gently took the gun. She recognized him. It was the same one who had visited weeks ago, bringing gifts from Peter.

He took Arno's pistol from Helene and tucked both guns into his belt. Then he yanked Arno from the floor.

"My arm," Arno cried, releasing a stream of obscenities. "What did you do to my arm?"

Helene gasped at the gaping wound. Then she remembered her children. She ran to the door and let out a sigh of relief. They sat safely in the army jeep with Henri.

"Mutti," Anika called, reaching her arms toward her. Helene ran to her children.

The GI yanked a screaming Arno into the daylight. The young man and woman staggered behind. Helene went to them, giving each an embrace. Their thin bodies reminded her of Michaela and Lelia when she first found them at the camp.

When Arno was secure in the jeep, Helene gave the soldier a hug, then stepped back. "Thank you. You saved us." She stroked Anika's head as the girl clung to her leg. "I'm sorry, but I forgot your name again."

"Clifton," he said with a tilt of his cap. "Dan Clifton."

"Oh, yes, the music major. The soldier who was going to be stationed by that castle," she said, pointing toward the mountain. "But I don't understand. How did you know I was here and that I needed help?"

"I've been stationed at the checkpoint for a couple of days. I happened to be walking up when your car drove past. I recognized you immediately, and you didn't seem happy. I followed, but lost you. Then this boy flagged me down, saying there was trouble with a former SS." Clifton scratched his head. "What are the odds that I'd walk up at that moment? Someone must be watching out for you."

Helene's hands trembled. She kissed the top of Petar's head. "Oh, Someone is."

Thirty-Six

Outside the cottage, Helene helped Anika gather wildflowers to put on her grandmother's grave. King Ludwig's castle cast a shadow over them as they strolled through the swaying meadow. Helene snuggled Petar on her hip. She couldn't help but wonder about her mother-in-law. How had she felt about her son? Had she known of his imprisonment? Did she realize how those castles on the hills had given him such a lust for treasure?

Later, in the cool of the afternoon, Helene sat in the small bedroom and watched Petar and Anika as they napped. She wondered if this was the same bed Friedrich had slept in as a child. The room was obviously his. And it looked as if his mother had changed nothing since Friedrich had left for SS training. A small sling hung on a nail. A boy's cap dangled from a peg.

When had her husband changed from the innocent boy in the photograph to a vengeful, hostile man?

Niklas, the camp survivor, shuffled through the doorway with a pile of letters. "These are just a few of your husband's letters. There are more under the bed."

If Arno was right, and some clue to mysterious riches was hidden within those pages, Helene was determined to find it. She had to know what treasure had caused her so much grief.

"Thank you, Niklas," Helene said, taking the pile. "How's your wife?"

"She sleeps," he said, smiling. "I will go get more of the letters for you."

Helene spent the rest of the day stacking the letters into piles, trying to find a clue. Because of Anika's song, Helene was most interested in letters where Friedrich made mention of operas by Wagner. She quickly discovered all of those letters originated from Vienna.

When she had sorted them all, Helene had found twelve letters that held the most promise. They were all dated within a three-month window of when Friedrich worked as a clerk for the Nazis. She read them each a few times, but nothing stood out. She read one again.

Dear Mother,

As you may have noticed, I have been drawn to Wagner operas as of late. They are a favorite of der Führer also, and I often search the private seats in hopes he might be present. I have been to 17 operas and have yet to see him. But I keep searching.

Last night as I watched a drama called The Ring, *I finally made the link between the Jewish race and Niebelungs, the demons and goblins, and their lust for gold. I know you think it is wrong to link people according to race, but I have found the symbolism relevant. As a clerk I record everything Jewish-owned that would provide value to the Reich. Personal items, jewelry, furniture, even Swiss bank accounts. The greedy Jews live like kings while many of our own starve!*

Helene rubbed her face. She'd been given a glimpse back to view the shaping of her husband's soul, and it wasn't pretty. She read some more. From there, Friedrich wrote about many trivial things. The price of bread. His weekly paycheck. The number of people attending certain events.

As Helene studied the letters more closely, she noticed something peculiar. *They all deal with numbers.* And the numbers were written numerically, not spelled out. She studied a few more letters, ones that didn't deal with Wagner. In those, numbers were written as words.

Helene grabbed a fountain pen and began writing down the numbers, until soon she recognized a pattern. She thought back to the map, with the route into Switzerland. She recalled the address in Chur, a Swiss town.

It could only mean one thing. Immense treasure, securely hidden where no one would think to look.

AUGUST 20, 1945

Helene sat across the desk from Captain Standart. She'd returned to Linz, leaving her mother-in-law's house under the care of Niklas and his wife. Henri, who had no family and had grown up idolizing Friedrich, decided to remain there also.

Captain Standart shuffled the papers in front of him. "Well, Mrs. Völkner—Helene." A smile tipped his lips. "You were right."

"Which means?"

"Your husband was a brilliant man. He had planned to escape through Switzerland. As you guessed, the address you found on that map led us to a Swiss bank. And the numbers from those letters . . . they led to over a dozen accounts."

The captain stood. "We believe your husband planned to use his friend, Mr. Schroeder, to help him withdraw the funds, believing it would be too suspicious for one man to extract from so many accounts alone."

"What will happen now? Can the rightful owners be found?"

"Due to the secrecy of these accounts, we can't say yet whether the owners survived the war, or if they can be reached. But the matter has been turned over to the proper authorities, and you can be sure the money will not fall into the wrong hands."

Helene wondered how many letters had been burned.

How many other people had been affected who would never be identified?

Captain Standart leaned forward, elbows on the desk. "Now, is there something we can do for you? For all your help?"

Helene tilted her head. "Actually, I was hoping you would say that. Do you have connections with the Red Cross stationed in Poland?"

"Poland?" He sat up straighter in his chair.

"Ja. You see, I have a friend there who needs help."

"A friend? I was talking about helping you."

"And I thank you for that." Helene tucked a strand of hair behind her ear. "But you see, she is in need of a building to hold church services and—"

He laughed. "Slow down. Write down all the information and I promise to check into it." He leaned back and opened his desk drawer, pulling out a stack of papers. "Young lady, you never cease to surprise me. I assumed you'd ask for this." He placed the papers on the desk in front of her.

"I don't understand," she said, seeing her name and her children's names printed on the first page.

"It's a visa for the United States. Our country welcomes you."

Helene's eyes widened. "Really? I'm allowed entry? But how?"

"Sergeant Scott asked me to check into it after the brick incident."

Peter. Her chest constricted just thinking about him. His help continued to reach her even now.

"If you'd like, I can have someone take you back to Gmunden, and you and your children can leave from there. It shouldn't take more than a month to make the arrangements." He leaned forward in his chair. "Speaking of which, where are your children?"

Helene laughed. "My ever-faithful friend Rhonda is caring for them. I'm thinking about hiring her as a nanny."

"You realize," the captain said, lowering his glasses, "you could have hired a private nanny and bought much more with the money from those accounts."

"I know." Helene shrugged. "But I've been taken care of time and time again by a God who can provide more security than any Swiss bank account."

Captain Standart nodded. "You have indeed."

෪   ෪   ෪

Peter hurried to the office. He had just jumped into his jeep, preparing to make another pickup of prisoners, when a soldier waved him down. "Scotty, you have a phone call. It's urgent."

In his time in the military, Peter had come to learn that a telegram may be bad, but a phone call was life changing.

Peter picked up the receiver, his heart pounding. "Hello? Peter Scott here."

He'd been so convinced it was Helene, calling to say that something had happened to one of the children, he was caught off guard when another female voice broke through the static.

410

"Pete? Oh, Pete, is that you?" The woman sobbed over the line. "He's gone, did you hear that he's gone!"

With the word *Pete* he realized who it was. "Andrea?"

"I didn't even get to see him. I should have found a way to get there."

Peter felt as if someone had just punched him in the ribs. He gripped the receiver with both hands.

"Pete, are you there? Can you hear me?"

"I'm here, Andrea."

"You saw him at the hospital, didn't you? He wasn't that bad, was he? He wrote and said he was fine."

Peter rubbed his eyes. What could he tell her? What words could he offer? His throat felt thick and tight. "Yes, I saw him. He couldn't stop talking about you. About how much he loved you. How much he wanted to see you again." He hated himself for not letting her know more sooner. "Oh, Andrea, I had hoped . . . I would have been there if I'd known. When did you find out?"

"Just today. I was visiting my cousin in Minnesota for a month, and there was a package when I returned. A box of all his stuff. He's been gone a couple of weeks, Pete." He could hear her trying to maintain control, her breath coming in gasps. "Why didn't I feel it? We loved each other so much; you'd think I'd know when his soul left the earth."

Peter pictured Goldie's face and the wave of his hand the last time he saw his friend. Neither had known it was a final good-bye. The phone grew loud with static, then became clear again.

411

"What can I do?" Peter asked. "Anything—just tell me."

"Visit his grave in Belgium. Can you do that? Pray over it for me. Tell him I love him." Sobs overtook her. "I . . . I have to go, but I need to tell you one last thing. I don't understand it, but maybe you will." He heard the rustling of papers, then her voice again. "There's a note here from the nurse. She wrote down his last words."

Peter held his breath.

Andrea's voice grew distant. "It says, 'Tell Pete I beat him home.'" The static increased. Peter stared at the phone through a blur of tears, but she was gone. The connection was broken.

"You always did have to win, didn't you?" He sobbed into his hands.

      🍂   🍂   🍂

The sun had just begun to set when Peter pulled up to the Henri-Chapelle American Cemetery not far from Bastogne. Peter stopped near the chapel to read a plaque.

1941–1945
IN PROUD REMEMBRANCE
OF THE ACHIEVEMENTS OF HER SONS
AND IN HUMBLE TRIBUTE TO THEIR SACRIFICES
THIS MEMORIAL HAS BEEN ERECTED BY
THE UNITED STATES OF AMERICA

A stoic soldier showed him to the grave of Lieutenant Donald Herbert Gold. He stood aside as Peter approached the marker alone. White crosses stretched as far as he could see in all directions. Goldie's grave was just one of many. Peter was sure an ocean of tears had been cried over the men in this place.

He wished he had the strength to cry out to God. To ask why. He'd spent the drive thinking about his time with Goldie, realizing that it was their mutual faith in God that had brought them together in the first place.

Peter ran his fingers over the fresh mound of dirt and thought about their early days of digging foxholes. "When you dig in, always dig a hole large enough for two," the instructor had shouted. Peter realized that, the last few years, he'd been digging for one. Just for himself. He'd left no place for God in this hellhole of a war.

The cynicism, confusion, and anger he'd created had heaped even more pain on his broken soul. He sank to his knees in front of Goldie's white cross, feeling the damp seep through his khakis. Peter knew he needed God. Needed to trust what Goldie believed, what he himself had believed long ago. He needed to have faith that Goldie had beat him to a better place. He now understood that, just like in a foxhole, God didn't always make the bullets of life disappear. Instead He provided a place of shelter with Him, and the strength to climb out of the hole and carry on.

Andrea had asked him to pray over Goldie's grave. And Peter knew what he had to say wasn't what she'd expect, but it was exactly what Goldie would want.

Peter's shoulders slumped as he collapsed on the mound. "I've really messed up this time, God," he prayed out loud. "I'm losing them one by one. Everyone who's meant something to me. Except You. I need You. I know that now." His voice broke. "Tell Goldie he may have beat me, but I know now it's my home too."

Thirty-Seven

Helene would visit Friedrich only once in Dachau before leaving for the States. She'd considered not bringing the children, but then changed her mind. Anika needed a chance to say good-bye, and Friedrich, she decided, should at least be able to see his son.

The first few days after getting her visa papers, Helene had done nothing but worry about Friedrich's trial. What if he had to hang for his crimes? What if he was released? What if he came to America, following her? Would she ever truly be free?

The train ride from Gmunden to Munich hadn't been as bad as she'd expected. Helene and her children had stayed in the city one night before catching a ride to Dachau the next morning.

The prison here was different from the first one.

Not only was it a real prison with walls and armed guards, it had previously been part of the former SS training camp.

"See that building over there?" the GI driver pointed out as they pulled up in front of the prison. Across a broad expanse of brown lawn stood a massive brick building with white doors and tall multipaned windows.

"That's where the military tribunals will be conducted. Kind of ironic, don't you think, that the guards will go to trial in the same building where they first swore allegiance to *der Führer?*"

"Yes," she said, thinking back to Friedrich's early letters and remembering what he'd been like back then. "Thank you for the ride," she added, climbing from the truck. A cold breeze hit her face. Helene tucked Petar's blanket closer around his chubby body, then took Anika's hand in her own.

Inside the stark prison, Helene snuggled Anika against her leg as she spoke to the guard at the front desk. Then, with only the sound of their footsteps on the hard, polished floor, they made their way toward her husband's cell.

Friedrich occupied the only chair. He was dressed in a striped prisoner's uniform. His blond hair was slicked back. He needed a haircut badly. Still, his face was clean-shaven, and he opened his arms at their arrival.

"My family," he called as they approached. The guard unlocked the prison door and let them in. "Anika, come to your papi!"

Anika looked to her mother. Helene smiled slightly

and nudged her forward. Anika approached her father, but remained stiff as he wrapped his arms around her. Tears rolled down Friedrich's cheeks as he kissed his daughter's head.

"My son," he called, stretching out his arms.

Helene held Petar up for his father to see. Large blue eyes peered at Friedrich with uncertainty.

Helene pulled the child back to her chest. "He doesn't know you."

"Ja, of course," Friedrich answered. She could see the pain in his eyes.

Anika glanced at her mother again, then climbed onto Friedrich's lap. He squeezed her close to his chest.

"Are you well?" Helene asked, sitting on the hard cot.

"As well as can be expected," Friedrich muttered. "I wish I had more reading material—something to pass the time. It seems memories are the only things that occupy my mind. Many of which I'd rather forget."

Helene bounced Petar on her knee. "I think the baby takes after you, don't you think?" she asked after a silent moment. "I wish I had brought that photo of you as a little boy in Füssen. You had the same pudgy nose when you were young." Helene waited in silence for several moments, watching her husband rock Anika back and forth.

"I received your letter," he said finally. "With news about my mother."

"And about the accounts?" Helene's heart pounded. She was certain she saw a flash of anger in his eyes.

"I don't understand why you did that." His voice was low. "All the planning. All the work. Years of effort. It would have taken care of us for years—"

"If it had been ours," Helene interjected.

Friedrich didn't respond, but she could see his hand shaking. He changed the subject. "Yes. I've been thinking about my mother. Especially about her prayers. But I can't remember the words." He tipped his head as if trying to recall a distant rhythm.

"I could write down some prayers if you'd like. I've been reading the Bible and—"

"Nonsense!" His fist pounded the arm of the chair. "It's foolishness. All of it. Religion is for the weak."

Startled by his outburst, Anika's lips quivered. She attempted to climb down from his lap, but Friedrich pulled her closer.

"Oh, forgive me," he murmured. "There is too much troubling me these days. Pray for your father, my beautiful one. Promise me you'll pray for your papi, won't you?"

"I promise," Anika said, and she relaxed again into Friedrich's lap.

A guard peeked into the cell, then continued on. Friedrich leaned close to Helene. "The trial date is set. Did you know it begins in March? That's still almost seven months away. Maybe it'll be over in a week. Then I can leave." He gently stroked Anika's hair. "Then I can return to my family."

Helene caressed her son's hands with her own, trying to hide her trembling. "Do you really think you'll get out?"

Friedrich spoke as if talking to a child. "Helene, have I not told you? I wasn't a bad guard. I supervised, made sure the prisoners were in order, ensured that my men were safe. Nothing more. Besides," he added, "I am a family man. That's why I need you so. I need you to visit often. They will see that."

Friedrich held his hands out for Petar again. Helene gave him the baby, and Friedrich held both children, giving each a kiss on the forehead.

"Don't they have witnesses?" Helene asked. "Ex-prisoners who could say otherwise?"

"As if any decent person would listen to the testimonies of half-crazed vermin. Nein. Besides . . ." A peaceful countenance swept over him. "I was a soldier. Trained. Loyal. What could they charge me with? I merely followed orders. It's those from Berlin who will hang."

Helene could see Anika trying to follow the conversation, but to no avail. The girl climbed off her father's lap and went to sit by her mother.

"I wanna go," she whined. "I'm cold."

Helene glanced at her watch. Only twenty minutes had passed since their arrival, but she felt it too. Not coldness, but oppression that overwhelmed her. She needed to leave this place.

Mostly, she needed to get away from this man. She'd hoped his time in prison would have helped him to understand the pain he'd caused others, even his own family. But that was not the case. It was as if the man before her wore blinders that filtered out any moral objections that might arise within his soul.

"We should get going," Helene said. "They set our limit at thirty minutes today."

"You lie." Friedrich pressed the baby's cheek to his own. "You think I am a horrible father. You always have. That's why you want to leave." His eyes began to tear again. "Don't you understand? You're all I have. My family is all that remains."

Helene rose, despite his pleas. "This place is too much for them, Friedrich. I'll try to come back alone before I leave. Then you can tell me everything. About your mother's prayers, about your thoughts—"

"Leave?" He stood, holding the baby tight to his chest. "What do you mean, leave?"

Petar let our a loud wail. Helene reached for him, but Friedrich held the baby even tighter.

"Tell me first."

"I have a visa to the United States."

Friedrich sank into the chair.

Helene motioned to the soldier who guarded Friedrich's cell, then lifted Petar from her husband's grasp. Friedrich didn't try to stop her.

She took Anika's hand and stepped through the cell door, trying to jog some memory of what she'd loved about him. But it was no longer there. The jovial smile, quick wit, handsome masculinity. All were gone.

"Friedrich," she said.

His eyes lifted, meeting hers.

"We are not all you have left. God is with you." Her voice softened. "Remember your mother's prayers. That's where you will find relief from all that haunts you."

She could see in his eyes that he considered clutching the lifeline she offered. The barred door slammed shut and Friedrich looked away, refusing her a glimpse into his soul.

As they shuffled back down the hall, Anika pulled on her hand. "Mutti?"

"Hmmm?" Helene said, deep in thought.

"That's not my papi."

The hall opened into a small waiting area. "Sure, he is," Helene said. "He just looks different. It's hard for your papi to be here. Hard for all of us."

"No," Anika said, shaking her head. "I want Peter. He was nice. I want him to be my papi."

Helene kneeled beside Anika and placed a finger over her mouth. "This is not the place to talk about that. Peter is gone. He was our friend, nothing more. We must be strong. We need to pray for your father. He has no one else now. Do you understand?"

"Yes, Mutti." Anika's voice was a near whisper.

Helene motioned to the guard behind her, who had followed her back down the hall. "Would it be possible to get a ride back to town? I know it's earlier than expected."

"I'll see what I can do."

As they traveled back to Munich, Helene couldn't help but feel sorry for Friedrich. He was so lost, so confused.

What can I do for him, God?

As quickly as she asked, a thought entered her mind. But she tossed it away. No, she couldn't do that. She refused to do that. She needed to go to America. To be safe. To be free.

Thirty-Eight

SEPTEMBER 7, 1945

A hint of chill autumn crept into the warm days. Before Helene knew it, the time had almost come for her to leave for the States. Although she'd promised Friedrich to return to the prison alone, she wasn't anticipating the journey. She especially hated the thought of leaving her children behind again.

As promised, she brought Friedrich's cause before God every day in prayer. Yet each time, she couldn't help thinking about her conversation with Anika at the prison. *"He has no one else,"* she had told her daughter. Helene also couldn't shake the nagging feeling inside. The feeling that told her to stay.

She purged that thought from her mind, and instead considered the voyage. Helene regretted not being able to see her father or Michaela before she left. The Russian zones were off-limits for personal visits, and that wasn't likely to change anytime soon. She had written both Lelia and Michaela twice, and she thought about writing Peter also. But as she held the pen, her lack of words stopped her. What could she say that wouldn't cause him more pain?

She allowed her mind to wander, visiting her home again. She imagined her father heading off to town with a quick step, and Michaela and Lelia on the front porch reading letters and sharing laughter. She pictured Peter stopping by for a visit. Why hadn't she realized how special it was when they were together?

Now that she couldn't go back, Helene set her mind on moving forward. She examined the meager items she'd packed for the journey. On the top of the pile was the Bible Peter had given her. Ever since visiting Friedrich she'd put off reading it, afraid of what God might ask her to do.

Someone knocked at the door. Helene opened it and was immediately pulled into Rhonda's embrace.

"Guess what?" the petite nurse shouted. "I'm going home too. I have my discharge papers. We'll be traveling together."

Helene welcomed the excited woman inside.

"So, I have this plan," Rhonda continued. "I'll travel to Dachau with you; then we'll leave from there. I already checked out the train schedule and bought the tickets. It's all arranged."

They sat in the kitchen together, making plans for the trip. Helene bit her lip as the woman chattered on.

If it's all arranged, Helene thought, *why am I dreading it so?*

⁊   ⁊   ⁊

The next day, the army jeep was nearly packed when Rhonda arrived. "I have something for you," she said, her red lips smiling. "It just came."

Helene took the large envelope, noticing the postmark from Poland. Plopping down onto the porch step, she tore open the package. "It's a letter from Michaela." She flipped through the other pages. "And poems." Just seeing the handwriting made her ache for her friend. Helene's eyes filled with tears before she could read a single word.

Rhonda sat beside her. "Look, sweetie, there's no way you can read through those tears. Would you like me to help?"

Helene handed over the pages and wiped her cheeks. "Thank you."

"Which would you like me to read first? The letter or the poems?"

"The letter. No—wait—the poems."

Rhonda cleared her voice and read.

> *In the shadow of the tower,*
> *I felt oppression, fear.*
> *In the shadow I longed for escape.*
> *Escape has now come—*
> *Or has it?*

425

Rhonda turned to Helene.

Helene nodded. "Please keep reading."

Why do chains still bind?
Why do memories again draw tears?
I seek God, and He answers,
"Forgive him."

Pain shot through Helene's heart. She lifted her hand.

Rhonda hesitated. "Are you all right?"

"I'm sorry." Helene stood. "Can I just read these alone?"

"Sure." Rhonda handed them back, her eyes filled with compassion. "Why don't I watch the kids for a while?"

"Thank you." Helene fled to the bedroom and sank onto the bed. Her fingers shook as she reread the lines Rhonda had just read, then continued on.

But if I forgive, will wrongs become right?
If I forgive, will I then forget?
So I cling to my pain
Until the heaviness grows too great.
And I give it to my Lord.

As He lifts the burden off my shoulders,
I look into my Savior's eyes
And see my enemy reflected in Christ's gaze.
He sits in darkness, hurting, alone.
"Now, go to him," Jesus whispers. "Go to him."

Helene lowered the page, knowing the sacrifice she was being asked to make. Yet how had Michaela known?

She read the other poems. One was about a woman and a girl escaping from the ash of the camp. Another was about two women—former enemies—sitting side by side as friends. These poems were about her . . . about them.

She wiped her eyes again, then opened the letter.

Dear Helene,

I hope this package arrives before you leave for the States. I've already filled two blank books with poems such as these. I'm no professional, but the words come from my heart.

You may wonder about the poem about forgiveness. Do you remember me mentioning how someone reported my family? Well, I discovered he was one of my father's dear friends. Someone who acted nice to me and Lelia when we returned to my parents' home. I wanted to scream at him. I hated him for what he did. I clung to my pain.

Then I felt God telling me not only to forgive, but also to love. To go to him. Helene, this will be the hardest thing I will ever have to do. Please pray for me. As I am also praying for your journey.

I am sorry this letter is so short. I must run to make sure it will be delivered on time. Please write, and send me your address when you get to the States. I love you, dear friend!

Forever,
Michaela

Thirty-Nine

It took less than three weeks for Captain Standart to cancel Helene's travel visa and find her a small place in Dachau. Like St. Georgen, Dachau was a quaint town that had been transformed into a final hell for many of the Nazis' "enemies of the state." SS barracks were now being used as housing for U.S. troops. And in a worn-out apartment not a mile from the prison, Helene and her children found a temporary home.

Helene did her best with what little she had. She made some money by mending, sewing, and doing laundry for the U.S. occupational soldiers. Her children kept her busy too, and she always tried to take time for games and songs.

She made friends with some of the army wives, most of whom were war brides from various parts of Europe.

One day, as the summer sun lost out to the autumn rains, Helene left Anika and Petar with one of her friends and trudged toward the prison. She needed to let Friedrich know that though she never approved of his decisions, she was staying by him through the trial.

Friedrich sat on a chair in his cell, equally gloomy. Helene entered and cast him a pleasant smile. He swatted the air as if she was of no consequence.

Helene ignored his gesture and sat on his wrinkled blanket, which smelled of sweat. She could imagine him tossing and turning through the night, perspiration beading on his body as he considered his fate.

After a few minutes, Friedrich turned to her, his face tight with rage. She was about to call a guard, but the look disappeared and impassive disregard returned.

"You took too long. It's been three weeks. Why do you despise me so?" He leaned forward in his chair and took her hands. She immediately pulled away.

"Don't you know how I long to see you?" he said. "To hear news of my children? To know that you are safe and well?"

"It's been difficult. I'm sorry." Helene looked away. His gaze was too intense.

"I hear you have been cooperating with the U.S. authorities. Speaking lies about my comrades." His voice was sharp.

Helene raised her hands in defense. "I had no choice. It was for my safety, for the children's safety. Besides, I only shared the truth."

"You didn't have to. You could have taken the money

430

from those accounts. That money could have saved me. You want me here, don't you?" Friedrich drummed his fingers on the arm of the chair. "Are you sleeping with the enemy too?"

Helene sat up straighter. "Of course not. I would never—"

"Never?" Friedrich lifted an eyebrow. He folded his hands and rested his chin on them. "Even for the sake of your children?"

Helene noticed the guard was watching Friedrich as closely as she was.

"I promise, that has not happened."

"Good." He sat back in his chair and smiled as if they'd just been discussing the weather.

An eerie feeling crept up the nape of Helene's neck. *Who is this man?*

"The trial is in six months. Will you be there?"

"Yes," Helene said softly.

"What?"

She'd caught him by surprise. She sat taller. "I changed my mind about leaving. I have a place in Dachau now."

He stared at her for a moment, as if trying to comprehend her words. "I don't think that is a good idea. Maybe you should go. Escape." He took her hand again, only this time without the cocky attitude. "They are going to say horrible things about me, like they said about my comrades in other trials. But you understand, don't you? You know the reasons I joined. The SS was different then. I was just nineteen. They were the *Schutz Staffel* —the Protection Squad."

Helene used her thumb to wipe away a tear that was collecting in his eye.

"Four hundred boys in my village were prepared to volunteer for the SS. I was one of only twelve who were selected. It was a great honor."

"Yes, you've told me."

"We received the best uniforms. Top-notch training. Then they sent me to St. Georgen. Why not the front lines? Why, Helene?" His eyes seemed to delve directly into her soul. "You're the only good that happened there." His voice quivered. "And you're with me now. How many other men can say that? Promise me you'll be there. I need your support."

"Like I said, Friedrich, I will be there."

Friedrich slumped to the floor near her feet. The guard started to open the cell door, but Helene waved him away.

Friedrich rested his head on her lap. "I have been trying to remember my mother's prayers," he said faintly. "Do you know them?"

Although Helene did not know a specific prayer his mother had spoken, she recited, "Our Father which art in heaven, hallowed be thy name. Thy kingdom come. Thy will be done in earth, as it is in heaven. Give us this day our daily bread. And forgive us our debts, as we forgive our debtors. And lead us not into temptation, but deliver us from evil."

Forty

Helene managed to survive the difficult fall and winter, despite the harsh weather, rationed food, and lonely days. She visited Friedrich twice a month to talk and pray. His soul struggled so. How would she ever get through to him?

The time had come. The trial was about to begin. Helene arrived early and found a spot along the rough maple bench near the window—one of six that lined both sides of the room. Bright sunshine poured into the chambers but did little to warm her. She could not shake the foreboding chill that caused her arms to tremble.

The courtroom was standing room only. Men in American uniforms circled the room. The defendants were all dressed in dark suits and white shirts. They looked like respectable gentlemen, people you'd do business with or sit next to at church. Except for the white cards around their necks that numbered them like cattle and reminded all present who they really were.

A wooden rail separated the observers from the participants. In the center of the room stood a small platform, crudely made of wood and covered with a thin carpet. A single empty chair awaited the first witness.

In the front of the room, facing the chair and the observers, a panel of uniformed American officers sat, acting as both judges and jury. A large American flag adorned the wall behind them.

Friedrich sat in the back row, third from the left. Number 55. Even months of worry and inadequate nutrition could not diminish his powerful presence.

Bright lights and a movie camera pointed at the defendants. Films of the trial would be watched all over the world. And Helene realized her husband's face would forever be associated with death and horror.

He sat tall and proud in the chair, boldly facing the American officers. There had been times in his cell when he had broken down trembling like a child. But here, Helene knew, he would show no weakness, seek no mercy. He'd been an officer of the Reich. His job had been his honor.

Arno was there too, his arm still bandaged. Number 14. Unlike Friedrich, Arno seemed terrified of what awaited him. For a moment his dark eyes bore into Helene's. She quickly looked away.

Even more numerous than the sixty-one men on trial were the camp survivors who filled the witness benches.

Frail, distraught, dressed in ill-fitted clothing, each one prepared to testify. Yearning to finally see some measure of justice.

Helene felt the hatred that seethed through the survivors as they stared at the lineup. She wondered what images went through their minds, which faces of those on trial tormented their sleep. She wondered what Michaela would say if she'd been forced to testify. Who haunted her dreams?

Helene squinted out the window at the rows of administration buildings. If she looked at just the right angle she could make out the large smokestacks beyond. Officially, Dachau had been selected as the trial site due to the abundant former-SS housing. But many also believed it was chosen because death still hung in the air. American prosecutors could easily point out the high walls, prisoner barracks, and human ovens. The place itself seemed to cry for vengeance.

The proceedings started in German. The prosecutors listed the crimes of the men.

"High casuality figures due to mass extermination."

"Gas chambers."

"Criminal enterprise."

The words swirled in her head.

One at a time the men took the stand to testify.

"We were only under orders," one officer claimed.

"Did you realize these were human beings?" a prosecutor asked, pointing a finger toward the man's chest.

The man, a former doctor at Mauthausen, shrugged. "When animals are no longer of use, they are killed.

Why not the same for people? Why should the state support such worthless creatures?"

Helene scowled and looked away. Many in the courtroom grumbled. The man beside her wrung his gaunt hands.

She held her breath when Friedrich was called to the witness stand. His casual indifference remained intact as he approached the chair.

"So, Mr. Völkner, you were a guard at Camp Gusen, correct?"

"Ja." He stuck out his jaw. "That is correct."

"It has been documented by former prisoners that numerous cases of severe ill-treatment, excessive beatings, and starvation of prisoners took place inside those walls. A great number of prisoners were murdered by SS personnel, were they not?"

Friedrich said nothing.

"You are required to answer, Mr. Völkner."

"We took appropriate action."

"Is that what you call it? Appropriate action? We have testimony that you personally beat a prisoner nearly to death for fainting during roll call. Do you remember that man, Mr. Völkner? Do you recall how he screamed for mercy? Cried for his wife and his children? Or was he merely one of hundreds of worthless creatures?"

Friedrich's jaw clenched.

"You remember the sick, don't you? The ones you loaded into a mobile gas van, and later unloaded their dead bodies? Do you remember their ashes falling from the sky? Those were human ashes, Mr. Völkner!"

Friedrich's chest rose and fell. "I was a loyal soldier," he spouted in anger. "I obeyed my orders. If you want someone to blame, try Himmler. Or the Central Security Office in Berlin."

"Are you saying that you should not be held responsible for your own actions? For killing men . . . *and women?*" The prosecutor held up a piece of paper. "Yes, Mr. Völkner, a transport of women was brought to Gusen in January of 1945. The entire transport disappeared." He glared at Friedrich. "Or maybe you'd rather talk about the children. Were there ever children in the camp, Mr. Völkner?"

Friedrich hesitated, then nodded slightly.

"Yet there were no children when the Americans liberated Camp Gusen. Where did they go?" The prosecutor stared at Friedrich, challenging him to give an answer. Sweat glistened on Friedrich's brow, yet his gaze never wavered. He opened his mouth to speak, then paused as if reconsidering his words.

Helene tightened her grip on the chair arm, haunted afresh by the memory of those cries from the cattle cars that cold winter night.

Friedrich's voice was calm. "They were vermin, sir. We exterminated vermin."

Helene could not hold back the sob that escaped from her chest. She rose from her chair and scrambled out of the room. The door closed behind her, and she ran down the empty hall, then out a side door.

Once outside, Helene leaned against a brick wall. Her body shook as she mourned for those who could no longer testify. Particularly for those whose murders her husband had played a part in.

The door opened and a man emerged. She caught a glimpse of his U.S. military uniform out of the corner of her eye. Helene wiped her face, her hands and shoulders still trembling. She faced the wall, hoping the man would keep walking. Instead he stopped beside her.

She glanced up. *Peter.*

It was really him, standing before her, his green eyes full of compassion.

"I knew you'd be here," he said plainly, "despite what it would do to you."

"Hello, Peter." It had been seven months since their uncertain parting, but not a day had passed that she didn't think of him.

A cloud passed over the sun, casting a shadow upon them. A cool wind blew. Helene felt her throat tighten, and her words came out strained. "I tried to stay away, but I couldn't do it."

"You don't need to be in there, to hear all that."

"But I do." The wind ruffled the hair on the nape of her neck. "Don't you understand? I lived it."

He reached a hand toward her. She pulled away. Peter backed off, and she felt ashamed for hurting him again.

"What are you doing here?" she asked gently. "I thought you were leaving."

"I knew you'd come. I thought maybe you could use some support. Besides . . . I always seem to end up near Landsberg."

She studied his face. "And?" she asked, her eyebrows raised.

Peter kicked a pebble off the sidewalk. "And even though the visa fell through the first time, I found someone to sponsor you in the States. If you're willing, you can still leave."

Helene's throat tightened. "If I could, I would have left months ago."

Peter shook his head. "I don't get you, Helene. Why would you want to stay in this depressed country? To mend officers' clothing for the rest of your life? Getting by on potatoes and bread? Is that the life you want?"

Helene didn't know whether to laugh or cry. "I wish you could understand. I'm supposed to stay here. As much as I'd rather be anywhere else." She paused, the implication of his words suddenly sinking in. "How do you know about the mending and the potatoes? Do you have spies watching me?"

"Call them that if you want. I call them friends. But I know these things for the same reason I know Petar is nearly walking and Anika is learning to read."

"And what reason is that?"

"Because I care about you."

Helene didn't know what to say. She had nothing to offer. "Friedrich's still alive," she stammered.

"I know," Peter crossed his arms and tipped his chin to a soldier passing by. He leaned toward her ear. "I know you don't want to leave until you hear his fate. But you have to think of your children. The United States has so much to offer. But I can't guarantee the passage beyond a month's time. I know it's hard, but you have to let go. You must move on."

She placed her hand on his arm. "I appreciate you being here. I really do. But until I hear otherwise from God, I'm staying. I made a vow to follow Him wherever He leads, and right now, this is it."

Peter's eyes reflected reluctant acceptance of her decision . . . and perhaps a little admiration. "I understand. Who knows? Maybe I can work something else out with your visa. Just let me know when the time is right."

Helene smiled weakly, but she didn't commit to anything. This was her place until God chose to release her.

"Can I walk you home?" Peter asked.

Helene faced the large windows. She could barely make out the backs of the defendants. "I don't think that would be a good idea."

Peter glanced that way too. His shoulders sagged. "I'll be around, off and on, if you need me." He shuffled back to the door. "Just call Captain Standart, and he'll get in touch with me."

"Danke," Helene mouthed, but no sound came out. *I'm so sorry,* she wanted to add. But before she could, Peter had walked away.

Forty-One

MAY 2, 1946

No matter how hard she tried to convince herself, Helene couldn't make herself go back to the hearings. Over a month passed, and she occupied her time with her children, her work, and finding a hundred and one ways to cook potatoes.

Many times during those long days, Helene considered taking Peter up on his offer. She thought of his kind, caring heart. How he'd come to the trial to support her. She wondered what it would be like to have such a man for her own. Perhaps she should leave. She wasn't even attending the hearings.

Yet in the still of the morning during her quiet prayers, Helene knew she couldn't go. No matter how useless she'd become, or how hopeless she felt, Helene knew God hadn't freed her from this place, or her husband. Until she learned of Friedrich's fate, she was bound to remain for the trial. Depending on his sentence, maybe even after.

Anika often asked about her father. Helene tried to explain that he was still in prison. Anika also asked why her papi did bad things—why he'd hurt so many people. Helene had no answer. How could she explain what she didn't understand herself?

One day, as Helene was putting her children down for an afternoon nap, she heard a knock at the door.

"I hear they're ready to give the verdict," the next-door neighbor said.

"But my children—"

"You go. I'll stay with them. Hurry, now."

Helene ran all the way to the prison, then burst into the courtroom. Several eyes turned toward her as she entered. Then the room quieted as an American officer stood.

Helene made eye contact with Friedrich as she slid into an open seat. His jaw tensed as he and the others rose to hear their fate.

The officer in charge read in a flat tone, void of any emotion. "The Court finds that the conditions and the nature of Concentration Camp Mauthausen, combined with any and all of its subcamps, were of such a criminal nature as to cause every official, whether he be a member of the *Waffen* SS, *Allgemeine* SS, guard, or civilian, to be culpably and criminally responsible."

Helene held her breath.

"The Court further finds that the irrefutable record of deaths by shooting, gassing, hanging, regulated starvation, and other heinous methods of killing were brought about through the deliberate conspiracy and planning of Reich officials."

Helene struggled to comprehend his words.

"The Court therefore declares that any official—governmental, military, or civil—is guilty of a crime against the recognized laws, customs, and practices of civilized nations, and by reason thereof is to be punished."

Helene leaned forward in suspense. Names of the accused were called out one by one. Of the sixty-one men, fifty-eight received the death sentence. The three others, Arno included, were given life in prison.

As the court adjourned, a wave of voices filled the air. Most shouted with joy. A few cried. All Helene could think about were the words swirling through her mind: "Friedrich Völkner, death by hanging."

☙   ☙   ☙

MAY 27, 1946

There was one stop between the verdict and death: Landsberg. Friedrich had been brought there upon his capture. And there he, along with many others, would breathe his last.

Helene had contacted Captain Standart. Not to reach Peter, but to see if a visa was still available. As soon as the verdict of Friedrich's death reached her ears, Helene knew her freedom would soon follow. But moving on

443

was something she had to do on her own, with God. No matter how much she desired Peter's strong arms around her, she must depend on God alone. It was Him she must trust.

Helene packed the last of Petar's small clothes. All they owned in the world fit into three satchels.

Anika ran up beside her. Petar, ten-and-a-half months old, crawled up behind Anika. "Tell me again about the big buildings in America," she said. "And the people that live close together like bees in a hive."

Helene paused from her packing and pulled the young girl onto her lap. Gone were the fat cheeks and innocent eyes. This girl seemed much older, wiser. Her hair was plaited in two long braids, one of them already half undone.

"Remember our trip to Munich, with the streetcars and people everywhere?"

"Ja."

"New York is like that, only ten or twenty times bigger."

"Do they talk like us there?" Anika asked.

"I'm sure some people speak German, but we must learn English. Remember the English words I've been teaching you?"

"Only a little," Anika said. Petar chattered on the floor as if already practicing.

Helene quickly unbraided Anika's hair and twisted it again. "Don't worry. We have a long boat ride on which to practice."

Anika ran to the front door the second she heard the

knock and swung the door open. Outside stood Captain Standart, hat in hand. The mood in the room instantly sobered.

"Your ride to Landsberg is ready, ma'am," he said.

Helene checked her appearance in the mirror one last time. She scooped Petar into her arms and smiled weakly at the captain.

Helene was nearly out the door when she realized she had almost forgotten the most important thing. Racing back in, she picked up her Bible from the table.

The occupants of the jeep were silent during the hour-long drive to the prison. Anika seemed to sense her mother's mood and sat motionless in the backseat.

When they neared the large building, her steps slowed. "Papi's in there?" she asked, staring up at the gray fortress.

Helene straightened the young girl's hair again. "Make sure you tell Papi you love him," she said, trying to keep her roiling emotions inside.

"I will, Mutti."

Helene took her hand. The baby rested in the crook of her arm. "Thank you again," she said to the captain as he led the way. "I know you're not supposed to—"

A wave of his hand silenced her. "Five minutes. That's all you have." He pointed to the second door on the left, a solid wooden door with iron hinges. A guard opened it for her.

As the trio entered the stark room, Helene saw Friedrich in the corner. He was a broken man. His long hair hung over one eye. He brushed it away and opened his arms to them.

"My family." His words were a sigh.

Helene moved into his embrace. He smelled like sweat, cigarettes, and steak. He'd apparently already partaken of his last meal.

"It's a miracle you've come." He held Helene at arm's length. His shoulders shook, and she had to look away.

"Beautiful one." He lifted Anika into his arms and breathed deeply of her sweet hair.

"I love you, Papi," she said, then looked to Helene for approval. Helene smiled and nodded.

Placing Anika on the floor, Friedrich took Petar from Helene's arms. "Grow strong, my son." He pressed the baby's face to his cheek. Petar squirmed, but Friedrich refused to let go. "Grow strong."

"Friedrich, there is something I must tell you."

He stared at Helene with a confused, haunted expression. Then he tucked the baby into one arm and caressed Helene's face with his free hand. "You are so beautiful." He leaned forward to kiss her. She tilted her head, and his lips grazed her cheek.

Unable to speak, she held her precious Bible out to him.

His eyes narrowed. "Are you going to preach to me, woman? I have one minute left with my family, and you preach?"

Helene took a step back, refusing to be silenced. "God will forgive you, Friedrich."

446

"I don't want to hear this."

It was as if she was at home again, confronting him, trying to talk some sense into him. Only this time she was not going to back down.

"Jesus loves you. Yes, you. He died for every horrible thing you have done. He will take away all of your sins, Friedrich, if you give your life to Him."

"My life?" he shouted. "What life? I'm dead in the morning."

Anika flinched. Petar squirmed and reached out to his mother.

"That's what I'm trying to tell you," Helene said. "There isn't much time."

Friedrich handed the baby back to Helene, his eyes reflecting his torment.

"Remember your mother's prayers?" she asked. "She prayed for a son who would love God. It's not too late for those prayers to be answered."

Friedrich faced the wall, trying to ignore her. Trying to escape her words. Helene heard footsteps in the hallway, and she knew her time was almost up. She had to find a way to get through to him.

She placed the Bible on the rumpled cot, then touched his shoulder. "I forgive you," she said, her voice strong. "And I love you."

He turned. His eyes, welling with tears, exuded a quiet wonder.

The cell door opened behind them. "I'm sorry, ma'am, but it's time to go."

Helene caressed Friedrich's rough face, then placed

447

a soft kiss on his scratchy cheek. She stepped from the room, holding Petar, Anika at her side. She couldn't stop the tears from flowing.

"Wait." She moved back into the room and picked up the Bible, placing it into his hands. He looked down at it, then up at her again.

She left the room. The door slammed shut behind her with a resounding thud.

"Just a few more minutes, please," she heard Friedrich cry, pounding his fist against the wooden door.

"This way, ma'am." The soldier pointed down the hall. Friedrich's sobs quieted as Helene and the children were led to the front doors.

Helene did not dare think about what would happen in the morning. An image of a hangman's noose flashed through her thoughts, and she pushed it away.

Captain Standart was waiting outside. While he drove them away from the prison, she prayed that somehow, during the night, Friedrich would find the only truth that could bring liberation to his soul.

When they arrived back at the small apartment, Helene addressed the captain. "Would you mind driving us to the train station? I'm already packed. I only have to grab my things."

"Right now?" he asked.

"The sooner the better. I cannot stay here while—" She did not finish. "Perhaps the children will ride better on the train at night."

Captain Standart didn't argue. He loaded her things into the jeep, drove her to the train station, and helped her board the train. "You've become my pet project," he said. "Europe will be boring without you."

She gave him a hug good-bye.

"Oh, the bank found three rightful owners of those accounts. They're still searching for the others, but at least those families can begin rebuilding their lives."

Helene smiled, silently thanking God that He had used her in that way. When the captain was gone, Helene examined the temporary visa papers and notes he had given her. Her hands trembled as she considered what starting a new life would mean.

"Take the train to Paris," he had written. *"From there you will be hooked up with a group of civilians emigrating to New York. The rest of the paperwork will be in order, waiting for you."* She studied the visa and other forms, then paused on his handwritten note on the last page.

> *Peter Scott*
> *P.O. Box 3470*
> *Columbia Falls, MT*
> *. . . Just in case.*

Shadows spread with the fading sunlight. Though she could not see them, Helene imagined the mountains beyond. And her father's little home in St. Georgen. North of her, in Poland, a dear friend was also attempting to reconstruct her life.

As the train lurched forward, Helene realized she was leaving behind everything she once loved. "Good-bye, Friedrich," she said, her voice hoarse, as she pressed her fingers against the glass. "I hope you find the truth before it's too late."

Helene pulled a thin, torn piece of paper from her pocket. She had removed it from her Bible just that morning.

> *To Helene,*
> *To help you on your journey of faith.*
> *Love,*
> *Peter Scott*

She held it to her chest, beginning to realize just how much faith this journey would require.

Before an hour passed, the children were asleep on her lap. Helene watched the lights from homes and automobiles flicker past until she too finally fell asleep. And as she slept, she dreamt that the swaying of the train was a thousand prayers rocking them as they made their final escape from the dust and ashes into the sky beyond.

When Helene woke, the sun was rising over the farms and meadows. She sat up with a start and checked her watch. She had missed it. She'd planned to pray for Friedrich during his final minutes, but it was too late. He was already gone.

Helene leaned back in the chair in stunned silence. Friedrich's body would be taken to the small cemetery near the prison. But his soul? Only in eternity would she learn his fate.

The conductor's voice sounded through the car, announcing their next stop. Helene realized that this *was* happening. Friedrich *was* dead. Her father far, far away. She would soon be in New York, alone with two children to raise.

Suddenly, Helene couldn't hold back the emotions any longer. A cry burst from her—and she tried to muffle its sound with her trembling hand. Through her sobs she was aware of Anika awaking, and then Petar. She knew other passengers gathered around, attempting to calm her. But the flow of tears could not be dammed.

Her mind spun back to four years ago. When Friedrich had promised her the world. With his position, they'd have status and money, he'd said. But the only thing his position had brought in the end was heartache. Heartache for her, her father, her children. Even for Peter.

"Oh, God," she sobbed. "You are all I have left. You're all my children and I have left."

She had no choice He had to be enough.

⁊ ⁊ ⁊

Michaela assessed the small group of people gathered around her. Kasia sat beside Marek in the shade of a large oak. Pawel and Rozalia tossed a large ball with Sabine. Even Filip had found a place among them after Michaela had approached him, offering her forgiveness.

Michaela smiled, realizing how much turning his acts of betrayal over to God had healed her own heart.

"Marek, can you please recite verses three and four of Galatians chapter one for us?" Michaela asked, running her fingers over the lush grass.

Marek cleared his throat. "Grace be to you and peace from God the Father, and from our Lord Jesus Christ, who gave himself for our sins, that he might deliver us from this present evil world, according to the will of God and our Father." He paused, glancing at something behind her.

Michaela followed his gaze. Two men approached —the mayor from their town and another man, dressed in a dark suit and wearing a Red Cross armband.

"Michaela Perl?" the Red Cross worker asked, stopping before them.

"Yes?" Michaela stood. Had something happened to Helene, to Peter or Lelia? Or were they doing something wrong by meeting here?

The Red Cross worker gave her a firm handshake. "Sorry to interrupt, ma'am, but Captain Standart of the United States Army has brought to our attention that your father's church building was lost in the war. Our organization is looking at the land, and we believe your property would be a perfect location for our new building. We would only need it during the week, and you could—"

"Are you saying you would build a church for us, at no charge?"

The man's eyes brightened. "Of course, we'd have to clear the former structure first, but building could begin in a couple of months."

Michaela covered her mouth with her hands. Her friends stood around her, asking a dozen questions all at once.

Marek placed a hand on Michaela's shoulder. "Some-one has friends in high places," he muttered.

"The highest." Michaela took a deep breath, inhaling the Polish spring air.

Tears streamed down Kasia's cheeks as she lifted her hands in thanksgiving to God. "Just imagine," she said, "a church rising from the ash."

Michaela raised her hands as well, reveling in the Lord's goodness and mercy. She felt her Shepherd's hand upon her, upon all of them.

"Yes," she said. "Just imagine."

$$\textrm{℞} \qquad \textrm{℞} \qquad \textrm{℞}$$

Peter wiped a stream of sweat from his brow. He gingerly lifted the canteen from the holder on his waist and took a long drink. Carefully returning the canteen, he took a deep breath of the thin, cold air. He readjusted his feet into his toehold on the marred rock face and clasped his gloved hands tighter around the rope that supported his weight.

"Are you ready to move on?" the voice above him called.

"Just one more minute," Peter answered. His feet dug even deeper into the wall, and a few pebbles bounced free from the rock, tumbling down the 200-foot drop. Peter turned his head, taking in the feel of the strong mountain wind against his face.

Scanning the peaks that surrounded him, Peter was again awed by the wonder of God's creation.

He looked up. His eyes glanced over the obstacles that remained, and then he saw it. Just above his guide, Peter spotted a low bush that seemed to grow straight from the barren rock.

"How amazing You are," Peter whispered to God. Peter had come here for her, but he had been surprised at how much God had for him on this journey.

"Okay, let's head up," Peter called in German to the guide. His fingers pressed into the rock, searching for a hold as he continued to scale the mountain wall. *Trust the guide,* his mind kept reminding him. *Trust the guide.*

His legs ached as he continued upward. Then, for a moment, Peter was sure he caught sight of the glimmer of white amidst the brush.

"Up. Keep going up," he coached himself, feeling the rope pull as his guide continued to climb. "Up, up, we go."

Sure enough, Peter caught sight of it again. The dainty alpine flower. *Edelweiss.*

She's worth it, he told himself, remembering the Austrian ritual. Soon, Peter knew, he'd be leaving for the States. And maybe someday he would be sure of her feelings. Perhaps before too long she would find a way to let him know. But for now, he'd continue to travel the paths laid out before him. He'd wait. Wait until it was time to show proof of his devotion.

Forty-Two

SEPTEMBER 17, 1947
NEW YORK CITY

Helene called in English to the boy toddling behind her. "Hurry, Petar, or we will miss your sister at the bus." She swung open the front door of her tailor shop and adjusted the hands on the little plastic clock. "Back in 15 minutes," it read.

Petar ran into her arms, and she swung the boy onto her hip. Although he was only two, he was almost too big to carry.

"We have to put you on a diet," she muttered, poking his belly with her finger. "Too much apple pie."

Petar laughed, and Helene joined in.

"What that?" Petar asked, patting her front apron pocket. Stuffed in with pins and a measuring tape, three envelopes poked out.

"Letters for Mutti," she said.

"Oh," he said with his mouth in a circle.

Helene mimicked the face, which made him giggle.

In addition to the monthly letters from Michaela and Lelia, for the first time in over a year and a half, she had received a note from her father. He was well. Busy feeding the Russians, he said. Though it was not written, Helene was sure he was equally busy resisting anything that threatened the good of his neighbors. And in a few years she hoped he'd consider joining her.

"Bus," Petar called, as clearly as if English was his first language. Actually, it was.

The school bus was just pulling away. Anika stood on the curb, waving. Helene waved back, then paused as she noticed a man approaching her daughter. She couldn't see his face, but she recognized his familiar gait.

Helene's chest filled with warmth at the sight of him. She kissed Petar's blond head and grinned to herself. Peter had come. He had not forgotten her, had not moved on.

Helene hurried her steps. Anika took the man's hand. Peter approached Helene with long strides.

"Cowboy," little Petar said, pointing.

Helene chuckled as Peter neared her. He did look like a cowboy in his Levi's and cotton shirt. Then she noted his "horse" parked on the street. "That dusty old jalopy made it all the way here from Montana?" she asked. Her heart did a double beat at the sight of his smile. She had tried to picture his face many times during her months of healing and waiting on God. But now he was here.

"You're worth every second on the road," Peter said, his voice husky.

Helene gave Peter a hug, then pulled away. "It's so good to see you. But what are you doing here?" *And how long can you stay?* she wanted to add.

He laughed. "My sister kicked me out. Annie told me to quit moping around and find you." He held up a slim silver watch. "And when I received this in the mail, I figured you were giving me a hint. Perhaps you were saying the time was right?" Peter chuckled at his pun.

Helene felt heat rising to her face. She'd mailed the watch with the dimmest of hopes. But he'd received it and had understood. She lifted her arm, and Peter wrapped the watch around her wrist for the second time.

"How did you get my address?" he asked, his big hands struggling a bit with the tiny clasp.

Helene thought back to that night on the train, and Captain Standart's note. "Oh, I have people in high places looking out for me." She pressed her lips together, holding back the grin. "So it looks like you figured out my clue and decided to follow it to me."

"Well, you're no Swiss bank account, but—"

She gently punched his arm.

"What I meant to say is that you're worth far more." He pulled a small Bible from his pocket and opened it. A petite white flower was pressed between the thin pages.

"Edelweiss," she whispered, her hands covering her mouth. "You remembered."

"I'm yours, Helene." Peter placed a hand over his heart. "If you'll have me."

Helene tucked a strand of hair behind her ear. "Ja," she said simply.

Anika squealed and Petar clapped his hands, although Helene was sure the young boy didn't quite understand what all the excitement was about.

Peter took the toddler in one arm and lifted Anika into the other. "That way?" he asked, tilting his head in the direction Helene had come from.

"Around the corner and straight to home," Helene answered with a playful grin.

Helene lagged a step behind, soaking in the sight of Peter carrying her children. He had come back, and she had no doubt that soon they would be a family.

Helene sighed. During the dark days in St. Georgen, she never could have imagined this. She lowered her head, thinking back to the camp. To those horrible days past. Things were so different now. Better. She was free to live and to love. But she'd promised herself to never forget.

Helene caught up and draped her arm over Peter's shoulder. "I can't keep up with your long stride."

"Don't worry, pretty lady," Peter said, slowing. "I'm learning to adjust my pace."

Helene stared into Peter's deep-green eyes. They were the same eyes she'd looked into when she first entered the death camp. Now, she was certain she could see new life in their depths.

The love she saw there reminded Helene of the love

Michaela had first given her a glimpse of so long ago. An eternal love. One that would be in Helene's and Peter's hearts forever. A love that reached far beyond the dust and ashes.

A love that had saved her. Saved them both.

Acknowledgments

Many thanks go to the following people:

There are two special people I'd like to thank—first and foremost, my husband, John Goyer, for loving me and believing in my dreams. And my best friend, Cindy Martinusen, who introduced me to writing, to Europe, and to World War II history. This book would not be here without you both!

To my children, Cory, Leslie, and Nathan. You are great (and very patient) kids!

To my family, Ron Waddell, Linda and Billy Martin, my brother Ronnie, and my grandmother Dolores Coulter. I can always count on your love. Thanks to my brother-in-law, Tim Goyer, for working with me on my website to get the true narratives of the WWII veterans available to all. Also to John and Darlyne Goyer. Thanks for the numerous days you provided me with quiet time to write!

To Anne de Graaf for driving Cindy and me around

Europe (road trip!), and for believing in this story. And to Jennifer Harmon (a.k.a. Kiki) and Lorie Popp for joining us on the second research trip.

Thanks to Annie Von Trapp for sharing the beautiful message of the edelweiss.

To my One Heart and Blessed Hope Sisters, always praying, forever faithful. And for my special friends, Tara Norick, Twyla Klundt, and Jamie Spaulding—your friendship is precious.

To my friends at Easthaven Baptist Church for your encouragement and your help with my kids.

To my writing buddies who read through the many stages of this manuscript, especially to Ocieanna Fleiss, Bob Burdick, Sharie Bonura, Marlo Schalesky, my fellow sojourners from Dennis Foley's critical scenes class. Your input was great! And to Robin Gunn who took time to care after that first writer's conference and has been a long-distance inspiration to me in so many ways.

To my agent-extraordinare, Janet Grant, and my editors Michele Straubel, Kathy Ide, and Lisa Bergren. You make me look good.

To Marta Gammer who first shared the true stories that inspired this book and who continued to help with information during the writing process. May God bless the work you do to preserve the history of the Gusen and Mauthausen camps!

To Willy Nowy. Thank you for sharing your experiences of growing up near a death camp. You are fantastic. And to Heidi Mahr, my wonderful translator.

To others who helped with my research, Gregg A.

Urda, Mararet Gerace, Vera Zanardelli, Bob Pfeiffer, and Art Venzin. Thanks again.

And a special thanks to the men of the 11th Armored Division who have found a special place in my heart. LeRoy Woychik, LeRoy "Pete" Petersohn, Charlie White, Thomas Nicolla, Ross Snowdon, Arthur Jacobson, David Wofsey, Charles Torluccio, Bill Mann, Al Dunn, Bert Heinold, Joseph Lawolki, Tony Petrelli, Ray Stordahl, Roy Ferlazzo, Tarmo Holma, Calvin Caughey, Alfred Ferrari, Lester Freeman, Darrell E. Romjue, John Slatton, Ivan Goldstein, Harry Saunders, Leonard Kyle, Barrington Beutell, and Wilfred McCarthy. I feel honored to share your stories.

Also, to George Brown, holocaust survivor. Thank you.

And, finally, may all glory go to God, who birthed this story in my heart and showed me the truth about His true, eternal libertation. In Christ there is freedom indeed.

SINCE 1894, Moody Publishers has been dedicated to equip and motivate people to advance the cause of Christ by publishing evangelical Christian literature and other media for all ages, around the world. Because we are a ministry of the Moody Bible Institute of Chicago, a portion of the proceeds from the sale of this book go to train the next generation of Christian leaders.

If we may serve you in any way in your spiritual journey toward understanding Christ and the Christian life, please contact us at www.moodypublishers.com.

"All Scripture is God-breathed and is useful for teaching, rebuking, correcting and training in righteousness, so that the man of God may be thoroughly equipped for every good work."
—*2 TIMOTHY 3:16, 17*

Only the **Wind Remembers**

ISBN: 0-8024-3324-3

Only the Wind Remembers is based on the true story of "Ishi," the last surviving Yahi Indian who emerges alone from the California wilderness in 1911 and is thrust into the bewildering world of San Francisco society.

Allison Morgan, an assistant curator at the museum where Ishi is put on display, quickly forms a deep bond of friendship with him. Haunted by her painful past and unable to open herself up even to her husband, Allison can identify with Ishi's loneliness and fear. But the secret fable he begins telling her gives Allison hope that things can be different. Will Ishi die before he can reveal to Allison the truth she was destined to hear?

MOODY
PUBLISHERS

THE NAME YOU CAN TRUST.

1-800-678-6928 www.MoodyPublishers.com

The Brother's Keeper

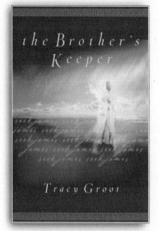

ISBN: 0-8024-3105-4

Thirty years after he followed a star to Bethlehem, one of the Magi is back on another mission. This time, he is sent not to an infant "king of the Jews," but to the king's brother James.

The sons of Joseph run a successful carpentry business in Nazareth. At least, it was successful until the oldest brother, Jesus, left home to tell the world He will forgive their sins and save their souls. Now everyone is hearing outlandish reports of healings and exorcisms. Business is suffering; not many people want a stool made by the family of the local crazy man.

Not My Will

ISBN: 0-8024-1413-3

Eleanor's secret love for Chad could mean losing her inheritance and giving up a lifelong dream. Although she worries about the cost of following the Lord, the cost of her own willfulness may be greater than she thinks. Will she follow her carefully laid plans, or make the hard choice to submit her life to Christ's leadership?

With more than 500,000 copies sold, *Not My Will* continues to inspire readers to consecrate their own lives to Jesus Christ.

MOODY
PUBLISHERS
THE NAME YOU CAN TRUST.

1-800-678-6928 www.MoodyPublishers.com

FROM DUST AND ASHES TEAM

ACQUIRING EDITOR:
Michele Straubel

COPY EDITOR:
Kathy Ide

BACK COVER COPY:
Stephanie Pugh

COVER DESIGN:
LeVan Fisher Design

INTERIOR DESIGN:
Ragont Design

PRINTING AND BINDING:
Dickinson Press Inc.

The typeface for the text of this book is
Sabon